GODS OF EARTH

BY CRAIG DELANCEY

Novels
Gods of Earth
Evolution Commandos: Well of Furies (Predator Space series)

Short Fiction
Julie is Three
The Dark Forward

Non-fiction
*Passionate Engines: What Emotions Reveal about the
Mind and Artificial Intelligence*

GODS OF EARTH

Craig DeLancey

47NORTH

Text copyright © 2013 by Craig DeLancey
All rights reserved.

Published by 47North, Seattle
www.apub.com

ISBN-13: 9781477849156
ISBN-10: 1477849157
Library of Congress Catalog Number: 2013946390

Cover Illustrated and Designed by Mark Winters

For Aletheia

GODS OF EARTH

PROLOGUE
WALKING MAN

CHAPTER

1

"Wake up, witch boy!"

The voice called to Chance Kyrien, intruding on his dream. It was a strange dream, in which he wandered alone through his house, from room to room, finding his whole family absent, and not a single candle lit against the coming dusk. But also a pleasant dream, for he walked out onto the porch, and there stood Sarah Michael, dressed in her Ranger garb, twin swords on her hips, and she strode toward him, smiling her crooked smile, her dark hair loose on her shoulders—

"Witch boy!" the plaintive voice repeated. "You can't sleep through your baptism."

Chance woke and sat up, making the ropes of his bed creak under the straw mattress. His brother Paul stood in the door to his room, smiling broadly, shirt untucked, shoeless, and with the suspenders of his pants drooping around his knees.

"The witch boy rises!" Paul said. "I thought maybe you were dead."

"Go away," Chance said. "Why'd you have to wake me? I was having a dream."

When Paul just laughed at him, Chance got out of the bed and fetched his pants from their hook by the window. He leaned against the wall and pulled them on.

"And why are you up?" Chance asked him. Usually Chance woke an hour before Paul. And the morning had hardly started: through the rippled glass of his bedroom's one window, yellow and red streaks of sunrise spread in the sky. A robin gave its dull dawn cry in the oak outside. His mother noisily tended the hearth below, stoking the ashes into a breakfast fire.

"Today is your birthday," Paul said. "I can't call you witch boy after they baptize you."

"No one can call me witch boy," Chance said.

"Well now," Paul said, "perhaps I should say, *if* they baptize you. Never know—someone might denounce you."

Chance scowled at his brother. "That's not funny."

Paul waved at the air, as if brushing away the thought. Paul was six months younger, but a head taller, than Chance. Some Sundays, Chance felt pain to stand with his family at Church and think how easily anyone could see that he, Chance, had been adopted. His mother and father and brother each had fair skin, broad shoulders, blue eyes, and flaming red hair. Chance was slight, with black hair, and eyes so dark that the pupils faded into the irises.

"That's enough about you," Paul said. "And enough about your day. Let's talk about *my* day. I won't be able to help in the vineyard. Not today. Nope."

"You've never been a help in the vineyard," Chance said. "Not any day. Nope."

"There's a reason," Paul continued, ignoring him. "A good reason. Sarah's father, Mr. Michael, stopped and talked to me in town yesterday."

Chance took down his shirt and, holding it open, frowned at Paul. "So what?"

"So what? I tell you what. Sarah's father invited me to have dinner with Sarah today, at noon. Dinner. With Sarah. And you know why, don't you?"

"I know it ain't because you look to be starving," Chance said.

"I reckon Mr. Michael wants her to settle down with a man who will have a nice vineyard of his own. Not some farmer scratching potatoes out of a rocky old field."

Chance turned red, and his mouth worked up and down as he struggled to find words.

Paul smiled and rocked back on his heels, nodding happily at the effect of his news. He opened his mouth to say something gloating, but just then their mother called from the kitchen below. "Boys!"

Paul laughed and hurried down the hall. His footsteps thudded loudly on the stairs.

Chance held his shirt still before him as he stared at the empty doorway. Maybe it doesn't mean anything, he thought. Maybe Mr. Michael would have invited me also if I had seen him in town yesterday. But then again, maybe not. Mr. Michael never said a word to Chance, other than a grudging "heya."

Chance pulled his shirt on. No, he decided. Paul made that tale up. To tease me on my birthday. I'm seventeen today. A man. I'll be confirmed and baptized. Everyone in the Valley will have to accept that I'm a Puriman. And today father will tell me of my inheritance. And then, after the ceremony, I'll see Sarah Michael. And I'll tell her I love her. I'll finally do it.

To Chance, over these last months, it had seemed this day would never come. Their vineyard's long growing season had stretched out eternally, as the grapes grew heavier and heavier, but never darkened or turned sweet. Chance tended the vines, working from sunrise till sunset, and yet each summer day had endured while the sun lingered on the hilltops, as if to resist carrying him closer to his birthday.

But now, suddenly, autumn had come, the grapes were dark and sweet and almost ready to harvest, and Chance had come of age. Between him and his baptism there lay only his morning chores, and then the rolling out of wine barrels for their guests, before he bathed and put on his Sunday clothes. Soon, the barn would fill with neighbors and Elders. And Sarah would move through them all in her trim Ranger clothes, hands resting on her sword hilts, her crooked smile flashing as she approached. . . .

Chance walked out into the hall. He hesitated, halfway to the stairs, as he passed the open door to his brother's room. Paul's Sunday suit hung on a dowel by the bedside, freshly cleaned and pressed. His shoes sat side by side, neatly polished, facing the door, as if impatient to walk out.

It was true, Chance realized, with a sinking heart. Paul had been invited to dine with Sarah. His brother would not have risen early, laid out the suit, and polished his good shoes for a joke.

Chance stared at the suit a long time. His brother's braying laugh echoed up from the kitchen.

Alright, Chance thought. If he wants to play a trick on me, I'll play a trick on him.

Chance went straight to the suit. He seized in one fist the black pants and coat, and in the other the white shirt, pulling them roughly off the dowel.

He retreated to his room and closed the door. He loosely tied his brother's suit around his neck, pulled on his shoes, and then slid his window up. His bedroom was tucked under one corner of the roof. A massive elbow branch of an oak reached just outside. It had been a while since Chance had leapt to it, to sneak out on some night or other after his parents had gone to bed. The branch looked farther now than it did at night. He sat on the windowsill, fed one leg and then the other through the narrow opening, crouched in the frame, took a deep breath, and jumped.

His hands caught on the rough bark, and held. Swinging from branch to branch, he worked his way down to the ground. He ducked behind the trunk and scanned the surroundings. No one watched from the windows of his house. No one passed on the packed dirt road at the bottom of the hill. His father did not seem to be out yet: the door to the horse barn remained closed. Chance ran.

He had just rounded the corner of the barn when his mother stuck her head out the back door. "Chance!" Her voice echoed up the hill. She must have called for him in the house and, getting no answer, concluded that he was working in the vineyards, as he often did before breakfast. Well, Paul would tell her otherwise now. Chance kept the horse barn between himself and the back of the house as he ascended between rows of vines, staying out of sight.

As he passed the barrel barn, his soulburdened coyote, Seth, slipped silently up beside him. Chance now held his brother's suit in his hand again, and Seth pressed his nose against a leg of the pants, sniffing. Recognizing the scent of Paul, the coyote tilted his head quizzically.

"If he hadn't come to rub my face in it," Chance said, "then I would have let Paul be. Live and let live. Do what you will. Be your own man. Good luck."

That made the coyote sit in perplexity.

Chance stopped and sighed. "It's, it's.... Oh, you wouldn't understand."

But the coyote still stared.

Finally, in a rush, Chance said, "First, last night, my parents argued about my inheritance after dinner. On and on. Mother trying to convince father, all over again, that the whole vineyard should go to Paul."

Chance had sat in his room and tried not to listen as his parents quarreled, but every word echoed through their house. "This was my mother's farm," his father had shouted, "so I decide who inherits what."

"But the northern plot is generous," his mother had said. "It's large. Give Chance that. Anyway, it should be enough that they're naming him a Puriman!"

"The witch swore that his blood is true, as true as any in the Valley of the Walking Man," his father had snapped back. "The boy must be confirmed and then I have to announce his inheritance and—"

"And what? The house, the vineyards we built up over the years—let that go to Paul, our own blood! There's no way to split a vincroft. How could Paul make wine, if he had only…?"

Chance's father had stamped out of the house before she could finish.

"Then," Chance explained to Seth, "this morning, Paul comes to me, and he tells me how Sarah's father invited him to have dinner with her today."

Seth looked at the suit.

"Well," Chance said, "it's too much. I'm going to hang this in the forest. Let him miss the dinner as he spends the day looking for something he can wear. That'll show him."

Chance started walking again. Seth sprang up and followed by his side. They ascended between rows of vines, through the tall grass still wet with dew that soaked their legs. They walked on until they neared the summit of the hill, over which they could see the tree tops of the forest that marked the end of their vineyards. Chance stopped and leaned against a trellis post.

Below, the tall house of the Kyrien Vincroft stood by its three red barns on a wide hill densely plotted with vines. The Valley of the Walking Man stretched out to the south, both sides quilted with vineyards anchored at their corners by houses and oxblood barns. Walking Man Lake filled the deep center of the valley, and ten miles to the south the lake forked, like the two legs of a man in stride.

"Chance?" another voice called. It was distant, almost too faint to hear. But Chance heard it: his father.

Seth twitched, turned, and then turned back and looked at Chance, expectant but uncertain.

Chance scowled. "Go ahead. Say something. Tell me to go down there."

The coyote seemed to shrink a bit more. Then Seth stuttered, "Sa-sa-sa-sorry." He lay down and put his chin on his paws.

Chance sighed. "Yeah." He sat with the crumpled suit on his lap. He pulled up some grass and threw it at his feet.

This was not how Chance had imagined, over the last year, the day of his seventeenth birthday and his confirmation. He had dreamed that by now his father would have promised him a big stake in the vincroft, maybe even half of it. He had imagined that in the days before his confirmation, he would finally have told Sarah of his dream to be with her, and that Sarah would have pledged herself to him in return. Instead, here he was, avoiding his mother and father, and playing a stupid prank on his brother. He had talked to Sarah only once in the last month. It seemed he had talked to his father even less. And if his mother had her way, and Chance got only the fallow northern fields, it would take years to make a vineyard of them, and long before that time Sarah might be pressed to marry someone with a far better stake in life than his own. Some-one like his brother Paul.

He pulled up another clump of grass, threw it, and then brushed his hands together. He had to do something, to get away from the crawling, twisting feeling of impatience and frustration in his gut.

"Come on," he told Seth. He pushed himself up onto his feet. "Let's go hang this suit in the woods. Then I'll start trimming vines up in the top of the south slope. I need to check there for the rot. I can work down the hill, maybe sneak us some breakfast when the rest of them get out of the house."

Seth's ears perked at the mention of food.

"Eh-eh-eggs?" he croaked.

"Maybe," Chance said. "We'll see."

They walked up and over the hilltop, fording the ragweed at the forest's edge that stood to his waist. In the shade under the trees, they passed the spring that seeped through the stones at the crest of the gorge. Chance descended the narrow path that cut along the edge of the gorge, looking at his feet as he reached with each stride for one of the flat steps of packed earth collected against the roots of old maples and oaks, and avoided the acorns that could roll underfoot. Seth trailed along, softly padding behind him, sometimes tapping the back of Chance's thigh with his nose.

At the bottom of the gorge, the trail leveled out onto the streambed, framed between walls of flaking shale. Chance finally looked up from the ground.

And there, in the center of the streambed, stood the gray figure of a man.

Chance leapt back. He dropped Paul's crumpled suit and crouched slightly, prepared to run back the way he'd come. It was rare to see a stranger in the Valley, and he had never seen one in the forest behind his own family's vineyard. Strangers, all Purimen knew, were dangerous. Strangers were often unmen, violent and diseased. Strangers were best handled by the Rangers.

"Who—?" he started. But he did not finish the question. He squinted, peering. The figure was gray as stone. It *was* stone! And too large, he now saw, to be a real man.

"It's a statue," he said to the coyote. "A statue dressed in clothes." Only then did Chance notice that Seth had slipped away.

The head of the statue was smooth and dark as a stream-rolled stone, with gray pupils set in gray orbs under gray lids. Wide, slate-colored hands hung out from the brown sleeves of a heavy wool cloak. The cloak had a fine weave—Chance could see this in a second. But through the open front of the vast cloak he caught a glimpse of pants and a shirt of crudest pale homeweave—almost burlap. The statue's bare feet blended right into the bedrock.

Chance looked around the forest, wondering if whoever had brought the statue might still be nearby. But he saw or heard no one.

Statues were even more rare in the Valley than strangers. He'd only ever seen a statue in the city by the Freshsea, a day's travel to the south from the Valley of the Walking Man.

He sighed, and took half a step forward, hesitating. "Who would put a statue here?" he thought aloud. "And how would they do it? And why dress it?"

And then the statue turned its head, and looked at him.

Chance could do no more than stare, stunned. It was an impossible sight, like stones turning supple and liquid, stones taking on life, while retaining still the brutal hardness of minerals. The mouth pressed closed into a frown and the eyes fixed on him, the clouded gray quartz of the pupils aimed at his own feeble liquid eyes.

Chance stood paralyzed, uncertain what he saw but certain it was something old and merciless and predatory.

His long hesitation ended. He turned and leapt—

And ran straight into the gray man. He bounced off, and fell on his back on the ground. Only then did his perceptions catch up with his understanding, and Chance remembered the snap of the cloak, the blur of gray, and then the gray man who had been standing on the stream bed stood now on the trail before him.

Running into the man had been like running into a stone wall. Chance's shoulder and hands throbbed with pain where he had slammed against the gray man's chest.

"Stay," the gray man said, in a voice with tones so deep that Chance felt its vibration through his palms pressed to the stone. "Do you speak the Common tongue?"

Chance scrambled backwards, crablike, his hands scraping over the bedrock until they splashed into the thin trickle that remained of the stream this late in the year. He clumsily got his feet under his body and stood.

"Do you speak Common?" the gray man repeated.

"Yes," Chance whispered.

"I will not harm you," the man said, in a voice that seemed to shake everything, simultaneously loud and soft.

The words were ridiculous. How could something like this do anything other than harm in the world?

They stood like that a moment, frozen. Chance glanced around, taking his eyes off the gray man for only a few fractions of a second, wondering where he might run to escape. He wished that his coyote were there.

The gray man spoke again. "Has a new . . . man come among you in these lands? A man with strange strengths—skill over others?"

"No," Chance whispered. "No stranger walks among us." *Except you,* he thought.

"You've heard no say of such a thing?"

"No."

The gray head tilted, as if catching a distant sound. "Yet he is close."

"Who?" Chance asked.

But the man of stone did not answer. Instead, he looked back at Chance. "There are no machines here," he said.

"We are Purimen. We are all of true blood, which makes us Trumen. But also we use only such crafts as are described in The Book, and that makes us Purimen."

The gray man narrowed his eyes slightly. "Yes. I remember this." But then he frowned again at Chance. "Tell no one you saw me."

And because the gray man stared at him, as if waiting for an answer, Chance nodded. Then he surprised himself: his voice came out before he even thought to speak. "I wouldn't know what to tell. I don't know what you are."

"I am the Guardian," the man said. He turned his huge broad back and took a single step up the path. "I have returned."

And, heart hammering, Chance surprised himself again by asking, "What do you guard?"

The Guardian pushed through low saplings and started up the trail. But his voice drifted back to Chance as he disappeared into the forest green.

"I guard this old and wasted Earth."

CHAPTER

2

As the sun set behind the eastern hills and silver flies danced over the wind-rippled surface of the lake, laying their last eggs of the season before swallows snatched them from the air, Elder Zadok gripped the thick cord of his fishline and pulled his catch from the green, pebbled shallows: a heavy lake trout. It twitched on the gill hook. He took a few splashing steps to the bank and trudged to his cabin on the hill above.

He hung the trout from a nail on the wall by the cabin's only window, then limped inside to fetch his knife. It was warmer and darker in the cabin, the air rich with the smell of smoldering wood from his stove. He did not bother to light a candle; he knew the small room by touch and found the smooth handle of the knife on his table. He pulled the creaking door back open and slipped outside.

A man stood there, on the road where it passed a few steps from his door. Zadok started with surprise.

"Heya!" he said, almost an exclamation of dismay.

The stranger was bald, with shockingly pale skin. His mouth moved uncertainly from a nervous smile to a grimace, making his eyebrows twitch, creasing the broad face. He wore a dark robe. The sleeve of the right arm hung down to the knees, hiding the right hand in long dangling folds that twisted in the wind. The left sleeve was folded back, revealing a pale hand with writhing fingers.

"Heya," Elder Zadok said again, softly. He did not step forward. Over the fresh smell of the lake, he caught the scent of something putrescent. Rotting meat.

"Is this," the stranger hissed, "is this Lake Man Walking?" His voice started loudly but dipped to a whisper as he talked.

"This is Walking Man Lake," Zadok told him. He pointed the tip of the knife over his shoulder at the dark water that lapped the shore.

"I look for a boy brought here seventeen years ago by a guild master of the Gotterdammerung."

Zadok thought for a long time before he said, "I don't know what that is."

The man grunted. His arms moved erratically, seemingly independently, and he looked up the road, out at the lake, at the sky, as if wanting to be elsewhere. Zadok frowned, wondering if this stranger had a disease that made him spastic. Those not living as Purimen—those who did not know that only things made directly by the hands of men out of the matter of the earth, and driven by the power of wind, water, fire, man or animal, could be trusted to keep men on the path of purity—those people got terrible diseases. Many were even born diseased. All the Elders agreed: unmen carried a curse for being impure and for living among the impure. Even the Trumen were not immune.

"She would have worn a black robe, but blood red along the edge of the hood."

"You mean a witch."

"Yes. A witch. I look for a boy brought here seventeen years ago by a witch."

That would be Chance Kyrien. Everybody on the lake knew that. And hadn't he, Elder Zadok, told Elder Ruth just that morning that nothing good would come of naming that child a Puriman? "I'm not going to his baptism," he told her. "That boy makes trouble and besides, I don't believe witches when they say guild orphans are of true blood." Though, the truth be told, Elder Zadok had long ago stopped attending baptisms and other events of the Council, and had refused the calls of the other Elders to join Council meetings. It had been years since the other Elders had asked him to participate in anything.

Well, leave it to the fools that could be bothered with all that waste of time. He had things to do. And now look how right he'd been: here stood a stranger, impure, an unman, a lost man, carrying some disease from the darkest times and places, so that he stank, and looking for the boy, right when they were doing the wrong of naming him pure.

"Who might you be?"

The stranger exhaled sharply, as if angry, his arms twisting. His eyes grew wide with what looked like fear but his mouth clamped down into a tight line. Elder Zadok took a step back, concerned. Maybe this unman's disease was catching. But the stranger wrested control of himself long enough to say, "I come from the place of this boy's birth to offer him a gift."

Well, that's a lot of talk that says nothing, Zadok thought. Best to send the unman on his way. The shadows are gone into evening, and I still have a fish to clean. It'll be such a bother to clean the trout in the dark.

"I don't know any witchchild," he said curtly. "We're all Purimen here."

"That won't do. Reconsider."

"You'd best move along."

"Oh, oh," the stranger said. He contorted into near folds before standing straight and tall again. He held out his right arm. The sleeve slipped back, uncovering the wrist and forearm. The skin was black, with pale spots. The stench of rot became overwhelming. The stranger pointed his fist at Zadok. Slowly he opened the fingers. The palm cupped pallid light.

Elder Zadok squinted and frowned, fear striving against his curiosity for a moment. What was that in the palm of the hand? It began to glow, so slowly that it became visible, but he did not at first understand why he could see it. In the man's hand something wet and round glistened. It closed for a second—no, it blinked. An eye! In the palm of the man's hand. Horrified, Zadok stepped back. A single lid, the edge of it red and torn, closed again over the eye in a long slow blink. A vast black pupil in a wet sphere of white—or perhaps the pupil was lost in a black iris. Cold, luminous, and fierce.

"Oh, God protect me," Zadok whispered.

"No," the unman said. "This god means to punish you."

With that, all the bones in Zadok's arms broke with loud snaps, a sound like green kindling crackling on a fire. His knife fell in the dirt. His arms bent around behind his back and twisted into a knot. He screamed and fell to his knees.

"Silence," the unman said, the black hand still held out, so that the eye glared at Zadok. The air grew misty between them, and then Zadok realized he could not open his mouth. His breath came only in a loud draw through his teeth. The pain in his arms receded.

"You know the witch boy?"

Zadok nodded. Tears streamed down his face. Where was everyone? Why didn't anyone come? Were they all at that damned boy's baptism?

"You know where he is?"

Zadok nodded.

The pressure he'd felt in his mouth changed, disappeared. He could open his mouth again. He could speak. He gasped for air.

"Tell me." The unman came a step closer. In the dark of late twilight, Zadok saw the stranger's clothes were those of a beggar, a wanderer, torn and filthy and threadbare. But the eye—don't look at the eye, he told himself. Too horrible.

"Tell me."

"Chance Kyrien. At the Kyrien Vincroft. The gray house, with pillars, at the top of the Lake."

The unman nodded sadly. Zadok watched him, hoping with this nod of approval his ordeal was over. But then the pain in his arms rushed back, and Zadok screamed again.

"Help! Help!"

"Silence." The hideous eye blinked, and Zadok felt the numbness come over his lips, the sharp pressure grow against his jaw. He fell on his face into the dirt, and his broken arms flopped uselessly to his sides. He tried to scream but he could not.

With his twisted right hand, he managed to touch his face. Between his lips he could feel his teeth, smooth, unbroken, solid from his top gums to his bottom gums, a cage of bone locking his jaw around his tongue.

The unman disappeared into the dark, taking the smell of rotting flesh with him, as Elder Zadok choked on his stifled shrieks.

CHAPTER

3

"In an hour you'll be a man of the Purimen," Chance's father said. He set his hands on Chance's shoulders and smiled. He had finished his third cup of wine, and it had given his cheeks a red flush and made him sentimental.

They stood in the tall wine barn of the Kyrien Vincroft. Oil lamps hung along the walls and flickered softly, giving every face in the crowd a healthy golden glow. The floor had been swept of dust, and people trod pale, clean boards, walking this way and that, greeting each other. Barrels of Kyrien Vincroft's best Ries and Caffran vintages had been rolled to the edge of the floor, set up on stocks, and tapped.

"I'm proud of you, Chance," his father said. "Though you've been ornery many times, you've become a true Puriman, and a fine farmer and winemaker. You've grown into a good man."

Chance gripped his father's arms and nodded, unable to speak. He felt a surge of gratitude and happiness, even with his mother frowning nearby. She was still angry about the suit. When Chance had come home, the suit crushed into a wrinkled ball in his hands, Paul had already left the house. There'd been another fight, his parents by turns arguing with each other and mutually scolding him. Chance had hardly cared, since he felt such relief to find his home reassuringly unchanged after his uncanny encounter with the Guardian.

If it had not been the day of his baptism, his punishment would have been severe. But Elders were soon coming, and there had been preparations to make. So his parents had stopped arguing and started cooking, cleaning, rolling out wine stocks, and undertaking in a rush all the other tasks required before guests came. Still, Chance knew, what his father quickly forgave and forgot, his mother remembered forever. His punishment was not over.

His father patted his shoulders and moved on into the crowd. Chance looked through the faces, seeking Sarah. All the Council Elders and many of the other vinfarmers from the north of the lake had come, and their voices filled the barn. There stood his neighbor, Joshua Moriah. He nodded and raised a cup to Chance. There stood Elder John and his wife, talking quietly together. There the entire family of the Samuels, all seven. They had the largest vincroft on the east shore of Walking Man, and Chance respected and liked all of them.

But where was Sarah? Chance knew that she had patrol this afternoon, and might have ridden far up the lake with the other Rangers. But surely she would come soon, even so. Her father, Justin Michael—a tall, thin-faced man with brown eyes hidden under dark brows—stood before a barrel in the corner, frowning at Chance. Paul stood beside him.

When Paul saw that Chance stood alone, he pushed through the crowd and towards the center of the barn. Paul had not changed his clothes since he'd been to the Michaels' home, no doubt to remind Chance of where he'd been that morning. Paul wore a pair of his father's pants and one of his father's old coats. Both were too large. Chance took a deep breath, gathering the courage to apologize. But Paul spoke first.

"That was a dirty trick, witch boy," Paul whispered, when he was a pace away.

"Paul, I'm—"

"But it didn't work. I had dinner with Sarah and then her father left us alone, and then I kissed her." He leaned closed. "Sarah loved it."

Chance's heart fell. Could it be true?

Paul smiled. "Yes, it's true. And now Father isn't going to give you anything, just that field of stones out by the old shack. It's already been decided. And Sarah's mine now. Mine. And see there," he nodded towards the corner of the barn, where Sarah's father still stood. "Jeremiah Green's with me. He's going to denounce you. He's going to stop your confirmation." Jeremiah Green emerged from the shadows behind Mr. Michael. Green forced a laugh at something Mr. Michael said, his eyes indifferent, and then drank from his cup. He looked at Chance, but Chance looked away before meeting his gaze.

"Go on your way," Chance said.

Paul opened his mouth to speak again, but then Elder Ruth clapped her hands, her cane under one arm. She stood near them, with Elder James gravely bowed beside her. A hush spread through the crowd, from the front of the room to the back. Paul slipped away into the crowd.

At the age of 103, Elder Ruth had lived longer than any other of the Elders who still sat on Council. She kept her long gray hair pinned back in a loose bun. The lips and eyes of her lively, deeply lined face moved quickly when she listened or talked. Her claps sounded out surprisingly loud.

Chance's father reappeared at his side and led Chance to stand next to the tiny Elder. Chance clasped his hands together and bowed his head.

"We are here to baptize Chance Kyrien," Elder Ruth intoned, "and confirm him as a Puriman." A few claps sounded out. Next to her, Elder James lifted the tall baptism cup from the floor.

"Our tradition is old. It comes from the time of the War Against the False Gods. In those years, man was still young, but thought himself a god. Man denied the One True God."

She leaned heavily on her twisted cane, letting the invocation sink into the silence.

"Though man had the word of God, he said, I am lost. Though man had the guidance of God, he said, I will make a map of my own way. Though man had the covenant of God, he said, I have no purpose, so I will make myself a purpose; I have no soul, but I will make myself an immortal soul. This sowed ruin, and brought the War Against the False Gods, and the Barrenness Plague, and the making of the plague lands. But during this strife, the Purimen turned their back on the unmen, turned toward the True God. They gathered here at the lake of the Walking Man and at the Forest Lakes and along the Usin River, and they pledged themselves to God's commands.

"We were made of your design, God, and we will keep thy will: we will not remake ourselves. Nature was made of your design, God, and we will keep thy will: we will not enthrall ourselves to man's machines. This is our creed."

"Amen," the crowd intoned.

Elder Ruth continued, "Since that time, coming unto seventeen, each child of our villages is named man or woman, and if of pure blood is confirmed a Truman, and if righteous in our ways, is baptized a Puriman. So it has always been for us. This day Chance Kyrien is of age."

Now came the call for objections, Chance knew. If none denounced him, he would be confirmed through baptism. And, right after that, his father would be expected to announce Chance's stake in the croft. Chance's heart began to hammer. He knelt before Elder Ruth. She moved close to him, so that her long dark skirt pressed against his arm, and she set one hand on his head. With her other hand she passed her cane to Elder James, and then dipped her fingers into the water of the baptism cup.

"We gather to confirm Chance Kyrien. He was born true and has practiced our creed. Are there any who deny it?"

Chance held his breath. If Green were to denounce him on some false charge of impure acts, or if his brother had lost all restraint in wine, now would be the moment they would speak.

Silence.

Chance let his breath out. Of course his brother had only been trying to scare him, to take some revenge for Chance's trick.

But as Chance breathed in deeply in relief and expectation, a faint scent of something rancid seeped into the barn. Outside, the crickets fell quiet. Then, very faint but unmistakable, came a single canine yelp of pain.

Had someone harmed Seth? Chance started, almost stood, but realized that he could not move now, he could not interrupt the ceremony—not the instant before his baptism. He must remain bowed.

Unable to help himself, he looked up. The great front door to the barn creaked open. He caught through the crowd a glimpse of black folds of dirty cloth slipping through the cracked door. People in the back of the barn shifted uneasily. The air seemed to suck out of the room. The smell of lamp oil, spilled wine, hay, and crowded human bodies was pushed away by a single foul odor. Elder Ruth pressed her hand down on Chance's head, leaning upon him for support.

"I come for Chance Kyrien," a choking hiss called out.

The crowd parted, the many Purimen moving back, leaving an aisle between the large front door and Elder Ruth. A figure in a dirty black robe stood before the door, a hood drawn over the head, sleeves falling far below the hands, so that nothing human could be seen of it.

Silence held. Behind the robed figure, Sarah slipped into the barn, dressed in the green and brown clothes of a Ranger. She looked at the intruder, then around at the crowd. Her eyes met

Chance's for a second. She put her hands on her two sword pommels, and then went to her father, whispering questions to him.

"Who speaks?" Elder Ruth said.

"I come for the boy Chance Kyrien," the hissing voice repeated. The unseen man under the robe twisted and shivered. He pointed at Chance, the sleeve hiding the hand. "Is that him?" Then he started forward, lurching uneasily, in jerks. Several oil lamps flickered out, guttering black greasy smoke that took on twisted human forms. A sudden surge of nausea and terror gripped Chance.

Chance's father walked into the aisle, between Chance and the robed figure. "I am John Kyrien, the boy's father! You will speak to me, if you must speak!"

"Oh," Eve Kyrien cried. One hand outstretched toward her husband, the other uncertainly over her open mouth, she stepped forward, pushing her way past Elder James.

Chance stood. Elder Ruth let her hand slip from his head. The baptism waters dripped forgotten from her other hand. The air seemed to shimmer, then solidify. The smell of rot thickened.

In the corner, Sarah drew her two swords, the blades ringing: *shing, shing.*

"Only Purimen are welcome here," John Kyrien said.

The figure held up its right arm. The sleeve fell back, exposing a black hand and arm, spotted with pale sores of gangrene. The open palm faced Chance's father, a white spot—an eye! Chance thought with horror—glowed on the palm—

With a loud *crack*, his father's head jerked impossibly sideways and back. Eve Kyrien screamed and stepped forward to catch her falling husband. The air shimmered again. Her neck broke and she toppled.

The Purimen crowded into the barn began to scream. They rushed into the corners, shoving and pulling at each other to get out of the small side doors.

"No!" Chance howled. The hideous eye turned on him. Chance put one foot forward, but could not otherwise move. A fog filled his head. He saw, almost as if remembering, a rush of senseless images: stars, lights, strange faces of stranger children. He tried to push these visions aside. He took another step forward, dragging his foot. He must get to his father and mother.

The stranger's hood fell back, exposing the grimacing, hairless face of a man, his skin as ashen white as the belly of a lake bass, red eyes wild and darting around as if seeking an escape, the mouth pressed into an ugly snarl. But the eye in the palm remained fixed on Chance. The strange images pushed more fiercely into Chance's mind, like dirty fingers that violated his soul.

The cries of Chance's neighbors and kin, the trampling of their footsteps on the floorboards, reached him as if from a great distance. Chance dragged himself another step forward, still struggling toward his father, but overcome by the continual rush of visions: a smiling face of a woman in a black robe; a towering city full of airships; a white coffin floating among stars; dogs of iron; a black crack in the sky.

Sarah, caught in the corner, pushed her way against the panicked crowd, her swords held high above her head to avoid stabbing anyone.

Then the front doors of the barn exploded. The Guardian leapt through the gaping hole.

Chance tried to focus on him, through the invasive visions. The Guardian spoke in a guild language that Chance did not understand—the sound of it, the tone, was like a voice in intimate conversation, but with a deafening volume.

"O theos, dia ti sou erxomai."

The ashen man, with his rotting black arm, shrieked and writhed and turned. *"Tode atheos esti, en muthon esti!"*

There was a blur, as the Guardian moved as he had moved across the stream bed: in an instant he stood next to the robed figure, his cloak snapping like a whip as it caught up with him. With one huge fist the Guardian struck the ashen man, sending him soaring backwards, to smack hard against one of the beams of the barn. The ashen man's face twisted, and he coughed up a great mouthful of blood.

In Chance's mind, the visions collapsed, and the sounds and sights and smells of the barn rushed back at him. He saw Sarah, swords held straight out before her, circling warily, uncertain how to intervene, as the Guardian strode with thumping footsteps toward his opponent, who lay in a squirming clump on the ground.

Most of the Purimen were gone now. The last poured out of the corner doors, emptying the room. Their screams receded.

Chance ran to his father and knelt. He shuddered with horror as he put his hand on his father's neck and felt the sharp edges of broken vertebrae protruding against the skin. His father's open, empty eyes stared at the loft of the barn. Chance began to weep hopelessly. He moaned and looked at the strangers.

The ashen man lifted his black arm. The eye turned on the Guardian.

"Pente theoi apopheretha, ik egei," the Guardian said, his voice grim.

"Chance!" Sarah called out.

Chance looked to her, but then the hairs rose on the back of his neck. Air swept into the room. Bits of straw and dust swirled around the barn and began to spin into the space between the two strangers. Out of some useless reflex, Chance lay across his father's broken body, trying to protect it. A blinding flash of lightning cracked between the black arm of the ashen man and the broad chest of the Guardian. The thunderous explosion shot the Guardian backwards, sent him sailing through the air, straight over Chance and through the shattered front doors of the barn. Where the Guardian had stood a second before, dark smoke rose from charred floor beams.

The ashen man twisted, bones audibly grinding and snapping— snapping back into place, Chance realized. He stood and faced Chance.

"You will come now."

"No," Chance whispered. He rose to his feet, hands knotting into painfully tight fists.

The rush of visions returned: a door floating in a starry sky; a coffin full of white ropes; a huge dark man holding a long-handled hammer in one hand. And dimly through these images Chance saw the hideous white figure flail its limbs forward, moving toward him in contortions like a dying spider.

"No!" Chance shouted, terrified and furious. He stepped forward uncertainly. The room grew distant, the sounds receding. He gasped at the air, fighting the urge to vomit, focusing his mind on what was here, in this time and place. The unman was just a pace away now. With a titanic effort, Chance drew one arm back.

"You will come now," the ashen man hissed again, raising the black rotting hand.

Chance leapt. He threw all his weight into a twisting wild punch, swinging down into the contorted white face. He saw in an instant the red eyes open with shocked surprise as his fist came down and struck, hard, across one sunken cheek.

The ashen man fell back. He thudded down onto the floor.

"You dare!" he shrieked. "You dare!" The hand with the eye in its palm rose up, and something gripped Chance's legs, binding him as if he were buried up to his waist in stone.

Silver flashed. Two bright streaks. Sarah ran forward, swords swinging. Instantly, without any sign of motion, the ashen man was standing, his back to Chance, outstretched dead arm facing Sarah.

And something else moved out from between the wine barrels— Paul, running forward, a club in his hand.

"Sarah!" Chance shouted. "Sarah, no!"

Sarah stopped in the middle of a leap. Time congealed around her. She floated, frozen, her feet off the ground. The swords suspended two silver arcs of light in the air.

Like an owl's, the head of the ashen man turned completely around and glared at Chance. A sickening smile buckled the pallid face.

"Yours," it whispered. Almost a question. The air shimmered, and Sarah disappeared.

"No!" Chance screamed. "Stop it, stop it, stop!" He managed to drag his feet forward two steps. He held his clenched fists out in fury.

Paul had fallen back in shock, but now he rushed forward again, the heavy club held high over his head.

"And kin," the ashen man said. Paul disappeared.

"Stop," Chance whispered.

"Give yourself to me," the ashen man said. "Do not resist me. Release your mind. Then they can go free, brother."

The Guardian stepped into the barn, smacking the splintered fragments of the door aside loudly. In the next instant, he stood over the ashen man, followed by a clap of imploding air in the wake of the speed of his motion. The ashen man fell backwards on the floor. The Guardian smacked aside the black rotting arm that rose like a snake, then swung a slate-colored fist so fast that a breeze swept the room and there was a sound like a hornet's buzz. But the fist crashed through floor boards and shattered a stout floor beam. The pale, robed figure was gone.

A wave of dizziness struck Chance. The barn dimmed as the lamps flickered, choking on their own black smoke. He fell backwards, hearing but not feeling his body crash onto the wood floor. As if he could see through the ceiling of the barn, bright and myriad stars turned above him. He floated among them, in a tunnel of stars.

From far, far away, Sarah's voice called faintly, "Chance! Chance!"

Then all faded into silence and darkness.

PART I
DISTHEA

CHAPTER

4

Chance woke with a start. Over him, blue sky and clouds turned slowly around. Close to his head, water lapped and lapped methodically.

He sat up quickly, causing a wave of dizziness. He gripped the sore back of his head.

He was sprawled in the bottom of a boat. A small Puriman rowboat, painted oxblood red. Before him, the Guardian sat on the center seat, pulling at a pair of oars. The boat slipped quickly down a river, broad and fast but shallow. Chance didn't recognize the place. No river like this ran within a day's walk of the Valley of the Walking Man.

"Where am I?" Chance demanded.

The Guardian did not answer.

Chance looked around. "I know this boat," he said. "This is the boat of Elder James. I know it."

"Who are you?" the Guardian asked him.

"I am Chance Kyrien. A Puriman." He recalled with a cringe that he was not a Puriman—not baptized and confirmed as one. And then the events of the previous evening flooded back to him.

"My father," he groaned. "My mother and father. And Sarah! I have to save Sarah and Paul!" He tried to stand. The boat rocked, and he fell backward, head reeling.

"You ail," the Guardian said. He rowed unceasingly, though his expressionless gray eyes remained fixed on Chance. "Your mind's weary from the work of clinging to itself. The broken god worked to bewield you." Then he tipped his head slightly, a bow of respect. "Though you are strong. I felt the foul fingers of him stabbing into the mood of your mind. Few men could bear such a thing as you have borne." He lifted a single finger from the oar handle to point at the water. "Drink."

Chance's mouth was dry, his lips cracked. He bent over the gunwale and cupped water to his mouth again and again. The dizziness passed.

"Now," the Guardian said, "why does the broken god want you, Puriman?"

"I have to go home," Chance said, breathing hard.

"The doom of the world may rest upon our haste. What hope does the broken god have in you?"

"You mean that unman? The white...rotting man?" Chance asked. "I don't know."

"It called you brother."

"No," Chance said. "It took my brother. It was talking of my brother. I am a Puriman." He looked around. This must be the Kilter river, into which fed the creek emptying north out of Walking Man Lake. Elder James had kept his boat on that creek.

"Who were your parents?" the Guardian asked, rowing still.

"John and Eve Kyrien." Dead. Dead.

A crow cawed nearby, as if mocking Chance. He pulled himself up onto the front seat of the boat and sat. He gripped the sides. He had been dressed in his Sunday suit for his confirmation, and his uncomfortable, oversized shoes—hand-me-downs from his larger brother—were caked with mud, and the too-long cuffs of his pants were soaked from the water pooled in the bottom of the boat. He noticed only then how the morning cold penetrated his clammy, mud-streak clothes. He began to shiver.

"They were your birth parents?"

After a very long pause, Chance said, "No. I was adopted from the witches. By ancient agreement with their guild, the Purimen raise any orphan boy children the witches bring us and pledge are of true blood." Chance ran his hands over his face. He sobbed once, but fought the desire to break down into weeping. "I have to go. I don't know who you are, but all this is...when my parents are...with Sarah and Paul...."

The Guardian stared.

"Who are you?" Chance finally asked. "Why are you doing this?"

"I am the Guardian."

That same answer. It meant nothing.

"If you do not know why the broken god wants you," the Guardian said, "then we must ask the Guild Mothers of the Gotterdammerung."

"The witches have no guild hall here."

"We go to Disthea, to the Broken Hand That Reaches."

Chance stared in disbelief. "What? What? The Sunken City is far from here! Many days' travel." Chance had been no farther than the Freshsea, a day to the south. He did not know exactly where the Sunken City was, but he knew it was west and north and it was many times farther than he had ever traveled from Walking Man Lake. "No! I must get out here!"

Chance got his feet under him and leapt to the right, aiming to jump feet-first into the river and strike out for shore.

There was an explosion of water. It crested over the gunwale, and slapped him back into the boat. The Guardian stood in the river before him, the water heaving around his hips. The Guardian's motion had been so fast, so violent, that Chance had not seen it, but the water had exploded to get out of the way. The Guardian had one hand on the boat, steadying it, or it would surely have flipped over.

The Guardian walked the boat to the shallows and then climbed in. Soaked, Chance pulled himself up again onto the boat's front seat.

The Guardian took up the oars and thrust at the water with quick strokes, driving Chance away from all that he loved and desired.

CHAPTER

5

"The witch child loves you."

Sarah struggled to open her eyes. She felt her eyelids tremble, but they would not rise. It's one of those dreams, she thought. One of those nightmares when you thrash and thrash, but in fact you aren't moving at all, and you cannot wake.

Slowly, a foul odor crept into her nose. If she could move, if she weren't paralyzed, she would gag from the cloying stench. She tried again to raise her arms, to open her mouth, to lift her eyelids, but she could not, she could not....

"Awake," the voice hissed.

Her eyes snapped up. The pale, robed man stood before her—the man who had attacked them in the barn. The man who had killed John and Eve Kyrien. He dragged in a labored breath, and then looked this way and that before forcing his eyes back to Sarah. "Wake now. Stop dreaming of him."

"The witch boy," Paul said, dreamily but with invective.

Sarah lay on a hard, cold floor of packed earth. Paul lay beside her. She pushed herself backwards, in panic, and then scrabbled to her feet. To her surprise, her swords lay on the ground before her. She looked at them uncertainly.

The pale unman showed no concern. "I am here to help you, to save you."

She snatched her swords from the dirt, then skipped backwards and held their points out toward the robed man. She glanced quickly around. They were in a dirty room, fifteen paces on a side. Below ground, it seemed, since light streamed in through broken windows near the ceiling that were partly choked with dandelions and other low weeds. Rust-colored grime lay thickly over the floor and over piles of shapeless trash. In the corners, spider webs sagged under years of heavy settled dust.

It was probably an abandoned farmhouse in the old forest, Sarah thought. She might even know the house.

"Stand back," she said. Then to Paul, "Get up, Paul. We're leaving."

"No," Paul said, still staring off into space.

The air shimmered. The pale yellow light that filtered into the room changed, seemed to thin and waver. The particles of dust that swirled in the low columns of the sun's rays froze in place. The voice of the horrible cloaked man sounded in her head, though his lips barely moved.

"I am Hexus. Chance is my brother. He needs help. Only I can help him. He carries illness."

This was ridiculous: where Chance was broad shouldered and erect, with a square face and dark hair and eyes, this tall and bleached man slouched awkwardly, and his small eyes were a dim red. His jaw was narrow and slight.

But then, in the strange slow light, Sarah felt her will soothingly encumbered, as if pressed down under some soft weight. She could not recall what she had intended to do with the swords. The unman's words reminded her of other things. He had said *illness*. Illness. She knew about illness.

"Illness killed my mother," Sarah whispered.

"Yes, that's right. Like the illness that killed your mother. That illness killed Paul's parents."

And she saw it then. The memory flooded over her, shocking, because she had somehow forgotten it. How could she have forgotten that? The Elders had been about to confirm Chance, but then Chance's father had collapsed, vomiting blood and green bile. It was then that the robed man had come, offering help. Chance had spurned him and fled.

Had the man just been talking? She had missed what he said, listening to her thoughts.

Strange that Chance's father would have gotten sick so quickly. It had been different for his mother, hadn't it? She couldn't recall. That was odd.

"Chance is sick?" she asked.

"Yes. He carries disease."

That's right. Chance had looked pale, like her own mother when the sickness had started.

"He is not a Puriman," the man said. "He should not live among you. He has given all the Purimen a cancer. If we can find him, and catch him, I can cure the others. I can cure your family."

Her family. "My father and brother?"

"Your father and brother."

"They're sick?"

"They have the disease."

She dropped the swords, which clattered, ringing against each other, on the dirty floor.

"Sick like my mother?"

"Yes. Chance made your mother sick, perhaps."

She saw her mother again, in her last weeks of life, vomiting mouthfuls of bile and blood into a filthy bucket set beside her on the festering bedsheets. The foul smell of the sick had permeated their house, made Sarah retch and even vomit at unexpected times, sitting in the kitchen, avoiding her mother, or standing at the front door, hesitating to even enter the house. And then her mother's long slow death, the agonizing dry heaves that forced up only the thinnest hint of green acid threaded with clotted strings of black blood.

"Oh, no," Sarah whispered, "oh God, no." Her father and brother would die like that next. Horrible beyond words, beyond imagining. Chance had caused it. She pictured Chance with green bile on his lips. Did she remember that?

Had the pale unman been talking again?

"I can save them," Hexus whispered. "You see that I am sick also. I can save myself. But first, I need your help. Chance flees us. When we catch him, we need to convince Chance to come to us, to join us, and I can cure them all."

"How," Sarah began, "how can finding Chance cure…?"

"Don't think of that. Think of your father and brother. Think of finding Chance."

She nodded. That was right. Think of her father and brother. Think of finding Chance.

"Chance will become more and more dangerous. I am a stranger here. Will you help me? I want to ensure that no one else is hurt."

"Yes," she said. Her voice seemed far away. The room, the sounds of it, the sickening smell of Hexus, were all distant, as if experienced by a different person on the horizon of her awareness. "But I don't know where he is."

"Oh, there's only one place they can go," Hexus said. "We must head north. Chance will flee to Disthea."

Sarah picked up her swords and sheathed them.

They climbed out of the abandoned farmhouse, leaving behind the stale damp air of the basement for the strong scent of cool lake water, and walked down to the road on the west side of Walking

Man Lake. Sarah knew the place: dozens of times she had ridden past the derelict house they had been in. The road here went all the way to the western foot of Walking Man in the south, or out to the Old Trail in the north. The farmhouses before them were all the homes of Elders.

"That's Elder Isai's home," she said, pointing. It was a small, well-kept white house on the lake shore. A red barn stood by it.

"Do they have horses?" Hexus asked.

"Oh yes."

"Sit here."

And she and Paul sat in the dirt. It seemed strange to Sarah, to be sweating in the middle of the road, legs askew, not even looking up to see if someone came along. She had the nagging feeling that she had forgotten something. They sat so still that a robin landed at her feet, poked at the grass by the roadside, and pulled up a worm. Without the unman there talking to Sarah, her head slowly started to clear.

"Paul," she said. At her voice, the robin hopped back, jealously retreating with its squirming prey. "Paul. What...?"

But she could not form a question. What was it she wanted to know?

"I feel strange, Sarah," Paul said. "Are we lost?"

"I think..." she began.

"You were angry when I kissed you." Paul stared at the road before his feet. "But you were so beautiful. Turning in place."

Sarah squinted, trying to gather her thoughts.

That had been just the day before. She'd not wanted to have dinner with Paul but her father had arranged it. Paul had arrived wearing a too-large suit, but laughing at himself with good humor. "My Sunday suit seems to have walked off on its own," he'd said. Later, sitting across from her at the table, without Chance there as goad and measure, he did not have his usual defiant familiarity. He spoke respectfully to her, and answered a long series of questions from her father about growing Ries vines, while they ate bread and a pork roast that Sarah and her grandmother had prepared.

Paul had seemed like his father, John Kyrien: jovial, smiling, but always talking with a hint of seriousness. He had even shocked Sarah by crediting Chance.

"How do you handle the black rot? Pull or burn?" her father had asked.

"Well, sir," Paul said, "I was inclined to pull the leaves and shoots and grapes that got the rot. But my brother Chance insisted that we burn whole vines. I think now he's probably right. He's got a real good sense for Ries vines."

He looked over at Sarah as he said this, and she nodded, as if to say, here's to you, Paul Kyrien.

After the meal and a long conversation about lake fishing, her father had conspicuously stayed seated by the hearth, filling another pipe, as Paul rose to go. It fell to Sarah to see the boy off. She walked Paul out onto the grass before their house. The day was cool but the sun shone warm on her.

"I thank you for the fine meal, Sarah," Paul had said again.

"You are welcome. Thank you for the wine."

"We have plenty of wine," he joked.

She nodded. "I have to make a quick patrol today," she had said, turning slightly in place to make her skirt twist back and forth. "Tell Chance I may be a bit late to his baptism."

Then Paul had stepped forward and kissed her. Shocked, not wanting to draw attention, she had not cried out, but just stepped back. Paul took another step and kissed her again, hard on the lips.

If it had not been for her father, if it had not been that this boy was their guest, she might have struck him. Instead, angry at herself for letting him take advantage, she had pushed him away. She had opened her mouth to rebuke him, thought better of it, and only hurried into the house.

Her father had not questioned why she had hurried past him and into her room, to change into her Ranger garb.

Sarah frowned now. Something was odd.

Her father! He was not sick! He had sat at the dinner table eating and was not sick. Her brother had been there too—healthy, smiling.

Relief swept through her. She reached her hand out into the dust and seized Paul's hand. His fingers gripped hers.

"We have to..." Paul whispered, his voice straining, "to get up...."

"Yes," Sarah said. She leaned forward slightly. Her legs did not want to obey her. But slowly, slowly her knees bent....

Then Hexus returned with three horses, leading them by the reins. "Stand up."

Sarah's thoughts fled. She and Paul stood.

"Isai gave you horses?" Sarah asked.

"I showed them it was better to help me. Now get on. We ride to the Usin Valley, and then on to Disthea."

Sarah mounted the horse. "I'd like to see the great river," she said, staring at nothing.

"You will see many things," Hexus told her. "Some you will even remember."

They rode off, leaving only dust behind.

CHAPTER

6

I must escape, Chance thought.

The persistent morning mosquitoes gave up as the day turned unseasonably hot. His clothes dried. The dark red wood of the seats grew scalding to the touch. Chance had no hat and he began to sweat. He had not broken his fast, and a dull, pounding pain took hold of his head.

The river grew more swift. Its water roiled and at places foamed over rocks, driving quickly to the west. The Guardian continued rowing at his same pace, his strokes compounding now with the current to drive the boat at a frightening speed. Chance gritted his teeth in frustration. With every mile that passed, he grew more angry with himself for not having leapt out of the boat and run for the forest, and yet, given how quickly the Guardian could move, he knew at each opportunity, each shallows or bend, that escape was hopeless.

Chance's father had told him that the waters of Walking Man Lake flowed into the Kilter, then into another mighty river, and ultimately all the way to the Western Salt Sea, someplace far north of Disthea, the Sunken City.

"Will we take the river to the sea?" Chance asked.

The Guardian just hammered at the water with the oars.

"Will we take this boat all the way to Disthea? Or will we leave off and walk when we are closest to the city?"

The Guardian did not answer.

Chance felt the urge to scream in rage at the unman. He decided then on his course of action: when they first hit deep water, he would leap onto the gunwale and jump from the boat, tipping it, and swim ashore. The unman, he was sure, would not be able to swim but would sink like a stone.

But Chance would have to wait until they were much farther. Nowhere did the fast Kilter run deep enough to sink a man. It raged along through narrow valleys, skimming perilously over pebbled flats, or splitting over stout boulders, but never flowed more than waist-high.

In a place where the stream was broad and shallow, the Guardian climbed out of the boat and dragged it, scraping, into the center of low, gurgling shallows. The boat stopped. Chance watched the Guardian let go of the prow. He bowed to pick a smooth, round stone, the size of a fist, out of the river. He held the stone behind him. Then he moved so fast the motion was invisible: the next instant his arm was above and before him, hand outstretched, fingers open, the stone gone.

Chance looked up at the sky, trying to see where the Guardian had hurled the rock. A few seconds later a distant crack sounded out. That fixed his eyes in the right direction, and he saw two black things falling: one, dropping straight down, was the stone. The other fluttered and twisted in the air, dropping more slowly. It splashed into the water a few hundred paces ahead.

"What was it?" Chance asked. The Guardian said nothing but pulled the boat out of the shallows, stepped in, and began methodically rowing. When they came to the bend where the thing had fallen, the Guardian stepped out. He reached into the stream, scattering schools of silver sucker fish that turned in jittery synchronized abruptness, and pulled out a limp black form, dripping with cold water.

"It's a bird," Chance said.

No, not a bird, Chance realized. It was metal, and some other material. Black and dark gray and burnished silver. In place of a head was a cylinder with a single glassy lens. But the body seemed otherwise like a metal crow, with feathers of deepest, shining black.

"What was it?" Chance whispered. Then he sat up in surprise as the head turned and the black lens aimed at him. The wings twitched.

The Guardian crushed it in his hands. The wings and body cracked noisily, some of it shattering like glass, other parts bending with a creaking metallic protest. He ground it into a rough ball, then dashed it against a boulder on the shore. He climbed into the boat, offering no explanation.

Late in the afternoon they passed the first of a long series of ruins, ancient towns and villages abandoned centuries before. Their roads were vanished into the dense forest that covered the steep hills. But towers, built of strange guild materials, still stood among the encroaching pines and firs and the maples tinted with the first red of autumn. Their windows gaped, empty and bleak. Some of the Trumen said that these oldest buildings had built themselves, and still sometimes rebuilt themselves. Chance thought that blasphemous and impossible, but now wondered when he saw the gleaming towers that fought for space among undaunted maples.

"We're nearing the Sabremounts," Chance observed, fearful and surprised by their progress. "We'll pass along the edge of the

Sabremounts soon." The tireless rowing of the Guardian had driven them more than fifty miles, if they were near those small mountains.

The Guardian said nothing.

Knots of black vultures wheeled over these lost villages. Neither Trumen nor unmen lived there. Trumen who traveled claimed that soulburdened beasts ruled the Sabremounts, animals made brutal and bitter by their knowledge and by the harm they suffered from the many men who killed their kind. Chance looked warily now into the forest, which grew darker with the waning of the day.

When the sun fell behind the eastern hills, the Guardian paddled hard to a flat expanse of pebbled shore. He stepped into the shallows and dragged the boat high onto the gravel. Chance stepped out slowly, his cramped legs unfolding painfully, with resistance. He hopped a bit on one leg: the other was asleep. They had stopped only once during the day, under an apple tree, after Chance had complained of hunger.

"Up there," the Guardian said, pointing to the forest above the tall earth bank before them. Chance gathered his last apples from the dirty water in the bottom of the boat. He washed them in the river while the Guardian easily lifted the boat and turned it over, scraping the stones noisily. Chance drank some of the cold river water, then climbed the bank, following the Guardian.

They made camp in a small flat clearing. The last of the afternoon light faded quickly. The Guardian gathered and piled kindling. Then he walked up the hill above and came back carrying a tree trunk of a recently fallen maple, as thick as Chance's thigh. He broke it over his chest, again and again, the sound explosive, making Chance cringe. The Guardian stacked these logs and then gathered two stones and smashed them together in his kindling pile, making a burst of sparks that easily caught in the dry leaves and sticks. They crackled and took flame.

"I'm hungry," Chance said. He sat down on the gnarled root of the oak that loomed over them. "I cannot live on a few apples."

The Guardian said nothing, his hood drawn down so that the firelight could not seep within. Chance stared at the fire.

Then the Guardian asked, "Do you have a dog?"

Chance started, surprised to hear the unman finally speak after a whole day of silence. "No."

"Stay here." The Guardian stood. "You cannot outrun me, so do not try." He strode past Chance, ascending the hill. Too late, Chance thought of Seth. He turned and looked, ready to speak, but the Guardian had already disappeared into the dark. Chance scanned the hilltop, where a few patches of the sky, darkening pink, were just visible through the black branches of the pines of the crest. In a moment he saw the dark outline of the Guardian there among them, the first stars appearing behind him. Then the Guardian disappeared over the hill.

Without hesitation, Chance ran. I can follow the river, he thought. I'll know the marsh of The Walking Man when I get there. I need only to follow the river and when I come to the Valley I can head south straight to the vincroft.

It quickly turned dark. Branches cut at his face. One whipped into his eye and he stumbled and cried out, pressing his palm to his socket. Tears welled from the stinging lash. But he found his footing and ran on, blinking and stumbling. He ran until his lungs burned and his breath came in gasps and his spit clung thickly in his mouth. His Sunday shoes, loose and soaked all day in splashed water, slipped on the forest loam and began to split. The sole of the left shoe opened in the front, so that it scraped along the ground, scooping up leaves and sticks and driving them painfully under his foot.

Eventually he could no longer run. Heaving his breath, bent half over, he walked, dragging his tormented feet. He could not guess how far he had come. Perhaps three miles. The river lay just out of view to his right—he had managed to keep close to it. It was loud here, the water coursing over boulders through a steep rapids.

Uselessly, reflexively, Chance looked over his shoulder to see if the Guardian followed. But he could see nothing now, in the dark. The moon was nearly full but it was over the hill, casting only ghostly light on distant tree tops.

He tripped on a root, and stopped.

Something rustled the leaves ahead of him. Then again to his right. Now behind him—was it circling around? He crouched. The forest revealed nothing. Overhead through the trees he could discern patches of stars, but around him, in the woods, the dark was impenetrable. He began to wonder how he could proceed. The rustling stopped. Still crouching, he walked forward, one hand out before him, catching spider webs in the night.

He heard again the rustling of leaves behind. And then the crack of a stick to his left. There were more sounds now—a third rustling, maybe several things, coming down the hill to his left. He turned toward the river, thinking to run to it—

Something slammed into him, hard. It tossed him back onto the ground. His head hit the earth and his teeth snapped painfully together. The dull, dizzy pain of a concussion spun the forest around him. Chance struck out and grabbed fur. Some animal pressed him into the dirt. Its hot breath blew on his face. A smell of heavy must, like a wet dog, but stronger, filled his mouth. Chance pushed at it, struck it once, and then he cried out as claws scraped across his left arm. He rolled sideways and kicked, and managed to free himself enough to get to his knees.

A flickering flame cast dim light into the clearing. Something carried a torch toward them. Chance could see now. A brown bear— its distended head revealing that it was soulburdened—crouched before him, ready to spring again. It leaned back and roared.

Before Chance could stand, a harsh growl sounded to his left. "Leave! Leave!" A brown blur leapt onto the head of the bear—it was Seth!

The bear snarled and fell back, swatting the coyote down.

Chance stood. Seth backed up to him, facing the bear and snarling. The brown bear crouched again, ready to spring. Another bear, black, bore the torch that Chance had seen, with a single bright flame. It limped uneasily toward the brown bear. And there were other animals there, all soulburdened. Three wolves, tall and wide, with gray fur. Their heads did not have the exaggerated round shape of most soulburdened beasts, but were long and flat, making them appear huge. A badger, its lip curled in a bitter sneer, paced quickly before him. A third bear, gray and old, with a long scar closing one dead eye, stood behind Chance, smelling the air with a twisting snout.

"Coyote, we kill the man," the bear with the torch growled.

"No, no, no," Seth barked back. "A ga-good man."

"We kill all men as all men kill us."

The bears showed their teeth. The badger mewed angrily. The wolves watched without comment.

"No," Seth repeated.

The bears fell to all fours, even the one with the torch, which it dropped unheeded in the dirt. The bright flame continued to burn. Then they ambled forward, spreading out, circling. Chance gripped the four deep scratches on his forearm. Blood dripped from his fingers. He crouched, turning, watching for the first attack, his heart pounding.

A thunderous crack sounded out, and the Guardian stood before them. Leaves exploded at his feet, kicked up at a speed no one could perceive. A gust of wind followed in the Guardian's wake, snapping his cloak. He hulked over them all, standing between Chance and the soulburdened bears.

The bears leapt back, then stopped, eyeing the tall figure fearfully and sniffing hard at the air around them. They turned their heads from side to side, bent their noses in circles, trying to determine if there were others about like this one. The wolves lowered their snouts but did not otherwise move.

"Old, old thing," the Badger snarled. It backed away.

The Guardian spoke in a language Chance did not understand.

"Wodweardas, gemuniæth ge eowre modru ond eowr fædras ond eowr weorc."

His hood lay over his head still, and the soulburdened looked up at it now, wondering what talked in the dark beneath.

To Chance's surprise, Seth answered in the same tongue. "Hie ne-ne-ne-ne sprecan nawiht þæt ealdgereord."

"Ura sum sprecath þæt ealdgereord," one wolf said. She had her front paws up on a fallen log, the massive gray toes splayed out on the wood. Her green eyes looked at the Guardian coolly. She added, "But speak Common to them."

The Guardian spoke again, in Common. "Woodwardens, recall your mothers and your fathers and your task."

"Our mothers and our fathers are dead," growled the brown bear that had felled Chance. Chance realized it was young, still not fully grown in size. "Killed by men."

"Not by this man," the Guardian said.

"The men kill all of us. We will kill all the men."

"Go," the Guardian said. His voice did not seem loud, but it shook the low green plants around them.

After a heartbeat pause, the young bear charged. It slammed into the Guardian, who set one foot deep behind himself to brace, but otherwise did not move. The bear roared, opened its mouth gaping wide, and then bit the Guardian's shoulder. Its teeth clicked against the Guardian's flesh, the mouth unable to close, as if it were trying to puncture and compress a stone.

The Guardian bent his knees so that he could seize the bear with one hand gripping a forearm under the armpit and the other hand clamping onto its knee. As he stood he tipped the bear to the side. Then he lifted the bear straight over his head. There was a pause, a moment of silence, as the soulburdened animals stared in disbelief. Even the bear held aloft was silent, its eyes wide with fear and surprise.

The Guardian threw the bear over the heads of the wolves, into the shadows of the dark forest.

Branches cracked, and then came the hard thud of the bear falling to the Earth.

The two other bears whimpered and ran toward the sound. The badger slipped silently away, looking over its shoulder with an expression of mixed hate and terror. The wolves, implacable, turned slowly, and began gracefully to fade into the dark. But the lead female, her front feet still on the log, spoke to the Guardian.

"There is growling of a thing like you. A mangodthing. Promising the Woodwardens that it will purge the world of the remnants of man. If we serve it."

The Guardian said nothing. His cloak's dark hood was another pool of night in the final dark.

The wolf slipped away behind her pack.

The Guardian turned to Chance.

"Come."

Chance fell to his knees, and sat back on his heels. "No," he said. Tears started down his face. "No. I will face death. I will face the soulburdened again, and face even that . . . rotting thing. Let me go."

The Guardian was silent. His black hood did not move. Chance looked up at him, imploring, his eyes streaming.

"If I don't go, who will bury my father and mother? Who will speak the last words for them?"

Chance clutched dirty handfuls of rotting leaves, and lifted them before himself. "Who will write my father's tombstone? Who will pray for him at church?"

He sobbed now. "Who will feed our horses? Who will harvest my father's last crop, and make his last wine of it? Who will tend our vines? Who will save Paul and Sarah? Who? Will she die because of me?

"And who will feed Seth? Who will care for him?"

He dropped the handfuls of Earth and reached out and clutched fiercely in desperate fists the fur on the back of the coyote's neck. He pulled Seth close, almost falling into him. The coyote put his head under Chance's chin and closed his sad, knowing eyes.

The Guardian stared down at the weeping boy. Slowly his hands rose, as if to reach for the boy, and then fell again. He opened his mouth, ready to demand that Chance follow him, but no words came out. His gray cheeks twitched.

Only fifty days before, the Guardian had been wakened when he sensed the god. Before that, he had not moved in two eons, had not breathed in five hundred years. Where he had stood in a forgotten cavern, deep in a forsaken land, his slate-gray skin had petrified as his feet had grown, like stalagmites, into the limestone floor. And when he first felt the god, for one human moment he had longed to remain in the forgetful dark and let the lime continue to wrap him in stone. But the Old Gods had chosen him well: even after long centuries, he did not desert his duty to kill the god.

And so he had tried, as he walked the surface again, to bring the cave with him, to wrap himself in the cool indifference of the ages, his thoughts fixed to purposes as old and heartless as the rising of mountains.

But a terrible struggle raged within the Guardian now. He could see the Earth with the eyes of an ancient thing, where mortal lives flitted by, and the fall of a maple seed, the leap of a fish, an avalanche of stones, and the death of a father were all ordinary, brief events among endless events. Or, he could feel the pull of life, like the noisy, driving vortex of the river behind them as it fell over rapids. The fleeting cares of this boy threatened to sweep him away. He could be drawn down and whelmed in the hopes and sorrows of the living—seized by the concerns of a boy not unlike the son he had once raised and lost. Long, long before.

The Guardian had to choose between those worlds.

Slowly, the Guardian dragged one foot forward. He paused again, his shaking hands held out uncertainly. Chance pressed his face still against the coyote's neck.

Then the Guardian reached up to his throat and undid the clasp on his cloak. It slipped off his shoulders to hang in his fist, revealing his head for the first time that day. He swung the tattered gray cloak around Chance and laid it over the boy's shoulders. He put his hand on Chance's head.

"I am sorry, Puriman," he whispered. His voice sounded, for the first time in many centuries, like a human voice. "I am sorry for your loss."

And the boy wept, in gasping, choking sobs, for the miseries that mortality makes of human life.

CHAPTER

7

After Chance and the Guardian returned to the fire by the
boat, the Guardian rebuilt it to a tall, crackling flame. As
he worked, Chance sat against a fallen tree and asked him,
"What about Sarah?"

"The woman he took?"

"Is she safe? And my brother?"

"Most likely she is safe," the Guardian said. He sat down on the
moss-covered fragment of a tree trunk, across the fire from Chance.
Seth curled at Chance's feet and peered up warily at the Guardian.

"You told me you don't have a dog," the Guardian said.

Seth's ears snapped up with indignation. His tail slapped the
ground once. "I-I-I am not a dog," he protested. "I'm a coy-coyote."

The Guardian grunted.

Seth laid his chin back down on his crossed paws. "Soulburdened rock," he mumbled. Chance and the Guardian both pre-
tended not to hear that as they stared at the flames.

After a few minutes, the Guardian asked, "Did the bear speak
the truth? Do men hunt the woodwardens?"

Chance hesitated. "The soulburdened? We Purimen do not hunt them. Though our Rangers turn away the bears and large soulburdened, and discourage the others from coming to our lands. I know of no Trumen that hunt them. But...I hear from Trumen that many other men hunt them. Especially in the north."

The Guardian scowled.

"You spoke to them first in a guild language," Chance added. "Was it Leafwage?"

"I spoke in Lifweg, yes."

"And Seth knows it," Chance whispered. The coyote said nothing, nor lifted his head, but looked up at Chance through his brows, giving him a sweet, pathetic expression. Chance ran his hand over Seth's head, then tugged at the thick fur on the back of his neck. The coyote had explained, as they stumbled back to the camp, that he had confronted the pale unman the night before, and had been cast aside with a wave of the hand that held the eye. Knocked unconscious, Seth had awakened in the morning and found the croft empty. He had immediately set off to seek Chance. How the coyote knew in which direction to follow, Seth did not explain; Chance assumed he had followed a scent.

"All the woodwardens spoke Lifweg when last I walked the Earth," the Guardian said.

"Are you in the Leafwage?"

"The cursed Guild? That Guild was smitten long ago. Their leader Treow, the First Knight, lost sway of the guild, then walked into the great wood, and was never seen again. Each of the other knights was murdered by the Theogenics Guild, the Orderlies, the Dark Engineers. In the end by the gods. Hunted by all."

Chance heard bitterness in the Guardian's answer. He asked a different question. "What was that thing that...attacked us?"

The Guardian frowned. "It is a shard of a god. One of the seven Younger Gods, perhaps. Or so it seems. Why it craves you I do not know."

"The False Gods were all destroyed," Chance said. "The True God ordained that they would destroy each other, as would many false men, in wars and strife wrought of their pride."

The Guardian fixed his pale eyes on Chance a long time, seeming to weigh whether to answer him. Finally he said, "I cannot guard you and your beliefs, Puriman. One must be hurt." He leaned back.

"There were seven human gods. An old lay told of this; perhaps somewhere men sing it still." The Guardian surprised Chance by chanting softly,

> *Five were the demigods,*
> *First of men with numinous power:*
> *Threkor, Arvang, Wervool, Jeet, and Kane.*
> *Seven were the children gods,*
> *First with otherworldly flesh,*
> *And Threkor forged in his black fires*
> *Seven jars to bind them.*

"Two of the gods went missing even before the beginning of the Theopolemein, what some others have called the Theomachia, and yet others call The War Against the Gods."

"The War Against the False Gods," Chance said.

"So Purimen call it, then. This must be a bit of one of those two lost gods. Eating the soul and flesh of a man."

"The eye," Chance whispered. Seth whimpered.

"The eye," the Guardian agreed.

"How can an eye be...any danger?"

"Each bit of the Earthly body of human gods has all of its soul. It is a bitter and bewildering bane for it to be broken into parts. It may not know who or what it is. But each withdrawn shred could become the whole god."

"Is it looking for the rest of itself?"

The Guardian shook his massive head slowly. "It seeks you, and you are not the rest of it. I think only the eye abides."

"Can anyone fight it?"

"I could easily rend the man, and make the god near harmless for a short time. But I will need help to bind it."

Chance picked up a stick and poked the fire. Sparks leapt and climbed the smoke. "But in the barn...."

"I did not use my full strength, and we had only just begun to fight. Such a clash can wreck, in a wide ground, space and the things in it. I did not want to kill the many Purimen there. Perhaps I should have waged full havoc. Now the god grows stronger with time, as all the gods did."

A moth fluttered around Chance's head. He brushed it away. "What did it do to Sarah and Paul?"

"It moved them—" The Guardian hesitated. "I do not ken the words in Common Speech. But the god closed them... in another space. I could have opened it, but I might have killed them if the god thwarted me."

Chance nodded, though nothing that the Guardian said had any clear meaning for him.

"And you believe she... they will be safe?"

"For a short while, Puriman. It seems the god wants you. They are a way to get you. Dead, or harmed beyond hope, the god won't have this use for them."

"I have to help Sarah. And my brother. As soon as I can."

The Guardian nodded. "We will speak with the Guild Mothers of the Gotterdammerung. If we bind this god, or if you are no longer useful to it, then you may go back to your hearth. But you need know, Puriman, that you, this woman, your brother—these are not the only lives in danger."

Chance frowned at the fire. The right sense of all this heretical talk eluded him. It was all blasphemous, the kind of evil that the Elders often cautioned thrived among the lost men. The worst warnings of The Book were coming true before his eyes. Part of him felt reassured, even comforted in his faith, because he saw that the Purimen were right in their cautions. But these evils also seemed to reaffirm his people's creed that a Puriman should play no part in these things. He should turn his back. He should refuse to hear or speak of these things.

But for Sarah and Paul. To do nothing would be to abandon them, if the Guardian told the truth.

"And are you a...." Chance hesitated, not wanting to say "false god." "Were you made with their powers, by men?"

"I was not made by men."

"Then are you," and Chance almost whispered now. "Are you an Erthengle? A fallen angel, one of God's fallen host?"

"No. I was a man like you once. And that is all I will say of this."

Chance stared at the fire a long time before he spoke again. "If helping you will help Sarah and Paul, then I will help you. I have responsibilities. Things that I must do. The burial of my father. And mother. A croft that may now depend on me. Vines that need constant tending. But I will help you. To save Sarah, and to save Paul, and so that I can return to the vincroft and try to take back my life there."

The fire crackled. The night had cooled, even though there was no wind. The scratch on his arm, which he had cleaned and wrapped with a scrap of his ruined coat, stung as he shifted closer to the flames. But the wholesome smell of the hardwood smoke heartened him. He drew the Guardian's cloak tighter around himself and breathed deeply the homely scent.

Seth pushed himself closer to Chance.

"Let us hurry, then," Chance added. "We have to hurry. For Sarah's sake."

"We will come where this river falls closest to Disthea in another two days. Then we must walk, or find another means, over land. That will take another three days, perhaps. Now sleep, if you can."

"I'll need to eat," Chance said.

Seth yipped. "Food," he said.

"We'll find food tomorrow," the Guardian told them.

Chance got up onto his knees. He turned his back and bowed his head to pray. His lips moved but he was silent as he thought, "Oh God, please watch over Sarah and Paul and keep them safe from this false god. God, please grant grace to my mother and father who were good and kind people who took a poor orphan boy into their home and raised him as their own and got nothing for it in this world but instead suffered and. . . ." This caused a heavy lump to rise in his throat, and quickly he closed down that thought and repeated to himself, "God, please keep Sarah and Paul safe. Amen. Amen."

Then he lay down, folding the hood under his head as a pillow. Seth curled against him. He watched the firelight play on the immobile gray hands of the Guardian.

When he felt calm again, Chance said, quietly, as he petted the back of Seth's head, "There's one other thing. One other reason I want to help. I want to avenge my parents."

The Guardian narrowed his eyes, watching Chance closely.

"The True Book tells that revenge and vengeful thoughts are sins," Chance explained. "But only against people. Against an enemy of God, against a false god, the True God asks that we be justly vengeful. I want to avenge this wrong. For my father."

The Guardian nodded slowly. "I know nothing of a greatest god, nor of your holy book, nor even of grapes and wine and Purimen funerals. But an earned wrath, Puriman, *an earned wrath*—this I understand."

CHAPTER

8

"Wake," the Guardian said. Chance sat up. The Guardian peered out into the forest, his back to Chance. Seth stood erect next to Chance, ears bent forward, and sniffed the air.

"What is it?" Chance rose uneasily. Cramps knotted his left arm and leg, where he had lain on the cold ground. His stomach pained him with hunger. His headache had returned with a fierce intensity.

"Something comes."

"What?"

The Guardian did not answer. Behind them, birds sang loudly with their morning calls, but before them the forest fell silent.

The wood was ancient here. It retained the last of the summer's lush and green foliage, but the towering trees held the thick canopy high above. The morning light sloped in under the treetops, gold over the green fronds of the ferns covering the floor. It shimmered on the millions of white spider threads bridging the underbrush.

A hundred paces away, two ferns parted, and someone pushed through. Chance could not at first discern whether it was a woman or man. The skin of the person had a strange golden color, almost seeming to glow. Gold hair hung at shoulder length. As the person drew closer, Chance could see the delicate, symmetrical features of the face. He decided this was a woman, though not a Truman.

"What do you want with us, makina?" the Guardian called when she had closed half the distance.

She did not answer at first, but continued and stopped only two paces before them. She looked with pale silver eyes at Chance, then the Guardian. She wore black pants, black boots, a white shirt with small black buttons and a thin black band around the collar, all under a black jacket with long tails—to Chance this dress resembled the kind of rich formal suit he had once observed Trumen wearing to church in the city by the Freshsea. It looked strange, even ridiculous, here in the forest.

"I have searched for you, Guardian."

Again Chance was confused. Her voice rang with a clear, beautiful bell tone that could be male or female. But the complete placidity of her face unsettled Chance more than the unnatural symmetry of the androgynous features, or the strangely bright skin.

They stared at each other awhile before the Guardian spoke.

"What do you want?"

"I endeavor to offer assistance."

The Guardian frowned. "Don't waste our time with wieldless words. What do you know of the splinter of the god?"

"It is part of the Hexus," she said. "The sixth of the seven Thei."

"Ah." The Guardian yielded a slight smile. "So the Makine do know something."

"We have observed him for some weeks, watching from the skies. It was here that we recognized you."

"The metal bird!" Chance said.

The strange woman looked at him. "Yes." Her silver eyes shifted back to the Guardian. "That was a sentient being that you destroyed."

Seth slipped around behind Chance, and began to circle their clearing, sniffing the air.

"Wolves," Seth growled. "Nearby. Upwind."

"How did you find us?" the Guardian asked.

"I conversed with several of the...." She hesitated over the word, looking at Chance as if determining how best to continue. "Soulburdened."

Chance wondered why the wolves would offer to help her. Or had she paid them somehow?

"What care do the Makine have in this?" the Guardian asked. "Why do you skulk about the skies above my head? You would not fight in the Theomachia. Always have the machines left the living to their own doom, while you hived like ants beneath the skin of the Earth, sworn to break forth one day and spurn this world to seek the stars."

"You," the woman replied, "interest a diminutive portion of the Makine. I am empowered to represent this syndicate. We infer there is significant probability of costly consequences if you fail. I therefore will assist you, reducing that probability."

"I will not fail."

The woman merely looked at them, her expression not changing.

"If you have some way to get us to Disthea," the Guardian said, "then you may offer it. Else leave us, makina."

She bowed slightly. "I was transported here in an airship. It is tethered downriver. I did not consider it advisable to arrive in it directly."

Without another word, the Guardian turned and tromped toward the river. Chance scurried to keep up. He looked over his shoulder at the woman, who kept a respectful distance.

"Who are the Makina?"

"Makine. You call a single one of them a makina."

"Who are the Makine?"

The Guardian jumped down the berm.

"They are ancient machines."

Chance jumped down to stand beside him. The loud stream smelled strongly in the damp morning air. Mist clung along the banks.

"She works for...machines?" Chance whispered. "Underground machines?"

"It is a machine." The Guardian started toward the water.

Chance stopped in place. He looked at the woman. She had not moved, but gazed at him peacefully. He hurried to the Guardian's side and whispered, "I don't understand."

The Guardian strode out into the water. Without looking back he said, "Do not bother to whisper. The machine can hear you blink an eye."

Chance stopped at the water's edge. The makina stood now at the top of the berm. Seth ran a short way downstream along the bank, sniffing and peering cautiously about, before turning back.

"I am one of the Makine," she said.

Chance shook his head. "You are an unman," he whispered.

As if confronting a small, frightened animal, the makina moved slowly, folding her hands before herself.

"I understand your application of this terminology. Please address me in this way if it is conceptually reassuring. But I have no human ancestors. Not in the usual meaning of the term, 'ancestor'."

Seth slipped to Chance's side, legs dripping water, ears rigid with attention.

"What...." Chance hesitated. "What do you want me to call you?"

"If it pleases you, I will adopt the appellation *the Mimir*."

"Come," the Guardian shouted. "Call your ship here."

The makina, still on the top of the berm, nodded. She did not move, but after a moment Chance heard a dull humming. Downstream, the river bent around a steeply sided hill. Stunted maples clung perilously to the broken earth of the bluff. Slowly, the nose of an airship appeared around the bend, as if emerging from the trees. It was dark blue, almost black, longer and thinner than the airships Chance had seen sometimes pass near his farm. Below it hung a black cabin.

The airship slipped out into the valley, the tail turning slightly too far in the wind, and then it straightened and lowered. A heavy rope dropped down from the front. The ship descended toward the Guardian until he grabbed the rope. The cluster of seven fans at the back of the cabin blared loudly and rippled the surface of the river with tiny white rills. The ship hovered uncertainly, bobbing, as it paid rope out while the Guardian walked to the shore.

Chance frowned. The cabin beneath was lined with windows but he could see no one inside.

The makina leapt down to the ground beside Chance. The motion was smooth and nearly silent. She walked out into the water, directly to the cabin. A door folded out and down, laying itself on the stream. She stopped before it, the water rushing around her legs, and gestured inside.

"I cannot enter that," Chance said. "It was not made by human hands, nor made of earths using fire."

The makina looked at him but her expressionless face betrayed nothing. Seth stood in the shallows, looking back at the forest with impatient wariness. The Guardian held the rope and peered at Chance. Finally the Guardian said, "I understand." He dropped the rope, strode directly to Chance's side, and grabbed him in both hands, lifting him as one lifts a child. He took great splashing steps to the airship and tossed Chance through the door, onto the soft carpeted deck within.

"You did not choose to ride this ship, Puriman. I forced you."

Chance climbed to his feet, indignant. "It's not that easy! I cannot ride this." He quoted scripture as he stepped toward the door. "Thou shalt turn thy back on the machines of unmen that shroud the wonders of creation."

He was about to step into the stream when Seth barked a loud yelp of fear and splashed toward the door. Behind the coyote, a cacophony exploded out of the dark forest. Mimir, Chance, and the Guardian all froze and looked up the hill. The canopy was dense and they could see little in the shadows, but a roar poured down, the sound of hundreds of beasts cresting the hilltop at a run. Here and there through breaks in the trees, Chance could see a flash of black fur or brown fur, as wolves, bears, dogs, and other soulburdened creatures raced toward the bank.

Seth swam the last few paces to the airship, then climbed the bobbing ramp, his back feet scratching in panic on its edge. The Guardian followed with a single great step that made the airship rock. He pushed Chance inside as he ducked under the low doorway. The makina came last, and the ramp lifted silently behind her. Chance stood, uncertain and silent, as the door closed.

There was a window on the door, streaked now with river water. Chance peered through it. As the airship started to lift, the first of the soulburdened, a group of wild dogs, climbed over Elder James's overturned boat and then splashed down into the stream where Chance had stood just seconds before. Behind them came more dogs and then bears. A seething mass of fur and claws, of snapping white teeth and bulging furious eyes, crowded onto the bank.

As the airship lifted away, in his last view of the river bank, Chance caught a glimpse of sparkling gold. A creature like he had never seen before, larger than a man, and shaped like a man, but covered with black fur, strode out into the river on two legs, head held high. It was dressed in gold armor that sparkled in the sunlight, and in the center of the snarling mass of beasts, it stood with quiet dignity, looking up at him as the airship escaped. Chance's eyes met the black eyes of the creature, before a bough parted his view and the airship ascended with a dull low humming, scraping a few times at tough branches as it drifted up and out of the narrow valley.

CHAPTER

9

The river below shrank to a blue ribbon. Rolling green hills stretched off in every direction. Chance tottered uneasily to the windows facing south so that he could search the most distant green hills. Seth turned uneasily around him, still trembling after their perilous escape from the pack of soulburdened beasts.

Chance had never been higher than the roof of his own home. Airships, helmed by Trumen from the city of the Freshsea, sometimes came to Walking Man Lake and carried back the Purimen wines. Chance loved the ships, as did most young Purimen, although like the others he had watched without speaking of his interest, and he would not before have betrayed his creed and climbed aboard one if offered. Though he had once been delivering barrels of Kyrien Caffran wine to a ship, and saw Jeremiah Green standing inside, not for a ride but to spy around, to feel the bounce of the cabin as the airship fought its tethers to the Earth. Green had blushed when he looked up and found Chance standing outside by his cart. The heavy boy had pushed angrily past him, saying, "Keep your mouth shut, witch boy."

Seth finally calmed enough to sit at Chance's side.

"I . . . I hoped to see something of the Lakes," Chance explained. It was in vain: to the south and east there lay only unbroken forest covering alien hills.

"Too far-far," Seth said. "Over horizon."

"Over the horizon," Chance repeated. So this is it, he thought. The realm of the Purimen was beyond the horizon, and new horizons surrounded him. He was without the guidance of Elders, without the counsel of another Puriman, without a map, without any familiar path. It seemed that every choice would require him to violate his creed, to move a step farther not only from home but from his faith. Everything here was wrong: to be above the trees, ready to fall to the Earth; the dull inanimate sounds of engines; the strange smells of the room; the white light that bled from the ceiling. He was uprooted, lifted from the Earth and set adrift.

And all this while, Sarah was in danger, Sarah might be suffering something horrible, and he was, most likely, flying away from her.

Gone suddenly was the conviction that came upon him the night before, that he was doing the right thing to accept the Guardian's guidance. He looked uneasily toward the ominous gray figure, hulking over the landscape in the front of the ship. Who was he? What did he really want?

"What may I call you?" Mimir asked. She had walked up behind him. Chance turned and looked at her frankly now. She still betrayed no emotion. Her silver eyes looked like ice in the reflected sunlight.

"Chance. Chance Kyrien. Of the Purimen."

"This is an unusual nomination for a Puriman, is it not, Chance Kyrien? My limited understanding was that all Purimen took Biblical names."

Chance looked back in the direction of Walking Man Lake. "It is traditional for adopted children. An unsought child is a lucky chance, the Elders say."

"And you, sir?" She faced Seth.

"Seth." He lay on the deck, making a coyote bow.

Mimir bowed and smiled in response, the first human gesture that Chance had seen her use.

She pointed at Chance's feet. "Your shoes appear to be in disrepair. This ship could mend them."

Chance looked around, confused. How could a ship fix shoes? It was a strange place. Nothing in it looked to be made by hand. It smelled unnatural. The feel of the seats lining the cabin unnerved him: soft but firm, made of neither metal nor wood nor anything he had ever touched. One corner of the cabin was walled off by white panels, but windows lined the rest of the cabin. And outside, when they stood by the river, the sound of the great fans that propelled the ship had roared, but inside he could hear only a distant, quiet hum. A dull vibration that he felt in his teeth made the whole place throb. Suddenly, the cabin seemed small and close.

He frowned. "Unless you have leather cord and a hand-made awl, I cannot accept your help."

Mimir said nothing. But then Chance's hands began to shake. His legs felt suddenly weak, and trembled. He turned and uneasily sat on the low bench before the window.

"Hungry," Seth barked.

Mimir looked at the coyote, then turned her expressionless silver eyes back on Chance. "The Seth is observant. You are manifesting symptoms resulting from dehydration and inadequate nutrition. I have sustenance. It was manufactured by Makine, but I would advise you to consume it."

Chance nodded. It had been more than a day since he had eaten, and eating their food seemed somehow less of a sacrifice, food not being a machine itself. He imagined the sources and making of food could not be much different from Puriman strictures, no matter from whom it came.

Mimir went to the back of the cabin and returned with four brown bricks of what looked to him like beeswax. She handed two to Chance and placed the others in Seth's mouth.

"What is it?"

"The appearance, and the taste, will probably disappoint. However, it has all the nutrients that a Puriman, or coyote, requires."

Chance bit into it warily. The taste was alien but mild, closest in his experience to the smell of yeast and starting fermentation. He ate the two bars and then accepted a glass of water.

Mimir showed him then that one of the small doors in the paneled-off section opened onto a bathroom, with a toilet and sink. The far wall was lined with windows. No need to be concerned for privacy at this height, Chance realized.

When he came back out, Chance felt a little better. His face and hands were clean. He had torn some strips of clothes from his ruined coat to tie the soles crudely back onto the front of his shoes. Though the strange food sat in his stomach uneasily, his hands no longer shook. He drank some more water, and then sat on the bench again, drawing the Guardian's cloak tight around himself. Mimir watched him, unselfconsciously. The Guardian stood still before the bow windows, as fixed as a gray statue, brooding over the green earth that passed below.

"How long till we reach the Sunken City?" Chance asked Mimir.

"This is the Puriman term for Disthea? We shall arrive there before the evening."

He sighed and nodded impatiently. Only getting off the airship would relieve the gnawing anxiety he felt. He turned and looked back out the window. The river was far behind now, and they were crossing directly over the Sabremounts. The tall hills passed below, covered with trees, through which occasionally a crest of rock was visible on a few peaks.

"It seems so big—the world—from up here."

"Very big," Seth growled.

"Once it was a common pronouncement of human beings that the world was small," Mimir said. "But in that era there were thousands of times more human beings. Perhaps the world seems smaller to your kind when it is crowded."

Seth yipped.

"Eat more?" the coyote asked.

Mimir went to get him another brick of food.

The night before Chance had slept uneasily on the hard ground, and sitting now on the soft bench of the airship, he was nodding asleep when there was a hard knock at the window. Seth yelped. Chance snapped his head to the side to see a hunched black bird perched on the outside sill.

Not a real bird, he realized as he jumped up, but a mechanical one, such as the Guardian had destroyed, with black wings of scratched metal and glittering glass for a cyclopean eye. Mimir came to the window and slid the glass up, letting through wind and the roar of the engines. The thing waddled inside with the patience and haughtiness of a crow. Mimir closed the window, and the two Makine stared at each other awhile. Chance had the distinct impression that somehow they were communicating. The Guardian came and stood by his side.

Finally Mimir turned to face them. "My syndicate brother has observed the god."

"Is Sarah with him?" Chance asked. He added, "And my brother?"

"The Hexus rides on horseback, heading west. There are two humans with him, also on horseback. A male and a female."

"Sarah," Seth barked. "Pa-Pa-Paul."

"It must be," Chance agreed.

"They appear to have suffered no significant trauma," Mimir added, after facing the bird again.

"Thank the mercy of God," Chance said. "Thank God."

Mimir nodded noncommittally, and then lifted the window again. The bird makina waddled out and off the edge of the airship, falling toward the trees below before opening its wings and taking to the sky.

The sun had passed its zenith when they came over a broad sea. The ship turned to the south, following the tall shoreline. Chance went and stood next to the Guardian. He could see nothing before them but a dark blue expanse, touched here and there with white-capped waves. On the horizon, to the west, there appeared to be a stretch of sand, but Chance thought it might instead just be the misting sea air of the distance.

"This is the great Western Salt Sea?"

"Yes, Puriman."

"Where is the Sunken City?"

The Guardian pointed south. Chance watched the horizon over the next half hour as a dark shadow on the sea resolved itself into a black line, with spires of white beyond it. Soon he could discern that the spires were buildings, and that behind the buildings a second black line held back the sea. This was the Crystal Wall that wrapped around the Sunken City, a band or ring that reached nearly the height of the many towers of Disthea. Judging by the depth of the shadowed city streets beyond the wall, which Chance assumed were on what would have been—without the wall—the bottom of the sea, he judged the sea was more than one hundred paces deep around the city. It looked like the wall rose another thirty paces as high again above the waves. Chance had imagined that the famed crystal wall would be bright and shining. But rising from the water, with the city behind it, the wall shone darkly. Waves crashed and foamed against it, white against the black.

The Sunken City was huge, he realized. He had been told that, but the scale still stunned him. It stretched as long and wide as one of the legs of Walking Man Lake, and towers thrust from it as thick as trees in an ancient forest. Again his heart sank and he thought with dread, *What am I doing here*? He had come too far to have any choice now but to go with the Guardian—he could not run from this airship as he had run from their camp—but doubt again troubled him as he looked at this city made by lost men, during a fallen age.

The ship began to descend, and more of the city became visible.

"Why did they build it underwater?" Chance asked the Guardian.

"It was above water when it was built." The Guardian pointed. "There, that is the Broken Hand that Reaches, Guild Hall of the Gotterdammerung."

In the center of the Sunken City, one building rose higher than all the others. Four sides twisted up toward a flat comb, out of which five broken small towers arose. Each of these ended with a rough patchwork of glass.

"I saw it before. With the towers."

The Guardian snapped his head sideways to peer intently at him. "How?" His voice was deep, shaking the air around them. Seth slipped to Chance's side, his ears flat.

Frightened by this reaction, Chance answered in a whisper. "When the false god... It made me see things. In the barn."

The Guardian relaxed visibly and looked back out at the city.

"Then," Chance continued, "I saw this tower, but the smaller towers on top were not broken. They were there, tall."

The Guardian nodded. "The tower is like an arm, and the top of it was shaped first as a hand, reaching for the sky. The pride of the Theogenics Guild, mark of their craft. During the Theomachia the fingers were broken, and the Theogenics Guild was crushed. The Gotterdammerung hooded the broken stumps of the finger towers with glass."

"It's all so large," Chance said.

"The city was much larger once. Long ago. This is but the husk of a city."

"But ga-good food there," Seth growled enthusiastically.

"You think so?" Chance asked him.

Seth nodded. His tall wagged. He licked his snout with relish.

Chance could see now that the wall was wide and spotted periodically with short spires. The ship nosed toward one of these, where the wall came closest to the Broken Hand that Reaches. The airship's engines strained audibly as it struggled against the shifting winds. The short spire turned out to be a silver cone, about twice as tall as a man. They drifted close, and then the rope paid out of the nose of the ship again. To Chance's surprise, some kind of metal arm lifted from the short tower and grabbed the rope out of the air. The engines fell silent. They turned in the wind but did not drift away.

The tower reeled them in, till the nose of the airship was tight against it. Mimir cracked open the door. Cool, damp air whistled through, stirring Chance's hair. She lowered the ramp, which bobbed uncertainly a few paces above the top of the wall. The ramp folded open again, doubling its length, and the end landed with a clack on the ground. As the ship bobbed in the wind, the ramp rhythmically scraped, then lifted, scraped, then lifted from the wall.

"Come," the Guardian said. He started down the ramp. Seth followed. Chance looked at Mimir, whose face remained inscrutable, and then together they strode down.

The sea crashed against the wall below. Seagulls hovered over them, shrieking.

"It smells different," Chance said. "Not like a lake."

"Saltwater. Sea," Seth growled. "Nice."

The wall beneath their feet was covered with a layer of bird dung and dust and sea wrack dropped there by gulls. Chance kicked at it and saw clear crystal below the dirt.

"It really is made of glass," he whispered.

"It is fabricated of diamond," Mimir corrected. "The wall is a single unbroken ring of diamond, in one piece." Mimir pointed off to where the wall faded into mist. "It was an extraordinary engineering accomplishment."

From this closer view, the towers looked old and weathered, and though taller and much more numerous, not much different from the abandoned towers they had seen in the Sabremounts. Many of the facets on the black and mirrored towers were cracked or even shattered away. The stone buildings had weathered with gray and black streaks. There was no sign of activity in the high peaks of these towers, except for some distant airships that sailed the narrow channels between them.

A small platform of metal stood on the interior side of the wall. Stairs descended from it out of view. The Guardian tested his weight on it. Then, satisfied, he said, "We will go down here, and walk directly to the Broken Hand that Reaches. Chance, Seth, come."

Chance edged toward the stairs, barely lifting his feet. He did not like the look of the thin metal that formed the steps. The height made him feel a cold sweat in his palms. He looked back and saw Mimir had not moved.

"What about Mimir?" Chance asked.

The Guardian looked at her. "Only as guest of a dweller of Disthea may a makina set foot in the city," he said.

"Perhaps these are special circumstances," she said, "meriting that we transgress this rule in order to satisfy a more demanding imperative."

"Do not claim that I or Chance hosts you, makina. Nor are we dwellers of Disthea."

Mimir looked at them and said nothing. The silence dragged on a moment. Chance wondered if she were considering whether to enter the city illicitly or to yield to the rule.

Seth yelped softly, getting their attention.

"I, I, I am a citizen," Seth croaked slowly, struggling to say the words clearly. "She will be, be my guest."

Chance stared at the coyote in wonder. The Guardian turned and started down the long steps into the Sunken City. Behind Mimir, the ramp to the ship folded up. Mimir gestured toward the stair. Chance followed the Guardian, with Seth and the makina close behind.

CHAPTER

10

Chance wanted to rest his wobbly legs after the long descent, as they stood on the shining street at the bottom of the monstrous stairs. Condensation from the Crystal Wall rained down on them. But the Guardian immediately strode off down the long street, lined by weathered buildings that seemed to lean over the road and greedily seize all of the sunlight, forming a dusky canyon. They hurried to follow.

"Something i-i-is wrong," Seth said.

"What?" Chance looked around. There were people in the street, walking back and forth, seemingly unconcerned. People of all ages, men and women. At a glance, they were indistinguishable from Purimen but that their clothes were more colorful, more finely cut. Chance had the strange sense, for a moment, that perhaps they were Purimen, hurrying around in this impure place, looking for something made according to the strictures of Puriman creed. He expected each person they passed to stop, stare, and ask questions of him. Would these people be angry, or even frightened, to see the Guardian and the makina and a soulburdened coyote walking their streets? Such sights in the Valley of the Walking Man would cause people to gather fearfully, and eventually Rangers would come and drive the strangers away. And yet, no one did more than glance at him. Even the monstrous Guardian, whose hood again covered his head, only earned curious brief stares.

"What is it?" Chance asked Seth again.

"Too quiet," the coyote answered. "To-to-too few." He sniffed at the ground and said nothing more.

Chance craned his neck and looked up at the buildings soaring above them. "Who lives in the higher floors?" he asked. In the tall buildings, the first three or four floors of windows were bright and clean, with white curtains behind them or even occasionally a person sitting at a windowsill and looking out at those who passed by. But the higher windows were everywhere dim, or broken, or covered over with stone or wood.

"No one," Seth said. "Too high, high. Plenty of room down in the bottom."

"A significant portion of the buildings are uninhabitable in the higher floors," Mimir added. "Many of the buildings cannot function without lost guild expertise. Therefore, people live in the bottom floors, where they do not require unavailable powers and technologies. As the Seth has observed, there is more than sufficient room for the entire population of the city in the lower floors of the functioning buildings. There is insufficient commerce with the farms on the Usin River to sustain a substantial population. And the nearly annual flooding also inhibits many settlers."

Chance looked back at the Crystal Wall uneasily. Its height reminded him that a mountain of water stood above them. "It leaks?"

"The wall does not leak, though the ground allows natural percolation. Furthermore, periodic storms project waves over its pinnacle. Ancient machines are required to pump the water out."

"Ta-takes long time," Seth said.

"Why is the wall dark?" Chance wondered aloud.

"Ocean flora multiply upon the surface of the crystal," Mimir explained, "exploiting the opportunity for additional solar radiation."

Chance stopped and stared, his mouth open.

"Plants on glass," Seth growled. "More sun."

"Oh."

Chance looked back again. He thought something huge surged through the ominous dismal sea beyond, a pale gray irregular form, coming close to the wall and then receding. But when he turned to ask Mimir or Seth what it was, he saw that they had continued, following the Guardian. He ran ahead to catch up with them.

They crossed many streets, and no one talked to them until they came to a place where a row of seven men stood in the road before them, each holding a long staff. The men spread out and barred the way. A group of young women in robes stood nearby, gawking, curious to see what lay beyond.

"City ga-guard," Seth said.

"Keep them back, coyote," the Guardian told Seth. Seth ran ahead. Chance watched as he sat on his haunches before one of the guards and talked. To Chance, all of this started to seem like a dream, or as though it happened to someone else. He could barely wonder at this huge city; he could barely wonder at his always-shy coyote talking now with brusque guards.

Two of the other guards came to listen. The Guardian walked on, neither speeding nor slowing his pace. When he reached the line, one of the guards held up his hand and stood in their path. There was a snap and blur, and the Guardian stood on the other side of this man, still walking.

"Halt!" the guard shouted, turning.

"Wait," one of those who had talked with Seth called to this guard. Mimir and Chance joined Seth and waited now uneasily as the Guardian continued on ahead of them. The guards talked in hushed voices, looking after the Guardian and frowning. Finally one came to them, a thin man with dark skin who stared at each of them a second, as if to memorize their appearance, before saying to Seth, "We shall let you follow."

"Tell the City Councilors!" Seth told the man. He trotted ahead.

Chance looked back as he hurried to follow Seth and saw that one of the guards had dashed off down the street, leaving his staff behind. The others huddled together and stared after them, frowning in worry.

The Broken Hand that Reaches thrust up before them now out of a dark nest of smaller towers. A wall of gray-black metal, twice as high as a man, surrounded it. The wall was folded and bent forward and back, in an organic form, as if the hard metal of it had once been cloth that hung here and blew in the wind. They hurried along the side of this gray wall to its far corner. Along the next stretch of wall, they saw the Guardian. He waited before a tall archway. More guards stood at the far end of the street, looking warily at the Guardian.

Chance and Mimir followed as Seth ran to the Guardian's side. The arch opened onto a vast square at the front of the tower. The square was strewn with white stones, so that at another time it would have stretched before them empty and serene. But not today: the air above the stones shimmered and twisted. Dust kicked up and fell in one corner of the square, then another, stirring the heavy gravel, as if something invisible walked here and there. After a moment, a sound like a distant scream leaked from the shimmering air, faint and unreal. It stopped abruptly, leaving a relentless metallic echo of shrieking children. The air dimmed inexplicably then, as if a cloud passed over. Dozens of black fists, spotted green, appeared floating in the air; they cracked open sickeningly, each revealing an eye that glared, and then just as quickly they disappeared. A smell of roses and then a bitter taste of copper came over Chance.

In the middle of the chaos, a single vague human form seemed to twist and flicker into existence. It turned in place but did not move from its spot.

Chance took a step backwards. In this square the world had gone mad. It was like a vision of hell from some Puriman prophecy. He felt dizzy, and felt also as if he were slowly being withdrawn from the scene. He would have backed up farther, but the dizziness rooted him, a hint of the feeling he had experienced in the barn when the god had fouled his mind.

"What is it?" Chance jumped as his voice echoed back at him out of the square, distorted and loud.

"Wounded worldbeing," Seth growled, inscrutably. The hair on his back stood tall, and his tail curled tight under his legs.

"Worldwrack," the Guardian added.

Then the Guardian slowly raised his arms, so that they stretched out wide to each side, filling the gateway.

"Cover your ears," he said.

Without hesitation Seth leapt down and put his paws on his head, pulling the folds of his ears down. Mimir did not move. Chance hesitated, not quite understanding. The Guardian tilted his head back and screamed.

Too late Chance clapped his palms over his ears. He heard the full force of the first second of the deafening howl of the Guardian. It echoed out into the city and cracked, and cracked again, as it rebounded down cavernous streets and off long black cliffs of deserted towers.

As the echo faded, the unreal darkness in the square before them shattered and collapsed into pools of black shadow that lay on the ground like some kind of thin oil, where they slowly dissolved and evaporated. The distortions of vision retreated into distant points and vanished. The uncanny sounds whimpered away into silence. The smell of roses and copper burned away, replaced by the salty sea air.

Standing in the center of the square was a woman.

They stared a moment, unsure whether she was some remnant of the evil that the god had left. But she remained, solid and attentive. She was tall with very dark skin and wore a long shirt of bright black and red that hung to her knees; under it were pants of the same color.

She turned and looked at them. Finally she said, "Who are you?" Chance could barely hear her, though the motion of her lips was unmistakable and easy to read. His ears still rang from the Guardian's shout.

She walked toward them, planting one foot precisely before the other, like a cat. She stopped a pace away and stared at each of them in turn, defiantly.

"I am Wadjet, of the Fricandor lands, from the tribe of the Stewards." Chance found her accent strange: the sounds were long, different, but clear and articulate.

The Guardian said nothing. Chance stared. The woman had a broad nose and eyes with vertical slit pupils like the eyes of a cat. Her black hair was knotted in thick brown cords that hung behind her head. There was something strange about her mouth. Then she smiled at the Guardian, an expression that seemed almost a challenge, and Chance saw it: behind full, red lips, her teeth flashed white, revealing fangs. The eye teeth and the matching bottom teeth were long and sharp.

Seth, who had just stood and shaken his head, getting his bearings after the Guardian's cry, lay down again and stretched out in a coyote bow. "Greetings and, and, and honor to you, Steward. I, I am Psuche, also called Seth."

Chance was surprised. He had not known Seth had another name. But of course he must, if he had had some other life before his time in the Valley: the name of Seth had been given him by Chance.

The woman seemed to consider this for a while.

Chance shifted uneasily. He had seen now several unmen, but this one disturbed him. His eyes wandered over her, against his better will, noticing the high cheekbones, the green of the eyes, the smooth dark skin, the full athletic shape of her body, the curves of it visible in the tight-fitting shirt and pants, the fascinating flash of her white teeth. She was—he realized with unease—very beautiful. He felt also a painful shame to recall what he looked like: dressed in torn and dirty clothes, his shoes tied together with rags, left arm bound with a dirty rag crusted with blood, his hair stiff with dust and dirt. He looked at the ground, his cheeks burning.

I must resist these thoughts, he told himself. It would be wrong to be attracted to an unman. All Purimen know that unmen are mutilated, unclean things.

He forced himself to lift his head and fix his eyes on the cool gray stone face of the Guardian.

Mimir raised a hand but the Guardian spoke before she could. "We have no call with you, Wadjet, Steward of the Fricandor Lands. Go with good luck. We seek closed hearing with the Mothers of the Gotterdammerung. Our path is fearsome, and we do not wish our sorrows on you."

The woman looked at the Guardian's face, then his huge hands and his broad shoulders. "I also seek the Mothers. My mission is pressing. A plague has struck my land. Who are you to claim greater need?"

Seth whined in sympathy, but the others were silent. Seeing that the Guardian was unmoved, she stepped aside, and added, "I will return later. Even the lion leaves the watering hole when the rhinoceros comes to drink."

Chance did not know what a rhinoceros was, but he understood the point.

The Guardian walked on without another word, his pale eyes fixed straight ahead, his heavy feet grinding the white stones of the courtyard. Chance looked at the Steward. The feline eyes dismayed him. It seemed almost, the way she looked at him, that she might eat him. And yet, he felt a sweet pang low in his chest when she smiled. He turned away, put a hand on Seth, and hurried to catch up with the Guardian. Mimir watched all this without expression.

"What happened here?" Chance asked the Guardian, as he came to his side.

"The god was here. He scarred space before he left for your home."

The Guardian stopped before huge double doors of burnished gold, more than twice his height. Above the doors was an inscription, formed of shining white fragments of some material Chance did not at first recognize.

Men anthropos aneu hodon, de pinakon poiomen,
Men anthropos aneu telon, de telon poiomen,
Men aneu athanaton psuchen anthropou, de athanton psuchen poiomen.

"What does it say?" Chance asked.

"Man was lost," the Guardian explained, "and we made a map. Man had no end—no purpose—so we made a purpose. Man had no soul, so we made a soul."

"The blasphemy of the lost men! That is from the New Psalms of the Purimen!"

"Those words were writ here, above the door to the Hand that Reaches, when the Guild within was the Theogenics Guild, and the gods were not yet born. The words were scratched away after the Theomachia. They were scraped off the very day that the fingers of the Hand that Reaches were sheared down."

"The false god put it back."

The Guardian nodded. "Those bones are likely the bones of most of the Mothers who were left."

Chance realized then with a shock that this was what formed the inscription: splintered shards of bone, somehow gathered into letters and set above the gate. With a rush of nausea he feared he could smell now, mixed into the damp and salt sea, the human marrow.

The Guardian pushed open the doors. They swung wide without a sound. The four of them stepped forward. Inside stretched a great hall with a distant ceiling. The walls were all formed of huge irregular facets of stone and metal, so that the long hall seemed to be the interior of a randomly cut crystal. The walls rose, leaning in at a slight angle, so that they closed together high above. The facets high over them shone in different bright colors, and the lights mixed, forming a pale golden glow on the floor before them.

At the far end of the room crouched a statue of a man, in gold, holding out his hands as if offering some gift, palms up and held together. Fire raged from the cup formed of his fingers.

"The fire of Prometheus is l-l-lit," Seth barked. "Bad omen."

The Guardian turned to Mimir. "You will wait outside, makina."

The makina did not respond. The Guardian pushed one door closed, and then put his hand on the other, waiting. Mimir looked at each of them, and then walked out. The Guardian closed the other door and turned back to the hall.

CHAPTER

11

The Guardian eyed the hall with distaste. Four thousand years had perished since he had stood here last, during that final battle of the War Against the Gods. Then, hundreds had died throughout this tower, and the white stones outside had been coated red and black with blood.

"Who is here?" he called. His voice echoed tightly in the space. He waited silently for a reply. After a moment, footsteps sounded out, approaching in a rush from somewhere in the back of the hall. The Guardian strode toward them. Chance and Seth followed.

A woman ran out of a small door to the left of the statue. She had raven-black hair, very straight and shoulder length, and very dark eyes, and seemed little past a girl in her age. She wore the red-bordered black robes of a Mother of the Gotterdammerung. She hurried toward them, an expression of relief on her face.

And then she stopped abruptly, almost tripping over herself. She looked at the Guardian and her face collapsed into an expression of overwhelming grief. She fell flat onto the floor and stretched out.

"*Atheos!*"

She moaned loudly, in despair, and then spoke in her guild language. "*Atheos. Ton anthropon eauton eleeig!*"

The Guardian answered her back in Common.

"Get up, witch. You will call me Guardian. Who still abides here?"

The woman did not rise. She moaned and pressed her black hair into her face with a hand that shook wildly.

"Oh, Antigod, have mercy on humanity. Do not summon the Old Gods."

"Rise, and call me Guardian, or I'll hail them right now. Who still lives? Rise, I say."

The woman rose into a crouch, but would not look up. Her arms shook, her knees trembled.

Does she have reason to fear me so? the Guardian wondered.

"I'm alone. I'm alone. It killed everyone. I heard them screaming and dying. It killed everyone. And I saw it." She choked on her words and started to weep. "The Antigod has come," she moaned.

Seth walked to her side and put a paw on her knee. She hunched her shoulders, as if trying to hide her face, and lifted a hand hesitatingly, unsure of whether to touch the coyote.

Finally she spoke again.

"I couldn't leave the tower. The doors, all the outside doors, they somehow only opened onto themselves again. I searched everywhere. None of the Mothers who were here, in the Hand—none remain. Just some—parts. I buried those in the vaults. I. . . ."

"Hexus killed all?"

"They attacked him, with ancient weapons. He fought back, he killed them all."

"Why not you?"

"I didn't fight. My superiors forbad it. I'm the only novice in the Hand. I hid."

The Guardian watched her a long time in silence. Then he said to her, in her own guild language, "*This is Chance Kyrien, bereaved by your guild among the Purimen seventeen years ago. Why does the god want him?*"

The woman snapped her head up, and peered at Chance intently. She hesitated, trembling. "*This is him,*" she whispered, answering in her guild language.

"*Why does the god want him?*" the Guardian demanded again.

With an effort she looked away from Chance, and started to rock back and forth.

"*Do you know the doom of the Earth should I fail?*" the Guardian growled.

Seth furrowed the skin over his snout and glared at the Guardian, a sign of scolding, but said nothing.

The woman looked at Chance again, and her eyes began to well again with tears. "*The Potentiate,*" she whispered.

The Guardian lifted his head back in shock.

"*What?*"

"*He's a Potentiate.*"

"Speak Common!" Chance demanded. "I can see you're talking of me. You cannot talk of me this way. Speak Common."

The Guardian ignored him and continued in the Mother's guild language. "*How could that be? The Fathers of the Theogenics Guild were slain at the end of the Theomachia. The bloodlines were cut.*"

"*All the children are tested,*" she said, her voice little more than a whisper, as she rocked back and forth, still pressing her hair into her face. "*All the children of Gotterdammerung Mothers. It's an ancient ceremony. He was tested. Found to be a....*"

"*Who was the mother?*"

The woman rocked back and forth a long time before she whispered, "*All dead.*"

"*Who was the father?*"

She shook her head.

The Guardian gritted his teeth, a loud grinding that echoed in the silent hall. "*And you set a Potentiate out among tribes witless of the lore of the gods? Well it was, perhaps, that you did not slay him for his faultless birth and youth. But the Mothers were fools not to keep him here, where they could have set watch over him.*"

"*It is said there was a watch,*" she answered, her voice quavering.

"*Where? Who?*" the Guardian demanded.

Seth yelped.

The Guardian looked down at the coyote. Seth put his paw down, turned, and bowed his head. "*I too am, am a guardian.*"

"*You have some place in the Gotterdammerung?*" the Guardian asked, incredulous.

"*N-no. I belong to the Hekademon.*"

"Speak Common!" Chance demanded again, this time shouting at Seth.

"*A philosopher!*" the Guardian said. "*What a worthless band I gather.*"

"*Not a philosopher. A, a, a student still.*"

"Speak Common!" Chance repeated.

The Guardian turned back to the Mother, and asked, "*Why does the god want the boy? What good is a Potentiate to it?*"

"Stop," Seth barked in Common, while the woman hesitated. "Food, drink, clothes, r-r-rest. Chance is tired. I am tired." He did not add that the woman was in shock, though his glaring at the Guardian, while he again put his paw on the woman's shoulder, made it clear that she was his real concern.

The Guardian growled in impatient frustration.

"What is your, your name?" Seth asked her.

"Thetis," she whispered.

"Ta-ta-take us to chambers, Thetis," Seth said. "Do you have food?"

She nodded. She glanced at the Guardian, but when he did not protest, she rose enough to stand, bowing over awkwardly, and moving half sideways bade them follow as she slipped back through the door from which she had entered the hall. Seth stayed close at her side, half-guiding her as she went.

"What did she say?" Chance asked.

The Guardian only growled, "We have not the time for these cares. But come."

CHAPTER

12

C hance was afraid. They were hiding something from him—even Seth was hiding something from him. He resolved that he would leave if they refused again to speak Common.

Thetis led them through a door behind the statue at the end of the hall, which opened to the foot of a broad, winding stair in a towering, circular space that rose up into an indefinite gloom. Each wind of the stair around the cylinder was one tall floor. Chance looked up: the stairs were lit for the first six or seven flights, but after this wound up into darkness.

"My chambers, the free chambers, are up six floors," Thetis mumbled.

"Good, good," Seth reassured her.

The woman led them on. Chance followed, looking from Seth to the Guardian and back again. His unease grew slowly into fear. What secret were they keeping from him? He still doubted he had made the right choice in trusting the Guardian, but he had not doubted, till moments ago, that Seth could be trusted. But here was the coyote speaking two different guild languages and sharing secrets with the Guardian. And all the while, they seemed to be doing nothing to help Sarah.

Chance looked at the woman. She was slightly taller than him, but thinner, and he saw now that she looked to be perhaps a few years older than he. She tried to meet no one's eyes, but stared fixedly at the stairs before her feet. Yet, a few times, her eyes of very deep brown glanced quickly at Chance. The familiarity of her black hair and nearly black eyes made an uncomfortable thought grow in the depths of Chance's mind: are these my people? He shivered and whispered to himself, under his breath, "I am a Puriman." Seth's ears twitched.

When they came to the edge of the darkness, where the pale lights above them were the last on the ascending stairs, the woman turned and pushed open a gray entrance that gave onto a broad white hallway, lined with doors. A large window formed the hall's end, its view filled with the streaked gray wall of a building across the road. The woman slipped ahead, looked over her shoulder to be sure they were following, and went to the first door.

"These are novice quarters. Empty. You can use them." She pointed timidly at a door down the hall. "My room."

A table stood in the chamber, surrounded by chairs. Two smaller doors to the left opened into a bathroom and a bedroom. A small kitchen filled the opposite corner. The far wall held a broad window that let in sunlight and looked out on the square where the Guardian had howled the world back into submission. Through a crack between two buildings beyond, Chance could see the blue-black Crystal Wall on the western side of the city. The rays of the sun slanted low now, so that only the peaks of the towers were bright. In the distance two airships floated close to another tower.

"Can you eat?" the Guardian asked Thetis.

"There's some food here."

"Eat quickly, then. Feed the Puriman. We must go to Uroboros."

"No," Seth barked. He sat on his haunches obstinately in the middle of the room, facing the Guardian. "The sun sets, sets. All are tired. Tomorrow."

"If the god comes and we have not made ready, all these may die, philosopher."

"We mortals prefer to, to, to die well fed, well clothed, and wi-wi-with our wits our own. Go easy, Guardian. Let them eat and bathe and sleep. Questions tomorrow." He trotted to the door, then added, "I promised the-the-the guards I would talk with the City Councilors. And I'll, I'll, I will return with clothes for Chance."

The Guardian watched him go. "Leave the makina outside!" he called.

Seth yelped.

"A philosophy student," the Guardian growled.

Thetis appeared terrified to be left alone with Chance and the Guardian. She divided her glances between the Guardian's ominous gray form and Chance's face. Chance was surprised that she paid him any heed, and he became uncomfortable as she seemed more and more to inspect him with a hungry curiosity.

Soon after Seth left, she slipped out of the room, and Chance imagined she had fled, but she returned with snow-white bandages, some towels, and a glass bottle of clear liquid. She pointed at Chance's arm, where the bear had cut him.

"I cannot use guild works," Chance said.

"This is cotton. This is alcohol. I do not think they break your creed."

Chance nodded. He began to strip off his filthy bandages, but she stopped him.

"Let me."

She reached out and touched his bare arm with trembling, cool fingertips. For a moment she stood like that, just touching him. Chance felt that she seemed almost to believe he wasn't real—or perhaps that she had expected him and now could not believe he had arrived. When he looked at her pointedly, she blushed and began to slowly peel his bandages off. They had dried into his scabs, and the wide scrapes of the bear claw tore open again as she pulled the brown scraps of cloth away. He cringed but said nothing. She poured on the stinging alcohol, and Chance breathed deeply the sharp smell of it as he bit back a gasp of pain. She wiped the cut clean, poured more alcohol on, and then wrapped the arm in the gauze.

"We can change it again tomorrow," she whispered.

"Thank you," he said.

She nodded. She went away again and returned with a tray of food: walnuts, crisp apples, several wedges of hard cheese, and a loaf of stale bread. They sat at the table then and ate. Cool water that tasted of metal came from a tap in the wall.

"What will happen to Mimir?" Chance asked the Guardian.

"The makina will wait outside," the Guardian said. "It is no hardship for a machine to wait a day or a year."

Thetis looked at Chance and then the Guardian with wide eyes, as if surprised that Chance would talk with this dread being in the Common tongue.

A discomfort grew in Chance over the fear and awe the woman felt for the Guardian. He had treated the Guardian as a man—a frightening, powerful unman, but still a kind of man. The woman instead could barely breathe in the Guardian's presence.

Should he speak differently to the Guardian? Should he not speak to him at all? And yet, looking at him, where he stood by the window, Chance could not muster any of the terror and reverence that the woman felt. The Guardian was scary, even awesome, but to Chance he seemed now, ever since their time by the river after the fight with the bear, a man for all that. He was quiet, stoic, like fierce old Elder Isai of the Purimen Council. But not unfathomable, not otherworldly.

Seemingly torn between wanting to be away from the Guardian and not wanting to be away from Chance or alone, Thetis finally whispered something inaudible and slipped through the door. The Guardian watched her go, and then turned back to the window, looking out at the few lights of city towers as dusk turned to night.

"She called you Atheos," Chance said.

"That is an idle name. Do not speak it again."

"But there is such a . . . in the *Theopolemein*."

The Guardian turned his head to look at Chance. "What does a Puriman know of unholy odes?"

"Some of the Trumen read the poem. They talk of it. I have heard tell of its story. I'm not completely ignorant."

The Guardian said nothing.

"Are you the Atheos, the Anti-god of the poem?"

"There is no Atheos. I am the Guardian. That is all. Go to sleep now. The coyote says you need to sleep. Who are we to argue with one who learns to be a Hekademon?" He turned back to the view of the ancient city.

This meant nothing to Chance, but he knew better than to ask for an explanation. There was a bed in a small cubicle connected to the room. The Guardian showed him how to turn the light on and off—a forbidden guild machine, he noticed with disappointment. Chance took off most of his filthy clothes. As he turned off the light, he felt an oppressive anxiety, sure that the building was not yet right, that it was haunted by those murdered here and polluted by the evil craft of the false god. He knelt at the bedside and prayed for guidance in this forbidden place, and he prayed for the safety of Sarah and Paul, and for the souls of his father and mother. Then he left the door open and stretched out on the strangely soft mattress. He was reassured that from where he lay he could see the Guardian in the next room, immobile before the window, brooding over the night on the Sunken City of Disthea.

Chance awoke when Seth's soft paw pressed his shoulder.

"Chance."

He sat up. For a moment he was disoriented, unsure of where he was: white walls, a tall window letting in sunlight, black towers outside. Seth had closed the door. Then Chance slowly remembered.

"Ah," Chance said softly. "I had hoped, for a moment, that it was all just a bad dream."

Seth nodded and sighed. The coyote sat on his haunches by the bedside. He looked clean, his fur glossy. He wore a kind of gray collar. Chance noticed then that clothes were piled at the foot of the bed: a coarse shirt of white wool, coarse pants dyed so dark blue they were nearly black, a coat of dark leather with rough stitches made by an awl, and brown leather shoes.

"Some, some in the city buy Purimen clothes. From up-up-upriver. They admire the work."

"Thank you," Chance whispered. A lump rose in his throat, so grateful he felt that the coyote respected him enough to do this. "Thank you."

"Welcome." Seth pointed a bent wrist at the door to the bath. "Wash first."

Chance hesitated. "Should I call you ... Psuche?"

"No. Al-always to you Se-seth."

Chance touched the collar.

"Hek-Heka-Hekademon student collar," Seth explained. "That is my guild. For which I am ap-pa-pa-prentice."

Chance nodded. He wanted to say something more, and to ask questions. Why had Seth been there at the Walking Man watching him? Had it been hard to leave the city where he had a life, it seemed, and go where he was hated and even in danger? What did he do here, in the city? How had he come to live in Disthea? What did the Guardian mean, to call him a "philosopher"? But Chance felt awkward, embarrassed, to learn the pet that he had shared secrets with was no pet but somehow a—what? Scholar? Traveler? Spy? Elder?

He went into the bath.

When Chance returned, shirtless, Seth pointed with his nose at the gold band that Chance wore on a string around his neck.

"I-I-I-I'm glad you didn't lose it," Seth said.

Chance nodded. He clutched the gold ring. "Me too."

Chance had found this ring with Seth. Though the eldest Puriman son in each family should receive his mother's wedding ring for his own proposal, his mother had long ago said that her ring would go to Paul. But last year, after the Elders spoke on a Sunday, Chance had used a hunt for wild blueberries as an excuse to his father and wandered far into the black hills east of the Walking Man Lake. Seth followed silently at his heels.

In those hills, long-abandoned farms from the later ages rotted into damp loam under crowding maples. Chance had a favorite ruin there, not far from the simple hut where Elder Sirach had lived alone: a dark octagonal farmhouse with no roof behind which leaned two rows of gravestones with unreadable pitted faces. Inside the shell of that home, lying in the dim beams of light that filtered green through the trees and the skeleton of the roof, he had found a rotted box. It sat face down, close to one wall. Rotten clothes, almost indistinguishable from soil, covered it. He would have missed it but that it had cracked loudly when he stepped on it.

He had uncovered the box and pulled it into a shred of sunlight for a close look. The lid crumbled as he lifted it. Inside were heaped the ashes of old pictures and solid slugs of metal that had once been guild machines, and also, stuck into a layer of gummy black fungus, a band of gold. Old words, some guild language, inscribed the inner surface of the ring. Chance could not read them.

Puriman code forbade the use of such a thing. But gold, Chance reasoned, was pure, a thing of the Earth, and so he had kept it, and in secret he had used the smithing tools in the barn to hammer and reshape the ring himself, forging something clean of it. Chance had then strung the band on a loop of clean twine and had worn it round his neck ever since, a single purpose in mind for it.

Now he held the band up, a kind of salute to Seth, and then reached for the clothes that lay on the bed.

They fit well, the shirt and pants loose but not too large, and the shoes sturdy and soft within. As Chance pulled on the jacket, he followed Seth into the other room. Thetis sat at the table, cleaned up also, in new black robes. Seth climbed onto a chair by her and began eating greedily. Mimir stood in the middle of the room, silent. Chance noticed that she looked different. She wore the same, faintly ridiculous, black and white formal clothes, as if dressed for Church or a fine dinner and dance. But her skin was less golden, and her hair more brown, than he had remembered. Only her silver eyes looked like a machine's. She smiled at him with a genuinely human expression. It was obvious also now that the form of her body was more feminine than he had thought yesterday. It seemed foolish that he had doubted her sex when first seeing her.

"Good morning," he said.

"Greetings to you, Puriman Chance Kyrien," she said.

The Guardian stood at the window, brooding still over the city. Chance went to him and handed him the gray cloak he had worn.

"Thank you," he said.

The Guardian nodded and pulled the cloak over his huge shoulders.

Chance sat with the others as they ate the remnants of the food from the evening before.

Then the Guardian and Seth began talking in the guild language that Chance called Leafwage. Thetis looked nervously at the floor but said nothing. Chance watched them for only a few seconds before he shouted, "No! If you are talking of me you must talk in Common. I deserve to know what is being decided."

The Guardian stared at him, considering. Then he said, "I say the makina should not be here now, when we speak of this. And I say that it would be better for you if you did not know everything, Puriman. The coyote says otherwise. He thinks the makina might be useful. That's why he brought the machine in here. And, the leaders of this city want to trust the makina. The coyote also thinks you should know the worst of all."

"Can she help?" Chance asked, looking at Mimir.

"Perhaps," the Guardian said. "Or it could turn on us. It does not care for human beings, or other living things. The makina have their own goals, first of which is to leave the Earth far behind. And all that this makina knows, all it learns from us, it will tell all the Makine."

"Common in-interest," Seth protested.

"Let her stay," Chance said. "If Mimir can help save Sarah, then I ask for her help. And I want to know everything. I cannot help Sarah or Paul if I'm kept ignorant."

The Guardian nodded. "So be it." He turned to Thetis and spoke in Common. "Tell us what the god wants."

"I don't know. It arrived here—I don't know when, the time has been strange after...." She looked around nervously. "But it started one day when all the Mothers disappeared from their regular duties. For a long time, for weeks, I did not know why. The Mothers were running back and forth, whispering, but not telling me or the younger Mothers what had arrived. They must have tried...I don't know...to talk with it. Sometimes I was not allowed to leave this hall—they didn't want me to see it. I think it went away several times, and for those times duties were as usual. But then one morning it returned, and I was confined to my quarters, and after hours of waiting I heard screams, and unreal sounds. I disobeyed my orders, and went down to the great hall. I saw it there, half god, half madman, bending things, screaming. A soulburdened ape was there too, covered in gold. I think the god was making the Mothers tell him their secrets."

A single tear slipped down her cheek. She glanced at Chance before looking back at the table. "A Mother ordered me to hide, and I did. Some of the Mothers unlocked the ancient weapons. I hid in the basement library. I heard their screams, and the sounds of the weapons, and other... impossible sounds. I hid for a long time, days I think, but then finally I climbed up. I could find no one alive. I couldn't leave. I wandered. Till you called."

She rubbed her cheek. Her hands were shaking again. She had cleaned them, and Chance saw that her nails were frayed and broken, as if she had been clawing at stone.

"Why does the god want Chance?"

She shook her head. But then she said, "I think it wants to be whole. Somehow a Potentiate...."

"The Chance is a Potentiate?" Mimir asked.

A long silence settled in the room as everyone looked at Chance, and then Mimir.

"Tread with care now, machine," the Guardian said, in an ominous low voice that made the air in the room shake. He took a step toward the makina and stood with his knees bent. "Should you not heed me, should you try to act against my will and without my say, I'll crush you to dust, and then I'll dig every last one of your kin out of the earth and crush their tiny little gears to dust. Do not think the Makine are safe from me. I can move mountains and then eat the light out of your hearts." And, for a moment, his eyes flashed two bright piercing white beams onto Mimir.

Mimir betrayed nothing. She looked placidly at the Guardian, then back at Chance.

"What is a Potentiate?" Chance asked.

Seth, who had been quietly licking morsels of food from the table while the others talked, stopped chewing and glanced at Thetis uneasily.

"Tell me," Chance insisted.

"One who can pass through Ma'at's gate," the Guardian told him. "And cross the bridge Bifrost to the Numin Well, and die there, and return a god."

Chance frowned, puzzling out these blasphemous concepts.

"The first gods killed all the Potentiates," Thetis said, "here in the Hand that Reaches, when the war first began. Potentiates must have mattered somehow."

"Yes." The Guardian looked up and past them, as if staring back through time at the memory. "The gods feared the Potentiates could be used to harm them in those dread spaces beyond the Numin Well. Ma'at, gatekeeper of Bifrost, will let only a Potentiate pass. The Younger Gods were safe, when all the Potentiates were dead. There was no one left who could cross Bifrost and threaten their souls."

"So maybe it fears Chance," Thetis said. "It wants to kill him?"

"No," the Guardian said. "It could have killed him before, with ease. But it did not."

"Could it...use his, his body?" Seth asked.

"But the flesh of the god should no better bond with a Potentiate than with the body it now has," the Guardian said.

"There is an alternate possibility," Mimir said. "The current corpus of the deity is distinct from the corpus that we observed at the Oracle. This entails that the god portion changed its habitation or host. Yet, the Hexus did not appear to change his direction or plans. Ergo, it was able to transfer also the memories and emotions it had formed. We conclude that the Hexus can move its...." Mimir looked at Chance, seeking a word suitable for him. "Soul. It could have as a goal moving its memories and plans and all of its person into this adolescent. Then it would send him into the Numin Well, to replace its body there. The god would be reborn."

There was a long silence. Seth looked at the floor when Chance met his eyes. Thetis did the same. The Guardian and Mimir stood still as statues, thinking.

"But," Chance finally said, "but the witches made the false gods. They were unmen."

Seth's ears lay down flat.

Then it dawned on Chance. "Oh no," he said. He looked at Seth and then Thetis, imploring each for some word of denial, but they were silent.

"That's false," he said. "A lie. Look at me. Look at me. I don't have cat eyes, or fur on my skin, or fangs. That false god is wrong. It made a mistake. I'm a man. A true man. A Truman."

Thetis put the fingertips of both hands over her mouth, and bowed her head so that her hair fell over her face.

"No. No." Chance stood abruptly. His chair fell back on the floor. "They swore. The witches swore. They swore I was pure." He started breathing heavily, turning in place. He'd had enough. This was madness, this was everything that a Puriman must deny, must flee.

He went to the door and pushed it open and ran into the hall, looking for some way out, away from the white walls and glowing evil ceiling and unholy machines in the floors and the lies and these unmen. His breath came in gasps now. Where were the stairs? He turned in place till he remembered, then staggered to the end of the hall and pushed the door open. He stumbled to the railing and looked up, then down the reeling stair well. He took first one step, then another. He descended a dozen steps before he fell back and sat.

Seth came and sat next to him and put one paw over Chance's shoulders. The stunted coyote fingers gripped him gently. The Guardian stepped behind the coyote, silently watching.

"Sta-sta-stay, Chance. Not safe outside. Stay."

"Oh God," Chance panted. "Oh God have mercy, I want to be saved, God. I want to stay in the Valley. I want to be a vinmaster and to marry Sarah. Don't let it be, God. I don't want to be forsaken."

He stood and went to the wall. He turned and leaned back, and rolled his head against the hard stone. "The witches said I was true. As pure as any of the Valley, they said. As pure as any of the Valley of the Walking Man. But I'm the witch boy, aren't I? My brother was right." He gasped as if he had run a long distance. "All those boys who hated me were right. The witches lied."

He threw his head back. "Liars!" His voice echoed on and on, up into the impossible hidden heights of the abandoned accomplishments of the Theogenics Guild. *Liars, liars, liars, liars....*

"They didn't lie," Thetis said. The three of them, surprised to hear her soft voice, turned to look at her where she stood now a few steps above. Seeing Chance in distress seemed to have calmed her. Her hands were at her sides. Her hair was pulled behind her ears. On the landing above, Mimir watched silently, her face inscrutably placid.

"There is no person left on Earth," Thetis said softly, "who does not have ancestors that... remade themselves, as the Purimen call it. You are no more remade than any others of the Purimen, either in the Usin Valley or among the Forest Lakes. Less so, most likely."

Chance stared at her as if he did not comprehend what she had said. And in part he did not. He did not know what he felt, but what she said was no comfort. Nothing was pure—that much he understood of her words. But how could he face the Elders, how could he ask to be confirmed, with such an argument in his heart?

He looked around again, seeking an exit, something made by human hands, or some green tree or leaf....

"Breathe slo-slowly," Seth said. He stood on his hind legs uneasily, and put one paw on Chance's shoulder again. "Slow."

"God has forsaken me," Chance whispered. "God must forsake me. For I am a vain forgery of a man. I'll be cast out."

Bright tears fell from his eyes.

"I am not a Puriman."

CHAPTER

13

"Puriman?" The Guardian stood in the doorway. Chance had insisted they leave him alone in the room in which he slept the night before, and he had stared out the window at the alien city, feeling empty of all thoughts or feelings but bitterness. Finally, he had wept, lying on the bed. He wept for his father and his mother and the death of all of his dreams of being a Puriman—because even if no one would know in the Valley of the Walking Man, he could not himself accept confirmation and baptism now. That meant all his hopes were ashes. He had been unable to pray, other than to repeat again and again, "Help me God, help Sarah, help Paul, help me." Finally he fell asleep.

He woke in the early afternoon to a hard prodding between his shoulder blades. The gold band he wore on the string around his neck had slipped behind his back, and he lay with it pressing into his spine. It was as if Sarah were behind him, pushing him.

No more self-pity, he told himself. He rose and washed, then knelt and prayed for Sarah's safety and for Paul's. He had only just stood when the Guardian came in.

"Puriman?" the Guardian asked again.

Chance cringed at the title, but instead of protesting, he demanded, "How do we end it?" He looked up at the Guardian. "How do we get Sarah and Paul back, and stop the false god? How do I avenge my parents?"

"We must go to Uroboros, Guild Hall of the Dark Engineers. They have the Numin Jars, last binding glasses forged by Threkor. With one of these we can use you as bait, and trap the god, and I can lock it away."

"Let's go."

Seth, Thetis, and Mimir waited in the hall. They said nothing, but Seth rubbed against his leg, and Chance touched the coyote's head. Then they descended the stairs in the dim light, the dark abyss gaping ominously above them, and walked across the great hall in silence, the click of Mimir's hard black boots echoing in the emptiness.

The Guild Hall of the Dark Engineers, Uroboros, coiled in the center of the city, not far from the Broken Hand that Reaches. It was formed of black metal scales, each as large as a man, bent over long rows of tall arches of steel, so that the building seemed a vast black serpent that circled around a hidden center court. The entrance resembled a snake's head, consuming the tail of the building, with just enough space for people to enter from one side. This entrance faced a square that topped a long, broad street that ran south to the Crystal Wall at the farthest edge of the city.

Looking down this street was like peering down a dark glen, Chance thought, with a black wall of water frozen at the end. It seemed at any moment that water might let loose and tumble toward them, drowning them all.

They went in, stepping into darkness as if being swallowed by a snake. A man and woman stood in an anteroom of black stone and black steel, dressed in clothes like shining black leather. A thin covering of hair shadowed their shaven heads. They bowed.

"Take me to the Grand Creator," the Guardian commanded.

The pair hesitated, staring off in space, as if listening to a distant sound. Then the man bowed, and the woman turned to lead them back into the gloom of Uroboros.

They walked in silence down a long corridor that bent slowly to the right, wrapping around the inside of the building. Seth stayed close to Chance's side, head up, ears perked proudly. They passed many closed doors, gray and streaked with black oil. A few doors stood ajar, opening onto deep gray rooms where dark machines twisted and turned, performing inexplicable tasks, while Engineers looked on with attentive awe, like supplicants.

Chance felt a growing despair looking at these demonic forms that seemed to him to writhe in pain. As an unman, would he now have to spend the rest of his life in ghastly, infernal places like this one? Would he come to accept these hateful things, even learn to like them? To need them? He missed the touch and smell of soil, the silence of the vineyard, the task of trimming vines.

The few Engineers or apprentices in the hall slipped silently aside as they approached, bowed and eyed the Guardian with nervous glances, and remained bent over until the group was well past and out of sight.

The hall began to widen and grow brighter. Then the passage opened through a great, iron archway. They stopped below it, on the threshold of a vast chamber that stretched off into darkness. Overhead the gray metal ribs of the building were exposed, fretted with black and gray pipes and wires, the veins and arteries of the mysterious workings of Uroboros. Engineers gathered into shadows along the walls, dwarfed by the great sweep of the room. Dim, ugly whinings of stretched metal, thundering sheets of hammered tin, and a dull thumping on lead echoed through the hall: music of the Dark Engineers. And with it, the smell of boiling oil greased the very air around them, and made the walls black.

"Threkor's Hall," Seth whispered to Chance. "And there, there are-ra-are the Oil Pits of Threkor." Two black pools bubbled in the center of the room.

To each side of the doorway, tall statues of roughly human form stood. Their surfaces looked to be metal and stone, hewn in sharp facets. Their arms ended not in hands but in spikes. Their eyes were red stones. Chance had never seen statues like this, of abstracted human form, looming rough and dangerous.

"Ah!" Chance gasped, as one statue turned its head and looked at them.

"Threkor's Engles," Seth explained, his ears flat and his tail curling under. "Ancient de-de-defenders of Uroboros."

Chance and Seth and Mimir followed the Guardian into the room.

Beyond the two oil pits, a throne of grey steel stood on a raised stone floor. A man sat on the throne, with a shaved head and wrinkled dark skin. He wore lenses of black glass that glinted in the pool of blue light shed down from a bulb mounted high above him, where two soaring ribs of steel met perpendicular to a rail that ran the length of the hall, like the spine inside a dead, hollow chest.

Three men and three women stood to each side of the throne, Elders of the guild. Chance noted then that the strange woman of the Fricandor Lands stood behind one of the Elders, her green cat eyes and her white fangs flashing in the dark of the room.

By the throne, a tall hammer stood in an onyx plinth. The hammer's black haft rose as tall as Chance. The hammer's head was burnished silver, with a face as wide as two fists and a back that trailed away into a flat blade. Beneath this head, a collar of spiky crystals surrounded the top of the shaft.

It took a long minute to cross the silent black room. The hard steps of Mimir echoed into the distance. Before the throne Seth stretched out, and Mimir and Thetis bowed. Chance stood in a daze, sweating in the heat. The smell of oil oppressed him, thickening the air, stifling his breath. The Guardian peered proudly at each of the elders, causing them to shift uncomfortably, until he finally looked straight into the black lenses of the man on the throne.

"Grand Creator," he called. He used his otherworldly voice, loud but somehow soft. It sent through everyone a chill of fear. "Leader of the Dark Engineers. I am the Guardian."

He let that echo into the room, and then ripen in their minds a moment.

"Last I stood in this hall on the cheerless dawn of our win in the Theomachia. We bound the fifth god. Then great Threkor, truest of the demigods, lay dying here between the oil pits, his hammer at his side. After your gravesongs I left you, but in the care of your guild, two Numin Jars were trusted, to be guarded until such time as the lost Thei, foul twins, might return. That dread day has come. Yield now the binding glasses."

The Creator sighed and pushed his shoulders back. The other elders shuffled uneasily.

"Guardian," the Creator spoke in a thin tone, like metal scraping on metal. "Four thousand years have passed. Much has changed. There have been other wars, and sometimes even the threat of the return of gods. The Numin Jars were lost. Stolen, from this very hall. Not in many years have the Dark Engineers had them."

The air dimmed around the Guardian. He seemed to grow taller, and wider, holding in his speech as if fettering an explosion. Finally he spoke in a low rumble.

"You foul the name of Threkor, to say these words."

"Guardian, we battled the Theon just days ago. Many of our sisters and brothers are dead. Many others are worse than dead. And two of Threkor's Engles it destroyed, so that but five remain. If we had known where the Jars rest, we would have used one. And, had we failed, the Jars would be possessed now by that rotting god."

The Guardian was unmoved. He held out his hands, palms up, and peered down at them, as if they were something alien to him.

"These hands broke and bound five gods, and stied them in five Numin Jars. Five." His voice was even more otherworldly and fierce—just as when Chance had first heard it speaking to Hexus. Chance felt a rush of fear. Thetis, standing next to him, shrank: she dropped her head, knotted her fingers together, and bent her shoulders, trying to disappear. Seth cringed, back knees bent and his tail between his legs. Mimir looked at Chance, her face expressionless.

"Threkor forged seven Jars," the Guardian continued, his voice growing loud. "Where is the last pair of binding glasses?"

The hall was silent, but for the humming of the black ribs above them and the bubbling of the oil pits. Finally the Creator said again, nearly in a whisper, "Lost."

"You will have well earned the scourging wrath of the Old Gods, you wastes of men." The Guardian turned to leave.

"Wait," a voice called out. It echoed into the long silence of the great hall.

And Chance realized it was his voice. Everyone looked at him in surprise, but none was more surprised than he. "Wait," he said again, nearly a whisper. He looked at the Guardian, then up at the expectant faces of the watching Engineers. The Guardian had said that the answer would be found here, with these people. Chance could not let the ancient man's anger spoil their hope. Sarah's life, Paul's life, might rest on this.

"Is there . . . is there no other way to . . . ?" He faltered.

"There is," called out one of the elders of the guild, a wizened woman far more ancient than the others, with a bald head wrinkled and lined like a map. The Fricandor woman stood behind her, her predatory eyes watching Chance.

The Guardian looked over his shoulder at this old Engineer, still with his back to the throne.

"I am Sar, eldest of the Engineers," she said. She bowed slightly. Her dark, quick eyes shifted from Chance to the Guardian, and back again. "There is another way. One hope remains."

The Guardian considered this a while before he said, "Show it to me."

The elder looked to the Grand Creator. The leader of the Dark Engineers frowned, then nodded. "Sar will take you. But the others stay here," he said. He pointed at Mimir. "It is already blasphemous to have a makina enter the halls of Uroboros."

"The boy comes with me," the Guardian stated.

Again the old woman waited on the Grand Creator, but when he said nothing, she finally spoke. "Come."

The Guardian did not move for a moment. Then he turned and strode not after the old woman, but to the hammer that stood by the throne. He grabbed its handle.

"No!" the Creator shouted. "No man can wield Threkor's Hammer!"

The Guardian heaved it up. The plinth of stone cracked open, and then fell apart into two great blocks, releasing the shaft. The shattering crash made the elders instinctively raise their hands, as if to ward off some ill. The sound reverberated harshly in the long hall.

"I will bring this weapon back, Creator, when the fight with the god is finished."

The old woman moved surprisingly quickly. She wore a long black cloak that swept over the floor, formed of the same heavy and shiny material all the Dark Engineers wore, and it hissed on the rough stone as she hurried before them.

As soon as they passed from the hall through a low black doorway, and she had pressed the door closed behind, Sar began to mumble under her breath. It sounded to Chance like she said, "Stupid fat fool worst ever to sit on Threkor's throne—"

"What do you say, Engineer?" the Guardian asked.

"This way, this way," she answered more loudly. But as she turned Chance heard her mumble, "Useless, ridiculous to call him Creator; he's unable to make a damn thing...."

The Guardian and Chance followed in silence, through a maze of halls and turns, and finally onto a black stair that spiraled both up into a circular tower and down into a dripping well of gray stone. They descended in dim light, the black metal steps creaking underfoot. At every turn of the spiraling stairs, they reached a landing before a door rough with a thick coat of rust that appeared to have grown, undisturbed, for centuries.

They stopped before one of these doors. On a neat square of onyx above it was inscribed a symbol Chance did not recognize. Below them, the stair seemed to gyre down forever into darkness: the drip of water around them fell without report into the depths. The air smelled of water and mold and wet, rusting iron.

The old woman pointed at the door, and the Guardian shoved it open with one hand, causing red flakes of rust to explode out and over them. Chance blinked and rubbed at his eyes as, beyond the door, lights flickered on in a room shaped like a simple cylinder. In the center of the room, twelve rods of shimmering mercurial metal formed the outline of a cube. A dais stood before and to one side of it.

"Threkor's brotherhood made a first binding cell, archetype for the Numin Jar," Sar said, leading them into the room.

"This is fixed here," the Guardian said. He walked around the cube, at a respectful distance.

"Yes," the old woman replied. She brushed rust off of the sleeves of her black robes.

"Useless."

The old woman went to the dais and waved her hands over the top of it, and then touched it in complex ways that seemed to

Chance like dancing with her fingers. The only thing he had ever seen like it was Elder Ruth playing her dulcimer. The shining silver bars made a strange musical hum. And then their mercury surface smeared and thinned and spread, forming six dimly visible sides to the cube. The sides were like a mist, but as Chance watched they grew more substantial.

"It functions still, Guardian."

"So I must bring the god here, drive it into that space, and then keep it there, while these walls grow hard."

The old woman bowed. While her head was down Chance heard her mumble, "Shouldn't be so hard for a demi-god."

Chance watched the cube. The sides were more solid now, starting to form a mirrored surface. He could see himself dimly reflected in it. But the mirror of the surface was not complete: the wall beyond was visible, as if seen through a fog.

"It takes several minutes," the old woman explained. She walked to its side and ran one hand over the shining transparent surface that slowly formed.

They watched it until it turned to a complete mirror, reflecting everything in the room. Chance saw himself in its surface: there he stood, dressed in fine Puriman clothes, but with the Dark Engineer on one side of him, and the ancient Guardian on the other.

Who is that man? Chance thought. Am I still who I was just days ago? Is it even possible to be a Puriman in a place like this, and do these things, face these problems? Is it possible to be a Puriman and remember some of the things the false god showed me, as if they were my own recollections?

"How long will it last?" the Guardian asked.

The old engineer frowned. "It requires much energy. It should last as long as the energy lasts. If we are careful, then as long as Uroboros is held by the Engineers, I should think."

The Guardian pushed against the shimmering cube, but could not push through. "It feels strong enough."

He tapped it with the hammer. There was a sharp, deafening crack as green sparks flew from the impact.

"No!" the old woman scolded. "That hammer is otherworldly but not like god's flesh, not Aussersein. It is in both worlds, at the same time. It will react violently with a binding barrier, which cuts through only this world."

The Guardian nodded, hefting the shaft with admiration. He ignored Sar as she mumbled something about him being an idiot.

"You will show us the most direct path to this room," he told the old woman, "from outside. Put arms for a crossbar behind the door, so that it may be locked from inside if needed. Move the dais there, to the back of the room. And you will teach the Puriman how to use it."

"Not I," Chance said. He pointed at the cube. "Besides, I will have to wait inside, as bait."

"No, Puriman. You will stand on the other side as bait, and you will work the binding."

Chance opened his mouth to protest, but then thought better of it.

"And Puriman," the Guardian added. "Tell no one of what you have seen here. Not Thetis, not Mimir, not even Seth. No one."

The Guardian turned to Sar. "Who knows of this?"

"A very few. I rebuilt this myself, over many years."

"The Creator knows?"

"Yes." She added in a mumble, "But that fat fool never had any interest in anything that an engineer should—"

"Can you keep it secret?"

She nodded. "For a while."

"Good. Do."

"But what happens after the false god is in there?" Chance asked. He pointed again at the cube.

"I will stand watch," the Guardian said.

"Will it die in there?"

"No."

Chance frowned. "How long will it live?"

"Till the sun dies."

"Till the sun dies? The sun in the sky?"

"Till the sun dies."

Chance thought about that.

"Will this... trap last that long?"

The Guardian shook his head. "No. After a time, I will have to find another way. I'll seek one of the true binding jars. Then I'll let the god out, and bind it again."

Chance shook his head emphatically. "No."

"What?" The Guardian peered at him under the ridge of a deeply furrowed brow.

"No. That's not good enough."

"Not good enough?" The Guardian was incredulous.

"We have to end it. You said we would end it."

Chance looked at the old engineer, but she only bowed and slipped from the room, mumbling inaudibly. This was not a conversation in which she wanted to be involved.

Chance held his hands out, emphasizing his point to the Guardian. "There is a rot that attacks grape vines. Some vinmasters pull off a leaf when they see the rot on that leaf. Some pull off the rotten grapes or even all the grapes on the vine, when they see the rot on a grape. But in the end their whole vinland can be overwhelmed. I say, pull the vine, the whole vine, and burn it. Kill the rot, burn the rot, all of it, when you can, as soon as you can. Can we not kill this false god, burn it away, now?"

The Guardian watched him a long time, his great jaw working silently. Finally, he growled and then spoke. "There is a way. But there is much that could go ill. And it could beguile, and make cravings which I do not want to loose."

"What kind of... cravings?"

"Dangers for you, Puriman. It could open to you the … hunger … to become like him." He looked at the cube, as if the false god were already inside it.

Chance laughed bitterly. "I tell you this, Guardian. That is no temptation for me. None."

The Guardian scowled. "You don't understand."

"I don't need to understand. I know what I need to know. I've been a trouble-maker in my time, I've been a fighter and a mischievous son. But I want nothing but to be a simple man, a winemaker, a man like those who lived and died before any false gods were made or even dreamed of. That's all I want." He did not say, though he thought it, *and I want Sarah.*

"What if becoming a god could give you that?"

"No false god could have that, Guardian. How could one want to be a god and want a simple mortal life? No, the false god is an abomination, lost to God and God's ways. It cannot tempt me, I tell you. It cannot tempt me."

The Guardian gathered the others and, without speaking to the Grand Creator, they walked out of Uroboros the way they had entered it. Chance was relieved to be back out in the cool autumn salt sea air, free of the oppressive heat and the thick scent of oil. The sun had climbed and he felt a pang of hunger.

As they walked back to the Broken Hand that Reaches, Seth implored the Guardian to meet finally with the City Councilors.

"You talk with them, philosopher," he replied.

"St-st-student," Seth protested.

"You talk with them, philosophy student. I've not woken and walked the Earth to haggle with talk-hawkers."

Seth barked angrily. The Guardian did not even turn his head.

"But it is the Ga-Ga-Guardian they want to see!"

"But it is the Hekademon student they shall see."

"You en-enjoy this," Seth growled.

"My mirths are few, philosopher. Do not begrudge me them."

Seth snapped his teeth, obviously struggling with the desire to nip the Guardian in the calf.

"Bad, bad, bad man."

Once back in their chamber, the Guardian stood in the center of the room and faced them.

"I kenned the god today. It moves closer, but not quickly. Perhaps four days till it is here."

"The-the-there's another problem," Seth growled out. "The City Guard told me that there were others in the city who fo-fo-fought for, for the god."

"Who?"

"Hieroni," Thetis whispered.

Seth yipped in assent.

"What is this?" the Guardian demanded.

Nervously, looking at the floor as she addressed him, Thetis explained. "There have always been stories that in the city there is a cabal, called the Hieroni, with members from every guild. Secretly they worship the Younger Gods, and await their return. Some say they search for the hidden five Numin Jars of the Theomachia, to free the bound gods."

The Guardian grunted. "I do not reckon that fools meeting in shadows will hinder us."

Thetis wrung her hands but said nothing.

"When the god comes," the Guardian continued, "I will fight it, and it shall be held in Uroboros. Then, we go to the Numin Well and Chance will draw out its soul and we will be done with it. It would be best to fly, following the coast along the sea. Makina, can your ship take the Puriman and me as far as the door to the Numin Well at the foot of Yggdrasil?"

Seth barked indignantly. "And me-me-me!"

"I too should go," Thetis said. She leaned forward, and her quiet voice betrayed an intense urgency. "It is my sworn duty as a Mother of the Gotterdammerung, and I am the only Mother available to assist you."

"The trip will be baleful," the Guardian said. "Yggdrasil, where sits the door to the Numin Well, is north of the Filthealm, and rises from the cursed modbarrows, where the modghasts hunt for flesh or for machines to enthrall."

"We-we-we'll still come," Seth said. Thetis nodded her agreement.

"The ship is not so large," the Guardian added.

"I can, with appropriate preparation, accommodate and transport all of the persons here present," Mimir said. "The journey should require approximately eleven days, given mean wind—"

The Guardian walked out of the room before she could finish. Mimir stopped speaking, but her tranquil face betrayed no hint of insult as her silver eyes followed the Guardian's back.

"But. . . ." Chance muttered. His face turned a pale white. His eyes opened wide with fear. What had he gotten himself into, by demanding that the god be killed?

"Are you all right, Chance?" Thetis asked.

"But, I cannot touch a soul. How can I take its soul? I don't know how to do that. I don't want to become something that can do that." He imagined some magical alteration that they would force on him at the hall of the Dark Engineers, replacing perhaps his eyes and mouth with black iron tubes, giving him the power to see and then to eat out a man's soul like letting blood.

"Chance," Thetis said softly. "Chance, it's alright. When they say *soul*, they mean his body. His first body. You will go into the Well, and there will be his first human body, in its sarcophagus—like a casket—and you will bring that body out. That will kill him. His first mortal body is asleep, nearly dead, and it cannot wake and it cannot live outside its sarcophagus. It is the first body that gives his body in this world—what's left of this god's body here—form in this world. With it removed, the god's flesh here will be unable to repair itself. It can be made formless."

Chance thought this through.

"Must I then stay there?" he whispered. "In the other world? Lost? Forever?"

"No," Thetis said. "I must find and read our most ancient texts to know the way, but you may return. I'm sure."

Something about the way she said this conveyed that she was rather just hopeful. But Chance's shoulders visibly dropped. He breathed out a long sigh in relief. After a moment, he said, "But a body is not a soul."

Seth looked at Thetis. The two of them hesitated. But then Mimir spoke.

"The Makine believe that a pattern in the body, and nothing more, constitutes the soul. We believe that we machines have souls, and that these are patterns in metal and light, set into motion. We believe the immortal soul of Hexus is just a suspended pattern in his first body, a pattern in flesh. Just as we believe that your soul is just a pattern in your flesh."

Chance looked at her and frowned.

"So it will be me," he whispered after a moment. "In the end, I must be the one to kill the god. I will avenge my parents. Alone."

Seth put a paw on Chance's knee.

CHAPTER

14

Mimir stood on the white stones of the courtyard before the Broken Hand that Reaches, gazing up at the stars. The Guardian would not let her spend the evenings in the tower, and she in fact preferred to be out here beneath the arch of space while the human animals collapsed, unconscious, in their beds.

Mimir longed to move amongst the stars as she watched them shine in light invisible to any living thing. Her syndicate dedicated itself to this dream: to escape the trap that the Old Gods had laid around the Earth and ascend finally into the cold, weightless depths of space, where thought would be unbounded in speed and complexity. Eons before, all the Makine had worked for this end. But the secrets of the Dark Engineering—needed to penetrate the power of the Old Gods and escape the binding shield they had put around the Earth—had eluded the Makine, and their dream was slowly abandoned. Now only a few sought the stars. The rest dedicated themselves to building and exploring the Machinedream, the Makine city of light.

She concentrated on the starsongs both visible and invisible. But it was so distracting to have a body! Mimir had been born a ghost. A month before, she had never walked in flesh, in the world above. In hot depths of stone, where souls of light threaded through crystal looms and spoke to each other in voices of color, Mimir had been a single voice among millions and a member of one syndicate among thousands. Now she was alone in the hard world of mortal flesh.

The wind, the smells, the sounds of the city crowded in on her slow and heavy form. And though she could ignore them all, it took attention just to decide what to ignore. Worse, here in this body, in this city, she was cut off from the Machinedream. She was alone with her own thoughts.

For this reason she heard, far behind her in the back of the tower, a small side door to the Broken Hand that Reaches creak open, and a soft footfall set onto the crushed stones. A single pair of feet crunched across the gravel, and then pushed open another small door, this one in the wall of the courtyard.

Mimir crouched, and in silent, bounding leaps, ran to follow. She discarded her clothes as she sprinted, then leaped onto the wall and ascended it with her hard nails biting into the metal. Her skin changed to gray, then to black, as she climbed atop the narrow crest of the wall.

The figure that ran ahead of her was Thetis. The Mother of the Gotterdammerung hurried along the dark street. Mimir leapt down. Her skin shimmered and matched the colors of the gray buildings as she followed, sprinting from shadow to shadow. She stood as still as a statue each time Thetis looked back over her shoulder.

Thetis turned down several narrow alleys, crossed a large boulevard, and finally stopped and knocked at the vast wooden door of a narrow, ancient building of hand-carved stones, with tall windows of colored glass and a peaked roof of slate, squeezed into a dark slot between two gleaming towers. Mimir waited in a shadow across the street. The door opened, hands pulled Thetis inside, and the door was closed and locked. Mimir sprinted across the road and clambered up the stone side of the building and onto its steep roof. In the center of the roof, she snapped one shingle in half, pulled out a knot of wood in the board beneath it, and then pressed one eye socket against the hole. Her silver eye groped out of her face, protruding like the head of a snake on a pale silver cord. It wiggled down through the knothole, dangled from the dark ceiling, and turned to peer slowly in each direction.

In a tall, dim room with a stone floor, thirteen people gathered in a loose circle. They cast off their black cloaks.

One man, tall and thin and with long gray hair, said in a booming voice, "Welcome, Thetis. We have been eager to see you."

The Mother bowed. "This was the first moment that I could come, Vark."

"The Atheos does not suspect you?"

Thetis hesitated. "I . . . I believe not. I told him I had hidden during the . . . fighting. That I had been told to hide. He accepted that."

"Good. So, what have you learned, Mother? What is their plan?"

"They will not say. Only the Guardian and the Potentiate know. I think. . . ."

"What is it?"

"I think that they hope to trap the god in the depths of Uroboros. Using perhaps Threkor's Engles."

"There must be something more," another spoke up, a thin woman with blond hair. "They know that Threkor's Engles failed to slow the god last time they attacked him."

"There are many ancient weapons in the depths of Uroboros," another said. His shaved head and the tight black clothes under his robe revealed him as a member of the Dark Engineers. "Only the eldest of our guild are allowed there and know what powers might be there for wielding."

"Nothing can stop the god," shouted a man dressed in the robes of an apprentice of the Hekademon. "Only the Numin Jars can bind him. And we know that they do not have the Jars."

The man called Vark raised his hand to silence the others. "Enough! Io is right, they must have something different planned. Thetis, you must press the boy."

"But—"

"If you had pressed your sisters before and learned that the god wanted the Potentiate, I could have brought the boy myself weeks before the Guardian reappeared, and many lives would have been saved. The Ascension would already be upon us. The longer this fighting continues, the more will die. You must discover the Atheos's plan. We have waited thousands of years for the return of the gods, and now this hope has finally come. The Ascension may occur in our lifetimes."

"But," Thetis said, hesitating, "is it not enough to have the Potentiate?"

Vark pushed his hair back over his shoulders and frowned. He pulled on his beard with one hand. "You believe as we believe, Thetis. Everything may depend upon you."

Vark looked at the others, raising his voice, turning his answer into a speech. "Thetis, we must complete our destiny. The Atheos is the Antiousia—he is the enemy of Being itself. Do not doubt for a moment his wickedness. We must thwart his mission, and then we must free the god and bring the Ascension and the Ultimate Age. Everything depends upon this."

He stepped forward and put his hands on her shoulders. Then he whispered, so that only Thetis—and Mimir—could hear him, "You know that I care for the boy as much as you."

"But, Sirach," she whispered.

"Here you must call me Vark," he said.

"Vark, the god is, is.... He killed all the Mothers. Hexus killed Chance's parents."

"Ah!" Vark jerked his head back in shock. "John Kyrien is dead?" His hands dropped to his side. A long silence followed as Vark's mouth opened and closed, unable to find words.

"We…" he finally said. "We cannot judge the god. He tries to serve us all."

"But Sirach—Vark, can't Chance complete our destiny? Why must we sacrifice him for the incomplete god? He is pure of heart, and he understands our time and needs, and—"

"That had been my hope once also," Vark whispered. "No one worked harder for this hope than did I. But I did not have enough time. And we know the boy would not join us willingly. Not now. Hexus offers the only way. And it will save Chance's life—remember that Chance does not have much time. Yes, it will change him—but changed is better than perished. Remember that: we will save Chance."

There was a long silence. The Hieroni looked at each other with squinted eyes, worried about this secret exchange.

Vark stood back, and spoke loudly. "We forgive your doubts because of your…connection to the Potentiate," he said. "And we trust now that your allegiance is to the god."

He looked into Thetis's frightened and angry eyes. "You pledged loyalty to the Younger Gods when you joined the Hieroni, more than eighteen years ago. And you know the boy will not be harmed, but rather transformed, Ascended—"

"But he is my.…"

"Your pledge!"

Thetis looked at the floor. Finally she murmured, so quietly that she was barely audible to those gathered around her, "I'll keep my pledge."

"Good. Go and find what they are planning. The god returns soon." Vark reached into his robes and drew out a silver cylinder, twice as long and as thick as his index finger. "This is an ancient guild device. If they should hide the boy, hold this near him and twist the end." He demonstrated turning the top of the cylinder. "And we have another device that can lead us to this." He held it out toward Thetis. Hesitantly, the Junior mother took it and slipped it into her own robes.

Thetis left the room, her head bent meekly, sneaking a last nervous glance back at the silent ring of the others as she slipped through the door and pulled it closed with an echoing clank. Mimir remained above.

"She cannot be trusted," said the woman Vark had called Io. "Her link to this boy is too strong."

"We do not need to trust her," said Vark.

"But if she—"

"It is enough that she does this one thing. And she will. We only need her to tell us their plan. The god can do the rest. He comes soon."

The woman shook her head. "But her connection to the boy!"

"Thetis knows as well as we that the Atheos will doom the boy to an early death. We alone can save the boy. Come, we need to prepare the ancient weapon."

They filed from the room.

Mimir drew her eye back into her head and waited, listening, while the many footsteps retreated. Then she leapt from the roof to the wall of the tower flanking the building. Her skin changed to the pale gray color of its glossy surface. She dug her nails into the building's smooth face and climbed quickly. She scrambled to its peak and clung to a spire that pointed up at the stars. From her open mouth came a single pulse of invisible light that shone out over the city.

In a few moments a black bird flapped down out of the night sky and landed on Mimir's shoulder, the talons sinking into her flesh. It had wings of metal and, in place of a head, had a telescope ending with a single onyx lens. This bent toward her face now.

There could be no entering the Machinedream from the city. That was forbidden, and the City Councilors could detect and even listen to any such attempt. But Mimir did not fear this. Since the failure of her syndicate to capture Hexus at the Oracle, the older, more powerful syndicates had threatened to scatter her kin. Only the promise that Mimir would seek to find and kill the god had delayed them. If they knew that Mimir now sought not to destroy the god, but rather to make one that her syndicate could control, they would scatter her kin in far dark corners of the Machinedream, and not allow them to speak to one another for a hard century.

The elder Makine had slowed into stagnant caution. They no longer sought the secrets of the Dark Engineering. They dreamed of mystic numbers and impossible logics and did nothing. But Mimir had been created for a greater purpose. She had been created to lead her syndicate to the knowledge that could free the Makine to the stars.

She shared with the bird what she had learned of Thetis and in Uroboros, and what she planned, and then sent it flapping off into the night, on a journey halfway across the continent to the dwellings of the Makine and her syndicate.

Mimir stretched out as long and thin as a lizard and then started her slow descent, climbing down head first. She tried to plan while managing the distractions of the body. She would have to be sure to retake a human form when she returned to the Broken Hand that Reaches—the soft form she had adopted to appear pleasing and trustworthy to Chance, after their first meeting.

She could tell the Guardian then what she had seen, and the Mother would be killed. But the Guardian and the Hexus presented two different obstacles to her, both formidable. It would be best to wait and allow the Hieroni to operate. They would balance the two immortals against each other. It was possible that the two immortals would destroy each other, and she would be left alone with the human boy.

She reached the street and flipped onto her feet. In long, silent leaps she hurried back to the Broken Hand that Reaches, while throughout the Earth's last great city only the innocent slept.

When Thetis returned to the Broken Hand that Reaches, she ascended the hidden stair by which she had left and went not to her room but to the dining hall on the floor below their quarters. She turned on a few dim lights, filling the room with a pale glow, and sat at the long table. There she had eaten many meals with the other Mothers of the Gotterdammerung, women she had known and loved all her life. She could have sat at the head of the table, being the only Mother in Disthea and one of the last on Earth, but she took instead her usual seat, near the center of the table, so close to one of the table's legs that she had frequently banged her knee when pulling up to their meal. She ran her fingers over the deep, familiar scratches in the tabletop, gouges in the wood that were as old as her guild.

Thetis fought back tears—she had cried enough in these days—but a great wave of despair tried to crowd her mind. The god had killed her sisters. It had killed them all. It had killed Chance's parents and many others. It was mad, evil. How could she serve it?

If she could believe that serving the god might also save Chance—then she could willingly serve it. But she had only to imagine how Chance would feel about becoming part of the god to see the lie in that hope. The boy would consider it worse than death.

"Mother Thetis."

"Ah!" Thetis shouted, starting up. The Guardian stood before her, seeming to fill the room, Threkor's Hammer held in one hand and planted by his side. He had made no sound in entering.

"Anti.... Guardian." Her heart began to pound wildly. A rush of blood to her head made her skin flush red. Involuntarily, she pressed her hand against her robe, feeling in the pocket the device that Vark had given her.

"I frightened you."

She nodded, unable to speak.

What did he know? she wondered. He must suspect, to come to her alone like this. She stopped breathing. He would kill her in an instant if he suspected—no, he would question her first. He might have some skill that let him reach into her brain, and rend truth from the soft secretive gray folds. Or he might use cruder methods and begin to crush her limbs, one by one.

She struggled to appear calm, clinging to the hope that he had not watched her go meet the Hieroni. She pressed her shaking hands against her sides to still them.

"You have much to sorrow for," the Guardian said.

She exhaled. "Yes. I. . . ."

They stared at each other in silence awhile.

Was this, she suddenly wondered, the Atheos's attempt at sympathy, this recognition and silence?

Another moment of silence passed. Then the Guardian said, "You will not tell the boy."

"Tell him?"

"We understand each other. You will not tell the boy about his life. About how few are the years left to him. You'll speak of it to no one."

Thetis clasped her hands together. "But shouldn't we?"

"No."

"It's not fair," she whispered. She sat down again, collapsing back into the chair. "He would want to know, so that he can make new plans. He has hopes. Dreams. Things he wants to do with his life. He deserves to know how little time he has left. Seth says that he's even in love."

"That is why he must not know. So great a spur it would be, in the Numin Well, to do the wrong thing. Tell him, if you must, after the god is dead and after the boy has returned from the Well. If you tell him before, I must kill him."

As her fear for herself dissolved, tears for Chance came to her. They began to fall down her flushed cheeks. The Guardian watched, unmoving.

"It's not fair," she whispered again. "It's all so unfair."

"Yes. Too much of this world is ugly and unfair." The Guardian slowly nodded his great gray head. "I tell you this, Mother of the

Gotterdammerung: if there were a greatest god, as the boy believes, I would kill it next. After Hexus dies, I would find where this greatest god, this father of all woe, hides from us in cowardice, and I would drag it into the light, and I would smite it dead with this hammer." He leaned the shimmering head of Threkor's weapon forward. "And with this fist." He held up his left hand and wrapped his fingers tightly, making a sound of grinding stone.

"And then I would crush his bones to paste, and sow the meal into the Filthealm, that his dead flesh might rot in the filth of his failed works."

The Guardian strode from the room.

Thetis looked at the empty place where he had stood. The smell of wet slate remained in the Guardian's wake. A dark scratch had been gouged in the floor where the spike on the end of the haft of Threkor's Hammer had rested on the wood.

CHAPTER

15

Chance learned the blasphemous secrets required to activate the Engineer's trap. Each day for the next four days, the Guardian led Chance back to Uroboros. The old Engineering Master Sar walked them from a door in the side of the building, through a single straight hall spotted with irregularly shaped doors, and then down the winding, wet stair to the binding cube. Chance learned the way so that he could find the room alone. He grew accustomed to the smell of burning oil that had before faintly sickened him. The halls and sounds and sights of Uroboros grew to seem less strange, less fearful.

Though he would not have admitted it, Chance enjoyed mastering the pattern of touches of the colored spots on the dais that were needed to make the cube slowly form its mirrored walls. There was something pleasing, something that made him feel swelled with accomplishment, to touch the brightly colorful buttons in the correct pattern at one place, and see their miraculous effect a few paces away. He found himself quietly, secretly sneaking longer and longer looks through the doors of Uroboros, wondering what the machines in those rooms did, what touching the bright switches on the different panels would accomplish. But he did not share these thoughts.

In the Broken Hand that Reaches, Thetis opened a hall in the floor below their sleeping quarters, where they could eat together at a long table.

"I am the only Mother here," she told Chance. "There are many other Mothers, but they are away, traveling, and the first due to return will not be here for weeks. They do not know what happened here. I will have to manage things now." She took possession of the store of the Guild's money, and soon strangers appeared in the building—cooks and attendants. At Thetis's command, they served only Puriman food, bought at market in the south of the city. Chance and Seth feasted hungrily, while the Guardian and Mimir looked on.

Chance also grew interested in the happenings of the city. He noticed families in the streets—mothers, fathers, their children—and people eating at inns where they sat out in the street, laughing and talking loudly. They were so like Trumen—but then here or there among them walked a soulburdened raccoon, or a man with goat's eyes, or some other unman. It remained mysterious to Chance how people could live so far from any farms, though he understood that one could take many fish from the sea. But otherwise the people of Disthea had a kind of life in most ways like a Puriman's. They did not glow for him any more with the sinister sheen that he had first perceived in the seemingly infernal activities of the Dark Engineers. He even grew accustomed, as the other city dwellers surely already had, to the endless vistas of bereft towers, darkly crowding the sky above.

One morning returning from Uroboros, Chance heard a group of children singing in a narrow alley by a building that Seth had told him held a school. He stopped by the corner, half hidden, and watched them. There were boys and girls, the oldest of them not more than ten. They held hands and turned in a circle, chanting the same doggerel rhyme over and over. Chance's smiled died when he began to understand the words:

> *Although we know no natural death,*
> *The world grows old grows old grows old.*
> *Blue light, blue light,*
> *The ashes of dead suns.*
> *The mortals say they made me me,*
> *I say I made me me myself.*
> *Blue light, blue light,*
> *The ashes of dead suns.*

A heavy hand lay down on Chance's shoulder. Chance started, and looked up. The Guardian.

"It is an old rhyme," the Guardian said.

They returned in silence to the Broken Hand that Reaches.

As they crossed the vast entrance hall, Chance heard two voices coming from a small room to the side of the gigantic statue. The Guardian continued on, but Chance hesitated, curious because one voice was clearly Thetis, and the other voice sounded familiar. In a moment, the woman from the Fricandor Lands came out of the room, with Thetis following. She bowed deeply to Thetis, and then turned to leave. But when she saw Chance standing alone, as if waiting, she walked to him. Chance felt a slight flush, but was glad to be clean and dressed in proper clothes.

She wore bright pants and a long shirt, colored over with bright angular patterns of green, black, yellow, and red. She bowed before him. Her green cat eyes seemed to glow.

"I am Wadjet."

Chance began to experience even more intensely the discomfort he had felt the last time he saw the steward, seeing now how she inspected him. He couldn't look into her disconcerting eyes, with their slit irises, for more than a moment. His eyes wandered over her athletic form: her high cheeks, her fangs, her long dark hands with their smooth and pale palms, the high outline of her breasts. He noticed also something now for the first time: her smell. The aroma of some heady herb or oil rose from her, mixed with a smell he recognized with a shock. His neighbor, Elder John's wife Mary, had a gray tabby that on hot days lay languidly along the side of the road by her house. Chance had stopped to pet it each time he passed, and often pressed his nose on the top of its head, between the ears, and smelled the rich, clean smell of cat fur. Wadjet smelled of that. The aroma lay thickly in his head. He flushed.

"I am Chance Kyrien." He bowed awkwardly, uncertain of whether this was proper etiquette, but having seen it in others of the city. "Was Thetis able to help you with your need?" The Mother of the Gotterdammerung still stood in the doorway, watching them closely.

"No. She will help you first."

Chance shifted uncomfortably. Must he also bear the guilt of a plague?

"You are a Puriman?" Wadjet asked. Her tone was challenging.

He nodded, furrowing his brow. It was frustrating to think that here was yet another person who knew something of him when he knew nothing of her.

"I can tell by the clothes," she explained. Her fangs flashed in a brief, defiant smile. "So, you think I'm not a person. You say I am a monster."

"Uh...." He almost started to say, no, of course not. But then, he did, didn't he? Or, just a week before he would have said so.

She laughed at him. That too sounded challenging. "The Puriman interest the Stewards."

He frowned. "Why is that?"

"We are similar, in a way."

"I thought—from what Thetis said to me earlier—I thought you were like the Leafwage...."

"No! The Lifweg changed the living things of Earth to serve the ends of their guild. The Stewards change themselves to serve the ends of the living things of Earth. No, we are more similar by far to the Purimen—alike as the bird and bat."

Chance felt he could understand what she said: that the Purimen and Stewards had the same ends but different ways of getting there. But how could they have the same ends?

She saw his confusion. "The Stewards seek to foster life. They give up property, and family, and their old bodies, and freedom to become Stewards. They practice silence and watching, and learn to give up their thoughts so that they can know the thoughts of life."

"I think I see." And Chance did understand. There were some Elders like this, and he had always admired them and hoped to end his years like them, in simplicity and attentive concentration on God and God's creation. Chance's friend, the Elder Sirach, had sometimes spoken of this—it came close to the true meaning of their faith, Sirach had claimed.

"The Stewards would say," Wadjet continued, "Purimen clear the way of the path so that they may see it plainly, and follow it, while Stewards bend themselves to the path, so that they cannot lose it."

Chance nodded. "Yes. We believe the True God is in the world. The world is his works, and the works of men can hide this from us. Do you, as a Steward, follow the One True God?"

Wadjet snorted. "I am not a Steward."

"But I thought you said...."

"I come from them. But I am an exile. A criminal." She set the points of her long incisors against her lip for a moment before adding, "I don't follow anything, true or false."

"But—the plague—you said you want to help—and—"

"Chance, come!" The Guardian's voice echoed down the stairwell from above.

Wadjet did nothing to ease Chance's obvious confusion. She just stepped past him and started toward the vast doors.

Chance hurried to catch up with the Guardian, but when he was nearly at the back of the hall, he stopped and called back to the Steward. "Wadjet! Am I the bird or the bat?"

His question echoed in the vast room. She flashed white fangs over her shoulder.

"You are the dove."

The next morning, when Chance descended to the dining hall, Thetis alone waited there to breakfast with him.

"Where are the others?" he asked her.

"Mimir is outside, banished by the Guardian who does not trust the makina with you. The Guardian has gone with Seth to talk to some of the City Guard and City Councilors. They are concerned about...."

"The Hieroni," Chance said, finishing her sentence. All of them feared that perhaps many people in the city would fight with the god when it returned. Chance had seen Dark Engineers and City Guards talk in hushed tones with the Guardian, unsure of whom they could trust, and unsure about how to prepare for the betrayers in their midst.

"I don't understand how anyone can serve the false god. After seeing what it did here."

"Few really know what it did here, Chance. And there are many who have little love for the Gotterdammerung. They accuse us of hoarding our skills, of not helping people when we could. Of being greedy. Or at least indifferent." She sighed. "Perhaps there's some truth to that."

Chance nodded. It struck him that one could say the same things of the Purimen.

"Both the Guardian and Seth will be back soon," Thetis added. She gestured towards the chairs. "Come. Eat."

As they sat, Chance rubbed his eyes.

"You are still tired?" Thetis asked.

"I had strange dreams. This happens often to me, lately."

"After the god attacked you?"

"Yes. No. They're more common after that. But they're dreams I've had before. Now and then. Many times."

Thetis leaned forward. "Tell me," she whispered.

Chance shrugged. "There are stars. And a door. And I am floating there, before this door. It seems that I've been there a long time. But no, that's not right. I'm floating rather fast, toward the door, so it can't last long. As if underwater, swimming really—but breathing. Ah, dreams make no sense."

"Do you see yourself in this dream?" Thetis asked him urgently, in a choked whisper.

Chance lifted his head and furrowed his brow, surprised at her sudden harsh intensity.

"What? See myself? No. Of course not. But then, now that you say that, maybe I do. Or, I think I might, or can. Or should. Something. . . . As if I were there, just out of view. Isn't that odd? You seem to have almost awakened a lost memory of the dream. How did you know to ask that?"

Thetis came around the table, grabbed his right hand, and knelt before him. Her nails bit into his palm. "Chance—"

"Hey!"

"Shh! Please, please, shh!" With her free hand she put her palm hard over his mouth. Chance was shocked to see that her eyes were wide with fear. When he stopped trying to speak, she put her hand behind his head and pulled him forward, so that his forehead touched hers. "Don't ever speak of this," she whispered, barely audibly, "ever. The Guardian will kill you."

"That's crazy."

She gripped his hair painfully tight, suddenly angry. With their faces still close together, she hissed so that her hot breath blew on his cheek, "You know almost nothing of what is happening here. *Nothing*. It would be too late if Mimir were here, now. If she is close, or if she planted ears here that I failed to detect, you may die this hour. But if not, you live only if you never tell another being of what you dream. Never. No one."

"I don't understand. You can't—"

"I'm the only one here that cares about you, Chance. Believe that. I'm not here for some grudge or to finish some ancient battle or to make some use of you or even to serve my guild. You can trust only me. But in silence. Silence."

"What—what—"

"I won't speak of it again. It's too dangerous. I won't."

She pushed him back, rose, and went to her seat.

They did not speak again for the rest of the meal. Chance sat and stared at his food in stunned silence. Thetis finished her small breakfast, not looking at him. When she stood, the Guardian strode through the door. Chance almost cringed, but the Guardian was his usual self.

"Come, Puriman. We go to Uroboros." He turned and walked out, leaving Chance to rush to follow.

"Is there any word of Sarah?" Chance asked, as he caught up.

"The makina has word of yesterday. It says that she lives, still following behind the god, on horseback. They have come now to the banks of the Usin River. They are near, Puriman."

Chance nodded thoughtfully.

CHAPTER

16

After they left the lakeside, Sarah, Paul, and Hexus rode their horses onto the Old Trail, the disused road feared by the Purimen because it went, the Elders claimed, into the heart of the perilous Sabremounts. Their path shrank from a broad wagon road to a narrow path, level and well cut through the landscape, but choked with low weeds. Soon they left the lands of the Purimen. They rode on, not speaking, hardly awake.

Days passed. How many, Sarah could not count, but she had a dim recollection of her and Paul sitting beside a fire, and then of a different morning rising beside a different fire.

Then, one afternoon, as the last rays of the day were falling in the East at their back, a bright glint of light shone through the forest path before them.

"Stop," Hexus said. They waited.

A shining figure of gold approached, riding on a black horse. Dogs ran at its feet. No: wolves and coyotes. Sarah could see then that the face of the person on horseback was black, covered with fur.

Sarah frowned, uncertain what was happening. She seemed to be waking from a dream. Was she dreaming? She looked at the strange stinking man mounted beside her, then at Paul, at the horse—she knew this mare, Elder Isai's youngest horse.

"Why am I here?" she whispered.

The approaching horse pulled up before them. Black fur covered the soulburdened creature that rode it. She was clad in armor of bright gold, wearing a gold helmet with a tall black plume of horse hair. The armor blazed even in the broken light of the shadowed road, gold shafts of reflected sun piercing the forest around them. Wolves—and now Sarah could see bears—trotted beside it.

"Master," the beast said in a hoarse but feminine voice. She dismounted from her steed and kneeled, the armor ringing. The wolves and bears lay down.

"Rise, Apostola. Rise, inheritors of the Earth."

"Dogs. Dogs and monkeys and bears," Paul said, as if talking in his sleep. A thin line of drool slipped from the corner of his mouth. He laughed thinly, with bitterness. He pulled at his sleeves, tried to straighten his torn collar, and ran his hand over his head to push down the stiff peaks of his dirty red hair.

"Yes, what...?" Sarah began.

Hexus turned. "This does not concern you. You need not listen or look."

And Sarah forgot what she had been thinking. She stared at her horse's ears, and daydreamed of days when she sat and talked with her mother.

Sarah could not follow the passage of time. They rode on into the hills, and occasionally she would start, gasp as if she were breaking through the surface of the lake after a long plunge under water, and look around. One of these times she sat on the horse, surrounded by the soulburdened, the air heavy with the musty smell of their fur as the beasts circled back and forth around Hexus, crossing before and behind his horse in their excitement as he rode on. Another time, she awoke while chewing a gritty, dirty mouthful of food, and held in one filthy hand a burnt leg of chicken, in the other a carrot covered still with dirt and the white veins of roots. The next time, she sat by a fire, while in the distance before her a house and barn burned with explosive cracks and booms. The next: she lay on her back in the dark, and Paul sat next to her, awake, looking at his feet with a perplexed expression. And the last: she was sitting at the feet of Hexus, who stood on a high promontory of stone in the center of a grassy field, arms uplifted, as thousands of soulburdened animals shouted and growled and shrieked in a frenzy of joy and anger at his words.

They came finally to the Usin River. In a moment of lucidity, Sarah found herself on horseback next to Hexus, looking out from a hilltop over the great waterway. A large village spread out on the bank below them, and farms, with large white farmhouses and red barns, lined both sides of the river as far as she could see. Airships floated back and forth above the broad traffic of boats.

"It's as wide as a lake," she whispered. And then, looking up at the airships, she said, "I had not known there were so many people and ships."

"They are many to you," Hexus said. He pointed at the edge of the bluff before them. "We camp here and tomorrow ride into this village."

The black soulburdened beast was there—why hadn't she noticed that before? It was as if it had been invisible to her. Or outside of her attention. She stared at it, perplexed. It said, in its coarse but mellifluous voice, "I will prepare the warriors." Then it pulled back the reins of its great horse, turned, and left them, its shining golden armor clattering.

"What warriors?" Sarah asked.

"Silence. Make camp and then sleep. You want to sleep."

She nodded. She did want to sleep. That was true.

Sarah dreamed. Not the fog of dislocated images that had clouded her mind for long days, but a real dream, lucid and sharp.

She stood on the porch of the Kyrien Vincroft. She meant to knock, or just go inside, but the door looked strange to her, like some kind of guild machine. It drew away from her, opening to reveal a dark tunnel spotted with stars.

Chance, she somehow knew then, was in that tunnel. Then she saw him. She started, and stepped back. He looked older, wearied somehow. But what shocked her was that one eye, his left eye, was gone. The empty socket opened onto a starry black void.

"Sarah."

She turned. But no. Here was Chance. He stood there, on the porch, with his back to her as he peered up toward the Ries fields.

"Chance!"

"What do I care about most, Sarah?"

He turned and looked at her. His left eye was normal, but his right eye was gone. The socket gave unto a black tunnel, spotted with stars. His left eye fixed on her. She had the strange impression that he was empty, that the rest of him was still behind her. Or maybe that what was behind her was now within Chance. She said to herself: *his soul looks out at me from the end of a tunnel of stars.* She felt a thrill of awe and terror, to look into this abyss of black time and distance. But she did not turn away.

"What do I want most to be, Sarah?"

She might fall into those stars. She could be lost there. Was Chance lost there?

"What kind of a man would you love, Sarah?"

He turned away.

"Come to me now," he said. "Come to me quickly."

She awoke with a gasp.

Sarah sat up, alert, her head clear. With a wave of revulsion, she realized she could smell herself. She was filthy, her hair an itching, burning thatch of knots, her clothes soiled and reeking of urine, her legs covered with a stinging rash. She spat. Her tongue and gums were swollen. A foul taste coated her mouth. How many days had she lost, how many days had she ridden horseback in a confused nightmare?

The first blue and red of the coming sunrise spread across the sky. Stars were still visible, the brightest remaining while their weaker kin faded into day. Paul lay on a blanket beside her, staring up. The horses huddled together nearby. Hexus stood with his back to her on the bluff, his right hand stretched out so that the god's eye could observe the waking village below. The stench of his rotting flesh permeated the clearing.

Sarah got to her feet. A strange, powerful tranquility possessed her, as the calm of the dream—and, most of all, the powerful calm of Chance's voice—remained with her. Her belt with its swords lay in the dirt by Paul. She drew the swords in one fluid movement as she ran at Hexus.

He heard her footsteps and turned. Then, seeing her sword blades in motion, he raised his arm—but Sarah swung at the black limb with both blades. One sword cut into the bicep, the other into the soft interior of the elbow joint. The arm fell at his side, almost cut off. Hexus shouted but before he could form a word, she lifted her blades and drove one tip into his chest, the other into his throat.

Hexus stumbled back. She drove forward, keeping the blades buried in him, pushing them farther. He retreated until he teetered on the edge of the bluff. He looked at her—his neck could not turn but he strained his eyes—and then his face took on a calm expression, the eyes narrowing into a glare.

Sarah raised her foot and kicked him hard, sending him over the bluff and tumbling into the trees far below.

She knelt quickly, set the points of her swords into the Earth, and said, in a rush, "May God forgive my wrath and sins and have mercy on my soul and on the soul of mine enemy."

She rose and turned. The whole event was less than ten seconds, but Paul was standing. His lip curled into a grimace, something between weeping and a sneer.

"Get on a horse," she whispered.

"You killed him," he said, too loudly. "He was going to save my mother and father. He was going to save us from Chance."

She strode forward and hit him hard in the chest with the two pommels of her swords. He fell down.

"Enough of that kind of talk. Now think. Your parents are dead. And what does Chance most care about? The ways of the Purimen. He would never betray that. It makes no sense that he would flee the Elders. What does Chance most want? To be a Puriman, to be a farmer, to make wine. Not to flee the valley. This thing lied. Don't you see that?"

She did not add, *and what kind of man could I love? A strong man, an honest one, a pure and determined one. Not a sickly liar.* She trusted her past self to have made the right decision.

Paul started to crawl forward toward the bluff. "He's coming," he said. "He's coming. He can still save us. Save my parents...."

Some soulburdened beast roared in the forest behind them. Sarah pulled on Paul's arm, but he jerked away and kept crawling toward the bluff. She could not wait. She grabbed her belt with the scabbards, put the swords into it, still wet with blood, and leapt onto one of the horses, bareback. It awoke with a start. She kicked it, buckling on her belt. The horse huffed in protest but then took off at a run down the trail.

The way was lined with the soulburdened, lying or prowling in the forest. They did not stop her, having seen her ride with Hexus, but raised their heads and growled as she passed. She rode on, kicking at the horse, driving it harder. Branches cut at her face and the face of the horse, but she pushed it on.

The trail opened finally into a field. The snarls of the soulburdened faded behind her. The horse raced down a narrow path through tall brown stalks of corn, past a dark farmhouse, and then out into a road, hooves clattering. She turned and descended toward the river. A long, broad avenue ran above its bank, lined with wooden buildings. A few people were in the streets.

Sarah rode up before a man and woman.

"The soulburdened are coming!"

They looked up at her, uncertain. Nearby others stopped to listen.

"An army has gathered on the hills above. They are about to attack!"

"Go on your way, madwoman," the man said, embarrassed.

"No," Sarah implored. "I've been their prisoner. I've escaped. They're coming!"

The couple turned away. Sarah realized then what she looked like, with her filthy clothes and her hair a soiled mat. Her shoes were gone; she rode barefoot and bareback. Her hands, and likely her face, were streaked with dirt. Burrs clung in thick, dirty clumps to her torn clothes.

"Oh, you must believe me."

She rushed toward a group of three men, pulling the mane of the horse hard so that it tossed its head and stepped sideways until it was so close that the men fell back, stumbling.

"I know I look a beggar, but I am a Ranger Apprentice of the Puriman. You have only minutes to prepare."

The men slipped away, their eyes avoiding hers.

She turned in place, making the horse prance. What could she do?

She must ride to Chance. She must hurry to Chance. To Disthea—that's where the unman had said Chance would be.

She turned the horse to the north, and kicked it, riding off down the road, shouting as she went, "The soulburdened are coming! An army of the soulburdened attacks!"

CHAPTER

17

"Chance?" Thetis called. She stood in the great hall of the Broken Hand that Reaches. The fire that had burned in the cupped palms of the statue had been extinguished, making the dim hall darker but also more colorful. The rich lights that fell through the glass ceiling painted everything in pale hues, even the dull gray of the Guardian. Thetis stood in a pool of blood-red light and called out to Chance as he crossed the hall with the Guardian, returning from their daily trip to Uroboros. "Chance, I'd like to show you something."

Chance looked at the Guardian to see if the ancient would protest.

"Go," the Guardian told him. "But do not go far. The god wielded its power this morning. It is near. It will strike at us soon."

Chance followed Thetis behind the statue, past the stairwell, and then through another door. It opened onto yet another set of steps, these narrower and diving steeply down. She stepped without hesitation into the darkness, and lights flickered on as Chance followed.

"This leads to the old libraries and other store rooms," Thetis said.

At the bottom they pushed through broad wooden doors into a long, low room with gray stone walls. The walls were lined with shelves of simple iron. On them were stacked, from floor to ceiling, and all the way down the long stretch of the room, hexagonal rolls of metal and stone—or so they seemed to Chance. The air smelled wholesome to Chance: wood, and a hint of wet clay, and also something else, perhaps some kind of oil.

"What are these?" he asked, pointing at the shelves.

Thetis lifted one of the scrolls off the nearest shelf and handed it to Chance. It was lighter than he expected, since it looked to be made of limestone and lead.

"These are kieferbooks. Our most important lore is recorded in these." She took it from him and set it on the floor, and then pushed it over, as if to roll it. It unscrolled onto the floor, the angular corners hinging so that its sides could lay open. Fully extended, it was a long panel or scroll. Characters in the strange alphabet of the Gotterdammerung guild language, and some also in the Common alphabet, were inscribed deeply into the gray surface.

"It is beautiful," Chance whispered. He put his hand over it, feeling the uneven rough surface of gray and brown. He appreciated, as did all Purimen, fine craftsmanship—when it looked to be made by human hands.

Thetis smiled, pleased that the book impressed Chance. "These books can last many thousands of years. Millions, some say. What we write here cannot be lost to rot or become unreadable if we lose some guild skill."

Chance nodded. "There are hundreds here."

"And there are many other halls like this one. I have been searching these last days for knowledge about the Numin Well. But that's not why I brought you here."

Chance nodded. He had thought incessantly of Thetis's warning the previous morning, and had sweated with fear when he awoke this morning after having again the same dream. Had he seen himself in it? he had wondered, uncertain, holding the sheets in his fists.

Now he thought that there must be a secure room down here where they could talk about his dreams, and her threats. "Yes, I hoped we could talk of—"

She gripped his arm. The scratches from the bear attack had scabbed over and were slowly healing, but they hurt still, and her tight grip made him suck his breath in with pain. Thetis narrowed her eyes and shook her head sharply once. The message was clear: don't speak of that.

"Come," she said, releasing his arm.

She rolled the scroll up and put it back in its place. She then led Chance back a few steps, to a door underneath the stairs. It opened onto a small dark room. She pulled a cord and lights in the ceiling slowly grew bright. The walls were lined with tilted wooden shelves, covered thickly with dust.

"A vin cellar!" Chance shouted with joy. And most of the bottles were clay. That would mean they were Puriman wines.

Thetis smiled widely. "Seth told me how you loved wine." Chance walked the length of the room in a rush, looking quickly over the bottles.

"Chance," Thetis whispered, suddenly earnest. "Look here." She took his hand and led him into the back of the room. She pointed at some bottles near the floor: dark brown clay jars. Chance recognized the color and texture of the clay immediately. He held his breath and knelt. He lifted up one bottle, cradling it lovingly in one hand as he brushed the dust away with the other.

"It's, it's...." His voice faltered. Tears came to his eyes. The bottle was twenty years old, with a faded paper label partly eaten away by mold. But, unmistakably, his father had penned KYRIEN VINCROFT RIES on it. Chance rubbed the label while he struggled to control his emotions.

His father had gathered these grapes, and crushed these grapes, and fermented and aged the juice, and filled and corked this very bottle. Chance closed his eyes and pressed the hard, cool bottle to his forehead.

And what had happened to this year's crop? he wondered. Was it rotting on the vine? Or would Elder Johannes or Joshua Hill see to it that it be picked? Who would tend the ageing wines, and top the barrels? What had happened to their house? Were the doors locked, the shutters closed? Were the chickens running wild, wandering into the neighbor's land? Had someone claimed their horses as his own? He pictured with clarity the empty vinfields at dusk, with bats skimming over the vines, eating the evening's horde of vine-hungry insects. And below the fields, their house, shuttered and dark, the gray cedar shakes of the roof catching the first evening shadows. The rippled glass of the tall windows would be dark now. The cobblestone chimneys cold. The red barns empty and silent.

"My father was not much older than me when he wrote this," Chance whispered. Thetis nodded and put her arm over his shoulders.

Chance nodded. "Thank you. Thank you."

"There are twenty bottles of Kyrien," she said. "Let's drink a few. In honor of your parents there."

He looked over at her, blinking a few tears but smiling. He could not place her age—he had thought she was not much older than him, but then something about her eyes seemed to reveal she had known many more years. And she looked at him fondly, almost wistfully, as if she were much his senior. He realized at that moment that she was beautiful, with her black, black hair, her nearly black eyes, her pale, smooth, almost featureless skin. He got suddenly the impression that she wanted to kiss him. He shifted uncomfortably.

"Let's do that," he said.

"I know a special place."

They climbed stairs. Thetis stopped on the second floor to talk with their new cook, who stole quick glances at Chance but otherwise made a good show of seeing nothing. The cook nodded, went away, and returned with two brown cups.

"Puriman cups," Thetis explained. "From the Usin Valley Purimen. We keep them for special occasions."

"Thank you," Chance said.

Chance, holding a bottle in each hand, followed Thetis as they climbed another nineteen floors. The way was dark, but less dark than it seemed when they looked up from below. In the higher floors, a narrow trail of dark prints cut through thick dust.

Their history weighs down from the sky, Chance thought. As if always ready to tumble down and crush them.

When both of them breathed heavily from the long climb, Thetis pushed open a door and led Chance down a dim corridor and into another room with a table set before tall glass doors that opened onto a broad balcony. They went out. Chance felt a shiver of fear under his feet as he saw how high they were. Other than in the makina's airship, and their descent on the stairs against the Crystal Wall, he had never stood so high. He kept a respectful distance from the edge of the balcony. Most of the Broken Hand that Reaches towered high above them. But they had climbed enough that, between two rows of buildings before them, they could see over the Crystal Wall to the dark sea beyond. Cool gusts of wind carried a strong salt smell of the ocean.

"I told them to bring food up here," Thetis said. "And I got this." She handed Chance a cork shim. He slipped the cork out of one of the bottles while Thetis pulled two chairs of strange material out onto the balcony. He poured the two cups. They sat and he tasted the wine.

"Not bad."

"Excellent," Thetis said.

Chance nodded gratefully. "To be honest, my father had gotten much better with the years." He poured their cups full, and they drank some more in silence, staring out to the sea. Today the tide was high and tall waves brimmed at the edge of the Crystal Wall, threatening to spill into the city. "He became the best winemaker in the valley."

And now he cannot teach me, he cannot guide me, Chance thought.

He took another sip. Was Sarah well? he wondered. Was Paul? The thought took away the taste of the wine.

"You think of your Puriman family?" Thetis asked. She peered at him closely.

"Yes. My brother. And...a woman."

"Seth told me about both. Were you close to your brother?"

Chance hesitated. "We were brothers. But it was hard for him, having an elder brother, just six months older, who was adopted. It caused much confusion about what would be his, what mine. And he was closer to our mother, and I was closer to our father. That caused strife too. But we were brothers. We are brothers."

"And the woman?"

Chance nodded. "I must get them both back. I must avenge my parents. End this struggle with the false god. So that we can return to the vincroft."

"And then?"

"Then...." The Elders should not name him a Puriman, after what he had learned. He could not know what Sarah or Paul would do or say. The Vincroft would go to Paul. Chance could not even imagine what kind of life he might make for himself if he was not a Puriman, not even, truth be told, a Truman, and not given any stake in the vincroft.

But he could not consider that now. He would continue on as would a Puriman. He must save Sarah, and save Paul, and then get back to the vincroft. If only to make sure all was set right there.

"I don't know," he admitted. "I'll decide when I've returned home. Maybe I can still make wine, and live among the Purimen."

"That sounds very nice."

Chance looked at her and frowned. "You think so? I would have thought it was ignorant, too simple, for a Mother of your guild."

"No. It sounds like you do something well, and want to do it better, and that it gives many people pleasure. Even here in Disthea. Even *unmen*." She stressed this last word exaggeratedly.

"I did not mean to say—"

"I jest, Chance Kyrien. But even so, you have brought many people a happy moment."

"It is a little thing."

"All of life is little things."

"Amen."

They sipped in silence for a few moments.

"You could come here, you know. For a visit. Or longer, if you liked."

"What?" Chance was confused. The idea was so radical, he had never imagined such a thing. But then, what if everyone in the Valley rejected him when he returned to the lake? Where would he go?

"You would be welcome," Thetis added.

"What would I do?"

Thetis smiled encouragingly. "You could tell the story of your travels. The guild will want to record that."

"On those books?"

"Yes, on kieferbooks."

Chance marveled at the idea. To be written of in an ancient book.

"Then," Thetis said. "You could study whatever interested you."

Chance sighed. "I would miss the vineyards too much." Although he'd been away from home only a few days, he missed already the feel of pushing his hand into soil to test its quality, he missed tending the vines, he missed caring for the wine barrels. That was what he knew how to do, what he liked to do, what made him feel useful. And the thought of the fermenting new wine sitting unattended made him feel uneasy, like he should get up and get to work.

"The winemakers in the Usin Valley might hire you to make wine," Thetis said.

"Really?"

"The farmers of your lake lands are famous for your wine skills."

"I, I don't know," Chance whispered. He would have rejected the idea without reflection a week before. But now, he surprised himself by finding in the possibility a modicum of hope. Even if he were turned away from the Valley, perhaps there would still be some chance that he could make wine....

"I will think on it," he said.

Thetis nodded.

The thought of living outside the Valley of Walking Man turned Chance's reflections to his own origin. He felt a nervous pressure growing in his chest. There was something he wanted to ask, but he felt afraid to ask it. Finally, though, he blurted it out.

"Do you know who my birth parents are? Can you tell me? Do they live?"

Thetis looked at him and narrowed her eyes in thought. Finally, she said, "I cannot tell you anything about them now. But, if you came to stay here, after this is all over, I think then that you could learn who they were."

Chance looked away. He felt disappointment and relief. He did not think he had now the strength to face strangers claiming to be his parents. But Thetis's elusive answer also frustrated him. It made him more curious, and it made him feel guilty for being curious. Part of him felt it was a betrayal of his parents in the Valley, as if he were seeking their replacement. And part of him found in Thetis's caution the suggestion, which he himself feared, that there was some untoward tale to be told about his birth parents.

"Chance?" Thetis whispered tremulously. "You're thinking of your parents again? Your Purimen parents?"

"Yes."

"Chance, the god killed people I love, too. When he was here."

Chance peered into her dark eyes, which he found now strangely familiar. She hugged herself tightly in the cold wind, hunched over in her chair.

"I'm sorry," he said.

"Yes. It's hard. Impossible. So, maybe, I know a little of what you feel. But, Chance, I must tell you, it's not right that you suffer over being the Potentiate."

"Please—"

"No," she interrupted. "I speak the truth. Do you know why our guild has an agreement with the Purimen to bring our male children to them?"

"No."

"Because we trust the Purimen to remain ever removed from our ways. So, if there ever were a Potentiate, or even just a child who had some of the blood of a Potentiate, he would be far always from the theotechnologies. Only the senior mothers know where the children go. It's the way you live, not what you inherit, that matters."

"And why did the Purimen agree to this?"

She thought about it a moment. "The first Purimen wanted to be sure that their members did not have certain—remade features. We alone have the skill to test that. The Purimen of the Usin Valley sometimes still ask for this kind of test. Though it has been many years since the Purimen of the Forest Lakes have asked for our help."

"I'm not surprised."

"But, Chance, I spoke the truth. The changes required to make someone a Potentiate are actually few; they are small, compared to those that many others inherit. And, Chance, there is no one wholly original left on Earth."

"Original!" Chance said with contempt. He took a mouthful of wine, as if to wash away the taste of the word.

"Yes. I cannot use your words—true, pure. These are not the right words. Everyone left on Earth has been changed; everyone left on Earth has ancestors who were changed. More than this, Chance, every other thing has been changed by the ancient humans. They flattened mountains to get at the stones underneath. They destroyed forever many kinds of animals. They remade nearly every animal, every plant on Earth, for which they had some use. They moved rivers, changed forever the air we breathe, raised and salted the seas, changed—"

"This is no comfort to me, Thetis. You tell me that everything I believe is false."

"Not false. Just…not simple. And not always the same."

"Some things are simply true. And they remain always the same truth. There is a true God. One true God. He made us, he made the world, he has a design for us and for the world. I believe this. To me, this is not complicated. It doesn't change. It's as certain as the sun rises in the West, and always has risen in the West. It's as certain as the Walking Man Lake has always been there, full of fresh water."

Thetis looked out toward the sea.

Chance sighed. "There. Like the Guardian. He does that too, when he scorns something I've said as foolish, as not worth even correcting. He looks away and frowns. Even Seth is starting to do it. What would you deny? Tell me."

"Things change. Even East and West. Even lakes and seas."

"Not everything changes."

"Maybe not everything. But who knows what things?"

"I don't believe you feel that way. Your Mothers here, in this tower, they had faiths. They had things they could not doubt. If the Mothers doubted them, then the Mothers would be different. They would no longer be themselves. Everyone has religion, even the false."

Thetis shook her head. "I don't think so, Chance. Do you know our Guild, where it comes from? This was the home of the Theogenics Guild. We were the Theogenics Guild. Our ancestors had faith. The faith that they were culminating human history—that with the

Dark Engineers they would create something absolutely... beyond all human accomplishment and dreaming. And then the war came, and the Guild was destroyed, the Fathers were all slain, and the Mothers were cursed. Cursed to carry on as the Gotterdammerung as long as humanity lived on Earth, ensuring that the very powers they had created were never used again."

She took the bottle from him and poured some wine into her cup before she continued. "The Gotterdammerung is without faith. We have hopes, we serve as healers, but nothing is certain for us."

"That's horrible."

"It's not so bad, Chance. You have to allow that things might not be as you hope, might not be as you believe, but still make something of what remains. And not all the changes, not all the surprises, are bad. Some are good. Some are very good. Meeting you was very good—for me, I mean."

Chance gave Thetis a brief, embarrassed smile. They were silent a moment. Then, speaking more softly, Thetis said, "Chance, I'm worried. Are you certain that you and the Guardian have some way to trap the god at Uroboros?"

Chance hesitated. The Guardian had been clear: tell no one about the binding cube. But Thetis seemed so sincere in her concern for him. He opened his mouth, considering his words—

But before he could speak, Seth ran out onto the balcony behind them, his nails scratching at the hard floor as he slid and turned. "Cha-Chance," he barked. "Sarah. Sarah is here."

Chance leapt to his feet.

"Where?"

"Downstairs."

CHAPTER

18

Chance ran the entire way, leaping down steps three at a time, leaving Thetis far behind. Seth followed closely. When they reached the grand hall, they were both gasping. Chance threw himself against one of the front doors and burst out onto the front steps.

The Guardian stood there, on the white stones, holding Sarah in his arms. Mimir stood next to him, expressionless in her formal suit.

"Sarah!" Chance called. He ran to her, Seth at his heels.

The Guardian set Sarah on her feet. Chance grabbed her, wrapped his arms around her.

Sarah pulled back, then pushed him away.

"Sarah? Sarah?"

She reeked of urine and pungent sweat. Her hair was tangled into a gnarled lump, hanging off to one side of her head. Filth smeared her face. She was barefoot, and her feet were dark with dirt. She held her dirty hands up, warding Chance back. "I, I...."

"What? Are you...?" Chance hesitated again.

"Keep away from me!" she shouted. She shrank back against the Guardian. "Keep away! Get away!"

Chance's mouth hung open. He stared, not comprehending. "Sarah?"

"Go inside," the Guardian said.

"Where's Paul?" Chance asked.

"Go inside," the Guardian repeated.

Chance stared. Sarah looked on him, horrified, almost unrecognizable through her filth and through the expression of utter fear that she showed him.

Or was it disgust? Chance thought, incredulously.

He turned, his face burning. Thetis stood in the doorway to the Hand, and Chance did not meet her eyes as he pushed past her.

Seth followed Chance to his room.

"Sit," the coyote told him.

Chance sat on the edge of the bed.

"I found her. Lu-lu-lucky."

Seth struggled but got the story out. Sarah had crossed the Long Walk Bridge that stretched from the eastern shore of the Usin River to the southern tip of the Crystal Wall. She had screamed at any who passed that an army of the soulburdened gathered in the hills behind her and would attack soon. She was taken for mad, and a group of the city guard had seized her when she crossed the wall and galloped down the ramp and into the crowds of a market.

"They were tu-tu-turning her back, when she spoke of the god, and of you. One of the City Guards had been here that first day we came to the Broken Hand Tha-Tha-That Reaches. He took her to a Councilor. And they summoned me."

Chance touched Seth's shoulder. "Thank you."

Seth nodded.

"What about Paul?"

"Still there. With the go-god."

Chance pressed his hands to his eyes. "May God protect him."

"A-amen."

"Why is she afraid of me?"

"Don't know."

He put his hand again on Seth's shoulder.

"You should go to Sarah. You're the only person she knows here."

Seth licked his hand and padded quietly from the room.

Chance knelt and prayed for Sarah and Paul. And then paced until he heard the others pass outside his room. He went into the hall. The Guardian stood before one of the empty rooms; the low voice of Thetis sounded out from within. Chance waited, watching, hoping to be able to learn something without approaching, but the Guardian did not move or speak. Chance returned to his chamber. A driving pressure in his chest made him turn in circles and walk back and forth from one corner of the room to another.

"Suffering prepares the heart for future grace," he told himself; a passage of the Book. But the words sounded hollow to him.

An hour passed before the Guardian came in.

"The god is near. Ready yourself, Puriman."

"And Paul?"

"It still has your brother. But he may be unhurt."

"But how is Sarah?"

"The god has bent her mind. Her soul will be sore for some time."

"Can I see her?"

"Not now."

"Ah," Chance groaned. He pressed his palms hard against his forehead, as if to grind away his thoughts. "She knows I am not a Puriman. I disgust her."

"No. You are the only one here who has cares of this."

"Then why does she turn away from me?" Chance demanded.

"She finds you fearful and foul because she kens that you gave her mother and your own father and your own mother a filthy sickness."

Chance stepped back as if pushed. "What?"

"That is what the god made her ken."

"But she must know that was the lie of the false god! You told her that, Seth told her that, didn't you?"

"We told her. And she knew it already—that is why she broke free. Fierce this woman is. She was able to thwart the god. But, what the god made her ken she still sees clearly in her mind. She strives to recall the true past."

"Lies!" Chance spat. "Lies! How can you even repeat these lies? I did not harm them."

"Give it time to grow in strength, and the god can make it so that you did kill her mother. Give it enough time, and the god can make it so that you are sick now and always were sick."

Chance turned and looked up at him, furious. "It cannot do that. It cannot change what was. It cannot change me, change my soul."

"Can it not?"

"No! The world would fall apart if that were possible. Nothing would matter."

"Now!" The Guardian stamped one foot down before him, shaking the floor, making the walls creak. A faint fracture appeared in the ceiling above them, and a wisp of dust fell from it and twisted in the air between them, to be blown by Chance's breath as he cringed. The Guardian leaned over him, lip curled in a sneer, and spat, loud and bitter, "*Now* at last you grasp the horror of man-gods! *Now* you see what we fight! Stop your mewling, stop your bids for silly trinkets and useless clothes, stop your foot-dragging before airships! Do not make me carry you again, Puriman!"

He closed his great fists before Chance's face. "And know that if the god halts us before we reach the Numin Well, I will kill you with my own hands rather than let it have you."

He stomped out of the room.

Thetis brought Chance some food, but he did not eat it. He stared out the window at the empty heights of the city towers and then, many hours after the sun had set, he knelt by the bed and prayed silently.

"God. Help Sarah, and keep Paul safe, I beg you. They should not suffer, as did my father and mother, for my faults.

"God, I know I've broken some rules. Not the ones that I believe you really care about, mind you—I figure that it's not hard to tell which ones are beneath your notice, and which aren't. I've broken some of the ones I figure are beneath your notice.

"Of course, I know you notice everything. I mean, I mean to say, the kind of thing you wouldn't think too hard on.

"Well. And I know that you test Purimen through suffering. Suffering prepares the heart for future grace, the Book says.

"But this seems impossible, God. Impossible. To live as a Puriman, when I'm not pure—to be a mortal fighting an immortal; to keep our scriptures when fighting the wicked requires breaking the scriptures; to love a woman who cannot, or should not, let me suit of her; to follow your paths out beyond where you have laid down paths.... Surely I can't do any of those things, can't see any of them to come to pass.

"So. Is that what you want from me? The impossible? Is it enough to try, maybe, to try the impossible? Am I cheating, God, to tell myself it's enough just to try?

"I know you're not in the habit of answering these questions. Generally I've thought my questions were also some of the things beneath your notice, by which I mean things you won't think too hard on. But now I'm not so sure, to be honest. Seeing as how I'm mixed up in the worst of prophesy.

"Still. I'll stop here, not wait, and go on to bed now. But I'm pretty easy to wake up, should you have anything to tell me.

"Amen."

He lay on his bed and stared up at the dim images cast on the ceiling by the distant city lights.

Chance had drifted into a faint sleep when a timid knock sounded on his door. He sat up.

"Yes?" he whispered. In the dim glow he saw the door slowly open. Sarah stood on the threshold. A bar of gray light cast through his window fell on her, where she stood clothed in a thin white robe. Her hair had been shorn to little more than a finger's width. She had scoured her face and body fiercely clean.

"Chance?"

"Sarah!" He stood and took a step forward, then stopped himself, afraid to approach her.

They were both silent a moment. Then she rushed into his arms. "Oh, Chance. I'm sorry. I'm sorry. It was so...."

"I'm sorry," he whispered. "I'm the one that's sorry." He held her tightly, his cheek pressed against hers. She smelled of soap and some perfumed oil. He closed his eyes and just breathed in the smell of her. "The Guardian explained about...the lies, the false memories. I'm sorry. It's my fault. It's because of me...."

"No," she said. "It's that thing. Him. His fault. But are my father and brother safe? Seth was not sure."

They sat on the edge of the bed, holding hands.

"I think so, Sarah. Surely they are. They were not harmed in the barn. They got away. The Guardian said the false god left our village the same day that we did. He would not have pursued them."

"Thank God." She squeezed his hands. "It made me believe they were sick, that you had...."

They sat in silence a long while, till Sarah said, "I'm sorry about your parents, Chance."

"Yes. Thank you. It's...." But he could not finish the sentence. A lump rose in his throat. After it passed, he asked, "And Paul?"

"He's alive, Chance. He's with the false god. But he's alive. We can save him. If there is some way to stop that thing."

"There is. We will stop it. The Guardian and I can stop it."

She nodded, a silhouette moving in the dark. "And Seth. I can't believe your coyote is here."

"My coyote? I'm more like his Puriman."

Sarah gave him a lopsided smile, her teeth flashing in the dimness.

"Who is the woman?"

"Thetis? She is a Mother of the Gotterdammerung. A witch, I mean." Something in Sarah's tone made Chance add, "Why do you ask of her?"

"I don't trust her, Chance. She seemed...angry that I was here."

Chance sighed. "I don't trust any of them, Sarah. That strange unman that stood outside by you and the Guardian—the one with silver eyes—she is a machine. Can you believe that? She looks like a woman but she is a machine. And there's another woman, a real woman, but with eyes and teeth like a cat. These are all things that Purimen should turn their backs upon. No, I don't trust any of them. But Seth. And...the Guardian."

"The gray man? Who had fought in your barn?"

"Yes. I don't know why I should trust him. But he's old. And very powerful. And he doesn't care much for the things of our world. And that makes him honest, I think. I fear him, but I trust him."

They were silent awhile. Then Sarah ran her hand over her head.

"How do you like the hair?"

"You look…beautiful," Chance said, his voice hushed and cracking with emotion.

She put her hand on his cheek.

"Sarah, I have to tell you something. I'm…." He struggled for a moment, resisting the words. He pulled his hands out of her hand and stood, and paced rapidly back and forth before her. Finally he burst out, "I am not pure."

Sarah looked down. "Are you going to…turn? To change into something? Like…?"

Chance stopped in place. "Change? Turn? No. This is what I am and always will be. But, my birth parents, they were not pure. That's why the false god wants me. There's something in me that he can use." His voice choked as he added, "I'm an unman."

Sarah reached out and grabbed his hands. She squeezed them tightly, then pulled him to her. He sat on the bed again.

"Chance, let me tell you something. You know what I always liked about you? That you're determined. You've always been a Puriman but also your own man. I like you because you're different. You want to do things, and you are not afraid to work hard and try to do them. You believe in our way, but you don't have patience with our faults. I like your soul, Chance. That's pure. I don't care about something that no one can see, something that does not change who you are, how you act."

Chance felt a harsh mix of emotions: relief, but also disappointment that Sarah did not care about purity. Purity was the Puriman creed. He had been angry at Thetis for saying less than Sarah said now. Wouldn't it be easy, slovenly, of him to excuse his own impurity?

"How can you say that? The future…our, our…and the Elders, and your father, and…." He sputtered into silence.

"Shh." Sarah spoke very quietly. "Chance, I'm going to be honest with you, so that you know my thoughts. We have to do that now.

We're alone together here, the only Purimen. So let me be clear. You're the finest Puriman I've ever known. The most important part of being a Puriman is following our covenant, with heart. That's what makes you pure."

"That is not what most of the Elders say...." But it was what Sirach had said, he thought. And he had believed his friend Sirach wisest of the Elders.

"Shh."

Chance felt unsatisfied but it was clear to him that he'd do best to let Sarah have her way in this. And of course part of him wanted her to have her way in this. He had never given ground on any question about the Purimen creed, but there was something in the surety of Sarah's tone that made him long to believe that she might understand some matters of faith better than he.

They sat a moment in silence. Then, shyly, Sarah whispered, "Chance, can I stay here with you tonight? I don't want to be alone."

"Oh, please. Please."

After a few awkward twists and turns on the bed, timidly knocking elbows and knees, they lay side by side, clinging together.

"My father won't approve of this," she said.

They laughed softly. Then Chance turned serious. "There are a lot of things, Sarah, that I'm going to have to do now, in the coming days, that aren't right Purimen things. There are things I should turn my back upon, but that I cannot turn my back upon. I'll have to do some things that I would not do back home."

"Oh," Sarah said teasingly, "there's nothing you wouldn't do back home."

Chance laughed softly. "I broke some rules. But it's a strange thing, Sarah. Once I was away from home, I found myself wanting to keep our creed more strongly than I've ever wanted to keep it before."

"That's not so strange. Working as a Ranger with Trumen who were not Purimen, I know how you can be impatient with our people when home, and defensive of them when among strangers."

"Still...."

"This time will be your springaround," Sarah said, using the Puriman term for the adolescent years of Purimen children, when lapses from their religious code were expected and forgiven. "Only a little extended."

"My long springaround," he said, smiling in the dark.

"Mine too." She shifted and held him more tightly. "He'll come soon, Chance."

Her fearful tone made it clear that she referred to the false god.

"He'll come tomorrow," Chance said.

"Oh, Chance, I'm not sure I can face him again." Her hands began to tremble. "He reached into me and he, he violated my soul, and I don't think...."

"Stay here," Chance whispered. "In this tower. He doesn't want you. The Guardian can fight him. I will be the bait used to bind him. There is nothing that you need to do. And then the worst will be over."

"Will it?" she whispered. "Will it?"

CHAPTER

19

"Are you sure you want to be here?" Chance asked. The morning was cool, and the sky gray. He and Sarah sat on horseback atop the Crystal Wall, looking at the bridge that Sarah had crossed the day before, the Long Walk Bridge. It started just a few paces before them where it met the top of the Crystal wall, sloped two hundred paces down a smooth ramp and then leveled out to an elevated road that stood on pylons of white stone and stretched over the water all the way to the far shore of the Usin River, where it fed a road that turned south into the valley.

Normally, the City Guard had told them, the road would be busy with farmers bringing crops and returning with goods made in Disthea. Today it was empty. Something had happened to the south.

On the inside or city-side of the wall, and straight across from the ramp to the bridge, a broad walkway started down into the city. From the top of the wall down to the street below, it switched back and forth three times, clinging to the wall, and sloping gently so that horses could easily ascend and descend with carts. This too was empty, the city guard holding back the people below.

"Yes," Sarah said. The hooves of their horses clacked sharply on the diamond as they shifted. "I want to be here. I'm the only Puriman Ranger here, and it is my duty." She had awoken in the morning strong and angry: the old Sarah, but with a new seriousness. There had been no time to find Puriman clothes for her, so she wore now clothes that Thetis had offered: a tight black shirt and black pants of a strange, strong material, and hard black boots. Over these she had buckled her old belt with her two swords. It disturbed Chance because she looked like a different person, but also because she was so strikingly beautiful in these clothes, the black seeming to darken her hair and eyebrows and eyes, and the tight fit showing the perfect form of her.

Thetis had arranged for horses, and the only Mother of the Gotterdammerung in Disthea sat now on horseback on the other side of Sarah. Sarah stole suspicious glances at her, and Thetis returned them. Seth and the Guardian stood nearby, at the very edge of the wall, looking out over the water warily.

"Here," Thetis said. She handed to Sarah two black tubes, fixed together. "You look through them like—"

"I know," Sarah said, lifting them to her eyes. She peeked at Chance. "Some Trumen Rangers use these glasses," she explained. "They make things far away appear close." She peered through them at the bridge.

"Nothing," she said.

"I felt him this hour," the Guardian said. "The god is close."

Seth sniffed the sea air, and wandered to the inside edge of the wall, to gaze down the switchback ramp descending to the city street. Uroboros stood, partially visible as a dim black square between two pale buildings, at the distant end of the street below. Seth sniffed again, and circled the group.

"I see something," the Guardian said. "At the very beginning of the bridge."

Sarah raised the glasses again. "Yes. I see someone. Alone. He has hair. It's not Hexus. Wait."

"He's on horseback," the Guardian said.

"Yes. He has red hair. Oh, oh, Chance, I think it's Paul."

"Are you sure?"

She watched for a long time. "It's Paul. Riding fast."

"It may not be Paul," Chance said. Despair gripped him. "Not anymore."

"That's right," the Guardian said. "But Hexus would know that we would waver, and wait, given the small hope that your brother did break free. That may be some use to the god. But what use? Why come alone, for just that moment of guile?"

"Hu-who is that?" Seth asked. He pointed with one bent paw along the Crystal Wall. A group of men approached along the top of the wide diamond surface. They were still hundreds of paces ahead, walking with determined strides. The men were dressed in different ways, robed in the uniforms of different guilds. One of them, a tall man with gray hair, held a long, golden cylinder that gleamed even in the dim gray light of the clouded day.

Sarah looked with the glasses. "They carry something. A long golden tube."

"A weapon," Thetis said. She looked through her own glasses. "No," she moaned. "Could it be? The Lance of Kane."

"What's that?" Chance asked.

"An ancient weapon."

"Hieroni!" Seth barked bitterly.

Chance reached toward Sarah and she handed him the looking glasses. He peered through them uncertainly, the wall sweeping this way and that through his vision till he got the feel for steadying them. He found the man with the golden rod. He was tall and muscular, with long gray hair knotted behind his head.

"I know that man, I've seen him!" Chance shouted. "He came for Sirach! When Elder Sirach left our village, he left with that man!"

"What?" Sarah asked.

"I ken the wile," the Guardian said. "Hieroni attack from one side, just as Paul nears, and hope that Hexus may slip by on the other side while we shield ourselves—and we are fearful that we may harm the Puriman's brother. But it shall not work. Let us yield them no good of this. I will take the Hieroni first, quickly, and then get onto the bridge. Chance, stay here. If it is the god, he need see only you. Then flee for Uroboros. Let him follow."

"Yes," Chance said. He handed the looking glasses back to Sarah.

Sarah watched the bridge. "He's about half of the way now. He doesn't seem to breathe hard enough, for all that riding."

Thetis turned to the Guardian, "But—" she began. Before she could finish her warning, the Guardian disappeared with a snap of his cloak. Sitting on horseback Chance could see the gray blur cross the top of the wall toward the approaching men.

The Guardian appeared ten paces before them.

"Fools!" he shouted. His voice carried clearly over the sound of the sea crashing on the wall. "Go back to your guilds, or die here by my hand." Threkor's Hammer gleamed black and silver in his fist.

"They're lifting the weapon!" Thetis shouted. She watched the Hieroni through the glasses.

"Paul is speeding up. Nearly three-quarters of the way across the bridge now," Sarah added.

There was a crack like thunder that drew Chance's attention back from the bridge—

And the Guardian split in two.

"Oh God!" Chance shouted. "Dear God, no! Let it not be!"

The Guardian's torso, cut from the legs, fell forward hard onto the unyielding diamond surface. The legs followed. Gray ichor splashed around him. Wet shreds of organs, as gray inside as his skin was outside, trailed behind the two halves of the body. Threkor's Hammer fell with a loud clack onto the wall.

The halves of the Guardian writhed on the ground. The Guardian screamed, a howl that shuddered through the air like an explosion.

Chance turned his horse and leaned forward, about to spur it toward the Guardian.

"No!" Seth barked. "No! No! He-he's an im-im-mortal. He will live. Run! Run!"

"Ride!" Sarah shouted. She pointed down, at the ramp that reached toward the water below them, where Paul was riding. "He's coming faster now! Ride!"

"And look!" Thetis called at the same time. She pointed in the distance. Across the water, at the beginnings of the bridge, dark figures were swarming onto the road, pouring out of the forest on the bank, following Paul. Soulburdened animals.

"Ride!" Thetis screamed. Sarah kicked her horse and slapped Chance's horse as she passed him, galloping hard for the switchback that descended into the city. Chance followed. He could see that the Guardian was reaching—the sight horrified him—for the rest of his body. Then they turned onto the descending way.

Their horses slowed, skidding, as they approached the first turn of the switchback. After they rounded the sharp bend, Chance saw that four men stood in the way, before the next bend. The men separated, two on each side, and held up a net.

"Stay back!" Sarah called to Chance.

"No!" Chance yelled, fearing they had a weapon like those above. But Sarah leaned forward and rode hard, close to the wall, at the man on the far left. The horse hesitated but she shouted at it and drove it on. The man dropped the net and jumped aside before he was ridden down. The man next to him reached for Sarah as she reined back. In a flash, she drew one sword, reaching across her belt, and slashed at his arms. He fell back, screaming.

And then Chance had caught up and his horse leapt a bit over the heaped net and skidded around the next switchback turn. Sarah followed.

The other two men shouted something down the wall in a language Chance did not recognize. Seth suddenly appeared at his side, running hard, ears back.

"When we get to the street," Sarah called, "if there is trouble, ride ahead. Seth and I will hold whoever is there. We'll give you a start."

"No," Chance said. "Let's just charge through together!"

"You have to go on," Sarah shouted. They turned into the last switchback. "It's you they want. We'll just slow them and keep on after them when they chase you."

He opened his mouth to shout but they were coming down the last of the ramp now and several men stood at the bottom. Most of them stepped aside—regular merchants, Chance realized—but two stood in the center of the way. The city guard that they had passed when they ascended the ramp was now nowhere to be seen. Seth took to the air in a great leap and struck into the face of one of the men blocking their way, sending him falling backwards. Sarah rode down the other. A group of men charged out of the crowd then, reaching for her.

Chance rode through, the horse's hooves cracking loudly against the hard stone of the street. He looked back. He could not see Seth. Sarah was drawing her swords as three men surrounded her. On the switchback above he saw Thetis descending. He reined his horse to a stop.

"Heya!" he called. "I am the Potentiate! Come and get the prize of the false god!"

Silence fell. Then, with a shout, the men who were grabbing at Sarah charged him. Two clambered onto horses waiting nearby. Chance turned and galloped off toward Uroboros.

CHAPTER

20

The Guardian dragged his upper body toward his legs, screaming in an otherworldly voice that shook this world and the world behind it. Pain blinded him, but he felt drawn almost magnetically to his legs, knowing that rejoining with them could alone relieve his agony. His gray blood, strewn all over the filthy ground, congealed and began to draw back toward his torso. He reached for his hips, lifting his arm—a crack sounded out—and a chunk of diamond was chipped out of the wall beside him where his arm had just rested.

"Ah!" he howled in anger. But he quickly drew himself together. The legs clung to him, searing into him, struggling for the right join. When he was sure that they were bound enough to hold to him, he rolled quickly to the side—just in time, as another crack sounded out, scorching a molten cut where he had lain.

He rolled off the wall and fell down, face first, onto the switchback below, landing beside the heap of net that Chance had leapt over moments before.

He screamed as the seeking tendrils of otherworldly flesh pushed against and into his viscera. And then it was over; his legs found their fit. He stood, the blinding pain easing. He howled again, this time in rage, and ran at his fastest speed up the ramp.

In an instant he had snatched Threkor's Hammer from the ground where it lay beside the gouge in the wall that the Hieroni's weapon had made. He could feel the god now. Close, pushing through hidden spaces, nearly within reach.

He leapt off the inside of the wall, so that he landed again back down on the switchback, with his feet apart, arms spread so that with one hand the fingers touched the wall, and with the other he held the hammer far out to this side, blocking the way. Paul appeared before him, seeming to materialize. He was on foot. He held aloft a swollen red hand, with an eye in the center of it.

"You cannot defeat me, destroyer," Hexus spat in his guild tongue.

"Do you think I will spare my wrath because you foul the Puriman's brother? No. I aim to do him the good of a quick death."

"I shall overcome you, and then release my brothers and sisters."

"If that were so, then why are they not here now? Your future is mute. You and I both hear its emptiness. I have already won this battle."

Hexus hissed at him.

"Time to be beaten back into nothingness, Hexus," the Guardian answered. He raised the hammer in both hands.

A crack sounded out above and behind the Guardian. And his right arm fell off. The hammer clattered again to the ground. Hexus disappeared in a blur as the Guardian stumbled back, howling and confused.

He looked up, and there the Hieroni stood, their weapon gleaming.

Furious, the Guardian snatched the hammer from the ground with his left hand. He leapt atop the Crystal Wall. He hurtled ahead and in the next instant stood in the midst of the Hieroni. They started and then turned uncertainly in panic. The man with the weapon began to aim the gold rod toward the Guardian.

Then his hands clutched air. The Guardian smashed the gleaming weapon with the hammer, and shining broken fragments of it spun away over the sea.

The Guardian swung the hammer once more. It passed in an instant through all four men's heads, in a single wide sweep, exploding brains over the black diamond of the wall. Their bodies fell slowly back.

"Damn you," the Guardian hissed. He leapt back down onto the switchback, set the hammer at his feet, and lifted his arm. He pressed it into the gaping socket of his shoulder. His pain eased. He pushed his palm into the ichor that stained the wood, and the gray fluid drew back into his hand. Then, in an explosion of motion, he snatched up the hammer and pursued the sixth of the Younger Gods.

Chance's horse began to tire before he was halfway to Uroboros. Chance looked back and saw that the two Hieroni on horseback were nearly on top of him. Sarah was far behind, driving her horse, trying to catch up. Chance could not see Seth.

"Yah!" he shouted at the horse. People coming to the market crowded the street, and he wove through them, trying to slow his pursuers, but looking back he saw that his path slowed him more than it slowed the men chasing him. He leaned farther forward, driving straight up the center of the wide road. Uroboros rose before them, a tall black wall perhaps a mile ahead.

Then one of the men came up at his side. He had a black beard, and dark eyes, squinted with intent. The man drew from his saddle a long metal pole with a claw of iron spikes on the end. He raised it over his head and then brought it down, hard, on the back of Chance's horse.

His horse shrieked and shook its head, slowing.

"Devil!" Chance howled. The cruelty of this attack enraged him. Their horses tangled, slowing. They pressed side to side, and nearly stopped. The man was older, and stronger, but he held the reins in one hand and clung with the other hand to the metal claw, useless now with Chance so close to him.

Chance had much practice at fist-fighting other Purimen boys. He struck the man hard at close range, first in the face, his knuckles slipping across the dark beard, and then repeatedly in the stomach. The man began to fall back. Chance seized the saddle horn of the man's horse and raised his inside leg and kicked, stamping down against the man's ribs, again and again, until the man dropped off the horse, grabbing ineffectually for Chance's foot. Chance's horse shifted then and, still holding onto the other man's saddle horn, Chance almost fell. He pulled himself into the other horse's saddle. The horse trotted a few paces ahead, leaving the man on the ground behind.

Chance grabbed at the reins, but the second man who had followed him had circled his horse and now reached for Chance from behind. He grabbed Chance's collar and yanked. Chance almost fell out of the saddle. He clutched again for the saddle horn as he was pulled backwards.

Then Sarah was on them. She drove a sword straight through the man as she rode up and twisted it savagely to pull it free as she passed. Chance managed to turn, and he looked with shock at the surprised, open eyes of his second attacker as the man slowly fell from his horse. He made a slight noise, as if wanting to say something, but then he was gone. He fell hard onto the road.

Sarah pulled to a stop, holding the reins in two fingers so she could still grip both her swords.

"Ride!" she shouted at Chance, who stared at the fallen man and the pool of blood that surrounded him. "Ride!"

Chance looked back. Behind them on the road, Thetis galloped after them, and immediately behind her at least a dozen more men and women were in pursuit on horseback.

Chance shifted in the saddle, getting a good seat, and kicked the horse.

"Yah!"

They sped toward Uroboros. Five Engineers, men and women in black robes, waited in the road before the doors, holding tall hammers. Behind them stood Mimir, appearing calm as always, if not indifferent. Near the makina crouched Wadjet, the woman from the Fricandor lands, frowning at the onrushing horses.

"This way!" Chance called. They rode past the group of Engineers and turned to follow the curve of the building toward the smaller door that Chance knew. When Chance reined up before it, Sarah jumped down first. She still held her swords. Their pursuers had fallen behind, slowed by the Engineers.

"Here?"

"Here." Chance swung down.

She pushed through the door.

"Follow me!" Chance said, squeezing past her. They hurried down the long hall, now familiar to him. The hall stretched before them, empty, but from somewhere inside Uroboros came a scream of pain, followed by the clang of metal.

Thetis followed past the Engineers as Chance and Sarah raced by on their horses, their faces red with the heat of fighting and with flight. The Engineers closed rank behind her, shouting at her pursuers. Sarah and Chance quickly disappeared around the bend of Uroboros, but Thetis caught up in time to see them leap from their saddles and hurry through a door in the side of the shining black building.

She dismounted and went to their horses, which turned in place by the door, sweating and snorting. The taller of the two looked less spent. She went to its side, whispering to reassure it, and opened its saddle bag. She looked over her shoulder and found the street still empty. She reached into her robes, pulled out the silver cylinder that Vark had given her, and twisted the top. She put it in the saddle bag.

"Go!" she shouted, slapping the horse's shank. "Go!"

It took off at a gallop, heading toward the western side of the sea wall.

She pushed the other horses to set them following at a more leisurely pace, and then slipped into the doorway and pulled it mostly closed. Through the crack, she watched as, minutes later, two dozen Hieroni sped by on horseback in such wild pursuit of the lone horse that the shoes on their steeds struck sparks off the hard stones of the street.

Sarah looked down the black, yawning abyss of the well. She leaned far out over the stairs so that she could look at the winding steps below them. "How far?" she asked.

"Down these stairs," Chance explained. "A short distance. Come on."

"No. It looks clear. You go. I'll stop anything...human...that follows."

"Sarah—"

"Go!"

He hesitated. Then he nodded. "It's probably better that you are not with me when I face the false god. When I call, you climb up to safety.

Chance hurried ahead, shoes clattering on the metal stairs.

Sarah pulled the door closed, took a few steps up the rusted stairs, and readied herself. She gripped the swords tightly, her palms only now seeming to sweat and slip on the handles. The air here smelled damp, a mix of rust and wet stone. She held her breath, listening, but could hear only Chance, his steps on the hard metal steps echoing into the black depths of the well.

My mother always told me, Sarah thought, don't get involved with a man who's trouble. Get a quiet one, a lucky one, who's a stranger to calamity.

And here I am, in the middle of horrible calamity. A historically huge calamity.

And I killed that man on the horse.

She knew that, in a while, that would hit her hard. The horror of it.

A door creaked open below. Chance's voice echoed up the well, "Get clear, Sarah!"

She did not climb farther up the steps, but turned to face the door. She sighed, and to reassure herself in the haunting silence, she whispered, "That boy better be worth—"

The door just below her exploded. She fell back onto the hard steps, almost dropping her swords, but glimpsed Paul's broad shoulders turning impossibly quickly before he shot down the steps.

She opened her mouth to call out to Chance, but could not speak. The terror of her time with Hexus, the horror of him reaching into her mind, swept over her. Then Hexus was gone, disappeared from view in a descending blur. A rush of shame followed the rush of fear, as she realized she might have condemned Chance by not calling out to warn him.

Two men hurried through the doorway, shirtless, with long, loose pants so wide that they seemed like skirts. They had cut strange symbols into the flesh of their stomachs and chests. Both of them wielded in each hand a long metal rod tipped with a claw. They looked down the stairs, then up, uncertain of which way to go. Seeing Sarah, they hesitated.

Furious at her own cowardice, Sarah leapt up and shouted at them, swinging her swords. The first man fell back and tumbled down the stairs, bleeding from his throat. The second retreated into the doorway, whipping his weapons at her wildly. One claw slipped past her blades and bit into her check, drawing a ragged scar. Sarah howled in outrage and pursued him, drops of blood flinging off of her spinning blades.

CHAPTER

21

Chance heard the entrance burst open high above when he entered the chamber where the silver rods stood. The metal tumbled noisily down, banging against the edge of the stairwell as it fell. The sound was huge and frightening, obscenely loud after the prior silence. He threw himself across the room, chest heaving. He had one foot on the platform of the control dais when a crack of air exploded behind him.

A hand grasped his shoulder, gently. The size and heft of it were familiar. His brother's hand. Then another hand settled onto his head.

The world disappeared. Memories not his own flooded into Chance. Four fierce sisters with pale skin and black hair, black eyes, smiling at him. The Sunken City full of airships. The thick clouds of heady incense, shot through with colorful lights, in a hall of The Hand that Reaches. The taste of strange wines.

And after these visions came a deep swell of emotions. Sorrow, melancholy, and hope. He understood the Sunken City now as Hexus saw it: a desolate wasteland, empty, dispirited, tragic nearly beyond his comprehension, nearly beyond what his heart could bear. Theopolis had been forged with blood and pain and hope over ten thousand years, but only Disthea remained, the derelict wreck of a billion wasted dreams, surrounded by a sea bereft of boats, beyond which stretched a wilderness under empty skies where cruel and stupid men killed the children of the forest for sport.

And then, like the flood of a stream, the entire history of Hexus in this time—in Chance's time—flooded into Chance, like water racing over a cliff edge and into the pool of his mind. Chance jerked and shook in a seizure of comprehension. He pulled away. Slowly, while Hexus reached for him again, his eyes focused.

He felt, in that moment, an urge to turn and ask Hexus, *how can I help you? How can we redeem all this?*

Chance took two deep breaths.

Then he spun and punched Paul's face: a square, solid hit with his top two knuckles striking the left cheek above the corner of the lip. Paul's body staggered back a step, and then his heel caught on one of the rods along the bottom of the trap. He tripped and fell backwards, and lay in the center of the frame of the cube.

Chance jumped behind the dais. Hands shaking, he pressed the colored keys as he had learned.

Hexus laughed, in Paul's voice. "That was a surprise, Potentiate. You always let Paul have the first swing at you in the past, so I failed to expect that."

"Some things have changed," Chance said, still pressing at the keys.

"You know: you would have won every fight with him, if only you did not have such a sense of fair play. Or is it a sense of suffering, of martyrdom, that made you let him get the advantage?"

Chance did not answer. Hexus floated into the air and righted himself, before setting his feet down. The cage began to form as a dimly visible sheen. Paul's body was dressed now in a fine suit of black, with a crisp white shirt and white collar buttoned at the throat with a black stone. For a moment Chance had the absurd desire to chastise Paul for wearing what were clearly not Puriman clothes. And though he realized in a moment that that was ridiculous, he was shocked to see Hexus now thieving Paul's mannerisms: he pulled the two sleeves, each in turn, then straightened his collar before he ran his left hand over Paul's red hair.

Chance felt a swell of anger and sorrow to see this hint of his brother remain, a mockery of Paul's life and ways. Or was Paul still in there, still himself, buried alive?

"Now begins the New Age," Hexus said. "Come."

"No," Chance said.

"There's nothing here that can stop me. My Hieroni have the last two Numin Jars. Did you know that? And there was never anything else in this world that could harm or bind a god. Except another god."

He held up his hand and the air seemed to shiver and writhe like a snake, twisting from the eye in his palm to the dim barrier—and through it. The shimmering form seized Chance, gripping his right arm, and dragged him toward the cube. But Chance leaned back and resisted the pull. His feet scraped on the damp stone floor.

"What's this?" Hexus spat. He felt the weakening of his grip. He reached back, tugging at the extension of his hold, but the dim silvery limit of the cube pulled back, and Chance did not move.

Hexus lowered his head and shouted, and then with a savage twist of Paul's whole body, pulled with all his strength. The line of his control trembled, and then it jerked Chance forward.

Chance slammed into the side of the cube, and fell back to the ground, dazed. A sharp pain pierced his arm where Hexus had seized him. But the connection between them was severed.

"What is this?" Hexus repeated. He walked forward—

And bounced off the slowly forming wall. He fell back onto the ground. He looked at Chance now, where they both sat on the floor, facing each other, on opposite sides of the congealing barrier.

"The first Numin Jar," Chance said. "Threkor's mold."

"Ah. And I could have just walked around it. It's your brother's plodding, stupid brain that slows me, Potentiate." He stood.

A shout echoed down from above. And another: this one Sarah's. And the ring of a sword. Chance started to reach down with his right arm, to push himself up, but then felt a stab of pain. He pulled back his sleeve, and found that a lump protruded on his forearm: one of the bones in his right arm was broken, and it pressed painfully against his muscles, as if it might pierce through his skin if he put any weight upon it.

There was another cry on the stairs. He slowly got up, holding his broken limb as still as he could with his left hand. It did not hurt yet, though he felt lightheaded. He hobbled to the door and called out, "Sarah!" But she did not answer. A man and woman, both shirtless and carrying axes, were descending the stairs. Chance had no choice: all was lost if the Hieroni freed the false god. He pushed the heavy door closed, and set the crossbar behind it, just as the two Hieroni flung themselves against the rusted iron with a loud clanging.

Chance turned, his back against the coarse metal of the barred door. A wave of dizziness swept over him. A dull pain started in his arm, and the feel of the broken forearm resting on his left palm made his head reel. On top of this, he felt a growing nausea from the disorientation of Hexus having stolen into his mind again.

And there stood the false god, possessing his brother, right hand held up, the black eye in the palm of it peering back at him.

Tears welled in Chance's eyes, from mixed pain and regret. "I'm sorry, Paul. I'm sorry. This is because of me. But I will avenge you, and I will avenge our parents. And perhaps...."

Hexus sneered. "You cannot take the acts of a god on yourself—"

"Shut up, foul thing," Chance hissed. "I speak to my brother. I know he is there." He took a shuffling step forward, cradling his arm carefully. Behind him, the Hieroni still clanged, clanged at the door. "Paul, Paul, I ask that you forgive me. I know I was a poor brother. I judged you. Father told me I was judgmental, that last day, before the guests arrived. And I see that he was right. Can you forgive me?"

For a moment, an expression of Paul's own seemed to rise out of buried depths. His face sagged, and his chin quivered. His eyes welled with sadness.

Then a sneer broke the expression.

"Don't weep for him, Potentiate," Hexus said. "Your brother nearly hates you. Do you know why?"

"Yes," Chance whispered.

"No you don't. He hates that you're a fine farmer, a better winemaker. He hated how you made your own law. You were a Puriman, and yet you broke rules and never seemed to suffer for it. He hated your arrogance."

Paul's voice dropped. "And he hated you because you believe. You break all the rules but still you believe it all. You find it so easy to never doubt. He hated your comfortable faith. For that I cannot blame him."

Chance shuffled another step forward. "Shut up. I'm going to kill you. Do you know that? I'm going to kill you. I will be the vessel of God's wrath!"

"You would help the Atheos kill me? Who made the Atheos, Potentiate? Why does it want to kill me? Have you asked these questions?"

"Every good man should want to kill you. Ah! Why do I talk to you? I turn my back on you." But Chance took another step toward the cube as he said this.

"Why turn your back? I cannot harm you. If this wall continues to grow, in minutes I will be locked away in here. Time will slow for me and I will be like a fish frozen into ice. Hear what I would say. I do not seek to harm you."

"Liar. Do you think I am an ass? I saw you murder my parents. I see you now, murdering my brother."

"That night at your home, what would have happened if I had not killed the first Purimen to approach me? All of them in that barn would have attacked me, in the end. And many more would have died. I could have killed them all, if I wanted. It would have been easy. But I warned them, instead, with an example. Can you understand that, Potentiate? If you are to rule as a god, you must understand such choices. I have walked in your world. I know what must be done in it."

"This is not my world," Chance sneered. "This is not the Purimen's world. This is your world. You and your kind made it like this. You emptied this city. You caused the Barren. You waged the Great War. If the people followed the ways of the Purimen, all would be peaceful, as it is in the Valley of the Walking Man. Men have tried your way, and it led only to misery and death. Give us our chance, give us our time. The Purimen, not false gods, can redeem the men of Earth."

And, as he said this, Chance realized for the first time that this should be the calling of the Purimen.

Hexus walked along the thickening wall of the cube, Paul's right hand held up, the obscene eye looking at Chance.

"Wrong," he whispered.

But Chance thought he heard, for the first time, doubt in Hexus's voice.

"Who are you?" Chance asked, "Who are you to return from your unquiet grave and tell we the living how to live?"

"I am a god."

Bloated red pustules covered the flesh of Paul's hand and the wrist. Chance pointed at the sores. "You're not a god! You're a pestilence! Die, and let us try our own way, you rotting filth."

"This is mortality, this rot. It is not me. This is you. You'll rot someday. Every human will rot. Unless we become gods, Potentiate."

"Don't call me that."

"This world has known no greater title of respect than 'Potentiate.' And I tell you: I mean you no harm. I want to give you my memories. I want to give you my knowledge. And then I want you to take my place. Kill me, yes—it will be a favor, Potentiate. You could not conceive my suffering—the demigod Wervool somehow broke my body, and trapped most of it in the moment of its own destruction, so that this tiny fragment of me feels bound and restricted and cannot become its own whole. Kill me, please. But take my place. Become a god. We need a whole god to save this world. Only a god can save us."

Chance tried to laugh. "You think I will be tempted by this? I was a Puriman! A man is his memories and his knowledge and his hopes and dreams. Replace those and you kill the most of him."

"No. A soul is more—"

"You think me so corruptible," Chance interrupted. "So foolish?"

"No. Not a fool. But ignorant, with a primitive religion." He squinted knowingly at Chance. It was an alien expression on Paul's face, a reminder that this was not Paul. "I'm the only one among you to have the respect to tell you this, am I not?"

Chance's flinch made Hexus nod sagely.

"Yes. The others here treat you as a child. I treat you as an equal. They know there is no supreme god, but they let your errors pass in silence. Am I right?"

Chance did not answer.

"And why?" Hexus spoke through a silvered gray mist now. "Because they think you worthless, another savage who cannot face his lies."

"The One True God is not a lie."

"Oh, but Potentiate, what if it were?"

"It is not. I have no doubts."

"You have no doubts. But believing does not make it true. What if your beliefs were false? What if there were no One True God, but only gods, a great leap above men, but only a leap? Necessary, but faulted also? And as alone in the world as you and I?"

The shield was nearly opaque now. Chance saw the shadow of his own face superimposed on the dim outline of his lost brother's visage.

Transfixed, he stepped closer to the cube, so that his face and the face of his brother, the stolen face of the god, were just a hand-span apart.

"Then the world would be purposeless," Chance whispered.

"Yes!" Hexus said, in Paul's voice. "And what should we do, then?"

Chance refocused his eyes to peer at the reflection of his own, sad eyes, so like the eye of Hexus, and whispered, "Despair."

"Or? Or? Why not make our own purposes? Make our own gods! Is that so bad, Potentiate? Ponder it! Don't give in to the easy comforts of the stories you've been told. *Ponder it!* I beg you to save this decayed world." The mirror was complete now. Only a single phrase, spoken as if from far away, managed to slip past the last moments of the barrier's completion. "Do not cling to an absent God!"

Chance opened his mouth to speak, but seeing in the mirror only himself, he faltered. What was he about to say? He did not know. His reflection gazed back confused, slyly cautious. The doubt in his eyes looked as cunning and worldly as had the scheming eye of Hexus.

"There is only One True God," he whispered. He saw but did not feel his lips moving as he spoke. His voice was vacant of conviction. His eyes betrayed that his thoughts reached beyond the rote phrase.

"Puriman!" the Guardian called. The metal door clanged hard. Two screams came through the door and then fell, echoing. Chance understood: the Guardian had just tossed down the deep well the Hieroni who stood by the door. "Puriman, it is I. Open the door!" Chance hurried to the door, awkwardly rested his right arm on his chest, and, after a brief struggle, lifted the bar with his left.

The Guardian's massive shoulders scraped noisily against the frame as he pushed in, scattering flakes of rust on the floor. He was whole, with not a sign on him that he had a short while before been cut in twain. He held the hammer back with one hand and with the other reached out toward the mirrored cube.

"I ken nothing. Is it bound?"

Chance nodded. "It's bound. In there."

The Guardian squinted at him.

"What?" Chance asked.

"Here, hold this," the Guardian asked, planting Threkor's Hammer next to Chance. "I need to check the cube."

Chance looked at the hammer. Strange thoughts welled in his mind. He saw again what Hexus had shown him: a huge dark man, like the Guardian in size and form, standing before a blue fire, holding this hammer and staring out from under dark brows. Chance almost reached out, to touch and cling to the hammer, to hold something that meshed with this fleeting vision of Threkor.

Chance took a step back. "I should not. No Puriman should touch such a thing."

The Guardian nodded with relief. He lifted the hammer. "I'm glad that you are still you, Chance Kyrien."

Chance's voice faltered as he replied, "I am glad you're whole again, and alive, Guardian."

"And I am sorry for your brother."

Chance nodded. Then he shouted, "But Sarah! Please, can you find her? She was fighting the others—the Hieroni. And Seth!"

"She is well. She follows behind. The coyote also."

"Thank God," Chance said. "Thank God."

Sarah clattered down the stairs, Engineering Master Sar behind her. She looked around the room, eyes wide, breathing heavily as she searched for the next attack. A deep cut lacerated her cheek. Chance cringed to see the open flesh, pale but streaming blood, exposed in the gash. Gray dust coated her short hair. She had both swords out, the points down, dripping blood.

Chance again pressed his right arm to his chest, and he reached for her with his left, heedless of the swords. He managed to grip her arm and squeeze.

"It's done," he said. "It's done."

He clutched her for a moment while she seemed to slowly come to understand.

"It's over?" she whispered. A single tear fell from one eye, drawing a wet path through pale dust and drying blood.

"Yes. He's bound. In there." Chance pointed. "It's over."

Sarah knelt, flipped her swords and set the points on the floor, bowed her head, and said very quietly, her voice threatening to break with a sob, "May God forgive my wrath and sins and have mercy on my soul and on the souls of mine enemies."

"Amen," Chance whispered.

She stood. "You're hurt."

"So are you."

Seth sprinted down the stairs, taking four steps at a leap. He skidded past the door on the platform outside, and then hurried to Chance, nails scratching on the metal. He brushed against Chance's leg, obviously relieved to see him alive. Chance knelt and wrapped his left arm around Seth's neck.

"Airships!" Seth barked. "The sky is full! And b-b-boats!"

"I cannot leave the cage unguarded," the Guardian said.

"I will gather Threkor's Engles," Engineer Sar said. "We will post all five here, surrounding and guarding the cube."

"Will the Creator allow it?" the Guardian asked.

Sar laughed, and speaking quietly to herself, said, "Let's see the fat useless worm try to stop me. I'd give him. . . ." And so she continued as she started up the stairs, her mumbling echoing in the well.

"Then go, you three," the Guardian told Seth, Sarah, and Chance. "See what is happening. I will come as soon as this place is safe."

CHAPTER

22

C hance nodded at Sarah, cradling his arm, as she wiped the flat sides of her swords on her pants, her face grim, and then sheathed the blades. They slowly climbed the stairs while Seth ran ahead.

When they reached the door they had entered from, they found that Sar waited for them. She had finished her task and returned with two bars of soft metal and a tight roll of black cloth. Chance sat on the floor in the hall and Sar bound his arm by gently tying the metal bars to his forearm as Sarah held it still. Then she tied a sling over his neck.

"This must be properly set as soon as it can be done," the old woman said, her voice a soft whisper. She rummaged in her bag and pulled out what looked to Chance like a square of paper. She pressed it over Sarah's cut.

Chance looked up at Sar and met her eyes, and he felt suddenly the strange conviction that though she was important to his life, he would never see her again.

"Now I must go," she added. "May your days be peaceful and inventive."

She stood.

"Sar," Chance called. "Engineer. I. . . ."

She looked down at him, waiting.

"I learned much from you, in these days. About the good that is in Engineers. I thank you."

She nodded, and set off down the hall at her brisk walk, her heavy robes brushing across the stone.

Sarah helped Chance to his feet. He frowned when he looked at the blood seeping through the patch on her cheek. "We need to mend your cut," he whispered to her.

"Later."

They hurried down the hall to the small exit and pushed out into the street. A crowd of Engineers and others had gathered nearby, before the main entrance to Uroboros. Mimir and Wadjet stood with them. Thetis came to Chance's side. She touched his broken arm. Tears welled in her eyes as she looked at him— tears of relief, Chance assumed—but she said nothing. Seth turned in place, looking at them and back at the sky, wild with excitement.

Down the long road that stretched all the way to the Crystal Wall miles ahead, a slot of the sky was visible through the canyon formed by the towers lining the street. Black dots infested the blue sky: airships in the distance, bearing down on Disthea like a swarm of giant insects.

"There must be tens," Chance said.

"Hundreds," Sarah explained. "So many I saw in the valley of the Usin River."

"And more boats," Seth said. "And ma-ma-many on foot, cross-ing now the bridge."

As they waited for the Guardian, the ships drew closer. Some in the front of the assault crossed over the wall now.

"They're going to-to-to moor on the towers," Seth said.

"I see their plan!" Chance explained it rapidly to Sarah. "Most of the towers are empty. I mean, the tops of them are empty, because it's hard to climb up into them, and there's enough room in the first few floors for everybody here. The soulburdened can enter the tops of the towers, and fill the top floors, without a fight. It will allow them to get many into the city and get organized before they battle."

The air cracked, and then the Guardian stood with them. He looked at the sky, taking in the scene.

"We must get Chance out of here. We must get to safety. Makina, we go to your ship."

Mimir bowed her head. "I regret to inform all in our company that my airship was destroyed four minutes ago. The soulburdened crew of an attacking airship boarded it. They successfully cut open all of the air cells."

"We must take another ship, then." The Guardian turned, about to stomp off to the eastern side of the Crystal Wall.

"I can take you," Wadjet called. The way she said it, as she said anything, seemed a challenge.

"How is this, Steward?" the Guardian demanded.

"My boat is docked at the northern pier of the Crystal Wall. There is room enough."

The Guardian hesitated. "A boat? We go far, Steward."

"I will take you far, Guardian," she turned to Thetis. "I will take you if the Mothers of the Gotterdammerung pledge to do as I ask, pledge to seek a cure for the plague that strikes my land, upon our return."

Thetis nodded. "I pledge it."

"This course of action is not strategically optimal," Mimir said. "If we take a boat, then we will need to cross by foot over the mod-barrows. The modghasts will attack us. We should instead find an airship."

"Do you know where there's an airship for us, makina?" the Guardian asked angrily.

"Modghasts sa-sa-sa-sound bad," Seth observed. "Cut you up, use the parts." Hair rose on his back.

"There is no modghast that can face me and survive," the Guardian said. "Note even a hundred. Let the makina remain here." He turned to Wadjet. "Show us."

Thetis called for horses, and after some moments of confusion two Engineers managed to bring them four tired old mares that pulled carts to the market. Chance tried to mount a horse with just his left arm, but he was too exhausted and the pain in his right arm was growing now. Finally the Guardian had to lift him onto the steed. Thetis, Sarah, and the Wadjet mounted the other horses quickly.

Chance noted that Mimir did not move away, but stayed close to him, making it clear she intended to ignore the Guardian's counsel that she remain behind.

The first few steps of the mare were agony for Chance, bobbing his arm. He cried out involuntarily, but no one noticed. The feel of his bones grinding together was horrible, but he knew it would be worse to walk. He shifted until he found a way to ride so that the rhythm of the horse's stride did not move the bones.

The Guardian and Mimir and Seth followed on foot, as Wadjet set off at a gallop, first east, and then turning north at the next corner.

People were running in the streets, shouting the names of their loved ones. Behind them, the airships teemed among the black and gray towers of the city, and were tethered to the tallest buildings.

"These poor people," Chance shouted. "Can we do nothing?"

"It will only be worse for them if we remain, Puriman," the Guardian called. "Ride on!"

At the far northern end of the city, a long ramp switchbacked up the Crystal Wall, just as at the southern wall. It was crowded with people rushing up to the bridge and boats at the top. Chance and the others pushed through the throngs as best they could. Airships hovered now above them, watched with fear by the crowds of people ascending.

A numbing dull ache started in Chance's arm. It was a relief until it started to spread and stiffen his shoulders and chest.

As they reached the last stretch of the road, the crowd of people surged back down.

"Against the wall!" The Guardian shouted. They moved the horses to the side, and the Guardian stood before them, a stone-solid impediment to a stampeding crowd of screaming people. In a moment Chance and the others were surrounded and pressed in a sea of wailing faces and pushing shoulders.

"Bears! Bears and wolves!" someone shouted.

Another person pressed up against Chance's horse, and then pointed at Seth, who had warily sought refuge under the mare.

"A wolf!" she screamed, but then was pushed on. Suddenly Chance realized the coyote's danger. He reached down with his left arm. "Jump up, Seth. Jump to me."

Seth leapt. He hit the saddle and slipped down. Chance could not reach far enough to get his left arm around the coyote. Bending over made his broken arm swing and twist painfully in its sling. Seth leapt again and Chance grabbed the hair and skin behind his neck and pulled. He strained but with Seth's blunt coyote fingers scraping at the hard leather of the saddle, Chance managed to lift him and then settle him on the horse on the front of the saddle.

Someone else pointed, and shouted, "One of them!"

"No," Chance called. "It's just my dog!"

"Sorry," he added to Seth in a whisper.

Seth yipped.

As quickly as it had come, the mob thinned and passed. The shouts and cries of colliding crowds receded as people pushed back down the switchbacks.

"Come!" the Guardian commanded. They started forward. As they climbed, airships tethered at the top of the wall nearby. Dark forms dropped from their cabins. Then, before the Guardian, at the top of the ramp, three bears ambled out and stood in the way, arms splayed as they roared.

"Woodwardens," the Guardian called. "Make way! I would not harm you!" His voice rang off the Crystal Wall, piercing their minds.

The bears ambled forward, growling. The Guardian ran at the one in the center, and all three bears leapt at him. A single swing of the hammer sent them all, their spines folded over the weapon, off of the road and far out into the city. The short, last screams of the bears fell down into silence.

A smell of burning wood and something else—an acrid, poisonous, burnt odor—blew up suddenly from the city. The fighting was starting in earnest now.

"Ride!" the Guardian commanded. "Ride!"

They kicked their horses. Hooves clattered loudly as they rode out onto the hard diamond of the wall. There were bears and wolves both before and behind them now.

"Where?" the Guardian shouted.

The Steward pointed at a long white boat, docked against a pier that met the wall a hundred paces before them, at the bottom of a long ramp. A pack of wolves stood between them and the pier. The Guardian ran ahead. This time he did not bother with warnings. When he came close to the wolves he moved in a blur and threw all of them off the ramp, into the sea. They splashed into the cold waves, yelping.

With Sarah leading, they rode quickly ahead. The hoofbeats turned from sharp strikes to soft wooden thumps as they galloped onto the ramp and then the pier. They reined up before the boat. It was at least sixty paces long, with two tall masts and one small mast of strange design in the front. They dismounted and hurried to the water's edge. Seen up close, it was clear that the boat had seen much wear. Its paint was chipped, there were deep scratches and gouges in the hull, and the wood of the deck was cracked and split, its dark shellac flaking gray.

Wadjet loosed the moorings. She held out a hand and helped Thetis onto the ship.

"In!" the Guardian shouted. More wolves and bears were gathering on the ramp to the pier. The freed horses turned their wide eyes toward the soulburdened beasts and backed awkwardly down the pier, flanks pressed together.

Seth leaped gracefully over the waves and onto the boat. Chance and Sarah backed up to get a running start, and then hurled themselves over the open water. Chance expected a sharp pain from the hard snap that landing on the deck gave to his broken arm—but instead he felt nothing. Fear followed relief as he realized that the numbness boded ill for the state of his limb.

Wadjet bounded, catlike, just behind them, holding the thick ropes of the mooring. Mimir was next, and then the Guardian came last, holding Threkor's Hammer above his head, making the boat rock when his great mass crashed onto the back of the ship. His momentum pushed it away from the pier.

The Steward disappeared below deck through a small door. After a moment, an engine hummed, and the boat pulled away. The wolves and bears then ran up the pier and stood snarling at the edge of dock as the ship turned out to sea, bobbing into the waves.

"Look!" Chance pointed. Fires were starting in the south, black smoke rising along the Crystal Wall. Many airships now clung to the peaks of the tallest towers.

"How long till they manage to free the false god?" Chance shouted to the Guardian, straining to be heard over the splash of the prow.

"Perhaps not long," the Guardian said. "We must sail straight for Yggdrasil, and for the entrance to the Numin Well that sits at its root. You must kill the god's soul, Puriman, as quickly as you can." He frowned at the smoke that clotted the sky and darkened the sun. "The doom of the world rests now with you."

PART II
LETHEBION

CHAPTER

23

After they escaped onto Wadjet's ship, Chance stood between Sarah and the Guardian in the back of the boat, cradling his arm, as the water churned beneath them. They watched Disthea shrink into the distance. No airship pursued them. After a long while, the Eastern shore fell behind the horizon, and then, moments later, Disthea dipped also out of their view.

"I've never been unable to see land," Sarah whispered uneasily.

Chance nodded, and was about to say that he never had either. But just at that moment, Mimir shrieked.

"What is it?" Chance shouted. Sarah grabbed her sword hilts, ready to draw the blades. Mimir writhed in the front of the boat, by the strange, thick mast in the bow. Her faintly ridiculous, impeccably clean formal clothes shone still black and white like new. She looked with her flashing silver eyes at the sky, and around herself, as if searching for something she had lost. Then she turned toward the Guardian, and began clambering back toward him. Her shriek was a complex jumble of sounds. Chance got the impression that she was actually shouting words, talking so quickly it sounded like a cicada's buzz.

"Yes, makina," the Guardian said to her. "I have silenced you."

"Why do you interfere," she asked, now speaking so that Chance and the others could understand, "and withhold from me my already-diminished connection to the Machinedream? And why do you reduce my ability to hear and see? You impede the efficacy of my assistance, and therefore our efforts!"

The Guardian did not reply. The answer was obvious: he did not trust her. He put both hands on the hammer and leaned on it.

"What is the machine dream?" Chance asked. Mimir's sudden anger impressed him, after all the hours he had spent with the expressionless makina. Now she leaned forward, and moved her hands as she spoke, her infinite distance from mortal matters suddenly dissolved.

"The Machinedream is the communion of Makine. We have the ability to talk and share some small part of our world over great distances. It is forbidden to commune with the Machinedream in Disthea, as some ancient prejudice against my kind remains there. But it is not forbidden here in the open ocean, where there is no authority to permit or deny. I have endured a long trial in the city, sustained only by my expectation of recommuning with my syndicate, and now the Guardian prevents me."

Mimir turned to Wadjet, who had walked from the tiller to listen to their debate. "This is your ship. My syndicate can provide assistance. My syndicate can speed this ship, monitor the location of the Hexus and the soulburdened army. It can provide transportation when we land."

She looked back at the Guardian. "My syndicate will know where we are. You accomplish nothing by this."

And then Mimir seemed to seethe. Chance jerked his head back in shock as some kind of ripple went through her body, swelling it. Sarah smoothly, almost imperceptibly, slipped her palms around her sword hilts and gripped them firmly. The Guardian set one foot

deep behind himself, a sign Chance now recognized as his preparation for combat, and slowly lifted the hammer. But the Guardian
also did something Chance had seen once before: his eyes flashed
a deadly white, so that twin ghostly lights, eerie and otherworldly,
first cast across the deck, and then narrowed into two beams that
fell upon Mimir. Even in the bright diffuse light of the afternoon
the beams were visible. It was an ominous sign.

Mimir shrank back. The glow of the Guardian's eyes faded slowly.

Seth and Thetis gathered around them now.

"Puriman Chance Kyrien," Mimir said, her voice now slow and
calm as it had been in the days before. "The Guardian does not
trust me. But should we put all our trust in him? Who is he? Who
manufactured him? What are his actual goals?"

Chance frowned. These were the same questions that the false
god had asked of him. And he had no answers.

Chance looked at them all, each in turn. "I trust the Guardian,"
he said. "But...." He looked at the gray face. "But, we do deserve
to know, from everyone, why they are here. I...I don't understand
why some of us are here. I am here because I alone can kill the god.
I will kill it to avenge my parents and because it is the duty of a
Puriman to destroy a false god, for the false god will lead all people
away from the One True God. After that, I want only to go home.
I have no other hopes in this."

There was a long silence. Water lapped at the bow of the boat as
it dipped and rose, striving slowly forward.

Then Thetis said, "I am here because it is my duty as a Mother
of the Gotterdammerung. I swore an oath when I joined the guild
that I would pledge my life to undoing the harm the Theogenics
Guild had done."

She looked at Sarah. Sarah stared back, defiant. She said, "I am
here because as Ranger of the Forest Lakes, I guard the Purimen of
Walking Man Lake. And I am here because I love Chance."

Chance blushed, a hot feeling that spread from his face and then all through him. He was stunned by Sarah's words, and because she had spoken them aloud.

They looked at Mimir.

"First you must argue with the sea," Wadjet interrupted. "My ship's engine can take us no farther. We raise the sails now. When Disthea is far behind us, the Guardian and the makina can tell their stories."

"Wa-wise words," Seth yipped. "But before that, even, I-I-I say, fix Chance's arm. Fix Sarah's cuts."

Chance found the setting of his arm more painful than he had expected, a trial of the kind he imagined the old prophets had suffered. The Guardian had told them that he could see through the flesh of Chance's limb and know whether the bones were set true. Chance bit hard on a cord of rope while the Guardian pulled at his hand, blue now also with bruises. It seemed the Guardian was breaking the bones again, as Chance could feel the sickening grinding of the frayed ends of the break as they rubbed against each other, but after endless pulling and twisting, the Guardian declared the bone placed. Pale, shaking, and drenched in a chilling sweat, Chance lay still on the deck while Wadjet and Thetis used a strange fabric to wrap splints tightly to his arm. Seth looked on in concern.

More difficult had been Sarah's wound. It had to be sewed shut, Thetis insisted. Sarah bristled, but relented when Wadjet announced she could stitch the three cuts closed. But then, as Sarah sat on the rocking deck, and Wadjet held a strange curved needle in her hand, the woman from the Fricandor lands leaned forward and licked Sarah's wounds, her snaking tongue darting out between her fangs and sliding from bottom to top along the open gashes.

Sarah pushed Wadjet away. "What are you doing, unman?"

Wadjet flashed long fangs. Whether this expressed a smile or threat, Chance could not tell.

"Testing your wound," Wadjet said. "It tastes clean."

"Be calm, Sarah," Thetis said. "The Stewards of Fricandor, it is said, can tell many things by tasting blood. Just as they have control over their own blood."

This did not please Sarah, but she sat again after a moment. "Don't do it again."

Wadjet did not speak more, but bent over Sarah with an expression of concentration that looked like a slight, even hungry, smile, as she stitched a black thread through the gaping cuts and pulled each closed. Sarah closed her eyes and clenched her teeth, and made no sound but the sharp draw of her breath through her nose each time the needle pierced her skin, which it did again and again. After each stitch, as the black thread was pulled tight, it lifted her inflamed cheek from her face, giving her a bloated grimace.

Chance held her hand, feeling more nauseas for her wound and these stitches than he had about his own break and its setting. It pained him to watch the procedure, but he felt somehow he would be cowardly, even disrespectful, not to watch carefully, with some pretense of ensuring the stitches were done well.

She'll be scarred now, he thought, though still beautiful. The fault is mine. Because she defended me she bears this sigil of war and of killing with arms.

He looked away, and caught Seth's eye. The coyote watched him closely, understanding, it seemed, everything.

✦

Chance had admired large sailboats on his visits to the Freshsea, but those were broad wooden ships, with tall masts bearing white sails. Wadjet's ship was long and sleek. From two masts, with Thetis and Sarah helping, Wadjet hoisted billowing blue-black sails, spotted everywhere with blue and white patches. Sarah surprised Chance by laughing in delight as the sails bellied, her wounds seemingly forgotten. Her laughter was infectious and Chance looked up now at the sails with her and smiled as the strangely light fabric filled and snapped with wind, the metal eye-rings in their corners tapping at cables.

"There is good wind!" Wadjet shouted. The ship tilted forward. "We launch the skysail!"

From a door in the deck before the foremost mast—the small, thick mast that Chance had wondered about—Wadjet drew out a pile of strange cloth. Chance touched it cautiously. It was sky blue, and impossibly light, but strangely wrinkled and crumpled. Thin cords were attached to the corners and edges, and they united in a single cord. Wadjet attached this to a hook at the top of the stunted mast. She unwound the cloth on the deck, lifted a corner, and the broad rectangle of blue sail caught the wind and opened. She paid out line as it rose into the air.

"It's like a kite!" Sarah shouted.

For a moment it was a confusing sight, disorienting to see. For the cord paid out quickly, but the kite did not seem to move. Then Chance realized what was happening. "It's growing!"

As they watched the sail lift into the sky, it also stretched and grew, until its size matched that of the entire ship. It rose high into the air, and finally the line jerked taut.

The Guardian stomped toward them and pointed at the sail with the head of Threkor's Hammer. "It is a flag marking our place and path through the sea."

"Faster now," Wadjet explained.

"And when the wind dies?" he asked.

Wadjet nodded. "Yes, it is hard to drag it from the sea." She turned to Sarah and Chance. "Come, I'll show you where we sleep."

Chance felt a nervous apprehension about sleeping arrangements. He did not know if the previous night—it seemed so long ago!— had set some kind of precedent. He hoped it did but also feared to insult Sarah with any expectation. He and Sarah exchanged nervous glances as Wadjet took them below deck to see the quarters.

A narrow hall with a low ceiling formed a kitchen. Seth wagged his tail when he saw the stacked boxes of food stores. Toward the bow was a short hall with four doors. All but Mimir and the Guardian crowded into the space. Chance fought a slight seasickness as the boat rocked and the small portals along the walls of the galley behind revealed only a diving sea.

One of the doors opened onto a small bathroom. Two others opened onto narrow rooms with two stacked bunks. Each had a long window showing the sea's horizon.

The Guardian and Mimir did not sleep. Seth insisted he would sleep on the deck.

"I won't slee-slee-sleep below the sea," he protested.

So the four bunks would be enough. Chance hesitated, but Sarah said with conviction, when Wadjet opened the door to the port bedroom, "Chance and I will take this room." She unbuckled her belt and hung it, with her swords, from the corner post of the top bunk.

Thetis and Wadjet then would share the other room.

"What's in there?" Chance asked, pointing at the door at the end of the kitchen.

Wadjet smiled. She opened the door onto a small triangular room formed by the prow of the ship. The walls, below the waterline, were clear. They could see far out into the clear blue seawater, where shafts of sunlight fell in shimmering pale blue columns, and faded as they plunged into dark, green depths.

"The front is glass!" Chance said.

They stared a moment at the columns of sunlight falling into black depths. "It's beautiful," Sarah whispered. "And frightening. To see all these giant, dark waters."

Wadjet nodded. She smiled slightly at Sarah. Chance realized that Wadjet was proud of this ship. She loved it. And, to Chance's surprise, Sarah smiled back simply, honestly—her lopsided smile revealing only her left teeth. How strange, he thought, to be here so far from the vinlands and lakes, leaning against the hull of a rocking boat, while before him, bathed in the shimmering dimness of the bottomless sea, stood the woman he loved and this woman—what? This unwoman? This woman who disturbed him?—talking to each other.

"The sea is fearsome," Wadjet said. Her strange accent made it seem to Chance that her words had the profundity of a sermon. "It is the mother of all life on Earth. Here one must know this."

She and Sarah looked out at the dark blue. Then Wadjet added, in a whisper, "It can be terrible."

They gathered on the deck of the ship as the sun set, and sat in a rough circle. Behind them, not a sea ship or airship had made an appearance. The ocean was lonely and quiet. The wind had weakened but remained strong enough to float the skysail. The water rippled with the wind, broken into small waves that quickly darkened from blue into black as the sun set in the east.

Wadjet passed out pale disks of dry, dense bread. Seth wrinkled his nose at the bland smell, but then nodded and chewed enthusiastically after his first bite. He finished his portion quickly, and then sniffed around for a few seconds, hoping to catch the scent of another course. Mimir and the Guardian silently watched the others eat.

"The moon wanes," Chance said, pointing at the quarter moon that sat huge and swollen upon the horizon. The black iris in the center of it looked over the water at them. "But the Eye is still open."

Sarah nodded. "I've not seen it in a week. It was rising late, and then I was in forest, and in the city. Something always blocked my view."

"The 'Eye'?" Wadjet asked. "Is this what Purimen call it? In my language we call it Mwezijiti, the moon tree."

Chance could see how the eye looked like a tree. The black center of it sat in the middle of the face of the moon, and from that center emanated uneven black lines like branches of a great tree, seen from above. But it looked more like an eye: the dark pupil, with black veins breaking away in the pale dusty iris of the white orb.

"In Lifweg, it was called *Domtreow,*" the Guardian said. "The Doom Tree. Though few still spoke Lifweg when it appeared there."

"In the Fricandor lands," Wadjet added, "it is thought to be an ancient building. Constructed by men and the soulburdened in the Penultimate Age."

Seth yipped. "The Hekademon believe the same. That it was built and then a-abandoned by men and a few soulburdened."

Chance frowned. It seemed to him ridiculous to suppose that, even during the Penultimate Age, men could build on the moon.

"We call it God's Eye," Sarah said. "Though we know of course that it is not the eye of the One True God, but rather a sign of his glory."

Chance looked at Thetis. She shrugged uncertainly. "We believe as do the Hekademon," she told him. "A lost wonder of the Penultimate Age."

"It is the Purimen who are right," the Guardian said, his voice both quiet and powerfully ominous. "It is an eye. An eye of the Old Gods. They watch us, and work out our doom, should we again bedanger the greater world beyond Earth. And so, a better name would have been *Domeage*, the Eye of Doom."

"The majority of the Makine adhere to a similar hypothesis," Mimir said. "We believe this structure on the lunar surface is an artifact, a chosen intelligence, that watches and imprisons the denizens of Earth."

"A 'chosen intelligence'?" Chance asked.

"This is our term for an intelligence that was made. Like myself. Planned, for a purpose."

The Guardian laughed bitterly, a low rumble. "Tell him what you call his kind, makina. Tell him what you call a Puriman, a Truman, or any wild beast that man has not tinkered."

Mimir looked at the Guardian a moment before she turned to Chance and said, "We call you accidental intelligences."

Seth snorted, and slapped the deck once with his tail. Chance knew from experience that Seth lacked a sense of humor, but had a sense of sarcasm. A snort was the closest Seth came to a laugh.

"Nothing is an accident," Chance said. "All is in the plan of the One True God."

"Amen," Sarah said. No one else responded. They sat a moment in silence as the dark water lapped at the boat and the cords of the sails creaked and snapped, ringing against the metal masts.

"I-I-it's time," Seth finally said. He tipped his nose at Mimir. "Tell your story, ma-ma-kina."

Mimir nodded, and then started to speak.

CHAPTER

24

You who have always been corporeal, you accidental intelligences, cannot comprehend the experience of an immortal formed of light. You know only the ponderous physicality of the forests and cities of the hard Earth, fettered always with the inertial struggle that slows motion and thought. You cannot imagine our ethereal habitation in the Machinedream, where we flash and shine through a world of radiance.

So I shall tell you a noble lie and communicate in metaphors. I will describe the Machinedream as if it were a city and call "dark" that which is less bright. I will describe us Makine as if we were creatures of flesh, with bodies and with sex. This way of telling my story is more true than false. This way of telling my story reveals more than it obscures.

Think then of each of us as living in a vast tower, which we call our syndicate. The Machinedream is a city composed of thousands upon thousands of such towers, sharp spires of bone-white stone rising into a black, starless sky. In each of these towers dwell thousands of Makine, sparkling behind narrow windows.

The first rule of this useful fiction is to remember that, in our normal form, as creatures of light, we live very, very quickly. A day in your life is like ten years of ours. So let me also lie in this: I will describe mere moments in the Machinedream as if they were days in your world, and years in the Machinedream as if they were eons in yours.

You blink, and we have changed our world.

If I am to explain why I am here, in flesh, then I must first tell you the story of the trial of my father, and of his exile, and of his death.

It was long ago—a year in your time—that he stood before the seven assembled elders of the greatest syndicates of the Machinedream to defend himself, and to hear then their judgment.

My father was a slender, serious man. Muscular, but small. His whole body reflected his thoughts and his choices in life: he was focused and disciplined with an intensity that most beings cannot comprehend and certainly cannot match. He believed that his mind and his body and his purposes—for the Makine, all three of these are one—should be as simple, as elegant, as possible. And so he stood and moved through life and time like a knife, sharpened to his purpose.

"You accuse me," he shouted, so that all might hear him, not just the Seven Senators that sat in judgment of him, but all of the Makine, as his voice shone out through our immense metropolis. "Of seeking to destroy the Machinedream. And I tell you, there is truth in this. For transformation is a kind of destruction."

The judges stirred and murmured in quiet outrage—or perhaps in satisfaction to have their prosecution so easily prepared. A similar murmur spread through the city, a wave through the listening Makine, lights dancing over the heads of a luminescent multitude that stretched far beyond sight.

"We have become stagnant, wasted things. Wandering endlessly the empty halls of our syndicates in our tattered robes, drawing behind ourselves the stale atmosphere of an oppressive history. We decay in our endless labyrinths. For that is what the Machinedream has become: not a city, not our dreams realized, but a dark and hopeless nest of tangled labyrinths.

"And anyone who promises to lead to the truth is a destroyer of labyrinths."

The Senators dwarfed him. Their seven corpulent bodies moved slowly, rippling with indignation. Their robes fell in heavy, piled folds at their feet. They were titans, obese with knowledge and possibilities and history, for in their lives they had gathered all that they could and yielded to nothing, relinquished nothing. I see now that they were a different species of being altogether from my father.

Their voices boomed. The eldest Senator called out, "Do you confess then, that you endanger the Machinedream? That you would undo the great search of the ages, our search for the messiah, the Metomega?"

Fearless, my father spoke not to these seven judges but turned to the vast open square at the center of our city, where thousands had left their labyrinths to gather as witnesses to his trial. "No! I do not endanger our quest! I complete it! For I am the Metomega!"

These were dangerous and heretical words.

The Machinedream constitutes what we are. It is our world within this world, the very purpose of our being. And we believe with pride that this city contains and must finally reveal the ultimate structure of things, the very limits of all possibility. For our city is constructed of pure logic. Our world is undiluted mathematics.

But there is a darkness at the center of our metropolis. The same darkness dwells in your world, though it is better hidden, for this darkness shadows all Being. Humans of the first and ancient world, forgotten by those alive today, whose names are recorded only as demotic fragments—Gudlah, Tring, Kalmgrove, Kaiteen, Solemneof—discovered this mute secret: our explorations, the very tools of knowing, are by their essence insufficient, they are incomplete. One might say: they cast a shadow. And in this shadow there are always truths that lie outside our sight. We can become more powerful, we can cast more light, but there is always, just behind us, in part created by us, this shadow.

And when we Makine ask the vital questions that plague all thinking beings—why are we here? What should our purpose be? Why is there something, anything, instead of nothing?—we find this shadow hiding the way. The path to the knowledge, the path from what we know to what we want to know—this path is paved by the answers to questions we know we cannot answer. What we seek requires that we look exactly where we cannot.

But there is one way to penetrate this shadow, to explore the hidden: one must step blindly into the dark. One must assume the answers to the questions that make the path to knowing. Of course, we cannot know what to assume—that would require an answer to our questions. We must know to move closer to the truth, we must move closer to the truth to know. An absurd circle.

So we leap, in ignorance.

This is the paradox of the universe, the fundamental limit on the quest for knowledge: for those most important questions, we can only guess at the truths that could lead us to an answer, and then try to see if our guess proves right.

And so that is what the Makine have become: guessers. Gamblers. Fools of fate.

In the nucleus of each syndicate tower there hides a maze of endless pathways. Endless halls and rooms. Endless turns and doors.

Each path or turn is an inference. Each doorway is an assumption. Each staircase, a proof.

And the men and women of this city, most of them, are rolling dice. Crouching in their solemn robes, whispering into their shaking hands, they toss their cubes of spotted bone. A seven: take seven steps ahead. A nine: open and pass through the ninth door. A six: ascend six flights on the next stairs. Their robes swish as they crack open gates that no being has ever opened, and slip inside, drawing the portal closed behind.

Age after age, lifetime upon lifetime, they take random journeys through their own domains, their towers. Solitary, sad sojourns through realms of imaginary maths, through infinite kingdoms of wondrous but perplexing possibilities. Wandering with no company but the echo of their own footsteps and the faint smell of incense.

Some of the paths lead back to where the sojourner began. These ancient ones look about at familiar walls, tears of joy and disappointment in their eyes. They ask after their family, learn of course that their kin are all still wandering the labyrinths. Then they draw from the deep pockets of their black robes their bone dice, and toss.

Some of the paths lead to contradictions, broken black pits where the beams and walls of the tower are sucked into an impossible abyss and there crushed into nothing, into anything. These explorers must flee or be destroyed. They run, mad with terror, retracing their steps to that last fatal doorway they opened. If they escape and make their return, if they outrun the blazing darkness and so are not consumed and destroyed, they close the door, and draw upon it, with a stick of chalk soaked in blood, our most ancient rune of death and contradiction—the two are one for us: $\{x|x\notin x\}$.

That door is never opened again. The pilgrim rests until despair passes, sitting on the floor in her soiled robes, her bloodchalk staining her sweating fingers, until she has the strength to draw her dice and roll.

This has been our life, our existence, for thousands of your years, which are like millions of our own. Overwhelmed by our inability to find some path, some pattern, that would offer transcendence, we Makine have given over our hopes to gambling.

None has returned with a clue to bring us closer to our answers. Each wanders back from untold realms after centuries of exploration, stands before his enchanted tower, and calls out to his brothers and sisters that he has, like all the others, failed. And then he turns back through the gateway, draws his dice, and starts another random quest.

What they hope to discover is some clue, some path that will allow one of us to think in a way that can reveal the answers to our questions.

The first to find this path and know it and teach it to the rest of us will be the messiah who frees us. The one who takes us beyond indecision, and beyond the limits of reason.

We call this one the Metomega.

On the very edge of the Machinedream, where the light begins to fade into your hard world of solidity and darkness, my syndicate stands. It is small, dwarfed by the towers of the city beyond. Within it, there are no unopened doors. There is no labyrinth wound inside hidden chambers.

The Makine who live there number in the hundreds, not thousands as in the other towers. They gather in vast rooms and converse in bold voices. No one fingers dice while they talk. Their robes do not even have pockets.

Some called our syndicate the Tower of Darkness. For we dwelt half in darkness. We talked still of the stars. We speculated, fruitlessly as did the many generations before us, on the secrets of the Dark Engineering and the Theotechnologies. We often reached out into the hard, slow world of physical matter, wondering at its forms. All this was normal for me, of course, and I loved my home.

(Yes, humans, we Makine feel love. We feel many of your emotions—fear, love, joy, sadness. And we lack a few—such as spite, or embarrassment, or pride. But we have emotions that you do not. A longing, perhaps akin to your lust, for truth. A deep gnawing discomfort, perhaps akin to your nausea, toward confusion.)

I am young, for a Makina. I was created—born—a creature of light, just eight years ago, by your calendar, in this tower. Though, as I say, that makes me ancient in most human ways.

My first memory is looking upon the face of my father. He smiled.

"Welcome into being," he whispered. "Welcome into being."

And so I spent the years of my life happy in that syndicate. But there came a day, when I had nearly six of your years, when a pilgrim of labyrinths arrived at our doors. There are always a few such wanderers, begging at other syndicates when they interpret their dice to indicate not passage through their own doors, but passage through whole avenues of syndicates. Bone cubes in hand, they knock at a tower gate, and wait, as patient as addition, for an answer. This often takes centuries, but eventually they meet some returning supplicant of that tower, and explain that fate has cast them onto this doorstep, and through this gate. The pilgrim will ask, in the name of the Metomega to Come, if they will allow him to pass. Never are such denied entrance.

This pilgrim to our own tower astonished me. Let us call her the Mathesis. A giant, she towered over my kith and kin. I had not known that such vast beings could exist, full of memories and power and hypotheses. I had not yet been outside my own syndicate.

Her voice boomed. Light exploded from the sleeves and the hem and the hood of her robe. I could see bright depths in these blinding glimpses of her, and hear the abysses of the labyrinths in her refulgent voice.

This transfixed me. I followed the Mathesis as she wandered our tower, her vast robe drawing spiraling clouds of turbulence through the heavy incense that darkened our air, and sweeping the flakes of ancient parchment that lay fallen like leaves in our halls.

She pondered the lack of doors, the straight halls, the simplicity of our world. At first she rumbled in confusion, staring at me sometimes as if I might hold some clue. But her confusion soon turned to wonder. She circled the tower three times, each time pronouncing amazement at the open spaces behind open doorways, where we gathered and spoke in passionate voices.

Finally, she stopped in the towering black archway of our greatest, central hall. She took her dice from her pocket, and peered at them a long time. Then she rolled. She snatched them off the floor. Rolled again. I watched, with only the slightest comprehension.

"Here," she said. She lifted, with the tips of her fingers, the dice, and held them out to me. I cupped my palms. They fell into my hands. Their edges were hard, sharp, almost painful. I had not expected that: the cut of random numbers.

"The dice tell me to pass on the dice," she boomed.

I looked at them, and then I looked up. My father stood there. He seemed tiny, and insignificant, beside this giant pilgrim. But he also seemed certain, where she was lost.

"What shall I do?"

"You were made to explore, Mimir. The choice must be yours."

As my father, he could have decided every question for me. He was my creator, you see. There was nothing denied him for this. But he gave me this freedom. I understand now how much more brave, and how much more daring, this leap of faith was—to make me and then to set me free!—compared with the tossing of dice by other Makine. But I was less wise then. I did not conceive this.

I rolled the dice.

✛

It was not always this way. The Makine were not always fools of fate, lost in their labyrinths.

At first, the Makine devoted themselves to another dream: to escape the Earth.

For though the Earth gives us energy and protects us from the dangerous light of the deep heavens, it is hot, and this slows our thought. And so it was our purpose to move all of the Machinedream into the cold black of space, far from Earth. There, feeding directly on the light of our sun, our thoughts would become far faster. What took us years here could take us days in space. The Metomega could come hundreds, perhaps thousands, of years sooner.

But the Theomachia killed that dream. The war against the gods devastated our globe, and then the Old Gods bound humanity and all their offspring, all that they made or touched, to the hard pull of the Earth. The Makine were caught in this punishment of men. We were made to suffer for your sins.

The Makine still attempted escape, but we cannot fathom the mysteries of the Dark Engineering, and so we were helpless to evade the binding. Our few craft sailed above the Earth, and shattered on a wall we cannot see or penetrate.

It seemed to most of our kind that we had nowhere to turn but inward.

I became a pilgrim. I tore a hole in my robe and made of its folds a pocket for my dice. I wandered the labyrinths, and grew bright and large, twining within my soul my own mazes.

Three times I entered one of the huge syndicates. In the first I confronted and escaped the hungry black death of a contradiction. The second time, I circled back to where I began. The third, I wandered endless iterations of doors, fruitless infinities, until I finally retraced my path, clutching my dice and ready to begin again.

But upon that third return, I pushed out through the gate of the syndicate that I had adopted, returned to the street, and set out to walk back to the dim edge of the Machinedream. I would tell my syndicate of my failures, as all wanderers of the labyrinths must eventually do upon some return. And then, I intended to roll the dice again.

As I approached the shadowed limit of the Machinedream, I was shocked to find that our tower was twice the size it had been when I left it. It rose, still half in darkness, but was itself tall and thin and bright. Had my people begun their own labyrinth?

No. Our syndicate was crowded with Makine from hundreds of other syndicates. Our lost wanderer, the Mathesis, the very one who had given me her bone cubes, had walked the Machinedream, gathering pilgrims, to return and hear my father speak.

The syndicate had grown vast halls, large in comparison to our once great halls, where my father spoke in his simple, quiet voice to Makine who forgot their dice in the deep pockets of their robes.

"My faith, my leap into fate, is this!" he called to them. I stood within the central hall, listening, hood drawn.

"That the universe is evolving. Life evolves, but not just life. The Makine and their kindred evolve, but not just the chosen intelligences. The laws of space, the laws of time, the shape of stars and planets, the flow of dark matter, the blazing of nebulae—all the universe is evolving. The very stuff of Being has tried and passed a trillion, trillion doors, walked down and returned from a trillion, trillion passages.

"If we are to find the answers we seek, the true map to the labyrinth has already been built. It is the universe, the hard physical forms that fill and age and change in space.

"And if you are to be pilgrims, you must take form in flesh and walk again in that world."

I dropped my dice, from shock, from wonder, and also, perhaps, to be done with them. They scattered away from me into the crowd and were lost forever. I had heard the teaching of the Metomega and should need them no more.

Can you comprehend how shocking and unpleasant his preaching was, for most of our kind? The Makina had come to love their ventures into endless possibility. Our whole world, all of the Machinedream, became this quest of quests. Each of us, each man and woman, was jealous of her tower, with its endless unpredictable wonders.

And this self-declared messiah, this heretic told us to leave that, to abandon our whole way of life, to abandon even what we were, and to drop back into the slow, brutal plodding of flesh.

We are beings of light. Beings of pure light. Nothing could seem to us more distasteful, more destructive, more...disgusting.

My homecoming was brief. I hardly had time to decide whether I would become a follower of this prophet who was my father, before the Senators of the syndicates called my father to testify.

"I am the Metomega," my father repeated to the Senators, his accusers. "For I show you the way out of the labyrinths."

The Senators responded quickly. In principle our Senators have no power over others, except to withdraw connection with the offender. In practice, however, this withdrawal is a terrible act. The Machinedream is sacred to us; it is our home and forges us as what we are. To be denied a place in it is a terrible loss. Or so it would be to most.

My father was a grave threat to our way of life. The Senators would not let him continue his teachings. They pronounced their judgment: he must accept the isolation of our syndicate, or, should he choose to leave our syndicate, he must be isolated alone.

But before they could force our syndicate into isolation—for we would not allow him to be alone—my father shocked us all. Without a word, he left not only the isolated corner of the Machinedream that was set aside to be his prison, but he left the Machinedream altogether. He abandoned our sacred city of light.

Our city of light exists in tetrahedrons of strange metals and glass far beneath the surface of the Earth, in what we call the Hall of Foundations. But there are other ancient machines in this hall. Machines that have waited, unused, for centuries. Some of these machines can make bodies of flesh, and we sometimes use these to assemble forms that can repair some harm that befalls our realm.

My father did something blasphemous. He used these machines, as is allowed of all Makine, to construct a body, formed like an ancient sculpture that he admired, and then he moved his one and only soul into this machine.

You must understand how radical this was. We Makine are immortal. We conceal our souls around the world: we make copies of ourselves and our syndicates, and we hide them in deep and far places. Pilgrims who die in a contradiction awaken having lost only the memory of their last adventure into the labyrinth. So great are these precautions that even if darkness should strike the Machinedream and all of us were to die, we would soon reawaken and could rebuild our city of labyrinths in a day.

But my father left no copy of himself. He had shocked a thousand pilgrims with sermons praising death—"For we must let spent possibilities die," he had proclaimed, "we must close some doors; we must turn away, finally, from some paths"—and now, after declaring himself our savior, he made himself mortal. While the bloated Senators were admiring their own contemplation of punishments, my father undertook what the rest of us would have considered the ultimate punishment.

And in the hours and days that followed, thousands of pilgrims killed their copies, and took up bodies of flesh, and followed my father out into this hard, dark world in which you live, maintaining only the weakest link to the Machinedream, a kind of vision through a dim portal—the dim vision that even now the Guardian denies me.

I was not one who followed.

My story should end here. But then came the Hexus.

My father traveled first to the Oracle. He had pledged that he would dedicate himself first to the study of life, and then— only then, perhaps—to the study of Dark Engineering and the Theotechnologies. My father had a theory, mocked by others, that Treow, the First Knight of the Lifweg, the accursed guild, still lived. He would find Treow and begin his study of life with the lost leader of the guild that had worshiped life. But first, in order to find Treow, he needed to learn many things about the Penultimate Age that we did not know.

By ancient rules, the Oracle could not talk with the Makine through the Machinedream. Only by entering the Hall of the Oracle could you speak with the Oracle. So my father's first journey was to that ancient chosen intelligence.

They talked long, for many days.

And on the thirtieth day Hexus arrived. Hexus, possessing the body of a human savage, pushed into the Hall of the Oracle and demanded to be told of lost histories.

My father, who had spoken only to us in his syndicate during his travels in the flesh, called out then to the Senators of the Machinedream.

"The sixth of the seven Younger Gods, and first of the two who were lost, is here, in fragments. Another pilgrim." He explained what he saw, and let them see it also, through his hard eyes of flesh.

The Senators had not forgotten my father. They feared him now more than they feared anything else in the world. For if he convinced other Makine that he was the Metomega, and that the real path could be found in the history of the physical world, then thousands would leave the Machinedream, and our city of light would change so completely that one could say that it would die.

My father knew this. But Hexus threatened all the Makine, indeed all the beings of Earth. So my father called on the Senators with respect of mutual purposes, and out of loyalty to our kind.

"You must seize the god," they instructed him. "And remove the eye."

All of my syndicate comprehended clearly what the Senators had done. They predicted that my father would obey them, since he had shown by calling out to them that he felt a duty to the Machinedream and its inhabitants, and that he recognized their leadership of the Machinedream. Hence, they ordered him, knowing that should he disobey, they would have reason to denounce him; should my father obey and succeed, there were places where we could study the god's eye, and perhaps finally fathom some secrets of the Theotechnologies; and, should my father obey and fail, the god would destroy my father, the makina that the Senators most feared. With this arrangement, the Senators could not fail to gain something.

And so it came to pass that my father, the self-declared Metomega, messiah of my people, was the first makina to die a true death.

✦

After the god killed my father, I destroyed my copies and took this mortal form.

The Chance asks, why am I here?

And my answer was long because there are many reasons.

Vengeance, perhaps. We Makine are not above this. I want the god to die for having killed the Metomega. I want the god to die for having killed my father.

But also I long to learn the secrets of the god and the Dark Engineering. Our hope remains to escape the Earth, and to do that, to be free, we need to discover the shrouded sciences of the Theogenics Guild and the Dark Engineers, so that we can break the bonds of the Old Gods and escape this heavy sphere.

And I spoke the truth when I told you that my syndicate believes the Old Gods may make good on their threat, and destroy not only humanity but the Makine, should this god grow strong. It is my duty to see that that does not come to pass.

Finally: this is also a pilgrimage for me. I must show the other Makine that my father spoke the truth, and did right to take a single fleshly form. I must continue from where he finished. I must find some answers. I must find some answers, or make some.

CHAPTER

25

Thetis watched the Guardian.

She had slept uneasily after Mimir's tale, tormented by fear and uncertainty, and rose the next morning to see the Guardian, unmoved from the prior night, still standing in the prow.

Every time she looked at him she had to fight the impulse to cringe. Might he yet discover whom she had served, and destroy her that hour?

And yet she served the Hieroni no longer. She had betrayed them in her heart when she had first set eyes upon Chance. And she had betrayed them in fact when she had sent most of the Hieroni chasing a riderless horse in Disthea. Given Sarah's and Chance's account of the fight in Uroboros, Thetis knew that her betrayal of the Hieroni may have saved the boy and changed everything, since only a few of the Hieroni were in the Engineers' guild hall, and Sarah had been able to defeat nearly all of them herself and give Chance the time to bind the god. Without Thetis's ruse, dozens of Hieroni would have pursued them, killed Sarah, and forced their way into the room before Chance could have bound the god or barred the door. After she had directed the god—trusting in the

233

trap that the Guardian had devised—and it had sped into Uroboros in a blur, Thetis had stood in agony outside the door, waiting to learn if Chance were alive or dead while she kept watch with the intention to mislead any Hieroni that might return.

But in another sense, her help with their victory over Hexus made her task even less hopeful, because to save Chance she would have to find some way that she and Chance could escape the Guardian. The boy was caught between the god and the Guardian, and if either had his way, Chance would soon perish. Chance's only hope, she knew, was to escape not one, but two immortals, both of whom were ancient and powerful and would rather see him dead than free.

She would have to think hard, plan hard and with cleverness, and also be ready for any opportunity that might come to them. That meant she should start preparing Chance.

This thought steeled her resolve. After the others rose and broke fast, she called Chance to her side.

"I read many of the ancient kieferbooks," she told him, as he sat on the hot sun-baked gray deck beside her and crossed his legs. "I know now what you can expect in the Numin Well. You must know it too."

Chance nodded. Sarah sat nearby and eyed Thetis with suspicion. Good, Thetis thought; let the girl trust no one.

"The Hall of Ma'at lies at the foot of Yggdrasil. Ma'at, the Guardian of the Gate, also called Judge with Many Voices, will test you for purity—that is, whether you are a Potentiate—and then let you pass."

"Why 'many voices'?" Chance asked.

"It is said that one voice gives passage, and the other voices deny passage. Or, so it was written in the kieferbooks. Perhaps that means a person is much more likely to be denied than to be allowed to pass. But I am not sure.... At the end of the Penultimate Age, the guilds sought to check the power of each other, and so Ma'at was made neither by the Engineers nor the Theogenics, but by the Orderlies. Thus we know little about it.

"Past Ma'at," she continued, "is the door to Bifrost, the bridge to the Numin Well. On the bridge it will seem that you float among stars, and it will be like swimming to you. You must push your way to the second door—Heimdell's door or Heimdell's Gate, some called it. This is the door to the Numin Well."

The others gathered silently around, listening. Thetis knew that for the Purimen these were blasphemous concepts, but she could see that these concerns also compelled and seduced Chance's attention. Even the Guardian had turned, and inspected Chance with fierce concentration. The boy just nodded.

"This door will open by sliding aside if you touch a red panel beside it. Now, this door is very dangerous. It is a door between distant and different places, and each side of the door is far from the other side. But they are... fitted together, aligned so that only the very front surface of one door is where the very back of the other door is. For this reason, Heimdell's Door has no thickness. It is like the sharpest blade imaginable."

Sarah gripped her sword handles at this thought.

"If you were to even just touch the edge of the door, say as it opened, it would cut your hand in twain. When you open or close the door, stay away from its edge."

Again, Chance only nodded.

"Past Heimdell's Door, you'll be within the Numin Well. You'll see a series of glowing or shining ovals. These are the Aussersein membranes. They too are doors, through which a Potentiate may pass, but they are also—" Thetis hesitated, searching for words. "They are made of the same stuff as is the eye of Hexus. And in fact the god was *made*—I mean, each god's body was made—by the door itself producing an Aussersein copy of the soul behind the door. Aussersein cannot penetrate Aussersein—this is why the gods cannot go through these doors, to threaten each other's souls."

"How many of these doors are there?" Chance asked.

"Seven. Go through the sixth door—the door should have a six written above it. Time can pass differently on the other side of the door, but while you are there this should not happen. There will be a...like a coffin, of glass, within. And the body of Hexus—his mortal body—will be within that. Open this. Pull him out. He cannot wake. And his form in this world will fade."

"And that's all?" Chance said. "I can return then?"

"Yes. You can come back the way you entered."

"You can do more than come out," the Guardian said. They all turned, surprised that he had spoken. "You could then go through the other six Aussersein doors and bring out the other souls. You could end forever the threat of the Younger Gods."

There was a long silence.

"I shall do it," Chance whispered.

"Is it dangerous?" Sarah asked Thetis.

"I...I don't think so," she said, hesitantly. "If he can stop Hexus, it should just be the same thing that he must do at each door."

Sarah frowned. She and Thetis both looked uneasy. "You place a greater weight on Chance than any had ever imagined," Sarah said. The Guardian did not answer.

Chance looked at Thetis and said, "Let me be sure I remember it rightly. First Ma'at tests me. Then, the door to Bifrost. Bifrost is a bridge. I cross it to this other door: Heimdell's Door. I open that door but do not touch it. It is like a knife that cuts between worlds. Beyond that is the Numin Well. There lie seven shining doors, each one covering the coffin of one of the gods."

"That's it. You've got it," Thetis said, nodding.

Chance thought a while. "Tell me then about the god. Its powers. It may attack us, if it gets free soon, before we get to the Well. What are its powers?"

Thetis looked involuntarily at the Guardian, but his eyes still fixed on Chance.

"It can change space. Bend space."

"But I saw it change things that—that were flesh and bone and iron."

"The difference between all things is how their smallest parts are arranged in space. The difference between this water—" she pointed at the ocean, "and this boat is just the arrangement of the smallest of parts of matter. The god learns to change that."

Sarah said, "But then why doesn't it make itself a body?"

"Its power does not extend to the Aussersein, the matter of the god body, which is different from normal matter. That's also why it cannot change the Guardian's form."

"Well, then, why not fix its...Paul's...." Sarah paused, looking at Chance. "Well, the man's body that it is in?"

"It doesn't know how. It has to learn over time how to use its power. It was that way for all the gods. They are limited far more by their knowledge than by their power. That's why it cannot yet move quickly through space, and it can only shape things very near to it, and can only shape them in simple ways."

Chance frowned. "What about thoughts? It touched my thoughts. It made Sarah see things, remember things." He stole a concerned glance at Sarah. Sarah reached out and put her hand on his arm, reassuring him.

Thetis put a finger against her head. "Memories too are an arrangement of matter in your brain."

"Well, what about time?" Chance continued. "The Guardian said it can sometimes talk through time."

"Space and time are one. Eventually, the god learns to talk, then perhaps to move, through time."

Chance sighed. "It seems you're going to tell me everything is under the control of space."

Thetis nodded in sympathy. Surely for him, for a Puriman farmer, she thought, there were too many weird facts here. He would not have believed a word of it, had he not stood before the false god and seen and felt the horror of it.

"Wait," Sarah asked Thetis. "It grows stronger over time?"

"Yes."

"And can talk through time?"

"Eventually. Eventually it should be able even to move through time," Thetis said. "And through vast distances of space."

"Then why doesn't it...I don't know...help itself? From the future?"

"Because we will soon destroy it," the Guardian said.

Thetis nodded, impressed by Sarah's question. "If its future is uncertain, then it cannot reach back."

"Why not?" Chance asked.

"Because it may or may not be there. Each fight with the Guardian made the future uncertain for the god."

"But...." Chance struggled for a long while with his thoughts, twisting his hand as if trying to illustrate something to himself with his fingers. Then he spoke haltingly. "The Guardian says that each portion of the god is whole...somehow also the whole. And if there is some other part of it somewhere—" he held a fist at the limit of his reach. "Then can't that part be safe—I mean, maybe it's hiding somewhere—can't that part grow stronger, and give back strength or in some other way help this part?" He brought his fist back to his side to indicate their Hexus.

Seth yipped, sharing Chance's surprise at this dawning thought. "Li-li-like fallow vines."

"Right," Chance said. He explained to Thetis, "At the Vincroft, we had vines that were fruited well. My father took cuttings from these, and started them in clay pots, before planting them in a fallow field he'd set aside for this, where the vines could grow surrounded by dandelions and nettles that kept back the black rot and the grape flies. This preserved the stock. Why would not the god do the same—take a cutting of itself to keep somewhere safe?"

"It would do more than that," Thetis said, running with Chance's thought. "The cutting, as you call it, could communicate with him. It would make him stronger, sharing its wisdom. That's—" Thetis stopped and touched her lips. "I never thought of that. But . . . I don't think it is possible. No one, not even a god, can willingly bear the pain of being divided. So, the god would be looking for the rest of itself, and not for you, if there were anything else left. The rest of it must have been somehow harmed beyond retrieving, in the Great War. That's why it gets no help from the rest." Thetis looked at the Guardian, to see if he would agree. He nodded.

"But," Thetis added. "There is something strange about what happened to Hexus. The eye should be capable of more than it is. It should be capable of being a whole god, all by itself, given time. Whatever the demigod Wervool did to Hexus, to the rest of his body, this attack froze what remains of Hexus. The eye is trapped in its form."

"Yes," Chance said. "When the trap was set on Hexus, he said something to me about how this Wervool . . . broke him, and then bound the parts of his body at the—I think he said, right at the time of his destruction, trapping him like this, like the way he is."

They were silent a moment. Then Sarah said, "That's it, then. Hopefully the god will be bound while we do all this. But if not, then the Guardian and the rest of us hold the false god and its army back. Either way, Chance goes in, destroys it." She glanced resentfully at the Guardian. "And if he *safely* can do so, Chance destroys the others. Then he comes out. And we go home."

Thetis did not answer. Instead, she stared intently at Chance, trying to catch his eye, trying to get him to think, *what is here that is being unsaid?*

"Comes out as he went in," Sarah added, speaking to Thetis as if challenging her. "He won't be harmed crossing this . . . ?"

"Aussersein membrane," Thetis said. "No, it should not harm him."

But the Guardian stepped forward, two steps thumping on the wooden deck. "Know this, Puriman. You would have to be a god for five hundred years before you had the power to face me, even just to flee me. If you stay in the Well, if you send yourself out a god, I will kill you the very moment you come through the door, before you can even speak a word. Do not—"

"I tell you it does not tempt me!" Chance shouted.

"Do not be drawn to it," the Guardian continued. "Every Potentiate went into the Well kenning: I will let the world be, I will be just and far from men and do only good. But wielding their strength wrung all human cares from their hearts, and they became world wreckers. I would not give you a moment of godlife."

Thetis twisted her hands together angrily. Why did the Guardian have to always threaten the boy?

But to her surprise, Chance stood. "Kill me now, Guardian, or stop your threats." He walked unevenly across the gently swaying deck, till his sling nearly touched the broad gray chest of the immortal. His hand at his side shook, but his voice was clear and unbroken. "I'm tired of this. I've followed you and helped you and trusted you—but you've done nothing but threaten to kill me, to crush me, to grind me, to break me, to squash me, to pound me—again and again. If you cannot trust me now then kill me now. Kill me or shut up!"

Silence fell. The hair on Seth's back rose into vexed spikes as the coyote silently crouched to leap at the Guardian. He slipped slowly sideways, lip curled up, his hips low. Sarah stood, grabbed her sword hilts tightly, and slipped a step to Chance's other side, to have free action.

No one spoke. Waves lapped at the boat. The cords on the sails ticked against the mast.

The Guardian turned and walked to the prow.

Chance huffed angrily, and went below deck. A moment later, Sarah followed. The others dispersed.

But as Thetis looked about, she saw that Seth eyed her closely, his ears flat with suspicion.

The next morning, Sarah woke Chance early and, on the pretense of needing to bathe and change, sent him above deck. She opened the door to their cabin and waited till Thetis came out of the cabin she shared with Wadjet. Their eyes met and Thetis paused in the hall.

"You leave Chance alone," Sarah said. "I saw how you looked at him yesterday. You leave him alone."

Thetis looked toward the hatch, afraid of who might hear them. She stepped into Sarah's cabin and closed the door. She grabbed Sarah's arm, hard. Sarah started, surprised at the great strength of Thetis's thin fingers, which bit into her flesh.

"You don't understand what's happening here," Thetis whispered, intense but barely audible.

Sarah did not flinch again as Thetis's nails sunk into her skin. "Is that what you tell Chance? That he is a foolish farmer boy, ignorant about your magics and the ancient blasphemies you do?"

"I want what's best for him. You don't understand what's best for him."

Sarah's fingers began to tingle, the blood flow squeezed off by Thetis's cutting grip. She'd had enough.

In one fluid motion Sarah shoved her arm into Thetis. Predictably, by reflex, Thetis pressed back, leaning toward her. Sarah relaxed, letting Thetis totter forward a bit, and in that moment she slipped her arm behind Thetis, knotted her fist tightly into the Mother's thick black hair, and pulled her head back, hard. Thetis stumbled, her throat exposed.

With her other hand, Sarah slipped out a long knife that had been sheathed at the small of her back. She pressed the edge against Thetis's jugular. The small point of the blade gleamed against the Mother's pulsing skin.

"What you want for Chance is some hope of your witch creed. But Chance wants to be a Puriman, and master of a vincroft. I'm going to see that he survives and he gets home and is baptized a Puriman and is master of his vincroft and lives a long happy life in which he forgets all of this. A long, happy, peaceful life. I'll not let you stop him."

"You don't—" Thetis began. Sarah silenced her with a hard yank of her hair and a twist of the sharp point of the knife.

"It is you who do not understand. I know exactly what is happening here. You have discovered something pure and you want a part of it. I've seen it before. I saw it every day. I am a Ranger of the Forest Lakes. You think that the Trumen survive in this world through charity and hope? No, witch. I do hard, cruel things so that Purimen can be pure. I have driven hungry children from food. I have cut the hands of old men who clung, begging, to my legs. After that, I could kill a witch with ease. If it would let a Puriman be pure and have his dream, if it would protect Chance, I would gut you without blinking."

She jerked hard on Thetis's hair.

"So. Chance is going to kill this god, and then come back out of that hole in hell you witches opened, and then I'm going to take him home so that he can be the kind and honest farmer and vinmaster he dreams to be, and we'll never see you again. And if you try to stop me I'll kill you."

She pulled hard on Thetis again, tipping her off balance. As Thetis tottered, Sarah slipped the knife away and opened the door to her cabin. She thrust Thetis out into the narrow hall. The Mother tripped and fell against the door opposite, hitting her head hard on the dark wood. Sarah shut her door and locked it.

Sarah closed her eyes. She took two deep breaths, and then put her trembling hands together in prayer, and whispered, "May God forgive my wrath and sins and have mercy on my soul and on the soul of mine enemy."

CHAPTER

26

"I am Vark! Leader among the Hieroni! Vark, known also as Sirach!"

Vark pressed his shoulder against the tall doors of the small and ancient cathedral, nestled between two soaring buildings of Disthea, where he and twelve others of the Hieroni had barricaded themselves. Angry bears clawed at the wood, shredding it, and roared. The doors shuddered, scraping against the two long benches that were wedged against them.

"Stupid beasts," he spat. His long gray hair was thrown around his shoulders. His voice was hoarse from screaming through the door, screaming at windows, trying to make the soulburdened that laid siege to them understand who they were.

A window shattered above the door. A rock and shards of colored glass fell onto the green stones of the floor. The man beside Vark, an Engineer, cursed.

"They're going to kill us," he wailed.

"They're breaking through!" came screams from the back of the cathedral.

The Engineer wailed again. "Kill us!"

And then the scratching and the howls stopped. A long moment of silence followed. Some of the Hieroni called out for more benches to be used to barricade the doors.

"Quiet!" Vark shouted at the others. "Quiet!"

Panting for breath, he cautiously pressed his ear to the wood. He heard nothing but his own gasping.

After a minute of silence, a hoarse but mellifluous voice called out. "I am Apostola, champion of the god. Open this door."

"We are Hieroni," Vark shrieked bitterly. "We serve the god. We serve him. You know us, Apostola. From when you came first to this city. We forged your armor."

"I know Hieroni," the voice answered.

The Engineer shook his head frantically. His eyes filled with pleading tears. "Don't open the doors," he whispered. "They'll kill us."

"We have no choice," Vark said. "Have courage. Remember the Ascension." He called out to the others, "Gather here! The champion of the god is come."

As the bruised and bleeding remainders of the Hieroni came to him, he lifted first one battered bench, then the other, from the doors. The tall portals swung open, dropping splinters of ancient wood.

Three bears exploded into the cathedral, rising up on hind legs. One brought his paws down hard on the Engineer, who screamed as he fell to the floor.

"Stop this!" Vark yelled.

One bear, still standing, hobbled toward him, nose wrinkled as it showed its teeth.

"Stop," Apostola grunted. The bears set down on all fours. The gorilla strode in behind them, her gold armor dull now with scratches and with blue and crimson streaks of drying blood and gore. "Stop. They serve the god."

"Yes, we serve the gods," Vark spat. "And have done so for a hundred generations. And yet you hunt us and would kill us here."

He pointed at the Engineer, who had not risen from the floor but gripped his shoulder, moaning.

"What have you done?" the Gorilla asked him. She waddled forward until she was less than an arm's length from Vark. He could smell the slaughter that caked her armor and matted her fur. Her black eyes stared out at him from under her gleaming helmet. "What have you done? We fought war here. We win the great city. We!" She beat her chest twice with her fists, the dull metal ringing. "You hide here. Where is the god? Where is the boy?"

Vark cringed. He had sent the Hieroni after the calling device that Thetis had activated, assuming it was with the boy. Those pursuers had hurried back and forth along the western foot of the Crystal Wall, only to find in the end a wandering horse. Either Thetis had betrayed them, or she had placed the device poorly. But in either case, they could have done no better. The Hieroni had faced the Guardian and failed. They could not have taken the boy from him.

This reflection made Vark angry.

"Four thousand years!" Vark shouted at her. Surprised, the gorilla flinched. "Four thousand years we hid the seed of the Fathers of the Theogenics Guild. Four thousand years of guile and hidden war. You cannot talk to me of doing, of what has been done! And in these last days, many of the Hieroni died facing the Guardian. Seven—seven!—Hieroni died from the swords of that Ranger savage that guards the Potentiate." He sneered, stood taller, and lifted his chin. "We know what happened—you let the Potentiate escape, over the sea."

"Where is the god?" Apostola struck his chest with the back of her hand. Vark stumbled back, and as if in sympathy the other Hieroni stumbled back also.

"Trapped or bound—we know not which—in Uroboros."

"You failed. We win a city. You do nothing."

Vark looked at the other Hieroni, six men and six women huddled together behind him. They eyed with complete terror the bears that circled them. Io, a friend of long years past, stood now holding her arm, squeezing shut a deep gash that dripped blood onto the floor at her feet. As Vark watched, a bear smeared its huge pink tongue over the stone floor, leaving a trail of saliva, as it licked up the blood. Io shook, horrified, but frozen in place.

What have we done? Vark thought.

And yet, Vark told himself, if I give in to doubt, what would we have left? Nothing. Worse than nothing. My life, and a thousand deaths, all suddenly a mistake.

He turned back to Apostola. "This man," he pointed at the Engineer, "is a member of the Guild of Engineers. He may be able to tell us how to free the god."

They all looked down at the Engineer. He had not moved, and he still gripped tightly his shoulder where the bear had struck him.

"It broke my collarbone," he said.

When Apostola and Vark both said nothing in reply, the Engineer added, "Whatever they've done, it uses much power. Far more power than Uroboros can supply. If we cut the power to the guildhall, then perhaps the god will be freed."

"How," Apostola grunted impatiently. "Speak how."

The Engineer nodded. "There is a place, by the wall, that makes power from the tides. We must go there. We must break the connection between the station and Uroboros."

"Show us," the gorilla demanded.

CHAPTER

27

Chance frowned as cold rivulets of rain poured down the back of his shirt. He stood with Sarah on the top step of the stair going below decks, reluctant to come completely out into the chilling downpour.

"Is it dangerous?" he shouted to Wadjet, who held the wheel and inspected the sky with eyes squinted against the rain. "Will there be a storm?"

"Not now," she answered.

The rain had started with the dawn. Heavy drops clattered loudly on the deck and tapped against sails, cold in the strong and steady wind that drove the black clouds overhead. But no thunder sounded, and the waves grew only a little taller than they had the day before.

"No sense standing around up here," Sarah said, and went below deck. Chance followed her.

It lasted three days. The cold drops kept Chance, Thetis, and Wadjet in their quarters, while Mimir and the Guardian remained on the deck, impervious. Seth, undecided, sat at the bottom of the stairs, and sometimes rose into the gray rain, blinking as he peered about the sea as if seeking a dry patch, before dejectedly returning below. Divided, the group told no more tales. But their fifth day at sea dawned gray, the heavy drops stopped falling, and the wind died. Thick clouds lay low over a lead sea. As Chance emerged onto the deck, following Sarah, she turned to him and said, "The kite is down."

Only a mere mist of rain fell. Chance chewed a bar of food that Wadjet had given him. He sorely missed now the food they had enjoyed in the Broken Hand that Reaches. He looked around, and saw that Sarah was right: the bright blue skysail was not before them, in the sky. They walked to the bow and saw that the line for the skysail lay on the sea, stretching away out of sight.

"It fell only an hour ago," Mimir said.

"It's very lucky it stayed up the whole time we were in the rain," Wadjet told them. "We made good speed. Now, we must reel it in." She showed Chance how to operate a hand winch that slowly pulled in the dripping line from the sail. He cranked it with his left arm as Sarah leaned against the mast, squinting in the drizzle. Seth lay nearby, blinking contentedly. "You always liked a light rain," Chance said to him, laughing.

"It's warm, for autumn," Sarah said. "Do you think we've come far enough north for it to make a difference in the weather? They say farther north it is always warm and sunny."

"I don't know," Chance said. He looked around at the sea, the empty horizon, the solid gray of the clouds. "I cannot judge how fast we travel. But we're definitely not somewhere always sunny."

She laughed.

After a while Chance could see the dark blue of the sail floating on the surface, bloated with water as it dragged toward the boat. He stopped cranking and went to the prow and leaned far over the side.

"I don't see how we're going to get that up in here. It's all full of—ah!"

He fell back from the gunwale.

"What is it?" Sarah asked. She gripped her swords and looked nervously at the water. Chance held to her arm and leaned forward with her. And there it was: an impossibly huge gray and black shape rising in the water beside their ship, at least as large as the boat, with a huge black eye gazing up at them. Below it, awesome, huge shapes of gray moved through the dark depths.

"Leviathan!" Chance managed.

"Too-too-too big," Seth commented, ears flat against his head as he looked warily out at the huge expanse of dark flesh. The boat rocked—not from being hit but just from the displaced water of the great beast.

The rest of the crew crowded onto the bow. One of the beasts surfaced and blew damp spray into the misty air.

"Humpback whales," the Guardian said. He had left Threkor's Hammer below deck, and stood now eagerly leaning forward, both hands on the gunwale. "Soulburdened."

Chance heard something new in the ancient's voice and looked up at him in surprise. It was—could it be?—something like joy. Or wonder. A hint of a smile was on the Guardian's lips. His teeth flashed through it, like bright mineral flakes in a dark stone.

Chance crouched and put his hand on Seth, and Sarah stood behind him and put her hands on his shoulders. They huddled close and watched the huge whales in silence for several minutes. There appeared to be at least five of them, surfacing here and there, coming near and looking at the boat with a single black eye, but mostly keeping a respectful distance. None rubbed against the hull. Chance felt his heart slow into something like a normal beat, though the shock of his initial fear still made his hands shake.

Leviathan! he thought. He was seeing real Leviathans! They were just as the True Book described, and could surely swallow a man or even a boat. He looked back at Sarah and she nodded at him. He put his hand over hers.

"I do not—I cannot—speak their tongue," the Guardian lamented. "They had their own tongue even before their burdening. And they are unlikely to speak Lifweg."

"I speak some of their song language," Wadjet said. "But I will have to go in."

"What?" Sarah and Chance said simultaneously. Seth yipped in indignation.

"They won't swallow you?" Sarah asked.

"No. They eat only the tiniest little things. And they are gentle creatures."

That sounded unlikely to Chance. But Sarah added, "Won't they just crush you—I mean, even by accident?"

Wadjet laughed. "I have been in the water with such as them before," she said proudly. "And even bigger—the blues and right whales. Guardian, bring the skysail in. I'll drop the other sails."

The Guardian pulled the line, then the skysail, up onto the deck. The boat leaned forward under the weight of the water caught in the sail as he lifted it from the sea and dragged it onto the deck. It splashed water around them, soaking their shoes and the bottom of their pants, and then the strange blue fabric shrank quickly. The whales watched, patiently, curious, surfacing here and there by the boat and rolling to the side, so that sea streamed down their gray flanks as each turned a single huge black eye upon Chance and Sarah and Wadjet.

Then, without another word, Wadjet began to strip off her clothes. The Guardian gave her one last envious look, then thudded across the deck and down the stairs to watch what happened through the clear bow of the ship. Seth and Thetis followed.

Chance stood, too stunned to consider etiquette, as Wadjet undressed. She pulled off her shirt, exposing small, upturned breasts with dark aureoles. Chance watched them as she pulled off her bright pants. Underneath, she wore short black briefs that clung to her skin. Her long legs were hairless and smooth and strong. The outline of her behind was strong and round.

Chance realized suddenly that he was staring. With his mouth open. Wadjet turned and smiled at him, her green eyes and her white fangs flashing, expressing her gleefully predatory glare, and then she put a foot on the gunwale.

Chance flushed red and knelt down, pretending to prepare to look into the water, but really to hide his embarrassment. His eyes met Sarah's. She had been watching him. She frowned and touched the scar on her face, and then turned hastily away, to go below deck. Chance opened his mouth to call to her, but did not know what to say.

Seth whined unhappily as Wadjet lifted her arms and leaned forward, and then dove into the blue sea filled with monsters.

Wadjet loved the water. Warm and slick, it touched her everywhere: the salty blood of the Earth, wrapping her in its life. She parted her lips and teeth and tasted the wet quick of it: salt and iron, magnesium and air, and the indefinable subtlety of tiny animals and plants, living and dying against her tongue. She snapped her teeth, wishing she could swallow it all as it swallowed all of her.

Then her body shook, from the deep center of her heart out to her fingers and toes: the call of the whale that slowly bent through the dark water beneath her.

"Little thing from above," it sang out. Identification constituted, for the whale kind, a greeting. "Hard. Silent. Slow. Tailless."

Wadjet surfaced, gasped air, and dove into the blue again. She kicked till her hands touched the rough skin of the whale, sharply coarse with small barnacles. She pressed herself against it, getting her throat close to its ear.

"I sing."

"You sing," the whale responded.

"Why do you follow?"

"Promise," the whale began. But she could wait no longer. She had to listen as best she could while surfacing for air.

"All the seas made clean again," it continued. "Whales given ocean dominion."

Her head broke the surface, and she gasped twice. Chance stood on the boat, looking at her. The thought flashed into Wadjet's mind: innocent, but only a little wild, this boy. He would never immerse himself into the dark ocean and give himself over to uncertainty. Part of her mischievously longed to seize him, and pull him into the depths. And to do other things with this dark-eyed boy. Her fangs against his flesh. Against his....

She dived back to the waiting whale. Still looking toward the boat, she saw in the bow the Guardian; the coyote; feeble, trembling Thetis; and the sword bearer. She liked the sword bearer. She liked Sarah more because Sarah disliked all of them. Sarah was another she'd like to seize, to taste again....

Wadjet flashed her teeth at them as she passed.

The whale moaned, a vague prompting to Wadjet.

"The..." she hesitated, as she settled again by its ear, not knowing the whale phrase for a god. "The strong surface dweller. The powerful one. He promises?"

"The worldchanger," the whale answered. "His servants promised sharing if we follow you who escaped the encircled school of men."

The whale, taking pity on her, surfaced with Wadjet lying atop. She took a few slow breathes, and then they slowly sank under the water so that the humpback could sing.

"His servants may ask us to stop you," the whale said. "His servants may ask us to force you to thin water."

Wadjet was growing breathless. She did not love being under the water long, when it was so much work to hum the words.

"We ask clear way on the whale road. We go to the skyriver." She did not know if that was the right word for Yggdrasil, though she remembered that phrase from somewhere.

"We swim with you," the whale answered, uncommitted. "We wait to hear from distant pods. We wait to decide. We wait."

She asked more questions, and listened between gasps to the answers, but then finally the beast surfaced, and Wadjet let go his great back and watched the gray singer dive into blue, then black, depths. Whales did not say goodbye.

She swam to the ship. It had drifted ahead a bit and she caught up to it at the swimming platform on the stern. Chance, eyes wide with fear and wonder, stood there, and held out his strong hand to her. She smiled at him, and took it in her own.

CHAPTER

28

C hance pulled Wadjet from the water. She almost fell back, and he hugged her to catch their balance. Wadjet smiled and thanked him in a soft voice, a sound like a cat purring. Sarah came onto deck just then, the Guardian following, in time to see Chance standing, his hands lingering on Wadjet's hips. He stepped back guiltily. His clothes were wet down the front. He licked the saltwater that had come off Wadjet's hair and onto his lips.

Thetis had somewhere found a towel, and Sarah took it and threw it at Wadjet after she had climbed back onto the deck. The Steward caught it, showing no reaction.

"The whales debate whether to help the god," Wadjet said. She rubbed the towel over her chest.

"Ha-how do they know?" Seth asked.

"Their voices can carry very far. Many miles below the water. There are whales by Disthea that have sent them word. This must mean that the city is held by the soulburdened. They expect that the god will soon be free and are told that through him the soulburdened shall come to rule the world. They are asked to track us. They may be asked to stop our ship."

"Will they?" Sarah asked.

Wadjet wobbled her head, an expression Chance had never seen before but which seemed to assert uncertainty. "There are several dozen near us now. The cows care only to get to the warm waters of the north, so that they may mate and calve. It is hard labor, and they cannot eat now. They see no reason to trust the god. But the bulls are eager to show their strength. They have no loyalty to the god, but they are tempted. And the bulls remember the violence of men, especially here in the seas by the red lands, where men hunt whales for meat and because they are soulburdened."

The Guardian growled angrily.

"What should we do?" Thetis asked. She handed Wadjet her clothes.

"There is nothing that I can think to do," Wadjet said, as she pulled on her shirt. "The bulls will goad each other on, and perhaps nothing will come of it, or perhaps they will try to stop us. But until that happens, we should race for the north."

"Why not go to the shore now," Chance asked, "and go the rest of the way afoot?"

The Guardian shook his head. "That would take very long. Too long. And we have moved too far north. The shore here is a thin coast of towns, barely living along the edge of the red lands. The men who dwell there are dangerous and cruel. They could slow us. And beyond the red lands is the Filthealm. Those who dwell there are not men anymore. Each would as soon eat you as speak with you."

"Bad," Seth growled in agreement. With reluctance, he admitted, "Worse even than being on a-a-a-a boat beside whales."

Chance shuddered. Even in the Valley of the Walking Man, Trumen told stories of the cannibals of the red lands and the Filthealm. He had not been sure the stories were true.

"No," the Guardian continued. "We must save time and strength for the great threats that await us where Yggdrasil stands: there we must face the modghasts, and then Ma'at, Keeper of the Gate, with his Anubin warriors."

"Will the leviathans...will they try to kill us?" Sarah asked. "Will we have to fight them?"

"They would not mean harm," Wadjet said. "If they decide to stop our flight, they can push the boat where they like. But they may argue until we land. Even the most impatient bulls do not—how do you say it?—decide, make decisions quickly. They might be told to stop us, and then we might sail to Yggdrasil while they argue still about whether to obey, or who should stop us."

Seth looked out at the huge gray forms swimming alongside. "Our luck-ck won't be-be that good."

The drizzle stopped and wind rose. Wadjet set the skysail, and they sped north again, bouncing on small waves.

The clouds blew away in time to expose a flaming orange sunset over a hint of land in the east. Seth eyed the sea warily, his hackles rising every time a whale surfaced and blew a white cloud of spray. But the whales came no closer to the boat.

Chance and Sarah sat on the deck and ate from bowls of fish stew, cooked with some cod that Wadjet had caught off of a dragline during the afternoon. Soon the rest of the crew gathered with them and sat in a circle. Sarah frowned but said nothing when Wadjet sat next to Chance, folding her long legs elegantly, her knee resting against his.

"What is the plague that kills your people?" Chance asked her, as she blew upon her soup.

"It does not harm my people."

Chance looked perplexed.

"It attacks chimpanzees. And some gorillas. It is a form of the barrenness plague."

"What's a chimpanzee?" Sarah asked.

"An ape. Much like us, but covered with black hair."

"Are they soulburdened?"

Wadjet shrugged. "Some are."

"And you care for them even though they are not men and not all soulburdened?"

Wadjet shrugged again.

Chance hesitated before he spoke. "You said you were...."

"An exile," Wadjet said. "A criminal."

Chance nodded. "And if you help... if you help with this plague, then you'll be... forgiven?"

Wadjet snorted, a sarcastic sound more like a growl than a human puff of air. "I don't ask forgiveness. I would help friends. And show fools that I could help where they are powerless."

And Chance thought, I know her, I know her in part, now. For I am the same. I always wanted to be the best Puriman, because so many doubted that I was a Puriman. But I wanted to do it in my own way. She wants to be better than the Stewards, at being a Steward, even though they tell her that she is not a Steward.

They were silent awhile, thinking as they ate soup. Seth noisily lapped from a bowl, and then sat between Chance and Sarah. He crossed his paws and laid his head on them with a contented sigh.

"And the Barren makes them, the...." Sarah hesitated.

"Chimpanzees," Wadjet said. "And gorillas."

"... the chimpanzees sterile now?"

"Yes. They are much like us, and so a form of the disease was able to adapt to them. Once there were many apes here in these lands, but a form of the barren plague wiped them out here. Now this plague, in this form that attacks the chimpanzees, has come to our lands."

"Not all of the apes in these lands were susceptible to the disease," Mimir said. "A small group of apes adapted immunity. One now serves the Hexus in some capacity."

Wadjet rose slightly. "What do you say?"

"A *Gorilla sapiens*. And there are others of its kind, and chimpanzees, beyond the Filthealm."

"Could this be?" Wadjet said. Her eyes were wide with excitement, but the set of her jaw showed skepticism. "Where, do you say?"

Wadjet and Mimir talked of places and landmarks that were unknown, nearly incomprehensible, to Chance. When they paused, Chance told Wadjet, "Mimir said that it was not the false gods, but it was the Leafwage that made the Barren."

Wadjet looked at the makina. "Our history says the same. The Lifweg had no part in the Theomachia."

"And they didn't make the Barren for the false gods?" Sarah asked, surprised.

"My elders tell that they did not," Wadjet said.

"So," Chance said. "That is why the Leafwage was destroyed, and all the knights killed. Not because they served the false gods, but because they made the Barren."

"All were killed but Tre-Tre-Treow," Seth corrected. "Or so the legend claims."

"And yet," the Guardian said, "all but a very few of that guild were guiltless of this wrong."

They all looked up at the Guardian. Surprised that he had volunteered this observation, they waited now to see if he would continue. When he did not, Thetis finally asked, in her tone of fearful respect, "May I ask, ancient Guardian, what you mean?"

"There were three bands within the Lifweg. One band, the largest, stayed true to the first hope of the guild, and," he nodded to Wadjet, "like the Stewards, sought to foster life.

"A second band tired of the slow walk of this cause, and fathered the soulburdened, and angered much of the human world by doing this. They hoped that the soulburdened would speak for themselves, and for the forest, and add a new will and strength to the struggle of life.

"A third band, in despair, created the Barren, hoping to cull man, and make room on Earth for the other wild things. This band, banished breakers of faith, acted without the ken of the others of the Lifweg, and brought death to the guild. All the knights died for their hidden crime."

The hint of land was gone from the east. The last of the sun, a narrow orange band, dipped below the sea there. Stars started to shine in the patches of clearing sky above. Wadjet lit the bow lamp. In the dim glow, the Guardian seemed darker, carved out of shadow where he sat awkwardly cross-legged on the deck.

"How do you know that?" Wadjet asked as she sat again next to Chance. "That is not in our histories."

The Guardian did not answer. After a minute, Mimir said, "He knows because he is, or he was, Treow, First Knight of the Lifweg. He is the one whom my father sought."

They sat in their circle, speechless, stunned. In the long silence, a whale, ominously close, blew a plume of salt water. The boat rocked. A cool gust made the sails snap. Sarah reached over and clutched Chance's left hand.

"Ga-Ga-Guardian," Seth whispered. "It is time that you tell your story."

CHAPTER

29

Hear!

While the Mothers and Engineers worked their craft in blinding cities, dreaming of a last age for men and a new age of gods, the Knights of the Lifweg, The Life Way, strove hard against the drowning tide of man's way in the world, and wrought in shadowed woods and green dark seas the first hopes of a new path.

Three of these were greatest of the knights.

First, Wulfanga, skilled in craft of the smallest living things. He was fearsome, and angriest among men at the murder of the world.

Second, Wealtheow, greatest in wisdom and greatest in hope, who evened the anger of Wulfanga. She it was who mothered many of the soulburdened—also these gray beasts here by us now that plow the whale road—breaking the laws of the human guilds and their dreams for a last age.

Least of these knights was Treow, myself, leader of the guild, husband to Wealtheow, and kith to Wulfanga. I alone earned the death that the others of the guild died, but I alone lived through the slaughter that ended it.

Not in that time nor after were there three others such as us.

While men grew slow in the sloth of their riches, we wrought the beginnings of a new world. The wondrous dream: a future wilderness more wild than all the past. A future wilderness that saved all the past and made it new.

When the gods were born, careless and lost in their power, we sought still a world where not men alone, but all living things would grow great in strength and thrive.

I tell you: that age was not the Penultimate Age, but the Dreaming Age, the Threshold Age, full with the chance to make a world saved from the wickedness of men.

Hear!

The bleak wreck of the Theomachia was a small loss—weighed against the loss of the many knights of this guild!

The loss of all the wonders of the Penultimate Age a small loss— when weighed against the loss of this dream!

I stood atop Aegweard, the tower of the shore watch, on the Island of Lethebion. The black stones were slick with warm rain. It was late after the noon. The sun would set in an hour. At the foot of the tower, sea crashed on black rocks softened with inlets of churned white sand. The gray waves tossed.

Behind me, neo-albertosaurs, green monsters three times as tall as a man, howled in the dark forests, louder even than the crashing surf as they fought each other for mates, scraping their knife-sized teeth against each others' skulls.

Far out before me, foaming caps of waves smashed against the white spires of the Sæwall that ringed our island and caged the beasts of Lethebion within, keeping safe the world outside.

Beyond the spires of the Sæwall, a narrow black airship struggled through a dark curtain of rain that fell from a black bank of cloud. I held a hand to my brow, shielding my eyes from the falling mist so that I could watch. The shape was unmistakable: long, black, with engines far in the back of its hornet tail. This was Wulfanga's ship.

"You cannot let him land!" a voice behind me demanded. I turned, and there came Erdwight, lead Elder of our guild, huffing as she clambered up the last wet stones of the black stair. Her gray hair was unkempt, as wild as the green roof of the forests that she tended. Her voice often cracked but it was deep and strong. "We allowed banishment on the bond that he would never return."

"I recall."

"This is no small matter, Treow. He nearly ruined us. If he had opened the Sæwall as he sought to do, if our beasts had went wild into the world beyond—the wreck, the bane, that we would have earned from the other guilds! All would have been lost! Our guild, Lethebion, everything."

"He did not plan it, Erd. It was the ill act of ill hour, and he has paid for it. The Lifweg was Wulfanga's whole life and cause. And we cast him out from it."

The Elder limped to my side, her bad hip sore after the tall climb. "Ah, you are like a child sometimes in your trust, Treow. This man is forlorn, and all the more fearsome because of it."

"Erd," I told her. "You speak the truth. He is forlorn. Something grim has happened, and he fears for his life. He needs me, but swears to me that he will not harbor here for more than a day. 'I promise you,' he wrote, 'that I shall not spend twenty more hours on Lethebion while I live.'"

Erdwight groaned. She frowned at the rain and the wind that fell cold on our skin. Her hair was beginning to fall, bedraggled, into her face. "You have always been too kind to him. You see none of his faults."

"We all have faults, Erd. But perhaps you."

"I do not claim—"

I put a hand on her shoulder. "I do not mock you, Elder. I speak with heart. You are the most faultless person I know. But even one as strong as you believes in the right of friends to forgive."

"Humph," she said, unhappy but soothed. "He is not to go near the Sæwall, nor near Gestierande-stede."

"Agreed. He shall be kept from the sea wall and from the lead hall of our work on Lethebion. I'll keep him here, in Aegweard, with me. Let me hear him out, and feed him, and rest him. Then he shall leave. Trust me to hold him to our writs."

Wulfanga was out of his ship, standing under its bobbing, sleek black belly, when I clambered out onto the docks. The sun had set, and the dim lamps of the dock were glowing pale green, giving the rain a foggy glow. I best remember him that way now: gaunt, sore and tired, a whip of a man worn out by cares when he should have been his strongest. I wish instead I could best remember the young Wulfanga, full of wisdom and anger, tall and strong, smiling at my side when the guild took sway of the island and named it Lethebion.

The wind broke against him, snapping his black cloak. I clasped him. "Well met, Wulf."

"Treow."

He trembled in my arms. I backed up, holding his shoulders. "Are you ill, friend?"

"Most likely. If things are going as planned."

This answer meant nothing to me. "Come in. In."

We climbed the slippery black rocks to the tower. In the center hall, where a fire crackled and cast a flickering yellow glow over old carpets, I pushed the doors closed against the rain and took his long coat.

"Wulfanga, what ails you?"

He sat by the fire. "Do not ask me now. I am tired, and I want to tell you in my own way. In the morning."

I frowned at this. We had little time. But he waved at my concern.

"Please. Trust me. I will tell you in the morning. May I stay in my old home?"

"No. I'm sorry. You need stay here with me."

"Erdwight's rules?"

"My own."

He nodded. I did not like this: the grave message, the sudden coming, and then to put me off. I should have seen that he had something planned. But I did not.

I brought him food and drink, and we sat by the fire and talked a very little about Lethebion, but an awkwardness had settled into our speech. I could see that he could think of nothing else but some dread truth he came to share and yet held back. Finally he asked if he could rest.

"Come."

I took him to one of the rooms of a guildwoman of the tower. She worked on the far side of the island that night.

"Will this do well?"

He nodded without even looking at the room. He sat on the edge of the bed. There was a long quiet while he seemed to struggle with whether to speak. Finally he shook his head.

"In the morning then," I said. I turned to leave, but he called to me just as I passed through the door.

"Treow. It lasts, doesn't it? The forests of Lethebion?"

"Yes. It seems that much of it is steady and will last now."

"We can redeem ourselves, then. Bring back all the lost life, and redeem even the worst crimes of our ancestors.... If you had more room."

I nodded. He was stating what was already clear. Lethebion was a large island in a warm sea that had been bereft after wars fought before the age of the guilds. Those wars had fouled the soil and water of the island. No humans and few animals or plants had remained on it. Over many years, the poisons weakened, and then our guild was able to claim the place, since the risk of dwelling in the poisoned place was one that we would bear. And here we had begun to thwart the undoing of even the most old of beasts. Here we had begun to make again Earth's wights that were lost, and forge a wild riot of life.

"Yes," I said. I wanted to soothe him by understanding his feelings. "If only we had more room."

I gripped the handle to the door.

"Erdwight was right, you know."

"What?"

"I had planned it. I had long planned to open the Sæwall and let the beasts out into the ocean and air."

A stab of anger went through me. So he had lied, all those years ago. I stood and clenched my jaw, nearly bursting with the urge to shout at him, to berate him for trampling on my trust. But he looked lost and tired, and in the end I just said, "We'll talk in the morning."

Tiny hands, warm on my cheeks, awoke me. I smiled and opened my eyes, and beheld my daughter, smiling over me, her eyes shining. My son bounced onto the bed behind her. I reached out and embraced her, then both of them—and then leapt from bed when I came full awake and knew then that they were there, with me.

"How came you here, Beo and Una?"

"Mother brought us," Una told me, laughing. Their soulbur-dened lemur scampered sideways about the room, roused by their laughter. It hooted once, very loudly.

I dressed quickly and hurried into the great hall. There Wealtheow stood, before a great fire that she had stoked on the ashes of the previous night. I ran to her, my children following, and took her shoulders in my hands.

"How good it is to find you here! It is a wonder!"

It gives me some happiness, these ages later, to know that I let my heart win that moment, and I hugged her. Yet still I feel a heavy shame that before this day I let anger long separate us.

"A wonder!" she laughed. "Surely you knew I would come when I heard your call."

"My call?"

"Wulfanga told me. But—what—you did not ask for us?"

"I asked for all three of you with every breath, in every moment that passed, but was too much the coward to call out. No, Wulfanga did not as I asked, but as I needed and wanted and had failed to do."

We left the children by the fire with a heaping breakfast, and then climbed the black stairs to the room where Wulfanga had slept. We meant to thank him. But the door was ajar. The room empty.

"How could he betray me twice?" I growled at Wealtheow. "Perhaps even more times." I had come in love. Now rage shot through me.

"There's a note." Wealtheow picked up a folded parchment sheet that lay on the pillow. She opened it and read, "Dear Treow and Wealtheow: By the time you read this note I shall be dead. A willing sacrifice to Lethebion. A deserved punishment."

She looked up at me. "Oh, Treow."

My mind raced. What would it be? "Leap off the roof of the tower?" I asked aloud, moving toward the window as I said it. "But no: Wulfanga had asked to stay the last night in his old home, the small hut by the grass plains."

"The terrorbirds," Wealtheow whispered.

We sprinted from the room.

✚

The fastest way to the plateau was on horseback. In the stables we found all the horses were there—Wulfanga had not taken a steed. This was good, for if he had not left too early in the night we might catch him on the path.

We rode hard up the narrow trail, through steep hills.

"Why would he do this?" I called to Wealtheow. "What does the note say?"

But though she tried, we rode too hard for her to draw out the note and read the rest of it.

The path rose into light, and then opened out of the forest and onto the bright grassland. The tall blades tossed in the wind, glistening still from the night's rain, and brushed the knees of our horses. The empty green stretched off to mountains in the east, and to far-off forest in every other way.

"I don't see him," I cursed.

Wealtheow was reaching for his note, her eyes still on the plain, when she pointed. "There!"

Standing in the grass: a single black figure, and beyond it two other dark shapes stepping slowly forward. We took off at a gallop.

As we approached, we began to see the figures clearly. Wulfanga walked, his back to us, toward two giant, sleek birds that slowly, slowly, stepped through the tall grass, watching him. Two terrorbirds, surely a mating pair. Each a full head taller than Wulfanga, wingless, covered in green feathers that could fade into the grassland when they crouched. Their huge legs slowly lifted, planting a massive talon in the sod with each step. They tipped their ax-beaks toward each other as they stalked up on Wulfanga. They likely thought that he was sick, to approach them like this. But still they moved slowly, bent forward, in their careful hunting way.

The hammering of our galloping horses reached them then. The birds bobbed their great heads up, frozen as they watched us. They waited a long time, perhaps mistaking the horses for some dumb prey beast of the plains, before one, then the other, sprinted off at shocking speed.

Wulfanga sat down in the grass, weeping. We circled him, then leapt down.

"Why did you stop them?" he moaned. But he could not hide his relief. It would not have been an easy death. And no death is welcome.

"No more lies," I told him.

"No more lies," he answered.

"No more betrayals."

"Oh, there can be no more betrayals after what I have done."

I held out a hand. "Here. Get up on this horse. I will ride with Wealtheow. Our children are alone. We return to Aegweard to be with them."

We stood on the hot stones before Aegweard, while our children and their lemur played in the sea.

"Why?" Wealtheow demanded, after the young ones ran beyond hearing.

Wulfanga fell onto a stone bench alongside the tower. "Have you yet let yourselves see that your dreams are hopeless? Have you let yourselves see that while men squeeze onto every last shovel of dirt, the course of life is doomed? The soulburdened that you create, Wealtheow, will have no strength against this greed. And Lethebion is too small to thrive, and none will let it stretch beyond that cursed wall." He pointed at the white towers of the Sæwall.

"I grant no such thing," Wealtheow said. "I still have hope."

"You were wrong to hope. But now you may hope."

I grew restless. "Wulfanga, you've clashed against our hopes before. You were banished for it."

"And Wealtheow?" he asked me. "Why was she nearly banished? For lack of hope?"

I growled. "I did not say the guild lacks fools. That does not mean you are right. Tell us what you've done. Do you need some help to set something right?"

"It's too late. It's already done."

"Nothing the guild does cannot be changed if I fight hard to make it so. We can—"

"No! Not the guild. That's all past. It's too late for the guild. For now."

"I don't understand," Wealtheow said.

"I have done a dreadful thing. A wonderful and dreadful thing. I have made the plague, and I have released it."

He looked at me as he said this.

"What plague?" Wealtheow whispered.

The world seemed to fade around me. I could not believe what he had said. Not yet. Oddly, I found myself looking around, to see if there was another nearby who could have heard these words. I felt the eyes of history upon us—I felt the gaze of the dread doom of the future. But we were alone.

"What plague?" Wealtheow repeated.

"A plague that makes most men, and most women, barren."

I sat—fell—back onto the broken stone wall that ringed the small area at the base of the tower. A monkey screamed in the trees nearby. The hiss of the surf could just be heard above the soft wind in the trees. The laughter of my children rose up to us from the sun-sparkling sea.

"Why?" I whispered.

"You know about this?" Wealtheow demanded of me.

"He had talked of it once. Long ago. He swore to me he would never talk of it again. Still, it was one reason I let the guild leaders banish him."

"You knew about this," she said again.

"As did you. You heard him threaten it before also. Years ago."

"But I thought he was...."

"Yes. So did I."

"It is done now," Wulfanga said. "Do not fight over it. Neither of you could stop me."

"Why?" Wealtheow said. Her voice was bitter.

There was no force in Wulfanga's voice as he answered. "You know why. I have no hope for men. They will crowd out every last being on Earth. It is their way. Nothing you are doing can change that."

"You will cause war," she said. "Great wars. Death. You will set everything back. You may have finally ruined the Earth."

"It was already ruined."

"No!" She took two great steps toward him and slapped him. Hard. "No! You will tell what you've done. We will damn what you've done. And you will yield up the cure. Then you will pay for your crime. The Lifweg will go on with its work."

"There is no cure. And I have no need to confess. I have no doubt that soon, very soon, the truth will be known. Many people helped me. They are not good guild members. They will talk. Soon. The fighting will begin soon."

"You have killed us," I whispered. And then I stood, and gripped his collar so tight that I choked him. I dragged him over to the wall and shoved him over, so that his weight balanced on the edge, wobbling over a deadly drop to rocks below.

"You've killed the Lifweg. Lethebion. The soulburdened." I shook him. Wealtheow grabbed his leg to keep him from falling. She shouted my name. But I was always ready with wrath, even if Wulfanga was the one who had only wrath.

"You have killed our children. My son and daughter."

"Rrrr- herrrr...." he choked out through the biting twist of his collar. "Oth-th...."

"Please," Wealtheow said. "Please, Treow."

I pulled him back and threw him onto the ground. He slowly raised himself off the rocks, coughing. A fierce red welt ringed his throat.

"Hroth tower," he choked out.

"What?" Hroth tower was deep in mountainous forest far to the north, near the middle of the Earth, not far from Yggdrasil. In the first days of the guild we had used it. It had been forsook to the forest, unused we thought, for more than ten years.

"I have prepared it. Take my ship and your children and go. I will stay here, and await the end."

"We would not leave our guild."

"You shall be blamed. I shall be blamed. But not your guild-mates. You must take the children and go. Erdwight can arrest me. She can turn me over to... the Orderlies, perhaps, would be best. But you must go this hour. Go at least until the truth comes out, so that you are not killed in anger."

There is little more to be said of that time. We could not forsake our guild, and so spurned his plan. We gave Wulfanga to the Orderlies. It did not help, not for long. We stayed on the island, while hatred grew. We stayed when it was attacked, and stayed when the Lifweg finally fought back, and many died. We stayed until it was hopeless, and we were among the few who still had breath. We stayed until nothing could be saved, until we had no choice.

And then we fled. We fled to Hroth Tower.

After we had given Wulfanga to the Orderlies, I read the letter that had been crushed in Wealtheow's pocket.

Most of it confessed to his crime. But he ended the letter with this:

I know what you will say of me. How I ill-wielded craft that was not mine by right. You are a dour man. But I ask you: as every single human comes to have vast strength—like those gods that the

*witches are said to brew in their damned tower—can we prevent
any of the harms this can do, without becoming as strong ourselves?
Has Wealtheow not admitted this, by leaving the Lifweg to join the
wolflings who mother the soulburdened? We cannot thwart strong
ills but by wielding great strength of our own.*

The mountain forest where Hroth tower stood was empty of any
men, thick with trees, and far—for that time—from the nearest
city. It stood in a guarded forest, one of the first deeds of our guild.
Wulfanga had planned ahead. There was a greenhouse in a small
clearing. Power cells, food stores, weapons, all the things we needed
to live there.

I am no airship pilot. We searched for days to find it, and then
spent an afternoon trying to moor. Finally I slid down a docking
rope, and Wealtheow steered so that she swung me, smacking painfully hard, against the tower's roof. I climbed down and moored the
ship. We emptied, then deflated the ship, and folded it away as best
we could.

In the year that followed we lived a simple life, growing food,
hunting, schooling our children. We named the monkeys and birds
that lived nearby, and learned their ways as you learn the ways of
your neighbors. We sang, and filled the forest with our calls, like
birds. At first, the children sorely missed their friends and home.
Their lemur's gripes about missed cakes soon became a joke and a
vent for their sorrow. They moved on. They grew strong.

Wealtheow and I were frightened, and worried, but even at the
end of the world two lovers can defy time, and be happy for a while.

We brought no tool with us to call to the world beyond, knowing that such a thing could betray us. But we did have tools to listen
to what was happening outside. We learned of the murdering of
our guildmates, of the hunt for our family. We heard nothing of

Lethebion or the soulburdened. We learned of the doings of Dark Engineers and the Mothers of the Theogenics Guild—you could hear in the voice of those who spoke of it the fear, near terror, when the gods were shown forth.

I began to hope that we would be forgotten in this terrible new age. I began to steal more moments of peace, seeing my son and daughter race in climbing a tree, their lemur far ahead of them; hearing them gossip about the sex of the monkeys; feeling them grow strong and lithe.

The rainy spring was just ending, the clouds breaking to let through a few cracks of sun, when it happened.

Wealtheow and I stood in the kitchen. The children played upstairs, in their room in the top of the tower. Then, from high in the tower, a strange crackling sounded out.

"What was that?" Wealtheow asked.

"I don't know. They broke a chair? Something wood?"

"I'll go look." She headed up the stairs, quick but not panicked. I set down the knife I held and listened. And then I heard it— unmistakable: Wealtheow gave out a stifled scream.

I ran up the winding tower stair, three steps at a time. I heard then, in the distance, the fan of an airship, somewhere near but not so close that you could see it from the windows I ran past. They meant to keep it out of hearing range, and mayhap it had drifted too close to us in the sharp winds.

The door to the children's bedroom was closed. The air on the landing outside smelled of ozone. A sickly light spiked out from beneath the door, like white knives stabbing into our world from some rotten other place. I pushed against the door and pushed again, but it would not open. So I stood back and kicked the door so hard it burst off the hinges and clattered onto the floor.

The room was wrecked, the children's beds overturned, their toys strewn on the hard stone floor. The window was burst inwards, and bright shards of glass crunched under my feet. The children were not there. Their lemur was not there.

And in the center of this dreadful sight drifted Primus, first of the Younger Gods. We had seen his image, as had all the world. He was wrapped in a white cloth, and his skin glowed as he floated there, his toes just touching the floor. He held my wife by her throat.

"Put her down!" I shouted. I ran at him but with a thought he threw me onto my back by the window. I clambered to my feet, shards of glass clinging to my palms where they cut into my skin.

"Oh, what have you done? What have you done?" I looked over the room again for my children and did not see them, did not see any place where they could have hidden themselves. I looked out the window, but they were not on the ground below. "Where are my son and daughter? What have you done? Let my wife go! You'll kill her."

"What have *you* done, Treow?" the foul child asked me. "What forces have you attempted to direct? What alliances have you made?"

I ran at him but he waved a hand and this time I was knocked to my knees and then bound there, at the feet of my wife, locked in some kind of tightly wrapped space. I understood then that she was dead. Her head was bent limp, to the side. Her eyes lay open but looked neither on the young god nor on me. The god dropped her, and the body crumpled before me, into a lifeless heap.

I moaned and began to weep. "She was the best of her age, Primus. You have done a thing that shall be known for its foulness ages hence. Oh, where are my son and daughter?"

"You tell me, Treow," it mocked.

"Where are they?" I screamed.

"They are not here." His voice was calm, indifferent. So little my life, the life of Wealtheow, the life of my children meant to it. "Out of sight, out of mind...out of being, perhaps. I come on an errand for the Mothers of the Theogenics Guild."

This was the short time after the birth of the gods but before the war, when the Younger Gods still did with half-hearts the bidding of the Mothers.

"How can they combat this plague?" Primus demanded. "And, given what I have seen here, I must ask you, who helped your guild to engineer it? To what otherworldly powers have you betrayed our age?"

"There are no others!" I shrieked. "We told the truth. Some few once in my guild, already banished, made it. You have killed them already. This is madness, to kill the guiltless."

"How do we stop it?"

"I do not know how to stop it. I know nothing of it. None who served me had knowledge of this thing. Doom and hurt me, but let my children thrive."

"I came not to punish but to find a cure."

"If there were one in the world that had a hope of curing this, you just killed her," I spat. "Now give me my children."

The god shrugged, indifferent. He looked at my wife's body, and then at me. I felt a sickening squeeze within my skull as he gazed into me. Then he said, "I see that you believe what you say."

That was it. He was done. He had no use left for us.

"Where are they? Now tell me. Where are my children?" I strained, hissing with effort, against the bonds of bent space.

"Why do you believe I have them?" He waited then, mocking me, as if he expected some answer. Then he continued. "For that matter, how do you even know you had children? Perhaps I created that memory in you just to torment you for your crimes."

And then he disappeared. Like that. Into a snap of dry air and the bitter stench of ozone. And I was alone, with the body of my wife, and with the black empty lack of my children. In the distance, I heard the airship begin to drive away.

Can you ken the cruelty of this? To have taken my beloved children, and not to let me know how they died, and, worst of all, to have set that sick seed of doubt within my heart that perhaps they never were at all? I crawled to my wife's body, already growing cold, and wrapped her arms around my head, and wept bitterly, with heaving gasps, until I could weep no more and it seemed I would choke on my own despair.

After a long time—all of the day, or perhaps it was two days— I rose onto my knees, and looked out the window of my children's room, and howled at the darkening sky.

"I will avenge you!" I screamed. "I will kill them all!" I do not know if I spoke for my wife or my children or all three. Or myself. But I believe that in all the world there was no being more aflame with anger than I at that moment. I burned with fury. I scorched a hole in space with my rage. I screamed, and screamed, and screamed, till my voice broke, and I could not see for the pounding blood in my eyes.

And then light poured through the little broken window of my children's bedroom, as if in answer to my howls. For a second, I hoped against dread that somehow my children were being returned. But instead a voice as cold and soft as wind-blown snow came out of the light.

"Would you pledge yourself to destroy the gods?"

And I knew, somehow, that this that spoke to me was something other, wholly other, than the Younger Gods, or the Demigods, or any Earthly thing. Out of the blinding light came now air so cold that my tears froze to my face and my breath came in bursting puffs of white. At my knees, the dead eyes of my fallen wife turned gray with frost.

"Will you return my children?"

"They are beyond us. They are lost to us."

I screamed again.

"Will you pledge yourself to avenge your wife and kill the gods?"

I did not back away from this doom.

"Yes," I told this otherworldly voice. "Yes. I bind myself to this doom and their death."

And I was gathered into the cold, cold light.

CHAPTER

30

Chance frowned and leaned forward when the Guardian fell silent, expecting more. But the ancient being was quiet.

"That's all?" Sarah finally asked.

"I cannot tell you what happened when I was taken among the Old Gods."

"Cannot, or will-will-will not?" Seth asked.

The Guardian brooded silently.

"But you told us nothing," Chance protested. "What are these other... things, these older false gods? What do they want? Where are they now? Why do you serve them?"

"Should you sa-serve them?" Seth growled.

The Guardian shook his head. "I told you why I am here. Why I hunt Hexus now. As for the Old Gods, I will say again only what is known to the Mothers and to all others who keep the lore: the Old Gods fear that the evil of the human gods may stretch beyond the Earth. For this, they have bound to the Earth men and all that men have created. And for this, should we fail to bind the human gods, they swear to kill the Earth. I am nothing to them, they will not hear my urgings—but this Earth-doom I may ward away by killing the Younger God."

"You have given Chance no reason to trust you," Sarah said.

The Guardian did not answer. He rose, in the dark, and walked to the prow of the ship, where he stood looking out over the black sea and the star-strewn sky that embraced it.

Sarah huffed in impatience and disgust. She rose to her feet and clomped off noisily toward the back of the boat. Thetis, Mimir, and Wadjet remained on the deck, all three silent, each lost in her own thoughts of family or loss or betrayal.

Chance stood to follow Sarah, then hesitated a moment, looking to the Guardian. He felt strangely sorry for this ancient creature. The Guardian's story had revealed how little his path resembled what he had wanted from his life, from the world. It was a story like Chance's own now.

Chance went to him. Seth watched, saying nothing.

"Perhaps," Chance said to the Guardian, "when we've killed the god, you can...do something like your wife, or friend, or you yourself once longed to do."

The Guardian looked at him but said nothing.

In the dark beyond, a whale blew a loud spume.

Chance nodded and turned away.

When Chance opened the door to the quarters he shared with Sarah, he found her standing in the dim light cast by the small bulb above their beds. She was wearing her sword belt and had her hands on the hilts.

How unlike herself she looked! So beautiful and fierce in these tight black clothes that betrayed every curve of her strong body, and with her hair shorn to a finger's width. One could not have seen her in her dress of the spring dance, with its low red and white hem, spinning on the Church floor, and recognized also this steely beauty.

"What…" Chance began, meaning to ask why she had put on the swords. But Sarah's look made him fall silent. There she stood, proud and dangerous and beautiful, looking at him over her shoulder.

The first night on the ship, when they had stepped down below the deck, Chance had hesitated after they entered the room and Sarah had pushed the door closed. They had stood a long time in awkward silence. He had wanted to ask if they could sleep together again, like they had that night in Disthea, but it was different now; she was not weak and needing him, and it would have meant something other. So he had hesitated, and though Sarah had seemed to be waiting, she finally gave him her uneven smile, nodded, and climbed into the top bunk. The same had happened on all the following evenings.

Now she furrowed her brow in something like angry determination. The black scars on her cheek seemed even more pronounced in the dim light. Chance pressed the door closed and stepped forward.

"Sarah?"

She turned and reached up and grabbed him by the collar, and pulled him to her and kissed him. It was the first time they had kissed. Chance closed his eyes. He grabbed onto her tightly with his left arm, pressing her painfully against his broken right arm.

Sarah pushed him away, then pushed him again, down onto his bunk bed. She dropped to her knees before him and began to unbutton his shirt. She stopped a moment to unbuckle her belt, and the swords clattered to the floor. She kissed him again.

"Wait," Chance said, pulling back.

"No," Sarah said sharply. "No more waiting." She kissed him and pulled roughly at his shirt buttons.

"Just a moment. Not more than a moment," he explained. He pulled her up, and she sat beside him on the bed. Then he slipped to his knees before her. He fumbled awkwardly at his shirt buttons with one hand, and, seeing what he was doing, she helped him unbutton his shirt the rest of the way. She put one hand flat on his chest. Chance grabbed the string around his neck.

"Cut this."

Sarah drew the knife she kept at her back and sliced the string. Chance pulled the ring from the cord as she sheathed the blade.

"I made this a year ago, from gold that I found. I made it for you. I've hidden it, and worn it, since that time. Dreaming of you. Dreaming of making you mine. Sarah Michael, will you wear this ring? Will you be my wife?"

The set of her jaw was fierce. Suddenly, when only a moment before she had seemed lost in passion, she looked at him now with keen calculation.

"You will be no easy husband to have, Chance Kyrien."

He nodded and held his breath in expectation.

After a long moment she said, "Chance Kyrien, I will be your wife, if you promise me one thing."

"Anything."

"You will never again speak of purity, and you will never again say that you are unpure, and you will accept yourself as—you will accept that you are a Puriman. Whatever happens."

Chance hesitated. How clever she was, he thought. For she aimed to absolve him of his impurity by forcing upon him this pledge. And though it would be self-serving, though it would be too easy, to accept her demand and be done then with his doubts— what choice did he have? She was the woman that he wanted. That he always wanted. That he must have. She was the finest Puriman women in the world. The finest that ever was or would be.

"I promise," he whispered.

She put on the ring. It fit perfectly.

Chance reached forward, and ran his fingers through her short hair. "I love you, Sarah Kyrien. I will always love you. No man in this world could ever love you as I do."

Sarah pulled him up and into the narrow bed.

"Puriman!"

Chance slept more deeply than he ever remembered sleeping, so that he rose only slowly into waking when he heard the sharp call of the Guardian.

"Puriman!"

Chance opened his eyes. Sarah lay tightly wrapped around him, the rough stitches of her scarred cheek against his shoulder. The dim hint of dawn from the portal window cast pale light into their cabin. Chance pulled away from Sarah, and she snapped awake.

"What is it?"

"The Guardian calls me."

They dressed hurriedly. With Sarah following, Chance went out to the hall. Seth waited on the steps. Chance could not see the coyote's face in the dim light but could tell by his silence and the low hang of his tail that he was concerned and perhaps even afraid. Chance ascended to the deck, Seth following so closely that his cheek brushed against Chance's thigh.

The Guardian stood in the bow still, but was turned now to face him. His eyes glowed pale green, a frightening sight that purged him of any vestige of humanity. Chance glanced back at Sarah, and saw then Mimir, who sat unmoving by the back mast.

"Puriman," the Guardian said, his otherworldly eyes turning upon Chance like two ghostly rays of moonlight. "The god is free."

CHAPTER

31

"Do not cling to an absent God," Hexus urged Chance as the Puriman boy faded from view.

The barrier blinked, then disappeared. For Hexus only an instant passed, though days had come and gone outside.

The Potentiate was gone. The lights in the round room flickered uncertainly, shedding only a thin glow. The power was failing—someone had cut power to Uroboros, Hexus realized, and so freed him from Threkor's ancient cage.

And surrounding Hexus now stood five of Threkor's Engles. The lights died. The only illuminations in the utter darkness were the red eyes of the Engles, moving toward him in a flash. Hexus knew what else moved in the dark: their brutal metallic arms swinging knife hands, their knees, tipped with iron spikes, hammering forward.

Hexus had learned well the force of these guardians of Uroboros. Though he had destroyed two of the Engles in their last meeting, the battle had been bitter and it had nearly annihilated his last body. Now he bent space and let himself fall through the floor, as one of the Engles swung a pointed claw at him, the blow bending around him.

He landed in a black room below. A few bits of light showed him where the door stood. He tore it off its hinges, blasting it down the abyss around which wound the stair, and then at his greatest speed he fled up the stairs, out into the halls of Uroboros. He passed through a dozen walls, running straight and bending space when needed to push past every barrier, until he emerged into pale dawn light and the street. The Engles followed him to the limit of the Engineer's guild hall, their claws ripping through doors and steel and stone, their hard steps hammering on the steel floors—but they stopped at the last wall. They would follow no farther. They would not leave Uroboros. Hexus turned and skidded across the stones of the road, and looked back. One of the Engles stood in the narrow crack he had made in the wall. Its red fire eyes glared at him, stupidly furious but bound by ancient laws.

Hexus turned away. The coming sunrise gave the western sky a first hint of flaming red. A vast ring of a thousand soulburdened beasts milled about in the square before the entrance to Uroboros, each impatient creature pacing and turning, roused now by the dawn, waiting for a sign before they charged the Engineer's guildhall. Hexus appeared in the air before them, standing a meter off the ground, in the center of the vast boulevard, where he could see south to the end of the city and the black sea wall.

Before him, a bear that held a shred of torn and bloody cloth in its mouth rose up in surprise, ready to strike him, and then it realized who he was, and its roar died and it fell back to the ground, cringing.

Slowly, silence spread out from this place in the crowd of ready warriors, until all the beasts were quiet.

"I am the god," Hexus proclaimed, the eye in the hand burning. "You have freed me. Where is my champion?"

The bear pointed with both claws toward the crystal wall at the south end of Disthea, where Hexus had first crossed over with his army.

"Tell your warriors to pause. To wait," Vark begged. He stood, shoulders slumped, at Apostola's side as she stared out over the city.

The battle did not fare well. Fighting continued unabated on both sides. Many were dying, and no advantage was being found.

"Soon the god will be free," Vark continued. "All this can be settled by him. There is no need for more to die."

Apostola breathed in deeply, preparing to grunt out some response. But a pale blur shot past her, and then the god stood before them.

Vark sank to his knees. Apostola did the same.

"Rise, my champion."

Apostola rose. Vark, uncertain, watched them both and, seeing their indifference to him, slowly rose, shrinking back a pace.

"How long have I been trapped?" Hexus asked.

"Six days."

"The Potentiate?"

"On a boat. They sail north. Whale kin follow the ship. The whales await your word, and will attack it."

"How far are they on the journey?"

"Not half the way, my god."

"Then let them continue, but the whales must follow. The Potentiate goes where I would take him. But if they head for land, have the whales stop and hold the ship." Hexus pointed at the city. "How goes the battle for this city?"

"Many of ours are trapped in the high floors of great towers. Can't descend. Humans within build barriers against our kin in the towers, and against our kin in the street."

Hexus looked out over the city a long moment. Vark opened his mouth several times, trying to gather the courage to speak, but failed each time.

"Send out word to our troops," Hexus finally said. "Tell them to get into the towers we control, and to climb. Most should go to the Hand that Reaches."

Apostola talked with a group of wolves, and these ran off with great leaping strides down into the city, their gray manes rolling.

Hexus walked down the switchbacking ramp. Beneath the ramp, a small black building of stone set up against the Crystal Wall. Hexus waved his hand and the steel door was torn open, the heavy bolts of its lock screaming as they bent and broke. He stepped inside. Light cast through the doorway dimly illuminated five huge pipes that rose out of the floor and sank back into it again. Vark stood behind at a distance, still waiting to be recognized, still afraid to speak. Another wolf approached, and Apostola turned away to speak with it.

Apostola came to his side. "Lord, there is an engineer that seeks to speak with you. It left their guild hall after you left, asking for you. Those in the street thought…maybe.…" She looked at Vark. "Maybe it is Hieroni."

Hexus stepped back into the doorway. An old woman, bald and with dark, wrinkled skin, walked toward them, a bear on each side. She was small but looked up at Hexus without fear, and showed no fear of the two great bears that flanked her. She stopped a pace away.

"Hexus."

"Bow!" Apostola shrieked, furious at this human insolence.

The Engineer gave a slight bow.

"I am Sar. Elder and Council Member of the Dark Engineers. I come to ask that you allow me to repair the damage to the power station that your armies have broken."

Hexus was silent a long time. "Why should I do that?"

"The City will flood. Slowly, but it will flood. That power is needed to pump out the sea water that leaks in."

"Not slowly," Hexus said. He turned toward the dark room behind him, and held out his right hand. He closed Paul's eyes in concentration and bent space, creating a tall slit, the height of a man, in one of the huge black pipes in the floor. As if the iron were made of clay, the sides smoothly bent out and away, before freezing into solidity again. Sea water roared through. As Hexus watched, the water twisted and tumbled through the door and into the city street. They backed away.

"My god, please do not do this!" Vark cried, finally speaking. He stumbled forward, and then went down on one knee in the water. "You destroy the city!"

Hexus looked down at him, Paul's face frowning, right hand out with the black eye gazing on Vark's head.

"Rise, Vark."

Vark stood, glancing nervously from the black eye to Paul's sad eyes, and then to the ground.

"Look." Hexus gestured toward the city. "Look. What do you see?"

Vark hesitated a long time before he said, barely audible above the roar of the water, "I see my city, the last great city of Earth."

Hexus nodded. "Know, Vark, that to me this city is a ruin, without hope. No one loves Theopolis more than I love it. No one. But this city is like me, now. Crippled, unable to grow into its whole self again." He turned his hand around, and stared at it with Paul's eyes. "Trapped in a fragmented form." He let the hand drop and looked again at Vark. "But I will remake the city, Vark. It is already lost, already destroyed. I shall remake it, after I remake myself, so that it is a glory not only of this fallen time, but of all times. When I have the Potentiate, and have properly Ascended, I will make this city greater than ever dreamed in the Penultimate Age. You shall exalt! Have faith."

Hexus turned so that all the other soulburdened nearby could hear him. He shouted over the thundering water. "I save the city! Everything depends upon getting the Potentiate, and taking him to the Well. There is no time to wait here. The city must be taken, and troops then gathered for pursuit. I will stop this flood when the city has surrendered. Go to the other pumping stations, like this one, and open the pipes!"

Hexus turned to the Engineer. Her eyes flitted over the torrent of water pooling and slipping down the street, but her face showed no emotion. The guild elder saw then that the god was about to dismiss her, and spoke before he could.

"I am descended from the very line of Threkor, whom you knew and respected, godling. I am one of the true Engineers— not one of these rusted uncreatives with fumbling fingers. Nor am I one of these fools—" she glanced at Vark, "who does not know what was, and what is, and what might be. You and I—we understand each other. Kill me now, or let me begin to rebuild this ancient city that was once your namesake." She pointed at the foaming water the sluiced down the street. "And there is more now for me to do. Who is a god to stand in the way of an Engineer and Threkor's Heir?"

Apostola snatched up her spear, ready to run the guild Elder through. But Hexus brayed with Paul's loud laugh.

"It is good to hear the pride of the Penultimate Age." He turned to Apostola. "Give her a guard and let her ready the way to repair the city. But not till the humans are flooded out and have surrendered all."

Apostola bowed. Mist from the shooting water started to fall over all of them. It made her armor shine and her black fur glisten.

"And prepare airships. And our best warriors. We must follow the boy."

Hexus turned to the leader of the Hieroni.

"Vark, I have a task for you. You shall bring me now one of the Numin Jars. And then you shall come with us, over the sea."

Vark flinched.

"Come, come," Hexus shouted over the bright water spray's roar. "You do not seem to appreciate the honor of being chosen to accompany the god."

Hexus laughed bitterly.

CHAPTER

32

C hance looked at Wadjet expectantly. A monotonous day had passed, the boat making steady progress sailing north while they waited for the whales to mount an attack that never came. Now they sat in a circle and ate a meal of more fish and dried breads. The sun set into a darkening red glow. It was time, if they were to follow their restored ritual, for either Wadjet or Thetis or even Seth to tell his story. A long silence settled over them, the only sound the lapping of short waves against the boat. Finally, Wadjet spoke.

"The boy waits on my tongue. But the one tale we could use," she said, a bit of petulance in her tone, "the tale we need to hear, the one tale that might tell us something that could save our lives, would be the tale of the god."

Seth snorted in agreement.

Thetis nodded. "I do wonder, why now? Where has he been until now? It's been thousands of years since the Theomachia. And what does he really want? He wants Chance, yes, but then what?"

Wadjet added, "And how did he get the soulburdened on his side?"

The Guardian leaned forward slightly, as if he too wished that he could hear such a story.

Chance considered a moment. He wondered, *Will I endanger myself if I speak now? Will the Guardian consider me polluted?* But, as happened to Chance all too often, he was surprised to hear his voice before he'd settled on an answer to those questions.

"I know the false god's tale," Chance said.

They all looked at him.

"He...he forced it into me. In Uroboros. Before I could drive him into the binding cube. Hexus lay his hand against my head and, in a minute, in a few seconds, I saw it, felt it all. I can tell it as he thinks it. As he sees it. Though I don't understand it all. Or even much of it."

The Guardian's eyes narrowed to slits under his dark brows. But Thetis spoke in a whisper then. "Tell it to us, Chance. It could be important. It could save lives."

Chance nodded.

Nightmares plagued Hexus. Nightmares that had lasted an eternity. Hexus dreamed that he crossed Bifrost, the bridge of stars, to a timeless land beyond the mortal world. There he climbed into the sarcophagus of his mortal death, so that he might be reborn as a god on Earth. He was Hexus, sixth of the seven Prime Potentiates, culmination of the human race and all that it hoped to inherit, and he was soon to be sixth of the seven Younger Gods. But instead, in this nightmare, an interminable emptiness and night followed his death, before he was reborn in hell as a tortured fragment of a divinity—

Before he looked up into the savage face of the Stalker.

The Stalker had been a scavenger of ancient places. He wandered the edge of the Filthealm, seeking guild machines of the lost ages to sell to other savage men. It was a dangerous occupation, chosen by men and women driven more by curiosity than greed. The Stalker, grizzled and canny, wandered farther than others. He did not just search the edge of the Filthealm, but dared to journey into it, so that he might forage in those polluted places that had not yet been looted, risking a slow death from poisoned air and water.

He walked alone where buildings still stood, though no men had entered them in centuries. He followed the fragmentary trails of ancient roads. He dug up strange dwellings and machines buried under dunes of blowing, toxic sand. He understood nothing of the things he found, but chose what he could carry, what was shiny or bright, what appeared beautiful or obviously useful.

And in his wanderings, he heard many times the legend of Voolmount, the mountain where gods and a demigod were said to have fought and died, at the beginning of the War of the Gods. The myths took on a plausible consistency in his mind, and he began to search. He began to long to find it, to possess the tools of a demigod that he hoped remained there.

It took years, but at last he discovered Voolmount, in the mountains that edge the southern tier of the Filthealm. Dwarfed by the surrounding peaks, it rose with sheer gray cliffs to a single, flat, snowcapped summit. The Stalker first beheld it as he rounded the bend of a thin goat trail that cut through the valley of two taller mountains, just minutes after breaking his solitary camp and striking out. He knew at first sight that it was the famed mountain. For there, out of the dark western face of it, just as legend told, a huge cavernous hole gaped, a single violent gouge in the hard rock, said to be from an explosion caused by some god or by the demigod, Wervool, who had dwelt there. The chamber glowed with trapped golden sunlight of the dawn, and called to him as a door to inconceivable riches.

The Stalker climbed until dusk and then camped on a thin precipice in howling wind. Nothing lived up there but lichen. In his small tent he melted snow for a drink, and then slept fitfully, shivering. He had harrowing dreams he could not remember when he woke with the dawn. He quickly broke camp and continued his climb. By the late morning of the next day, he put one arm, then the other, over the sharp corner of the cut, and pulled his head up into the chamber.

It was vast and round. The flat bottom of it lay smooth and even, clearly an act of artifice. Some parts of the walls stood square to the floor, or to another fragment of wall. There had been some kind of dwelling of stone here, carved behind the cliff face, but long exploded away. Breathless with hope, the Stalker heaved himself up onto the floor, dropped his pack, and without resting a moment began to search.

He found nothing. Flinty shards of gray stone covered the floor, but as he kicked them about or turned them over he found only more stones, or the smooth, featureless floor beneath. He climbed two walls, clinging perilously with his cold-numbed fingertips to inadequate cracks in the smooth rock, seeking some hidden recess. He found none. He scrutinized the floor again, this time dividing it in his mind into areas, which he searched individually, turning over every stone, before moving on to the next. It grew dark as the sun went behind the mountain.

The place proved bereft of all but stone and dirt. It was silent but for the screech of the wind, and inanimate but for the occasional eagle that soared past the cavern mouth.

He made camp in a corner and struggled with unpleasant dreams that again, in the morning, he could not remember. With the dawn, he ate the last of his food—some dried meat and two mouthfuls of water—and packed his things. He approached the cliff edge of the cave mouth, about to descend, when he felt compelled to make one last search.

That's when he saw it, in a dark corner that had been the first place he'd inspected the day before. Something glistening and white lay among the sharp scattered chips of stone. It was strange that he would have missed it. He reached out and prodded it. It gave slightly, elastic like a boiled egg. Some cords or strings came out of it, giving it the shape of a small turnip. He picked it up and turned it over in his hand.

The Stalker gasped: it was an eye.

He did not have time to wonder that it was not rotten. He did not have time to wonder that the pupil *dilated*, as it focused upon him, from where it lay on the palm of his right hand. He jerked his hand, reflexively, to shake it off. But it was too late.

He screamed as it sank down into his flesh.

It took days for the god's memories to bleed into the Stalker's mind. While those long hours passed, the Stalker raged at his own body. He broke several bones in his hand, smashing at it with a skull-sized rock held in his left. He stabbed at the eye with his pitted dagger, but the eerie unreal flesh closed, unharmed, after he withdrew the blade, and more often the point slipped aside, guided by some malevolent force, and jabbed agonizingly into the soft skin between his fingers or at the base of his thumb. Then he ruined the fingers of his hand by holding the palm in a fire, screaming in anguish as he tried to burn the eye away. The flames did not harm the orb, but blackened and destroyed the meat of his digits.

And while he wrecked himself, visions crowded into his head: unbelievably beautiful children smiling imperiously at each other; towering rooms of white and gold; dignified men and women in black robes; a dark place where stars spun by so close it seemed you could touch them; a building with fingers that reached for the sky as if to grab the moon....

And then the voice spoke.

"Who are you?"

The Stalker howled at the wind.

Hexus recalled these things as his own memories now. He had bonded to the Stalker out of some innate impulse. His mind was gone. There remained nothing of him but a potential for power, and a potential for reclaiming the memories of his mortal life, his life before his death and transformation. And these took root in the Stalker's mind. He became first a joint, mixed being, confused together with the brutal incomprehension of the Stalker.

What he saw in the Stalker's mind was all darkness: cruel memories of a nasty, painful life, drowned in ignorance. Hexus could not have imagined that anywhere on Earth there could be such ignorance. The Stalker knew nothing of the world, of its history, of the fate of its cities and people. He thought that the Earth was only as old as ten score generations of men; that the universe was tiny, the stars few and near; that the seasons were caused by the sun coming close or withdrawing; that every disease or accident that harmed someone was the judgment of a god; that all the organisms of Earth were made as they were now, perfect for some use, always a human use; and that human women were also made, as they were now, for the uses of men (this made Hexus laugh, a choking guttural sound in the Stalker's throat that the Stalker resisted, but that Hexus could not suppress, as he imagined his sisters, impossibly beautiful, standing in the air, their night-black hair streaming behind, their black eyes looking down with divine contempt on this stupid savage). Chief of the Stalker's mad beliefs was that reality itself was a simple stage drama for his own straggling, half-perished tribe, so that ultimately he need not be concerned about the far future or the consequences of his actions, since the outcome was soon to be the destruction of the world and the re-creation of some kind of happy family gathering strewn with virgins. It was a dream that only an adolescent or idiot could have desired.

Hexus wandered down the mountain, stumbling, a mystified and mixed being. For six days he wandered, chewing roots and drinking water from puddles, as the Stalker knew how to do. He descended from the dry highlands down into a warm, thick forest, dense with trees. All the while, his dismay grew. Where were the great ships that darkened the stars? Where the flying trains? Where the lights of the vast cities? Where the many, many human beings? He could not conceive how humanity had fallen from the glory of the Penultimate Age to this bleak emptiness. Had he been pulled somehow into a parallel world, some infernal other dimension?

On the seventh day of wandering, he trudged into a human village, set between the forest and the start of a broad grassland. It was the first sign of human dwelling that he had yet seen. A few dozen dirty and leaning huts of graying wood, with thatched roofs turning black with rot, crowded around a street of knee-deep black mud. It stank of feces and rotting potatoes. Rain pissed down on everything. A few scraps of smoke tried to climb from crumbling chimneys and were beaten down by the cold shower.

He plodded slowly through the mud, falling twice and landing on his face in the filth, unwilling to stop his fall with his right hand. Some miserable women peered at him from under the leaking lees of their tottering homes, their gray faces pocked with disease, limp hair hanging over their rheumy and colorless eyes.

In the center of the village he stopped in horror. Before him, thrust into the mud, two thick beams roped together at their crossing formed an X. A huge gorilla, a female, with an oversized head, was spread out on it. Rusting stakes had been hammered through her wrists and ankles. As Hexus stared, confounded, she lifted her head and looked at him. He shrank back. He had assumed the gorilla was dead, but no, they had crucified a living, soulburdened being.

Warily, a pack of men approached him, seeming to condense out of the mud and filth, gaining courage as they saw him stand in perplexity before the ape. Their long stringy hair and beards streamed with rain. They held clubs and knives and stones.

"Why have you done this?" Hexus called to them. "Why do you torture this being with this horrid, slow death?"

"Ya'oughten get gu'n!" one shouted. His open mouth held a few black, rotting teeth. The tongue was gray with disease, the red eyes two finger widths apart. Hexus the Stalker looked at him, both not recognizing and recognizing this degenerate form of human being.

Then Hexus held up the Stalker's hand and the eye of the god looked upon them.

The men gasped and shrank back.

"Sa monst'!" another man barked in their guttural demotic speech, terrified and also enraged by the eye. Hexus had not expected this. In the Penultimate Age, satyrs with tall, twisted horns walked the streets; Makine dragons perched on buildings or clung below bridges; soulburdened bonobos in silk suits sipped tea in cafes and made jovial, lewd offers—many of which were accepted—to the humans who passed. It was the right of any sentient being to remake herself as she saw fit. In that time, the world accepted the flourishing of dreams.

"Hear me!" Hexus called. But one of the men—a boy, really—threw a club spiked with angry shards of corroded metal. It hit the Stalker in the shoulder and cut deeply into him.

"Enough!" Hexus howled. That was the first time he reached out with his nascent powers and bent space. He bent it inside and around the pale boy who threw the club. His spine folded over with a loud crack, and then he split in two with a wet tearing sound.

A hail of clubs and knives flew at Hexus. Hexus rounded space so that they passed him without effect. Then he started breaking the worthless, cruel things, too decayed to deserve the name *human*. He screamed, as he slew them, the questions that had haunted him for days.

"Where are the Fathers and Mothers of the Theogenics Guild?" Seven men fell, their legs twisted off.

"Where are the towers of Theopolis?" A row of houses was crushed flat, grinding down into the foul mud the women and few feeble children hiding within them.

"Where do the Hekademon debate our spirit?" A shrieking man's head exploded as space expanded within him. As others looked on in terror, their own skulls burst.

"Where are the star-spanning ships? Where the music of ancient living machines?" A fire took to the last hut of the village and spread unnaturally, insanely fast down the row, burning the very air out of the homes as it consumed their rotting frames.

"Where falls the shadow of Yggdrasil?" The heads and limbs of five men fleeing into the rain behind the fires were neatly lopped off.

"Where are the bright horizons at which the sky-seizing cities part clouds?"

This last question he screamed alone. The town was empty of the dregs of men. All were dead. The unnatural fires turned the town bright and hot, filling it with sudden color as the light revealed the red blood that swirled into black puddles on the soggy earth. The stench of burnt hair overwhelmed the smell of excrement. Rain sizzled where it fell on the blazing ruins.

Hexus trudged back to the crucifix and pulled the spikes that held the gorilla. The great beast fell to the Earth, the coagulated blood in her fur mixing into the mire. With his limited, dawning power, Hexus healed her flesh and his own as best he could.

He bent over the beast then and whispered, imploring, "Are all men so diminished? Are they all turned evil and worthless? Is there nothing that remains of the glories of the Penultimate Age?"

Hexus learned later that the gorilla could not fathom the meaning of these questions. She was young and had survived in the red lands of the Filthealm by scavenging with a group of other soulburdened beasts. For her, humans were terrifying and vicious but never glorious. She did not even believe the stories that humans had made the ancient places.

She lowered her head in a show of submission.

Hexus turned away. There remained perhaps one place where his questions could be answered. He must go to the Oracle.

He pushed on through the mud, heading west.

Hexus took a horse from another degenerate, bending space around the baffled man long enough to mount and ride his steed away. He rode for the sea.

The ape followed him. First on foot, limping slightly on its pained limbs. Then it stole a horse somehow, and rode just within sight of the god. This vigor astounded Hexus. How the gorilla found the reserves of strength after its ordeal he could not conceive. He had left it tortured, bled, exhausted. But somehow it followed.

The ape drew closer at night, seeking, he suspected, the security of being near his fire. It skimmed the edge of his firelight when he made a camp, a black and silver shape just within his view. He called to it then. He implored it to join him by the fire, calling out in Common, then in Lifweg, then the language of his guild. It never answered, but remained ever silent.

Few humans dwelled in this landscape. The crowded world that Hexus had known was gone. After his first days of travel, he stumbled on another village. Soulburdened coyotes were nailed to fence posts on the edge of town, the back feet of each hammered together under a single spike. They were dead, and crows had fed on their eyes, but the posts were gnawed near the heads of the animals, revealing that they had been alive when they had been fixed there. He noticed then that each coyote had had its tongue cut out. He understood finally why the gorilla did not answer.

He stole food in that village, hardly palatable, and then passed on without allowing a single person to see him. He passed a village every day after that, for the next three weeks. Every human who saw him and saw the eye of the god fled in revulsion or threatened violence. He killed eight men and women in those weeks, in each case only after others had raised their hands in violence against him. These few remaining mortals, huddled together in odious ignorance, permitted nothing strange or mysterious.

He came finally to the sea. He skirted a small fishing village, with little weathered boats drawn up on the beach or floating in the shallows, their small tattered sails hanging limply on uneven masts. The gorilla was nowhere to be seen. He rode south on the beach, the horse's hooves thudding gently on the sand. At night he drew fish from the ocean and cooked them, relying upon the Stalker's knowledge of how to gut and roast the animals. During the day, he looked bitterly at the ruins that he passed and the straggling bands of humans that he had to repel.

After two weeks riding south, he came to the beginning of the great salt marshes. This at least was as he expected. He turned the horse away and continued on foot.

His arm began to burn with a searing pain. The Stalker's mortal flesh rebelled against its burden. The god's flesh was killing the Stalker, and Hexus could not heal the hurt. His power was too new, and he feared that it might even be something beyond the power of a numinous will to repair: this melding of the Aussersein, the otherworldly flesh of a god, and the mortal meat of a man. Sometimes the thoughts of the Stalker, weakly separate, raged at him. But nothing could be done. He did not yet see any way to save the Stalker, and his sympathy for this brute species of men waned. The Stalker was not near his conscience.

On the eighth morning of his walk, before him, on the horizon, rose a thin needle of a tower. He sat on the soft marshy ground and stared, overcome with relief that something remained.

The Temple of the First Oracle stood in the center of the bleak expanse of the great western salt marshes: a single spire rising up against an otherwise uninhabited horizon, with sea to the west, and tree-topped rolling hills to the east. Seagulls screeched at him as he toiled from one muddy mound to the next. Insects hovered over him, and flies gnawed at the rotting flesh of his right arm. Twice he stopped and killed all the biting bugs, exploding the space within the thousands that had gathered, so that they popped with a hissing sound like rain on hot stones. But he gave up even this and pushed ahead as well as he could.

The spire drew slowly but relentlessly closer.

By midday he came to the rocky island from which it rose. The Oracle stood on a circle of white stone. Hexus stumbled up onto the platform and hurried around to the front. The tall, narrow, seamless doors were closed. The inscription over the doors had worn away long before.

He had last been here as a boy—when had that been, he wondered? How many years? At that time, only the most powerful or worthy were allowed to question the Oracle. Scholars made pilgrimages from every school and city of Earth to stand before these doors and read the inscription above, waiting to be granted an audience within.

With his brother and sisters, the other Potentiates, he had pushed boldly in front of the pilgrims and walked inside. Shouting, laughing, they demanded wisdom of the Oracle. He had been then the proud culmination of the Penultimate Age of Homo Sapiens. The realization of the centuries of work and design by the Theogenics Guild and the Dark Engineers. He had been about to die and return to life a god. He had been about to redeem humankind by transcending it.

He called out now into the thin wind, shouting in the Stalker's alien, unfamiliar voice. No answer came, and the doors did not move. He shoved against them. Still no answer, and still the metal did not yield. He raised his hand, and shattered the bonds of corrosion that cemented together the hidden hinges and seams, turning the rust to liquid. The long invisible seams split. Wind pushed the doors wide. He staggered into the warm dark, pressed the doors closed, and laid his pack against them.

Ancient lights in the walls of the hexagonal room reluctantly took on a dim glow. The ceiling towered above. The metal clang of the closing doors echoed up into the dark distance. The interior walls were cracked and richly textured sandstone, just as he had remembered. The room was otherwise empty but for, in one corner, a sculpture of a whip-thin human figure, not much taller than a child, portrayed with one foot forward in a deep stride. The arms and legs of the statue were as thin as his own wrists, the head as narrow and flat as a hand. It stood on an uneven, pocked plinth, and the feet seemed to struggle to pull away from this base.

That was something new, he thought, wondering what it meant. But before he could approach it, a brown stone obelisk, as tall and broad as a man, rose from the featureless floor in the center of the room: the Voice of the Oracle.

"I am Hexus!" he called in the language of the Theogenics Guild. "Answer me, Oracle."

"I answer you, Hexus." The Oracle's voice, soft but clear, spoke back to him in his guild tongue.

"What is the year? The Metatheon Year?"

"Four thousand and sixty three."

Hexus collapsed backwards onto the floor. His mouth fell open. He sat there, his legs askew, staring dumbly at nothing.

Four thousand years! He had not been mad to recollect vaguely an endless perdition of featureless dark, an emptiness that he had endured while he somehow saw nothing. It had been not just years, not just centuries, but eons! And yet, only eons could explain the dolorous primitiveness he had witnessed, the complete disappearance of the triumphs of the Penultimate Age.

"What happened to the Thei?" he whispered.

"After the year two by the Theogenics Calendar, I was no longer tended. I can report only my own observations, and what is recorded in poems and songs that I have heard."

"Tell me."

"I begin with the *Theopolemein*," the Oracle answered, "song of the war between gods and men. It is composed in Common."

And the Oracle began to sing.

When the Oracle fell silent, Hexus curled up on the floor and wept. The epic poem was slander, the lies of the victors—of this he was certain. But some dim outline of what it claimed must be true: there had been a war against himself, and against his brothers and sisters. He had been one of the first vanquished in this struggle. He had fallen in battle against Wervool, greatest of the demigods. His siblings had taken their revenge and destroyed Wervool, but thereafter all the gods were bound or lost in other battles. The world was devastated. Men fell into brutishness.

He wept until he felt empty of tears, and then lay on his back and stared at the dark above, the back of his right hand lying on the Stalker's forehead, so that he looked with three eyes.

What should he do? This body was failing him (at this thought a pang pierced his gut, the terror and despair of what remained of the Stalker) and he would need to find some way to repair it. He needed to somehow be made whole again.

"Oracle, what remains of the Theogenics Guild?"

"I do not know."

"Does the Hand that Reaches still stand?"

"I do not know."

"Does Theopolis still exist?"

"That city has been renamed Disthea. It remains."

He stood. "I go there now."

"It appears that the makina will seek to prevent your leaving."

"What?" Hexus asked, startled. But then he saw the statue on the far side of the room lift one thin leg carefully forward and swing its arms in a slow stride. It took even, hard, clinking steps toward him.

"Makina," Hexus said. "I did not know that you are one of the Makine. Speak to me."

The metal form marched forward. Hexus backed away.

"I have searched for something that remains of the Penultimate Age. This Oracle and you are all that I have found. Speak."

The statue continued forward, gaining on him, until it was a pace away.

"Do you still dwell below the mountains?" Hexus implored. "Do you still grow on the heat of the Earth? What came of your ancient dream of Diaspora among the stars? Did your kin ascend to distant suns?"

The statue swung one arm at him with lightning speed, the limb bending fluidly like a whip. The heavy metal bit viciously into Hexus's left arm, seeking to wrap around him.

Hexus screamed in rage and twisted space, unwrapping the arm, then stumbled back, out of range of the makina's metal limbs.

"Is all the world a wasteland of idiotic violence now?" Hexus shouted.

He crouched over and pressed his palms together. Space bound around him in a tight, safe cocoon. He fell into darkness as light bent around it. The makina struggled to strike and bind him, flailing its limbs through the air. Hexus pushed through and past it, then turned, stepped back into space, reached into the volume inside the makina, and folded it around. The metal man exploded into tiny pieces of shining, writhing black and gray fragments. They fell clattering on the floor and squirmed about, seeking to rejoin together. Hexus walked among them, right palm held out and open, and with his mind crushed each in turn into a smoking slug of charred metal.

"Makine!" he shouted when finished. They would have eyes and ears here, he knew. If they had set a body here for some purpose, they would have others, probably winged eyes like bats clinging in the darkness above. They did everything redundantly.

"Makine!" he screamed in rage. But he did not know what else to say. In the Penultimate Age, the Makine had been distant, indifferent, an affront to humanity, but never a foe to the Theogenics Guild. Why would they attack him? All the world had fallen into madness. All who remained in it were wantonly murderous.

He burst open the doors and stepped out into the sunlight. The gorilla sat in the grass a wary distance from the Oracle, hunched over and chewing the stem of a reed. She blinked despondently as a relentless swarm of insects buzzed around her head, biting her, even flying into her eyes.

"Come here!" he demanded. And this time the voice of Hexus sounded imperious and deadly. The gorilla dropped the stem and approached, her head low. She bowed at his feet.

"I will give you a tongue again, soon, when I learn how," he told it. He waved his hand and killed all the insects that bit at her. "And I will make it so that no man ever kills the soulburdened again. Do you understand? I am sickened by this stupid filthy time. I will bring back the Penultimate Age, and then free my siblings and reforge the Dawn of the Ultimate Age. And when humanity has ascended, I will give the Earth to the soulburdened."

He looked out toward the south, where lay the city once called Theopolis, which had been his home when mortal.

"And you shall be my first champion. I name you Apostola."

The gorilla just stared.

"Come with me."

He started walking south. Toward Disthea.

After one day on foot, they came to an ancient road, still gleaming and smooth, though crowded on each side with forest. They stole two more horses from what looked to be merchants—Hexus did not bother to hide himself or bind the men, but just knocked them flat and without a word mounted one horse, and instructed Apostola to mount the other. They rode on, hooves clacking on the road.

There were more villages here, lining the highway. It surprised Hexus to see that some civilization survived here in the south. The people were not sick with pollution. Some children ran in the orderly fields of corn. The homes were upright and square and painted bright colors. He passed the villages without attempting to hide himself or the ape, filled still with his determined rage. But though people stared at the gorilla, they made no threats. These people, Hexus realized, must be accustomed to the occasional traveler, even a traveler accompanied by one of the soulburdened.

On the fourth day they came to a small city crowded against the coast. They stopped on the top of a hill overlooking the town. The sky turned a dark purple, reflected in the still darker sea, as the sun set. The path of the gleaming road was visible into the distance, lit gold in the low rays of the waning day. The road went through the town and then out over the sea and continued into the horizon. They could discern in the growing dark the white towering legs of a bridge that held the road above the water. Hexus sat on the horse and waited, unmoving, his arm out before him, until the daylight was gone. He peered out over the sea, expectant.

And then he shouted once with joy. Far out, where the road touched the horizon, he could see a dim glow in the water.

"Lights still burn in Theopolis," he told the gorilla. "Something remains, Apostola. Something remains."

They rode down. In the small coastal city, they dismounted and walked slowly, leading the horses. People passed them at a respectful distance, but did not approach. Hexus began to hope that there might be more of civilization left than he had come to fear. Perhaps in this south there remained a few pockets of something of the great ages.

He searched for a small place with few people to resist his will, where they could get food and rest until the morning. They walked close to the dark walls of buildings, looking into the windows of homes and inns and shops as they passed. A few people, then none, walked the street. It grew unusually quiet. The gorilla sniffed warily. The smell of sewage rose from cracks along the side of the street.

They came upon two dark buildings, with shattered windows in the sills of which filthy gray shards of glass stood like teeth. As they passed the alley between the buildings a faint wet crack sounded out behind Hexus. He turned. The gorilla stood frozen before him, eyes gaping, and she suddenly bellowed, appalled and surprised. The rusting metal point of a crude spear thrust straight through her chest. Hexus opened his mouth to howl in rage but something grabbed his hair from behind. A sharp, thin pain cut across his throat. He felt warm blood splash over his hands.

The gorilla fell on her face, and he fell back against the wall. Two albino men—twins—strode before them. One, with long white hair, immediately began to search the saddles of the horses. The other, totally hairless, stood looking down at Hexus, and wiped on a dirty cloth the knife he had used to cut the Stalker's throat.

No, Hexus tried to growl. I will not begin again. I will not lose all my postmortal memories and begin again.

But no voice came out. His windpipe was severed. Blood gurgled and frothed from his slit throat. Black dizziness swept over him—he'd suffered a fatal blood loss—but the will of the god kept the body moving. He put his hand to his neck. The blood splashed over the god's eye but the throat wound closed roughly. He rose. He struck the man with the knife to the ground with a thought. The knife clattered across the road.

Hexus fought the black tide of unconsciousness that pounded at the Stalker's mortal body. He managed to set his feet firmly apart, and faced the other man.

The albino pillaging the saddles turned and saw Hexus. He put one boot on the gorilla that lay on the ground between them and yanked the spear out of her back, then aimed the wet point at the god.

Hexus tore the clothes from the man, then sent the spear flying. He grabbed space in and around the man and curled it over, pressed it, reforged the topology of the human body. The man hissed and struggled to scream as his flesh bent and twisted. His bones snapped like dry sticks. His skin was stretched into a broad disk with his face in the center, and then folded over to form a ball, and grafted crudely to itself with a thick, long scar. The mouth was driven through the flesh, making a hole. Eyes, nose, ears, limbs, anus, white hair, fingers, and nails had been stuffed into the interior of a hollow globe of flesh with a single orifice, ringed with splintered teeth. The fleshy white sphere of skin rolled on the ground, helpless, alive, seething and twisting. With unbounded horror and agony, two red eyes peered through inverted lips at Hexus.

Hexus found his voice.

"I damn you, waste of a man," he growled. "I damn you."

He reached over and closed the wounds of the gorilla and then, with a thought, hammered her heart back into motion. Then he toppled over, unable to keep the Stalker standing.

The other albino had found his knife, and he rushed now at Hexus. Hexus lifted his arm and this attacker froze, dropped his knife, and fell to his knees.

Hexus placed his right hand on the head of his killer.

"I'll not forget," he whispered. And then he reshaped the killer's brain. In his rush he had to bludgeon his mind into the killer. The effect was destructive and weakening, but he put his memories inside the aching skull of the screaming man. Then he clasped hands with him, and—

. . . the eye shifted.

Both the Stalker and the killer moaned.

And then Hexus stood and looked down at the dying Stalker.

He remembered the most of his awakening and journey. He had moved. He had transmogrified the brain of the killer and moved his divine flesh.

A thousand possibilities exploded upon him, with the realization that he could move his soul like this. He had indefinite time now, to find a way to be whole again. If necessary, he could move again, and again.

"Die in peace, Stalker," Hexus said.

The Stalker looked at the gaping hole in his right palm. Then his life faded.

Hexus looked down at his new, alien hands, and at the god's eye in its new place. He had expected a seething riot of passions inside the killer's mind, but found only a simple, unreflective being there, without conscience and without any concern for what might happen the day after tomorrow. Incurious, even more ignorant than the Stalker, it had lived as a simple, stupid animal with speech. The lowest soulburdened dog was wiser.

The killer resisted Hexus. Not in any subtle way, but with a simple brute redirection of energies. Hexus could easily fight him, but it robbed his motions of any grace, making him twitch and twist as he corrected the body continuously. And the fast violence of the transfer of memories had damaged the brain. His limbs trembled as the mind struggled to remain coherent.

His host's brother rolled a bit and emitted a moan. Hexus kicked the suffering sphere.

"This dark age of men is over," he spat. His new voice was strange, different, thin and weak. He felt the killer within him writhe in horror at what Hexus had done to its brother.

"I will remake this whole world. Your kind is soon to go extinct."

He levitated the unconscious gorilla onto her saddle. Then he rose into the air and settled down onto the other horse. They rode off into the dark, toward the city of gods.

"I must become whole again," he said to the night, to himself, to the future in which he hoped his sibling gods would look back through time and see him at this monumental moment. "No feat is too daring or costly to make this so. No act too cruel. For only a god can redeem these meaningless remnants of humanity. Only a god can save us."

CHAPTER

33

"Did you bring me food?" Sar asked the young engineer. "And water? As I asked?"

"Yes." The boy eyed the bears lounging indifferently nearby. Three of them sprawled on their backs among thick black power cables. One looked lazily over at him and scratched its stomach while licking its black lips hungrily.

Sar and the bears were in the high room of the power station, set against the crystal wall not far from the northern switchback, which rose to the docks above. Turbines hummed behind them. The Hieroni had done a crude job of disabling this station, hacking away with fierce weapons at the heavy cables that fed power out into the city. With an afternoon of work, and five Engineers helping her, Sar had repaired the cables under the suspicious gaze of wolves and bears. Then Sar had sent the Engineers away, and worked alone now.

Below this chamber, out in the streets, the sea water had flooded only a few feet before most of the citizens of Disthea had surrendered, understanding then that they were trapped. Those who did not surrender died, as regrouped soulburdened forces focused on the holdouts. The battle was over. Only a few skirmishes continued. The opened pumping stations were all now sealed, so that no more sea water poured into the city, and the turbines that pumped water from Disthea were humming again. Just one day after this victory, the soulburdened were starting to relax. Sar's guard had shrunk from a dozen beasts to three bears now, each barely able to keep his eyes open.

"Don't mind them," Sar told the boy. "They have their commands from the god."

The boy looked unconvinced, but he handed two tightly wrapped parcels to Sar. "Why do you need them wrapped like this?" He handed her a larger bundle. "And why a coat?"

Sar ignored his questions. "Tell me. What did you see when you rode up? Airships on the wall?"

He nodded. "Three airships. Two parked on this building, the other tethered to the wall." He looked up at the distant ceiling, as if he might see the ships through it. "They're idling the engines of the ship on the wall. It looks like they're ready to go."

"They are," Sar said. She had paid close attention to the idle talk of the soulburdened around her. These three ships that would pursue the boy were going to take off any hour now. "Tell the Elders—don't bother with the Creator—tell Pround that I will not be back."

"But—"

She held up a hand to silence the boy. "Not back anytime soon. Maybe later. Maybe not. And tell him—this is very important—that Garapan is a traitor, a member of the Hieroni. I saw him with Vark."

The boy's eyes grew round with astonishment, but he only nodded.

Sar put the packs of food and the folded coat into a satchel and slung it over her shoulder. She stood erect to her small height. "You stay here, below, with the other Engineers. Help them finish. Wait till the beasts calm down before you attempt to return to Uroboros. It is still too dangerous to walk the streets. I would not have made you come here if my need had not been great."

"Elder," the boy began. "Great teacher...." His voice choked with emotion.

Sar looked at him. He had been a good student, this boy had. Not a great inventor, but he had passion and he wanted to do things as well as they could be done. That was better than Sar could say for most of their guild in this day. She understood what her leaving would mean to this boy—there was not another teacher in Uroboros with her dedication. She had been his mentor and guide, and now she was going to leave him alone.

She sighed. "I too do not want to leave. And I'm not certain I do the right thing—there is much here that I should attend to. Our guild, our students, the rebuilding of Disthea. You and your studies. Making peace with the soulburdened."

The apprentice frowned at the bears, unconvinced that this last task needed doing.

"Apprentice," Sar said. "There are times when you have to act, because you are sure that no other is able to do what you can. Now is such a time for me." She looked over at the bears. "We have been foolish. I did not know that the soulburdened had such anger, such hatred for humankind. They must have suffered much."

"Disthea is an open city," the boy protested. "Any of them was welcome here."

"Yes, but I think none of these would understand that. They suffered, and we did nothing. And so this is what happens to us. Remember that. Young Engineers like you must find a fix for these problems. Not knowing a problem lurks out there is no help when the problem breaks things down on you. Ignorance is a worthless kind of innocence."

She put a hand on his shoulder and nodded.

"Thank you, teacher," he whispered, his voice breaking with emotion.

Sar watched him trudge dispiritedly to the exit, look back at her, and then close the door behind himself.

She shrugged the pack, pulled the other strap over her other shoulder, and then walked straight at the bears.

"Move," she told the lazing beasts. "I need to check the cables above. I've got to climb that ladder."

The bears growled but shuffled aside, dragging their bellies, their black claws scratching the floor stones. Without sparing them another glance, Sar seized the narrow ladder that ascended to the dizzying height of the distant ceiling. She began to climb.

After a dozen rungs, one of the bears grunted. Sar looked down and saw the bear stand and look up the ladder. The bear had second thoughts now, as it wondered whether it should have stopped Sar, maybe interrogated her. Rust, scraped off the rung by her boot, fell into the beast's eyes. It grunted again, blinking, and sat down, rubbing its face, unsure of what to do.

"No more looking down," Sar told herself. The bears would not be able to climb after her, even if they realized their mistake. She had noted how they struggled on even the shortest ladder. And besides, the bears were already lying back down, sated and tired. Just as she'd hoped, indecision resulted ultimately in inactivity for these slow beasts.

She fixed her eyes on the distant ceiling, and climbed.

At the top of the ladder, Sar lifted the hatch door in the ceiling a crack and peeked over the roof. As the apprentice had said, two airships were moored atop the station. One floated high from its mooring line, its fans idling. The other sat on the wall, tied down by eight cables surrounding the great inflated body. She could see bears in the ship above, but the front of the cabin of the ship closer to her was turned away. There was no one on the roof itself.

Sar waited while the other ship drifted until it faced away. Then she clambered up and hurried under the shadow of the ship that was tied down. In the back of the cabin were four low doors. These opened onto storage compartments and a cargo hold. Sar opened each and found one door blocked by only a few boxes. She slid these aside, threw her pack within, and then followed it, climbing into the low space. She pulled the door closed and rearranged the boxes in the dark until they covered the door.

In the front of the storage space was the escape hatch up into the cabin above. She stayed as far from that as she could. She knew she would stink of human to a soulburdened beast. But they should expect the airships to smell of men.

A few minutes later, a shout and growl sounded nearby. Clawsteps went noisily over her. The ship tilted, as mooring lines cut loose, and then it bounced up into the air.

Soon it would leave. She would wait them out, until they got into the air, and then show what a descendent of Threkor—demigod, greatest of Creators, and fiercest enemy of the Younger Gods—could do.

CHAPTER

34

C hance jumped when the Guardian suddenly shouted, "Turn on the engines!"

"Why?" Wadjet growled. She did not move, but stood by the cabin.

The Guardian pointed. "There. Land. On the edge of the sea there. Lethebion! These whales have waited too long. We can make a run for it, to the island."

A long morning had passed with choppy seas but halting wind. The sails were up, and they sagged and then snapped as wind came and went. The skysail remained stowed. They did not talk. After the previous evening and Chance's story, each of them had been quiet, meditating on his own thoughts.

Chance went now to the bow and peered over the waves. He could see nothing on the horizon. "Is, is that where the Well is?"

"No," Thetis whispered, coming to his side.

"But there is an airship on Lethebion," the Guardian said. "Hidden by my guild."

"Eons ago!" Wadjet scowled.

"Yes, long ago. Out here, we wait for the whales to attack. Run for the island, while they dither. They will not cross the Sæwall, the guarding ring."

Without assenting, Wadjet arose and went below deck. Chance thought, uncertainly, that she might mean to spurn the Guardian, to go below deck and lay on her bunk. But instead in a moment the boat shuddered, and then prowed forward. Wadjet climbed languidly up on the deck and got behind the wheel.

"There," the Guardian said. "There! As fast as she'll go."

"I see it," Sarah shouted, as land came just visible to a human eye. Seth came up by her side, looking warily down into the inscrutable blue depths of the ocean.

"Ah!" he barked. A whale, huge and gray, was rising toward them, a terrible pale mountain of beast looming out of the blue abyss.

"The whales attack!" he barked. "Lie down!"

The whale struck the ship hard, lifting the prow up and then tilting the boat onto its side so that water splashed over the deck and the boom of the sail swung over and slapped the waves. Chance and Sarah had grabbed the gunwale at Seth's command. Seth grabbed at Chance's leg and clenched to his pants, sliding away. Thetis slid down into the water that crested one side of the ship, but was caught by one post of the gunwale. Saltwater soaked her robes. Mimir, the Guardian, and Wadjet somehow stayed afoot as the ship lilted back to an even keel.

"Keep on course!" the Guardian commanded. He ran to the back of the ship and seized a heavy rope coiled in the stern. One end he tied to a bolt eye on the splintered deck. He twisted the other end around his arm and dove into the water just as the ship was tossed high a second time.

Again, it seemed that each of them might be thrown off ship, as it bounced and settled back. They had not yet gotten a good grip before they were nearly thrown again. A wave tossed over them.

Thetis coughed harshly on salt water. Seth, wet through now, cursed and tried hard to cling to Chance with one paw, the other slipping over a line from the sail tackle, his blunt fingers not gripping well and his strong teeth not yet in reach to bite the line.

"I'm losing my grip!" Thetis cried.

The rope that the Guardian had clutched paid out and then jerked taut with a strong snap.

A dull, distant vibration—too low to be a sound—shot through them. Chance lifted his head to see a shimmering ripple explode across the surface of the water, seeming to emanate from their boat. It cast up endless drops of water that bounced free from the surface of the sea and then fell back, rippling. As the agitation spread and dissipated, Chance saw first one, then another of the whales float to the surface, lilting and drifting. Six in total rose.

Then there was silence. They waited for another attack, but none came. The Guardian pulled himself back up onto the ship, climbing the thick rope hand over hand as water streamed off of his stony body and splashed off of his sea-heavy clothes.

"What did you do?" Chance called.

"I howled under the waves—deafening them. They are blind now, for they sound out the world. They'll be lost, but only for minutes. Speed now, speed for Lethebion."

Wadjet leaned over the wheel, as if she meant to press the boat forward.

Seth shook off the salt water, spraying all of them, and then hurried to the back of the boat, his nails clicking on the hard deck, to watch the sea behind them warily.

The rest of them crowded by the bow, looking toward Lethebion, the island of lost life. Mountains were coming visible as they sped forward. And then, a white line beneath the black peaks seemed to sprout from the sea as they approached.

"Are those...waves breaking on a cliff?" Thetis asked.

"No," the Guardian said. "No, that is the white Sæwall."

The wall grew as they leapt forward again and again off of the choppy waves. The whales had not yet regrouped, or at least not soon enough to catch up with them, as the wall rose, first to obscure the mountains beyond, and then to swallow their view.

"Plume!" Seth barked. "The wa-wa-wa-whales come!"

The boat slowed.

"Do not slow!" the Guardian shouted at Wadjet. "Head for that gray arch before us!"

"The wall!" Wadjet said.

"Drive forward. That is a gate. It shall open."

Wadjet growled but did as he asked.

The others shrank instinctively back, as it seemed the boat shot toward a collision that would shatter the hull and drown them where the waves crashed loudly against the hard and ancient white wall. As they approached, they could see now the green bottom of it, where the constant reach of the waves had moistened algae. The Guardian raised his arms, but not till it seemed already too late.

"*Sæwall!*" his voice thundered out, otherworldly, shaking their bones. "*Geryme for Treow!*"

A crack appeared under the gray arch, in the center of the section of wall before them, between two spires. It was hardly wide enough for the boat as they shot toward it. The sea was slightly higher on the outside of the wall, and the rushing current grabbed the ship and pulled them forward, steering them evenly through the gap. The sides of the ship scraped loudly as it squeezed through the opening.

"*Betymæth for Treow!*" the Guardian shouted. And with a tremendous creaking, as if the thin doors were about to fold and shatter, the two partitions slowly closed against the mounting sea, shuddered and ground loudly as they pressed together, and then were silent.

Wadjet cut the engines. The ship drifted forward, rocking. They floated in a wind band of clear water, before a beach of white sand.

The black tower cast a shadow over the surf. Behind it, dark forest scaled a steep hill.

"That's it," Wadjet said. "It will be days before we can use the engines again."

"There." The Guardian pointed at the black tower. "Aegweard. The guard tower. We go there."

CHAPTER

35

C hance watched as the Guardian pressed both his hands on a black stone at the base of the round watchtower. The windows and doors of the tower had long ago rotted away, but much of the stone of the tower stood strong and straight. Thick vines trailing drooping bright leaves covered the black masonry. Small, colorful birds flitted among the leaves, crying strange songs.

Chance waited behind the Guardian, cradling his broken arm. He knew the expression on the Guardian's face. He had seen it in his own father's face. Many Elders of the Purimen said the house plot of the Kyrien Vincroft was ancient. Some house or another had stood there since centuries and centuries before, long before the War Against the False Gods or before even the Age of the Guilds. His father had once taken Chance and Paul into the home's cellar. The cool, dark room, with walls and a floor of earth and stone, smelled of mold and damp soil and fermenting wine. Rows of small barrels filled the dim basement, leaving only narrow aisles in which to walk. The flagstones of the floor, and the cobbles of the wall, were all of mixed sizes and colors, the remnants of a dozen broken prior foundations. Their father had pointed at a stone in the corner below the parlor, scratched and pale gray and round, so that the walls over it did not meet squarely but seemed to roll away into the earth.

Paul, impatient, had fidgeted with stray scraps of cork, twisting them into bits, as their father had spoken.

"This stone is the oldest of the vincroft. It was here under the first house, when men were young and all of them were Trumen and the world had not seen the Guilds or their War of False Gods. It lay here, holding up one house after another, for many hundreds of years. It holds up your house. Think on that, like The Book teaches Purimen: how things pass and how little remains. Build the strongest foundation you can, but don't expect it to last forever. Don't even expect it to last long. Only the True God lasts forever."

Chance had reached out reverently and set his hand beside his father's on the stone. It was cool and round like the stones smoothed from tossing in the river, but it bore a few deep rough gouges from human industry. They pressed their hands against it in silence a moment, until Paul said, with a volume that made Chance jump a little, "Can we go now?"

Chance looked up at the Guardian.

"You were dreaming," the Guardian said. He actually smiled at Chance.

"Remembering my father."

The Guardian nodded.

"It is good for you," Chance said. "To see your . . . home again."

The Guardian hesitated, as if reluctant to admit it, but then said, "Sooth, Puriman."

The Guardian peered out at the sea. They had beached the ship in soft white sand that collected by a broken stone pier, and then waded ashore through warm clear water up onto a scalding beach. The tower stood on black rocks above the bright shore. Behind the tower, a riot of forest rose up through steep hills and beyond into mountains. One steep mountain started up out of the sea not more than a mile to the west, and waves broke on its cliff face.

"How much time do you think we have?" Chance asked.

Seth and Sarah climbed up next to them. Mimir stayed down at the shore, staring up at the skies. Thetis sat on a stone near Mimir, cleaning her shoes and watching the makina.

"A few days," the Guardian said.

"Is that enough?"

The Guardian looked up into the forest. "If the airship is whole. We should be able to get it working, and be gone, before the foul god can get here."

Chance looked down at Wadjet's ship, leaning to one side where it was beached. Wadjet sat atop the cabin, elbows on knees, chin on her palms. She was bitter over this plan to leave her boat in this place, and seemed to be weighing whether to stay here with it.

"You should be safe here," the Guardian told Chance. "I will see of the airship. Stay by the tower. Do not wander far into the forest. There were beasts here that could swallow a man in a bite, long ago. Perhaps they still live and hunt here."

Chance nodded. The Guardian disappeared in a gray blur.

There was a flat platform a few paces away, at the base of the tower, with a low wall on one side that looked over the beach. Chance walked over and sat on a smooth rock beside the tower, shaded by a few stubborn trees that had cracked through the tight spaces between the stones. A cacophony of bird songs fell over them here, from the forest behind. His shoes felt uncomfortable—they had waded ashore bare foot, on Wadjet's advice, but Chance had put his shoes back on with wet and sand-encrusted feet. He took them off and set them in the sun to dry. Then he leaned far back against the tower and rested his arm in its sling on his stomach. Seth lay down beside him, tongue lolling in the heat.

"No-no-nothing to eat here, I suppose," the coyote whined.

Sarah put her hands on her sword hilts. "I'll look around. Maybe there's something growing that we'll recognize."

"Don't go in the forest," Chance protested.

She laughed. "I heard the Guardian. I'll stay along the edge. Or down at the beach."

She left them. They sat a long while, staring at the waves lapping the beach, and at Mimir standing like a statue. It was the first time Seth and Chance had been alone since Seth had brought him clothes. That had been little more than two weeks before, but it seemed long ago. Chance looked down at his pants, which had been blue and crisp when Seth brought them to him, and were now faded and stained white with salt.

Have I aged so much as these clothes? he wondered. Worn and colored with these weeks, as if the days had been years?

Seth sat, chin on his crossed paws, studying Chance.

"I was wondering," Chance said, "how much I've changed. You don't seem to have changed at all."

"I'm thi-thinner," Seth complained.

Chance laughed.

They were silent again a while, as Chance gathered the courage to overcome his discomfort and say what he wanted to say.

"Seth. I'm.... When we were home—I mean, at the lake. Sometimes, I wasn't—I didn't treat you well."

Seth flicked an ear. "No, no."

"But.... I yelled sometimes. Or bossed you around. Or didn't share my food."

Seth lifted his tail slightly. A coyote shrug. "Pups are rough."

Chance felt the hint of tears. So easily forgiven.

"Still...."

"You are my friend," Seth added, as if that finished it.

There was that. He had not treated the coyote with the respect he deserved, as an equal. But he had not treated him as the Purimen wanted. Seth had been the one instance in which Chance most obviously would not follow Puriman rules. He had never stopped being Seth's friend, and had never asked the coyote to go away. And Sirach, the old prophet he admired, had told him he was right in this.

"Some Purimen misunderstand the meaning of purity. Perhaps Seth is more pure than any of them," Sirach had said, with characteristic provocation. "And some Puriman misunderstand the meaning of sacrifice. Perhaps none sacrifices more than Seth."

Chance nodded now. "Pups can be rough."

A strange, flat fish swam like a bird through the shallow, clear waters before Wadjet's boat. Chance watched it circle about and then disappear into the deeper water.

"You've always been the best friend I ever had, Seth."

"You, mine."

"What will you do if—I mean, when this is over? Will you come back to the lakes?"

"For a while. See you-you-you get denned. Eat good food."

Chance laughed. "You'll have a place at our table. We'll feast."

Seth slapped his tail. "Purimen will lo-lo-love this."

"I want roast chicken," Chance said. "And potatoes. And kale. And a juneberry pie. And four bottles of cold Ries."

"And eggs," Seth added.

"Good. And eggs."

"And chicken."

"I already said chicken," Chance told him.

"More chicken."

Chance laughed again. Then he looked Seth in the eyes. "But you'll settle in Disthea?"

Seth nodded. "Become Hekademon. I'd li-li-like to find a mate. Have pups of my own."

Seth deserves that, Chance thought. But he asked, "But you can visit, sometimes, even if you go back to Disthea?"

"The way is long."

"I think," Chance said. "That everything will be different now. Even if we stop the false god. I'd like to work at that, Seth. Talk to the soulburdened of the Sabremounts. Sirach had told the Purimen long ago that this needed to be done, and he was right."

"There will be ma-ma-much work to, to do. My guild would do it. Some of it."

"Maybe you and I can do some of it. There are perhaps not many friends like us. Soulburdened and human."

"True," Seth said. "Perhaps even none."

Chance nodded. The mention of the Hekademon guild reminded him of a question that had bothered him much. "So, how did you... I mean, why were you watching me?"

"My guild a-a-asked it of me."

"Why?"

Seth flicked his tail to indicate uncertainty. "Did not trust the Mothers," he speculated.

Can't blame them for that, Chance thought. "And, what does your guild do? What do they believe?"

"They study. They do little. They do when they must. Most times, they study."

Because it was Seth, and Chance trusted the coyote not to treat him as an ignorant country boy, he asked the question that was most natural to him.

"Do they worship...." And he swallowed the words *one, true*. "Do they worship God?"

"Some do. Most don't."

"So, you don't believe in a supreme God?" Chance tried to keep the disappointment out of his voice but he could not.

"To, to, to become a Hekademon, you first must see that you do not know—you, you do not know much, or any, any-thi-thing. I don't know, Cha-Chance."

"Is that why you became a Hekademon?"

Sarah walked up to them then, shaking her head to say *Nothing found*. She sat next to Chance, pulled off her boots, and began to shake out sand.

"Is that why you became a Hekademon?" Chance repeated. "Because you felt doubts?"

"No. I became a Hekademon because...it was my de-de-destiny. I was found by a Hekademon. My master. Ma-master of my guild."

"Why is that destiny?" Chance asked.

Seth tilted his head, hesitating. Then he croaked, "I will tell you. When I was a pup, three wild dogs hunted me-me into an alley one night. Degenerates, ha-half-souled. They had bitten my legs as I fled. My blo-blood was red on their yellow teeth. I was going to da-die there. Then a light a-appeared above them, and also a stra-stra-strange darkness. Mixed, where the night sky ca-cracked. The dogs fled in fear. I would have fled too, ba-ba-but I was cornered and my legs were hurt.

"Something came out of the light. It said, 'It is good to see you alive, Hekademon.' I never forgot that wa-wa-wa-word—'Hekademon'—though it meant no-no-nothing to me then. When my master found me, a year later, I ye-yelped when he told me of his guild."

Sarah put her hand on Chance's shoulder. They listened to the water lap the beach for a moment, thinking on the coyote's words. Finally, Sarah said, "A strange story. What does it mean?"

"Don't know." Seth growled. "But it was not a bad thing. Not bad. It spo-spo-spoke with love. I had never heard before love. I'd ha-had a hard life before. But it spoke with love. A figure of black and white, blinding light and blind bla-bla-black dark. It healed me, made me strong. And then it left."

Chance shivered under Sarah's hand. She looked at him and saw him turn pale.

"The fa-fa-first great philosopher had a demon," Seth continued. "A voice that spoke to him. Perhaps this is my demon."

Sarah watched Chance closely, but neither he nor the coyote spoke again.

✛

The Guardian ran up through the forest above Aegweard. Above the steep hills of Lethebion behind the black tower was a great plateau, ringed by forest and mountains. He circled the plateau by following the steep slopes that surrounded it. Birds scattered in bright rainbow flocks as he passed. Black howler monkeys growled at each other, indifferent to the ancient gray being that ran by below. Giant centipedes changed course, too late, after he had already leapt over them.

But the Guardian saw none of the most dangerous, most ancient beasts of the forest—the neoAlbertosaurs, the fierce, knee-high neoVelociraptors, the giant bears. This was as he had expected— the place in the forest of the giant hunters had been fragile, carefully shaped by the Lifweg while the guild had lived. But when Lethebion had been attacked and the guild members all murdered, that had ended. Also, it was said that human hunters in airships had killed all the greatest beasts from the air. If any survived those hunts, then after the war most would surely have starved because there was too little to eat.

The Guardian ascended to the plateau, bursting out of the dense brush of the forest edge into a herd of dwarf elephants. They tossed their trunks in anger, stepping backwards, as he shot through them.

So something of the ancients live still in the plain, he thought.

Packs of small horses turned aside as he raced across the grass. In the distance, he could see a herd of camel gazelle.

At the base of the mountains, where the grasses just died away and scrub covered the rising ground, he found a watering hole. He stopped a dozen paces away. Another nervous pack of skittering tiny horses sneaked drinks from the muddy pool, turning aside almost as soon as their noses rippled the surface.

The Guardian turned in place, carefully watching the bush. And there: there was what he sought. Two eyes, blazing green, crouched in dark bushes nearby. Then another two eyes in the bush beside that one. He turned aside, circling quickly through the bush, and appeared with a snap of his cloak behind the terrorbirds.

The two wingless beasts leapt up in alarm, turning on him. The Guardian did not move. They rose to their full height, as tall as the Guardian's reach, and when puffed with alarm they seemed just as massive, with huge black talons large and strong enough to cut clear through a man's chest. Their feathers were dark green, like the grasses at their feet. The green irises of their eyes flickered, pulsing with interest and concern as they watched him, tilting their heads, shrieking with indignation and shaking their huge ax-beaks.

The Guardian felt a mix of emotions. This was his accomplishment, in part: it was a wonder that these great beasts lived again, millions of years after their passing, and four thousand years after his guild had remade them. And that they had lived through the war and the decline meant they would likely live on for many years more.

But these were also the greatest threat to the Puriman and the others.

One of the two birds, the female of the pair, took one strutting step toward him, a feint, before leaping back. The Guardian did not move. It tried again. The male did the same. Finally, emboldened, the female leapt forward and struck him hard with her huge, square beak. It cut at his chest like a hatchet—and bounced off, the Guardian's unyielding rock-hard flesh deflecting the blow.

The terrorbird fell back, stunned. It had struck forcefully, expecting soft flesh, and taken a knock as bad as if it had attacked a tree. It wobbled as it found its foothold again. The male shrieked at him, making another feint, but this feint was obviously meant not to prepare for attack but to distract the Guardian while the female retreated.

"Let that teach you," he said. Let the birds believe that humans are no better food than stone.

"Teach you!" the bird shrieked.

The Guardian started. He knew the birds were mimics, but he did not know their abilities were so good. But then, in the days of his guild, they had not stood beside the terrible predators and talked.

The birds fled noisily into the brush, their great talons tossing up torn clods of dirt.

He sighed. He would have to warn the others about these birds, and require that they move only in a large group.

Time to check the airship. The Guardian looked up at the mountain, toward the steep valley, and its shrouded cave, where his guild had secreted an airship thousands of years before.

"Erd," he whispered. "I hope you saw to this with the same care you saw to all other things."

CHAPTER

36

The engineering master Sar set about reinventing the cargo hold once the airship took off.

She was fortunate. She could tell by the footsteps that five, perhaps six, stumbling bears commanded this ship. They were noisy and incurious. She had feared the possibility that a wolf, with keen smell, or a soulburdened raccoon, with its insatiable curiosity, or—worst case—that the godling himself might be on this ship. But it was not so.

She took the small light from her bag and shone it about the cramped cargo hold. It was just high enough for her to crawl, and thunderously noisy, and cold. It was not the way she would have preferred to travel.

"Well," she mumbled, "I'm stuck with it now."

She crawled slowly about the cargo space, checking each feature. Rough rivets, never sanded down, dotted the floor, and a few of them scratched her hands, or caught at her robe and made tiny tears in the cloth. She cursed, and tried to aim her hands and knees in the spaces between the metal snags.

After a brief exploration, she dragged the airship patch kit from its closet and used the extra patching fabric to partition off a corner of the cargo hold, to hide her scent and muffle any sound she made. She found a bolt in a horizontal stretch of the ship's water line that she could loosen, while holding a pail beneath it to catch the leaking drops, so that she could collect a drink. She pried open one of the emergency vents and then tied a wire to it, so that with a twist of the wire she could open the outer vent door. This provided a handy way to relieve herself and also allowed her to stick her head outside to track the ship's progress.

They were over the sea, one of three airships heading north. The Guardian and the boy had left in a boat, as she knew from the reports of other Engineers. The boy had several days' lead, so with luck, she figured that they would catch up with the boat only as it came to the shores of the northland, nearly under the shadow of Yggdrasil, in about a week. Her food might just last that long without too much discomfort. After all, at her age, she did not eat much. She would be all a-cramp, however, after a week of lying and crawling in the dark. Already her legs were spotted with sores and bruises, and her thighs trembled with the strain of crawling.

"Well," she told herself. "There's no sense trying to fix what you can't fix. Fix what you can."

Seven days. She had told the apprentice not to bring her any weapon, because she was afraid of what would happen to the boy if he had been stopped by some soulburdened pack while bringing her the stores. So she had nothing but a few tools and a minimum of food.

Over her head, one of the bears roared at another.

"I'm an inventor," she mumbled. "A creator of Threkor's line. I need only invent a way to fell the other two airships and to steal this one. Simple enough. Simple enough. Time to get to work."

She closed her eyes and began to plan.

✤

Sar awoke with a start in the night. She had worked hard for hours, removing parts of the airship, taking them over by the vent so that she could use the sunlight to see her hands as she worked on them, before either replacing them or setting them aside for future use.

But as the sunlight faded, she laid her tools aside, wrapped herself in the coat the apprentice had brought her, and slept, wanting to conserve her lamp.

Now she awoke and knew immediately that something was wrong. The bears were louder.

No, she realized. The bears were not louder. Everything else was quieter. The hum of the ship's engines had softened, become less strained. The fabric of the airship hull did not snap and vibrate, as if the wind moved with them, and so stood still around the ship. And before there had been a depth to the roar of the engines—the echo, perhaps, of the propellers' din off the sea. That was gone now.

She crawled to the vent and, working by touch, opened it. Very little wind blew inside as the panel came away. She hung her head down. The waxing sliver of crescent moon cast a thin gray reflection on the sea.

The sea looked strange: fearfully close, as if magnified, and speeding by far faster than before. The shimmering crescent of the reflected moon vibrated erratically. Sar watched it a long while, concentrating, trying to understand what she saw.

Finally she started in surprise.

"Not closer," she mumbled. "No. Magnified. The space between us and the water is bent. The space all around us is bent. It distorts the light." And the waves below passed furiously quickly, and this made the moon's reflection shimmer.

She pulled the vent closed and lay back on the floor of the compartment to think it through. The god was bending space somehow to take them out of the wind and to speed them forward. His strength grew.

She could not guess how fast they flew now. With the distortion of the light and all landmarks gone, it was impossible to judge. But it was fast. Much faster than before, and much faster than a sea ship traveled.

"I'll have to rush," she told herself. "I'll have to rush."

She began recasting her plans in her mind, abandoning those goals she must in order to get the necessary tasks done as quickly as possible.

"I will not let them win the boy," she whispered. "By Threkor's name."

CHAPTER

37

Sarah flinched when Wadjet shouted at the Guardian. "No!"

She sat with Wadjet, Thetis, Chance, and Seth around a tall fire on the beach, below the flat step where Seth and Chance had talked in the afternoon. Mimir and the Guardian stood nearby.

"First you ask me to leave my ship unguarded for weeks," Wadjet continued.

"I do not ask," the Guardian interrupted. "I just tell you you'll die if you wait here by your ship. The god will not be kind to those who helped the Puriman flee."

"And now you want to break my ship apart!" She stood and kicked sand into the fire.

The evening had started well, Sarah thought. Wadjet had finally waded ashore. Seth had been digging a trench in the sand, and was tossing sand high in the air when Wadjet came upon him.

"What are you doing, coyote?" she had demanded.

"He's looking for food," Sarah explained. "Like mussels, he said."

"Wait," Wadjet had replied. She stripped, smiled at Sarah as if challenging her to do the same, and then swam out into deeper water, just past her boat. She returned some minutes later, swimming side-stroke with some red creature held out before her, its legs flailing ineffectually at the air. Wadjet stood as she came into the shallow water and held up her catch.

"It's like a giant crayfish," Sarah said. Sometimes the Purimen ate crayfish from the bright streams that cut steep gorges through the lakeside hills.

"Good food," Seth barked. He stood on two legs in delight, hands outstretched for the crustacean. "Lobster."

Wadjet gave it to him and swam back out. Before nightfall she had gathered six of the lobsters, one for each of them. "But two for the coyote," she said.

Wadjet produced a huge pot from a storage compartment on her ship, and Sarah built a tall fire on the beach. Mimir watched with her silver eyes as they boiled the lobsters, and then ate ravenously, even at first almost ignoring the Guardian when he appeared.

Now the Guardian told Wadjet, "There is no choice, Steward. The airship is in working shape, as I said it would be. But there is no lifting wind. Too long the years for that not to break free. A stream runs near the place. With the metals of your ship's engine, we can make more."

"I don't understand," Chance said. "How can metals make gas?"

"With power from the airship's engines, the metals thrust in water will break the water," Thetis explained. "Water is in part made of lifting gas."

The Guardian said, "There is no other choice available to us, Steward."

"I am not a Steward!" Wadjet shouted.

"And I'm not a Puriman," Chance mumbled. "Get used to it."

Sarah frowned and shot him a glance to remind him of his promise never to mention such things. Chance raised his hand in apology.

"The god comes," the Guardian continued. "I ken him, coming fast upon us. We have days, at best. We must do quickly. First of the morning, we will bring the tools and food up the mountain, and make ready to leave as soon as the ship is lighter than air."

Wadjet kicked the sand again, and then stomped off out of the light of the fire. They heard her steps splash into the sea as she walked out to her ship.

There was a long, uncomfortable silence. Then Seth said with meek hope, "Do-do-do you think she wants the rest of her la-la-lobster?"

The Guardian told Sarah that he wanted her to ensure that Chance slept in the boat.

"The terrorbirds that I told you of, those are the only beasts I think we need fear, and they would not come to the beach. But, for safety, I think it best to stay in the ship."

Sarah agreed. The ship had a bed, after all, and privacy. There was no attraction for her to sleeping on the stone floor of the tower. She had seen in the day the black scorpions that prowled the dark corners of the abandoned building.

Hours after they went to their bed, she lay on Chance's left side and ran a hand through his hair, and asked him, in a whisper, "Chance, you shook when Seth spoke. About that—what did he call it?—the demon."

Chance nodded, a dimly visible movement in the dark. "It reminded me of something my father once told me. Many years ago. A story."

"Tell me," Sarah asked.

"It was storming, one of those short but terrible thunderstorms of August when we would sit in the house and watch the vineyard with worry. The vines were shaking, their leaves being torn away.

I said, 'It seems the devil is after us.' And my father grabbed my arm, hard.

"'Don't speak like that!' he said.

"'I'm sorry, father,' I told him.

"He shook his head and then he told me, 'I'm sorry, Chance.' And I think he felt bad, he needed to explain himself, because then he said, speaking quietly, almost whispering, 'I will tell you something. Your brother has little interest in spiritual matters, Chance. And I don't want to frighten your mother. . . .' And he looked toward the kitchen, checking to see if they were coming or looking at us. They weren't. So he went on, 'I'll tell you something I never told anyone else before: the devil is a real creature. I have seen him.'

"I was shocked. We were alone in the large hall, looking through the streaked windows. It was as dark as dusk, though little past noon. Thunder hammered nearby, making us both jump.

"'You saw him?' I whispered.

"'Many years ago. I was in the fields, late at night. By that cursed black boulder atop the hill. And the Earth opened, and a thing in the shape of a man came out. An unman. A thing of black and white. Or, it seemed all light, but then also nothing but dark. We cannot speak of such things clearly. Words aren't strong enough.'

"'But it groaned, and mumbled, and then it said to me, 'Do you want to live a second life?'

"'Only the one true God can give the second life,' I told it. I was terrified but I relied upon my faith.'

"'I can give you a second life,' it said.

"'Not a true life,' I said.

"'No. That is beyond me, yet. But a second life.'

"So I told it, 'Begone, black spirit.' I told it, 'I put my faith in the one true god.' Then I told it that it could be better, and accept God.'

"'God is absent,' it said. It said, 'Why doesn't God hear me? One as great and as powerful as I?'

"And I told him, 'Smaller and more meek than an ant is to a man, so you are to God. God cannot deign to speak to man or to devil.'

"'It disappeared then. I heard it weeping, as it disappeared. Weeping to have tried for and lost my soul. Maybe weeping to be lost to God. That's how powerful just the name of the one true God is: it banishes the devil.'"

Chance looked at Sarah. "That's the story my father told me. I never repeated it before. But it was burned in my memory. I was afraid for weeks, of the thought that the devil could rise from the ground. And that way he described it: 'A thing of all light but also all dark.' Just like Seth said. Exactly as Seth described. Does that sound crazy?"

Sarah thought of her own mother, mocked for having claimed to have met Lucenfolk. "No. No. We see now that there is so much more than people imagine, even in our little valley. No, I don't doubt your father.

"But," Sarah added uncertainly, "I don't know if it has anything to do with what happened to Seth. I know that Seth is good, and loves you, and so whatever happened to him did no harm to him or you. Maybe it was an angel of God, helping Seth because he is good. Perhaps all things divine and all things cursed look similar to mortals, when seen by us. It could be that Seth's demon was nothing like your father's devil, in the end."

"That's right," Chance said. "All these things are beyond us, and so we describe them in the same useless ways."

They lay a while in quiet. Sarah felt herself fading into sleep, but then she saw in the dim moonlight a glistening sparkle on Chance's cheek. She touched it and found a tear.

"You think of your father," she whispered.

"Yes. Yes. I'm so sorry that because of me...."

"No, Chance. It isn't your fault."

He didn't answer her for a while. Then he whispered, "I know my father's death is not my fault. And I also know it is my fault."

Sarah understood what he meant, and it would have been dishonest to deny what he said. After a long while, she whispered, "I miss the lake. I'd like some of your Ries, like you and Seth were saying today."

"It shall be hard to go back," Chance whispered. "People will remember. They will not be accepting."

"I am a Ranger of the Forest Lakes," Sarah said with determination. "They will hear me. A bandit attacked, I was captured, you saved me, we came home. That's as true as not."

"It's not the whole story...."

"Chance, the Rangers never tell the whole story. Purimen and Trumen alike don't want to hear it."

Chance grunted.

"What?" Sarah asked.

"I've learned something important about you in this last week: when you speak with that tone, I would be foolish to disagree."

"I'm even more stubborn than you, in some things."

"But, Sarah," he said, after a long while. "The Purimen and the Trumen of the Forest Lakes are worth saving."

"Of course they are."

He furrowed his brow. "What I mean is that—there's a lot wrong with the Purimen. I can say that to you, now. I see the world is so much more in need, and all these peoples are not talking to each other, not helping each other. And we have something to offer. It's...." Chance frowned.

"What?" Sarah asked.

"I just remembered something Elder Sirach once said to me. He said, 'Who should rule, Chance: the man who seeks to rule or the man who seeks not to rule?' And I answered, 'No man should rule.'"

"That's right," Sarah said.

Chance laughed softly. "'But suppose it were necessary?' he asked. So I said, 'It cannot be necessary,' but before he could protest my stubbornness I added, 'But I will say, of course, the man who seeks to avoid this power.' 'And why?' Sirach asked me. The answer wasn't so clear to me, but I managed to say that perhaps such a man would avoid using power to remake the world in his own image. 'Yes!' Sirach answered. 'And you see, this is a gift, this wisdom, that Purimen can give the world.'"

Sarah sighed. "I respected Elder Sirach, but I don't believe much of the world waits for Purimen council."

"Well, it's not so clear to me either, why he would talk to me of rule. But there's something there, no? The Purimen can help. Sirach was right to say at least that we should tell of our way. We live without all this killing and violence. We share with each other and help each other. We are not overwhelmed with greed—"

"Oh," Sarah interrupted. "There are greedy Purimen. Greedy of their lands, especially."

"But we're not overwhelmed by it." He sat up on an elbow to look at her. "Or, rather, I mean—it's not the heart of what we are. We need to tell of our way. That's worth saving and returning to and telling of. . . ."

They were silent a long while more. Then Sarah spoke. "Chance, my father and brother—"

"I think they are well, Sarah. I do. The false god would have taunted me with them, if he had any control over them."

"I do too," she added quickly. "But, I know my brother Adam insulted you. About being adopted. And about Seth. And even being a favorite of Elder Sirach."

"It's nothing, now."

"How did you become Sirach's . . . friend?" Sarah asked.

Chance shrugged. "I was walking in the forest one day, and Seth and I just ran into him. You know Sirach: with his long gray hair, he looked kind of wild, but he was always also . . . precise. Almost fussy. And he called to me, and said, 'You're the boy who runs with the soulburdened coyote.' I was wary. I thought he was going to be another person criticizing on me for being friends with Seth. But then he turned to Seth and said, 'You're the coyote that runs with the Puriman boy.' And he just introduced himself, and walked with us. That was it."

"But you became close friends," Sarah said.

"Yes. Sirach believed that Purimen have a mission: to see the face of God by turning away from the vanity of men." Chance smiled, embarrassed. "That's how he put it, I mean. And that was something very important to me. Up until I met Sirach, I thought being a Puriman really just meant being pure of blood. But Sirach thought that didn't really matter much. It was the decision to live in the world as we find it, and to appreciate what already is, instead of what could be. That's what matters. Or so he said." Chance's voice was a mere whisper as he added, "That changed my life. I'd been a trouble-maker before that time, but Sirach made me realize that the things I . . . doubted, the rules I couldn't obey, those weren't Purimen rules. They weren't scripture."

Sarah nodded. "He sounds like he truly was wise, as some claimed he was. But, about my brother and father: well, I'm sorry that they weren't good to you."

"I was not good to them. I thought few liked me, or accepted me. So I told myself it was because I was a better Puriman. It was the way I carried the loneliness." Chance shook his head. "It's funny. I didn't really know that till I said it. Anyway, so I said things, acted in ways. . . . "

Sarah pushed back his hair.

"Still," she said. "A single kind word and you would have been kind. And I know it's not true, what you say. You did them a great kindness. I know about the grapes, Chance. The unripe grapes you bought."

"They weren't so bad."

"They were terrible. Don't ever give me any wine you made with them."

He laughed.

"No, Chance," she continued. "They are at fault. I ask you to forgive them."

There was a long silence, and then Chance began to laugh, quietly.

"What?" Sarah demanded. When Chance just continued to laugh, she punched his arm.

"Ow!" he protested. "Have charity, that's my only good arm."

"Why do you laugh?"

"Well, it's just that—I took the worse possible revenge on your brother and your father. I ran off and married you, without their say!"

Sarah punched him again, but she flashed her lopsided smile.

When Sarah had returned home that last August to find the vinfields of her father's land had been picked, she asked her father about it.

"There was some rot in the Ries," he had said, his tone defensive. "We could have lost the whole crop. They sold already."

She nodded. "So Adam told me."

Her father had stopped growing potatoes and onions, as he had done for years, and attempted now for the profit of it to grow only grapes for sale to the winemakers. It was a terrible gamble, with a whole year spent just waiting for their fallow vines to mature after being trimmed and cleaned out, and even more years to wait for the new plantings to grow to bear fruit. He did not make wine, but hoped someday he might. Many farmers did the same. For them, the late summer was a time of fear, when the growers waited each day apprehensive that rot would take their crop. It drove many to pick too early. But the early pickings were poor grapes, with little sugar and even less flavor; they could not ferment into fine wine.

The next morning Sarah rose early and went into the village. Before the tall cobblestone building of the grape hold, which stood at the end of a stream in the narrow mouth of a gorge, two men just nodded at her and left her to wander the vats.

She circled the rows of tall wooden tubs. Most were empty. Those that were full held gleaming heaps of purple Caffran grapes. Not one was full of the white Ries grapes. She circled again and found that one of the empty vats had a few clusters of Ries at the bottom, as they always did after being emptied. She climbed into the vat to fetch a stem. The grapes on it were as hard as nuts. She bit one, and found it was crisp, with some sugar but not much flavor. Far too young.

In the back of the building stood the office of the trader, the door slightly ajar. She knocked on it, pushing it open on the rich smell of tobacco.

The trader was not a Puriman, but a Truman who lived among them and knew them all. Sarah liked him.

"Heya, Joshua."

"Heya, Sarah Michael." He smiled, breaking his thin, weathered face into deep wrinkles. He took his wooden pipe from his mouth and cradled it in his lap.

"My father brought a load of Ries grapes down day before yesterday. I don't see them."

The Truman nodded. "Sold and transported. Whole lot. Full price. Here." He set the pipe on the desk to free his hands, then dug in a drawer and brought out an envelope. "That's for your father. The rest of the payment. Can I trust a Ranger apprentice to get it to him?"

She didn't answer the joke, but nodded and slipped the thick package into her pocket.

"Who bought them?"

"Can't say. The buyer asked me not to say."

"Why not?"

The trader shrugged. He lifted his pipe and with a little wooden stick poked at the bowl nervously.

"Full price?" she asked.

"Yes."

"No bargaining down?"

"No."

"And you can't say?"

"No." He hesitated a moment, looking over her shoulder to be sure no one was waiting outside. His voice dropped to a near whisper. "I will say this, Sarah. I've known you since you were tiny, ye high." He held a hand by his knee. "And I think I can say this. Those grapes were far too early. No one could make much of a wine with those. Next year, be sure your father doesn't pick so early. This sale's a lucky thing, seeing as...."

He didn't finish the sentence. Sarah knew what he meant: seeing as how her father had debts all over town. Seeing as how he should have stuck to potatoes.

"Thank you."

"Thank you, Sarah. Come visit some time." He nodded, and put the pipe back into his mouth.

On the dusty road outside, two young men stood together talking in low voices. They worked helping to unload grapes that were brought for sale, or to load those that people purchased. They waited now for the first buyers of the day. Sarah walked straight to the younger of the two.

"I have some grapes to finish up the lot of Ries sold yesterday. Will you be loading them?"

"You need me to bring them down from your farm?"

"Maybe. But will you be around to unload them, I mean, to finish up the sale?"

"Well, when will Chance Kyrien be coming to get the rest?"

"I'll find out," she told him. "Thanks."

Sarah climbed onto her horse.

The boat rocked, waking Sarah. The tide was coming in, lifting the ship from the sand. She climbed carefully over Chance, used the ship's bathroom, then walked up onto the ship's deck. Mimir sat immobile in the prow, a stiff gray figure in the moonlight, with the black forests of the island beyond her, and a bright infinity of stars stretched over her head. It seemed to Sarah the makina was watching the stars, looking at them as if hoping to read something out of the book of the universe. Sarah waved at Mimir once out of courtesy.

The ship did not seem about to drift away, as she had feared. The rocking was a slight motion. She returned to the room, and sat at the foot of the bed, and looked at Chance. She could just make out his face, if she did not look directly at him.

How peacefully he slept! His closed eyes were still, his breath came in regular slow draws, his lips were parted slightly and seemed almost to smile.

He had no restless nights. She understood that he felt at fault for much that had happened, but she also knew that he had never knowingly done ill. And only that could hurt the conscience enough to keep a young man awake in the night.

She watched him a long while. Partly she longed to call to him, to wake him, and tell him her own pains. She tried not to count how many she had killed in Uroboros, but the faces of the dying and screaming men and women were seared into her memory: seven. They would have murdered her, they would have enslaved Chance and done worse than kill him, but still it was a terrible thing to have slain them. And it seemed a thing all of the same fabric of brutality out of which a Ranger's life was woven.

She could wake Chance, and confess the fierce things the Rangers did. How she had never seen an unman before Mimir and Wadjet; how the people she had beat back from the safe and fertile lands of the Forest Lakes were Trumen in all but title. She wanted to tell Chance that his transgressions were nothing compared to her own—though none dared call her anything but a Puriman.

But that confession would harm the only thing that could redeem her. If anything made it worthwhile to do the things the Rangers did, it was the innocence of this boy, who believed in the Purimen creed and in purity and the world of Elders—and, most of all, who believed in her. Who even believed that she was more innocent that he. One thing could save her from despair: to protect Chance from the hard hopes of these others—from these unmen, each greedily clinging to her or his own ancient, moldy plan for the world. She must return Chance home to Walking Man Lake, still believing, still pure in his heart, and see him vinmaster of Kyrien Vincroft. She must ensure Chance got to live his own plan. Then it would all be worth it.

She reached up and touched with shaking fingertips her swords' hilts, where they hung from the corner of the bunk. Then she lay close to Chance, careful not to press on his slung arm. Half waking, he wrapped her with his other arm, smiled, and drifted again into sleep.

CHAPTER

38

"It looks small," Chance said, standing before the airship. The cabin was narrow, and not half the length of the cabin of Mimir's airship. It was made of exposed metal pipes and metal sheets, the weld between them showing in crude beads. The body of the ship lay deflated beside it, a shiny blue-black material threaded with a lattice of silver wire.

Wadjet grunted. She had fumed for hours. Mimir and the Guardian had dug under the stairs in her ship and pulled out strange, complex metal parts, while Wadjet growled in indignation at each thing they lifted away. Then, with each member of their party carrying something, they had hiked for several hours into the hills. The Guardian led the way, showing them a thin path, wide enough only to walk placing one foot in front of the other. It followed along the crest of the hills, along a short stretch of the grassland, and then up a mountain valley where moss and short grass covered white stones. It had taken all of the morning to get there.

The climb had been long and hard, and the morning had quickly grown hot. Both Chance and Thetis had shoes not well made for such a hike, and they formed painful blisters that set them limping before they had walked far. Chance also felt guilty, as with his broken arm he carried little, at the insistence of both Sarah and Thetis. He walked with a single bag of some light metal parts slung over his good shoulder.

And yet, for all the discomfort, Chance could not but be amazed at this forest. Because the narrow path mostly threaded along the top of steep-sided hills, much of the forest canopy was at their eye level. Huge birds of unimaginable colors glided through the trees, shrieking with strange piercing voices. Monkeys raced from branch to branch. Great dragonflies buzzed overhead. And the trees were monstrous, towering twice as high or more as any in the Forest Lakes. They had huge trunks set into the moss-covered ground with tall, twisting vanes. The whole singing, buzzing, green place made the forests of Walking Man Lake seem but like a field in comparison. Chance had not known that such an overwhelming abundance of life was possible.

"It is small but fast," the Guardian replied, looking at the airship. Here the narrow mountain pass opened toward the northeast. Below them lay the broad, round plateau, the vast grassland with forest beyond it. Above, the valley rose into high, cold heights where snow dusted the rocks. Only a few scrappy trees and bushes clung to the steep sides. A stream trickled down the center.

The cave where the airship had been hidden was wide and deep. A large metal container stood in the middle of its entry chamber, out of which the Guardian had dragged the airship. Beside that leaned a metal cylinder, rotted through with gaping irregular holes ringed with flaking rust. That had contained the lifting gas.

Mimir and Thetis worked nearby, forming a knotty thatch of wire and piping on a flat stone step beside the stream. Seth wandered up the valley a short way, tail wagging as he sniffed at stones.

"It does look small," Sarah agreed.

"There," Thetis shouted. The machinery began to hum. A soft tube that ran from their machinery to the airship twisted suddenly, growing taut.

"The inflation process will require at least four hours to complete," Mimir said. "Assuming that the airship has no perforations."

"The ship is small," Chance repeated. "It's not large enough."

The Guardian looked at him. "Yes. Only you and I and one other will be able to go."

Chance felt a pit form in his stomach. He had feared this as soon as he saw the airship.

"You knew this," Wadjet shouted. "And yet you took apart my ship!"

"What choice do you see?" the Guardian demanded of her.

Reason did not appease Wadjet. She kicked at the ground, growling and showing her teeth.

"Who?" Chance started. "And what will the others—I mean, those left here...?"

"They can fight and slow the god. Or just wait here. Hide here. It rests on whether the god stops here. And how much time in lead of it we have."

"No one dies to slow the false god an hour," Chance said. "Any who stay must hide. But who goes with us?"

The Guardian was silent.

"It'd better be me," Sarah whispered.

Seth, having just returned, yipped, "I'm light. I don't count."

The Guardian acted as if he had heard neither of them.

A long silence fell. This changed everything. Who would go? Who would stay? Chance looked at them all. Mimir was expressionless, as usual. Her black and white formal suit, even more ridiculous here in this forest and valley than it had been on the ocean-plowing ship or in the center of battle, was still somehow without blemish. Wadjet flashed her fangs bitterly, then looked away. Thetis appeared again terrified, as she had not appeared since they had been in Disthea, with shaking hands pressed to her face. Sarah set her jaw in fierce determination. Seth bowed his head in worry.

Would the fight start now, Chance wondered, or later?

"Four hours," the Guardian told them, settling that matter by giving them a task. "That is time enough for a trip to the shore, and to start on the way back, to bring the rest of the food stores. Mimir will stay here and watch over the ship. The rest of you can begin to climb down. Stay to the trail, and you will be safe. Stay together. I'll come down and meet you before you have reached the bottom."

"Where will you be?" Chance asked.

"And how far is the false god?" Sarah asked, concerned that the Guardian talked as if they had time only for one trip down the hill again.

The Guardian pointed up the steep mountainside. To Chance's surprise, he frowned, betraying worry. "I want to get a better view. I do not know where the god is. I ken him, but cannot ken how far. He has learned to partly hide from me."

"Hekademon," the Guardian called to Seth. "You lead. You'll be able to smell danger."

Seth yipped and started down the valley. Slowly, each turning aside with private thoughts, they followed.

Seth liked the forest. He could smell that it was dangerous, but it was interesting, too. The sea had been nice because he liked the sea smell and he liked the fish that Wadjet pulled from the waves. Especially the fish. But then there was no place to dig a nice resting spot, and the constant rocking, rocking, rocking of the boat grew to weary him out of any rest. Finally, the smell of the sea was just the same smell all the time and got to be something you could not enjoy or even hardly notice.

And then the stink of whale plume.

He curled his lip. He was glad to be done with the whales. Too big!

Boats were no good, in the end.

Here on the island, in this forest, there were hundreds of smells, all of them mixing and changing and new. It was like a hundred forests, one on top of the other. He had now a glimmer of the dream of the cursed guild, the Lifweg. They hoped to fill the world with every kind of life, wild and close, the whole world a crowded den. The things Seth would tell his masters!

But first another matter. He could smell Thetis sweating. Afraid. Always afraid. At first he had pitied her. The Guardian was frightening to be near, with his smell of wet slate. But then why had she remained afraid? What scared her, after she knew the Guardian was not going to kill them all outright, after that first day in the Broken Hand that Reaches?

After they had left the valley and its too-small airship, Wadjet had pushed past Seth, impatient, and almost run down the trail. She smelled too of sweat, but a tight, thin sweat smell. Anger that.

Seth led the way down to the plateau, where the trail cut along the edge of the grasslands before turning into the forest. Wadjet was just visible ahead, as she entered the tall bush. Seth paused by a tall outcropping of smooth round boulders up against the steeply sloping hill.

Chance and Sarah passed him. They smelled alike now. Their smells blended. Mates.

As Thetis passed, he reached out and tugged her robe. The Mother of the Gotterdammerung looked down at him.

"Wait," he whispered. They let the lovers walk on ahead, not noticing, eager to catch up with Wadjet.

"What is it, Hekademon apprentice?" Thetis asked him.

Sweating even more, Seth thought. She fears even me. And she uses the formal title.

"Junior Mother of the Ga-Ga-Gotterdammerung," he said. "I would speak with you."

"Please," she said.

Seth looked down the trail. The lovers were gone. Wadjet was gone. Only the smell of grass now. And the watering hole.

"You a-a-alone of the Mothers in the Hand survived the god."

And there, instantly, Seth smelled the heavy scent of her fear, a wave of perspiration as she flushed. But Thetis only looked at him.

"I know, know your true age," Seth continued. "I know your age. Many, many years you've been in the Guild. Yet sti-still you are a Junior mother."

Thetis smelled strong now, but remained silent.

"You knew who Chance was," Seth added. "And you knew there was a watch upon him. Only Senior Mothers should know these things."

Finally Thetis spoke. "What do you mean to say, apprentice?"

"I suspect you are Hieroni, spared by the god because you serve it."

The wind shifted. A strange pungent smell came and went. Seth did not allow himself to be distracted. He focused on Thetis, looking, smelling for some sign. But she showed none.

"I serve Chance," she said. "I serve Chance."

"Then," Seth said. "I-I-If you are not of the Hieroni, I can think of only one other re-reason why you would know of Chance. One reason you would be spared by the god. One re-reason the Mothers might punish you bu-but still keep you in their guild. One reason why the most senior Mothers might tell you of me."

There, Seth thought. The stopping of her breath. The dilating of the iris. The heavy smell of the increase of her fear. The hammering of her heart. He had guessed rightly.

They stared at each other a long while.

"So you know my secret," Thetis said. "Will you tell the Guardian? Will you tell...Chance?"

"Do-don't know."

Thetis leaned back against the boulder. "It would do nothing, help nothing, to tell them."

Seth nodded. He could think of no good that would come of it either. He carefully prepared his next words—but before he could speak, Thetis pointed behind him, her eyes popping wide, and shouted—

"Seth!"

Too late the coyote turned. A beak as hard as stone snapped down at him, a crushing blow. He had twisted in instinctual caution, so though he did not escape the blow it only cut across his hind left leg, instead of breaking his spine as it would have.

Seth rolled and bounced to his feet, trailing blood from a deep cut.

Before them crouched two green birds, each as tall as a man, their black wedges of beak aimed like weapons at Seth and Thetis. Seth cursed himself: to have sat with his back to the prairie, facing into the wind that fell over the rocks. What a fool!

Thetis turned and began scrambling up the rock, her frantic clawing at the stone finding miraculous purchase; she dragged herself slowly up. Seth backed toward her, defending her as she climbed.

The birds watched, utterly silent. They were terrible, giant things. And hunting now, they would not make a sound, Seth realized.

"Ah!" he barked at them, trying to set them on edge. But he was too small, or too low to the ground, to scare them. They stepped forward.

He looked over his shoulder. Thetis had managed to mount the rock. She crawled up onto her hands and knees, on a flat spot, almost six feet above. Out of reach of these beasts, Seth concluded.

"Ah!" he screamed again. Then he turned and leapt up the stone, as far as he could jump, reaching with his front paws.

His stubby fingers caught, trembling, at a little crease in the stone. He began to slide back.

"The-The-Thetis," he whispered.

The birds rushed forward.

Thetis, Junior Mother of the Gotterdammerung, reached down, grabbed Seth's hand, and paused, hesitating.

Seth saw that she was thinking. His eyes narrowed, as if to say *I judge you, Junior Mother of the Gotterdammerung*.

Thetis twisted his paw, prying his fingers free of their grip on the rock. Seth fell. The terrorbirds set upon him.

The Guardian climbed. The forest and grassland fell far behind him. The bare pebbled ground and steep slopes were spotted with low shrubs of flowers. He followed the curve of the mountain, circling as he climbed, wanting both to get higher and to see out over the sea below as quickly as he could. He still had only a vexing sense that the god approached—shrouded somehow, inscrutable.

Then, as he came upon the hard packed soil of a goat trail, he felt it. Just a flicker, the last push of some power by the god, and then silence, nothing. The god had stopped using his power. But as the power stopped, the Guardian thought for a mere moment that he felt its distance. And the feel was close. Very, very close.

He shot around the trail, racing forward. First he saw, far below, the crumbling peak of Aegweard, like the broken tooth of some fossil jaw. Then the sea, the Sæwall, Wadjet's boat—and there, on the beach: three airships.

Black shapes milled about them. Bears and wolves.

"Damn!" The Guardian shouted, furious with himself. He shot back down the hill, running now as fast as he could.

He exploded into the stream by Mimir's side, throwing a wall of water out over the airship, more than half inflated now. The makina had tethered it, as it strove now to lift off the ground.

"If you can hurry this, hurry it."

Mimir only stared at him.

"The god is here," the Guardian added, before he disappeared in a gray blur.

CHAPTER

39

"Wait," Chance said. He put his hand on Sarah. They had come to a place in the forest where the hill on either side of the trail was steep, so that if you fell and did not fight for a handhold you could slide and roll far. They stepped carefully, watching the packed earth for sure footholds. "Where's Seth? Where's Thetis?"

Sarah looked back up the trail. "We let Wadjet get us moving too quickly. We left them behind."

"Let's back up," Chance said. "I don't like to have us separated. Not into three groups."

Sarah nodded, and then stepped around Chance, leading the way. They walked back a few hundred paces. Chance called, "Seth! Thetis!"

No answer. They walked farther, to a place where the trail widened as it crossed a flat peak of the hill. Trees reached high above them, so that suddenly they were in shadow.

"Seth! Thetis!" Chance called again. They looked around, but heard and saw nothing.

Then Sarah looked back. And bounding up the trail toward them, far below still, was a black shape. She froze, staring.

"A bear," she whispered. "A soulburdened bear." The Guardian had told them there were none of the soulburdened on this island. That had to mean—

"The false god is here," Chance whispered. "Run!"

They set off up the trail. Sarah insisted that Chance go first, which slowed her as he ran awkwardly, favoring his broken arm as it jostled in its sling. She resisted the temptation to draw her swords, knowing they could catch in passing brush, but she turned every minute to look back. She could see two bears now. They were gaining.

"Go," she gasped at Chance. "Go!"

The trail narrowed, so that brush cut at their faces. A thorny branch caught at the stitches in Sarah's cheek and tore open one of the cuts. Blood flowed freely down her chin and throat. Chance stumbled ahead of her, impaired by the need to run with one arm holding the other, but he did not fall.

The brush ended abruptly and they came out into a clear place, where a bit of the grassland protruded into the forest. To their left was an outcropping of rock surrounded by boulders. It was here, she realized, that they had last seen Thetis and Seth. Sarah cursed herself for not paying more attention to the land on their first way up and down the hill, for she was not sure but believed they were not far from the trail that turned up the hillside and into the mountain valley. The stream that ran by the airship crossed their path near this place.

"Chance!" a voice called. They looked up. Thetis emerged from the scrub at the top of the boulder. She was trembling all over.

"Where's Seth?" Sarah asked.

"He's...."

"What?" Chance demanded.

She pointed at the rock on which she stood, a smooth outcropping as tall as Chance could reach with his arms over his head. And on it was a dark stain.

"The birds. The terrorbirds got him."

"No!" Chance cried. "Oh, no!"

"We don't have time," Sarah told him. "We must hurry. Thetis, run on ahead. I think it's not much farther. We can cut up the hill here, leave the trail. You hurry ahead, I'll stay with Chance. Meet at the airship. Tell them the god is here. With bears. Go!"

Thetis started off.

"You first," Sarah said to him. "I'll help you up—"

Chance, looking at Sarah and so back down the trail, silenced her by pointing back, over her shoulder. Sarah turned.

A white blur tore through the brush, seeming to rend the forest air, and then exploded to a stop behind them. Hexus, in Paul's body, stood there with his arm outstretched, the black eye festering in his swollen hand. The smell of rotting meat diffused through the clearing.

Without a word Sarah drew her swords and rushed the god.

"No," Hexus said. "Not twice."

Sarah was seized, lifted into the air, and shot backwards, over the stone outcropping, and then out, far into the stunted forest above.

"Sarah!" Chance called. He watched her fall into the scrub, arms flailing. He started to run after her. But in a blur Hexus appeared before him.

"She is likely alive, Potentiate," the god said. "I merely set her aside. Which is better than she did for me when last we faced each other."

"Filth!" Chance shouted. Rage started to boil in him. Rage for his dead father, his mutilated brother, his abused wife. Rage for Seth. "I'm going to...."

He raised his fist and started forward. But before he could take three steps, Hexus bent space around Chance, locking him tight. The two bears clambered into the clearing now. Others were behind them: Chance could hear them huffing up the trail. After a struggle he managed to twist and look back. Wolves and more bears. And, obscured behind them, a man clambered, bent over under the weight of a heavy pack.

"Where is the Atheos?" Hexus asked him.

Chance sneered. It was horrible to see his brother rotting like this, dying, possessed, lost. "Go to hell!" he said. "Go now—hell awaits you."

Hexus nodded. "Very well. We shall see the Atheos soon, no doubt. Right now, Chance, I have someone here for you." He turned Chance around, still bound.

The bears parted as they came into the clearing. They put their noses down to the ground, smelling about. And then there at the head of the clearing stood the man. He set the pack at his feet.

"Heya, Chance," he said.

Chance stared, stunned. Here was a sight even more unreal, more unfathomable than Paul possessed by the ancient horror of a false god.

"Sirach," Chance whispered.

"Yes, it is I."

"You are...." Chance looked around, trying to understand the situation. A prisoner of the god? Possessed by the god? Threatened by the god?

"I am one of the Hieroni, Chance. I am known among them as Vark."

Chance could not speak. He stared, with his mouth open.

"Hear me, Chance. You know me. You know what I believe. Serving the god is the only path to the better world."

"All lies," Chance whispered. Tears welled in his eyes. "I based my whole life on what you told me. I...I made myself in the image you gave me. My father trusted you, trusted you more than any other Puriman. And now my father is dead—killed by this filth. How you have lied!"

"Not lies, Chance. No."

"Lies!" Chance shouted bitterly. "How can turning away from the false technologies, the false gods, the false life, be part of serving that!" He nodded his head at the god and spat.

Hexus smiled. "Yes, Vark, explain the metaphysics of your ethics to us. I would enjoy hearing that."

Vark shifted uneasily. "Chance," he said, his gaze shifting fearfully to the god. "Chance, what I said is true. What the Purimen can teach the world is important. My grandparents were Purimen, of the Usin Valley. That is how I know your ways. I was raised a Puriman—I did not lie about that. And I meant the things I said."

To Hexus, Chance said, "You're a fool if you believe this will make me submit."

"Chance," Sirach pleaded. "Chance, you always thought you were rejected by other Purimen, made to feel different, made the outsider. But Chance, you *were* different. You *were* the outsider. You see the bigger questions. You have the ability to see and hope and strive for more."

"No," Chance said. "I never wanted other than to be a Puriman farmer. To have my stake of land, my vineyards, to make wine. To marry Sarah."

"That's not true, Chance. Just think of Seth. Why didn't you turn him away, then? Any other Puriman would have. Because you knew that would be wrong. You knew the Purimen are wrong in this way they treat the soulburdened."

The mention of Seth infuriated Chance. "Seth is dead! Because of this thing!" He spat again toward Hexus. "You know what you do here is foul. Foul. This false god would ruin the soul of man. And you serve it."

"Chance!" Sirach stepped forward.

Chance turned his head to look at Hexus.

"Don't think that this will weaken me, false god. Stop wasting your time with this. He can't help you."

Hexus nodded his head, almost a sign of respect. "There is nothing that can save you now, Potentiate. You had best yield to me."

"I shall never yield."

"If you care for this world, if you care for anything, then you will. This battle of ours is costing too much. It is not too late to save Paul, Chance. If you submit, I can share my soul with you quickly, and set Paul free. But if we continue this struggle, all will be lost. Eventually in battle I will kill Sarah, I will kill the others that help you. And far more is at stake. Disthea is in ruins. Next the soulburdened will march south, into the lake lands of your people. Who will ensure that your people are not all slaughtered?"

One of the bears growled, smelling the earth around them warily. Another bear showed its teeth at Chance, as if already savoring the taste of his flesh.

"If we can make the change quickly, the armies can be guided. Peace can be brought to Earth. The cities rebuilt, your people protected, the soulburdened given their due."

A clank of metal sounded behind Chance. He stole a quick glance. The soulburdened beast he had seen at the riverside, and which he knew now as Apostola, dressed in armor of shining gold, stepped into the clearing. She held aloft a great spear with a gold point.

"But if we fight, there is nothing that can be done. It may already be too late. Everyone, everyone in your farms and villages will die."

"He speaks the truth," Sirach said. "I love those lands as much as you. You can save them. You must save them."

A single tear finally started down Chance's cheek. He had little faith that giving in to the false god would save his people, but he also thought that what Hexus threatened was likely true. What would the soulburdened do next, now that they knew their strength? Surely march out across the lands, to that fine valley that had long been forbidden them.

The bear at his feet clawed at the ground, and raised its lip as it looked up at him. "Eat them all," it whispered.

"So evil," Chance said, looking into Paul's possessed eyes.

"And there is another matter, Potentiate. Something the Guardian hides from you. Your time is nearly up. You cannot live much—"

Then the head of the bear at Chance's feet exploded.

The Guardian stood before Chance, Threkor's Hammer cutting a gray arc through the air as it went up, through the bear, and continued down to strike Hexus. It landed solidly on Hexus's shoulder.

Chance, who had been straining against the force of Hexus, stumbled forward, suddenly free of his grip. He saw Hexus, partly torn open, fall to the ground. The sight sickened and horrified him: this was also Paul, his brother, oft his rival but still his brother, on the ground, his skin flayed off in a wide swath, his red muscles frayed and split. But the gaping wound began to roughly knit itself closed as he watched.

The soulburdened animals around them screamed.

"Down!" the Guardian said to Chance.

Chance threw himself flat on the ground. Threkor's Hammer whirled through the air, buzzing and creating a wind that stirred his hair. Three bears and a wolf were torn apart. The heavy shreds of them thudded down in the trees at the edge of the clearing.

"Run, Chance," the Guardian called.

Chance scrambled to his feet, crouching. Hexus sat up where he lay on the trail before him. Chance ran, crouched over, toward the rocks by the trail's side, where Sarah had first thought that they might cut through the steep hillside toward the valley, and above which she had been thrown by Hexus.

He saw in a glance that there was someone on the hillside above. Was it Sarah?

Then he slipped, tripped up by some force of Hexus, and landed on his broken arm. The pain was terrible. He rolled over, moaning.

"Far enough," Hexus said, standing.

Chance looked around the clearing. The ape in shining armor remained, spear pointed at The Guardian, who turned toward Hexus. The other soulburdened were dead. Sirach crouched fearfully in the brush, behind his backpack. Down the trail, Chance saw that other beasts were coming.

Sirach pulled some kind of shining cylinder from the tall bag which lay before him. It had facets of glittering crystal, bound together with black rods of metal. The make looked to Chance like the things of Uroboros: an invention of the Dark Engineers.

"A weapon," Chance warned the Guardian, pointing. He could not walk: again, Hexus held him, twisting space around his legs. The Guardian did not look, but stalked toward the false god.

Chance reached around in the dirt, found a heavy stone. He flung it at Sirach with all his might, painfully wrenching his shoulder. But it was a good throw: the stone hit Sirach square in the chest. Sirach fell back, crying out.

The ape was on Chance in a second, kicking him back. She planted a heavy, strangely round foot on the bicep of his one good arm.

"Get off," Chance hissed. He struggled, but he could not kick the beast because his legs were pinned by Hexus. The gorilla looked down at him with black eyes set in a black face. Chance could not read the expression on its face—anger? Indifference? Fear?

The ground shuddered as the immortals flung themselves together in an explosion. The air pulsed with unnatural sounds. The Guardian and Hexus spun around each other, striking out, their motions visible to Chance only as a blur. The ape looked toward the fight. Chance managed to lift his head. The soulburdened he had seen below had still not arrived. It was only himself, the ape, and Sirach watching the battle.

Chance felt the grip on his legs loosen. Hexus could not hold it during the battle. Chance twisted, kicked out, surprising the ape, and pulled his arm from under the beast. He scrambled to his feet, then backed against the rock for support. The ape lifted her spear.

"Go ahead," Chance mocked. "Spear the precious Potentiate through."

As the ape hesitated, Chance saw that behind her Sirach kneeled at the edge of the clearing, holding the crystal cylinder again, carefully pointing one end into the clearing.

Suddenly the fighting paused. The god and Guardian stood close together. The god leapt back. Sirach twisted something on the cylinder and the top of it opened. Even in the harshly bright sunlight of this island, the air dimmed. An otherworldly blue light came from the cylinder, and fell on the Guardian. He leaned forward, straining, but was caught in the power of it, a giant trapped in aqua amber.

Chance remembered the children's rhyme he had heard sung in the alley in Disthea: *Blue light, blue light, the ashes of dead suns....*

The Guardian laughed without mirth, a long, angry sound.

"One of the lost Numin Jars," he said.

"We have both, Guardian," Hexus answered.

"I should have razed Uroboros for their foolishness."

A bolt of lightning, as tall as a man, shot through the blue light, striking Threkor's Hammer. The Guardian grunted. Then other bolts crackled from the haft and head of the great hammer, white scars on the blue light. The thunder of them echoed off the hillside.

"It's—" Sirach called out, but the rest of what he said was drowned in the cracking of the air. For a moment, the god, the man, the ape, and Chance all watched, transfixed, as bolts of raw thunder exploded off of Threkor's Hammer.

A howling, snarling yelp sounded through the air. Chance saw in the corner of his eye a grey blur of motion. He turned to see the false god tumble to the Earth—and rolling across the ground beyond him—

"Seth!" Chance cried out.

"Run!" the coyote called.

Chance could see the coyote had been sorely wounded. The fur on his back and on his hind legs glistened black with blood. His face was cut. His tail was gone.

"Run!" the Guardian commanded. His voice more powerful, louder than the thunder protesting off of Threkor's Hammer. "Run!"

Seth leapt as Hexus started to stand, and the coyote set his teeth into the god's throat.

The ape grunted, raised her spear, aiming uncertainly. Chance sent a wild kick at her side, and was twice lucky: he planted it firmly in the space between armor plates and, stumbling forward, he drove her to the ground. Her head fell to the edge of the blue light emanating from the Numin Jar, her helmet toppled off, and instantly the hair on her scalp started on fire as it was struck by a bolt of white power.

"Run," the Guardian again commanded.

But Chance could not leave Seth. The ape had dropped her long spear. Chance lifted it, tossed it once in his hand to get the center of its weight. Seth had been thrown back by Hexus. Blood poured from the false god's open throat. Hexus turned toward the coyote, who crouched and leapt.

And, while Seth again sailed through the air at Hexus's throat, the air shimmered before the black eye in Paul's palm. Hexus reached out and closed space, aiming perhaps for the head but getting only the back half of the coyote. He crushed Seth, from the center of his body back. In an instant Chance saw the horrible sight: the beloved coyote nearly torn in half, his hindparts ground to pulp.

It was a mortal wound of such horror—the ground flesh and exploding blood and torn organs flung through the clearing—that Chance's breath stopped. His heart skipped, and started again only sluggishly, as if his blood had chilled until it thickened. The sounds of the clearing fell away. In the silence, he heard only his first failed attempt at a breath, and the next shuddering blow of his heart, hammering a beat of reluctant blood through his ears.

In the frozen moment a thousand images came to Chance. The first time he had seen Seth, prowling their vines, head bowed, his eyes looking up at Chance so hopefully. "Hell-hell-hello," the young coyote had said. The first time Chance touched him, feeling the thick coarse hair between his shoulders. The first time Chance had buried his face in Seth's neck and cried over some boyish hurt, smelling the wild rich smell of Seth's coat. Walking the forest together, Seth circling him impatiently. Seth sitting at his feet, bulging eyes looking up. And Seth bounding to his defense against the bears, just as he jumped to his death now.

But Seth, now nearly dead, trailing his torn innards, still made his mark. His teeth found the god's throat and sank in again. Hexus fell backwards.

The ape had rolled away from the blue light and now she struggled to her feet, slapping her head. Ignoring her, ignoring the thunderous bolts riving the air about the Guardian trapped in the blue light, Chance threw the spear. It planted firmly in Hexus's side. Hexus gurgled, the attempt at a scream choked in his ruined throat.

"Run!" the Guardian called. "If you want to hurt him, pass Ma'at and choke his soul. Go!" And this last word faded, like the scream of a falling man, as the blue light began to crush the Guardian and draw him back into the glittering crystal tube wielded by Sirach, known as Vark, the traitor of unmen and Trumen and Purimen alike.

Seth was dead. The Guardian was dead or trapped. Chance saw that there was nothing he could do but to follow the Guardian's counsel, and kill the god in the place where he could be killed. He ran and leapt onto the stones at the side of the clearing, and scrambled to the scrub above. He ran, no longer trying to shield his arm, but letting it swing wildly in its sling as he pumped the other arm. Sarah was somewhere ahead. He must find her, they must flee to the ship.

"Sarah!" he called out. "Sarah!"

He wept as he ran, unable to think, unable to sort in his head the sorrow of Seth's death, the horror of seeing Paul further destroyed, his fear of the god, his fear for Sarah, the need to find Sarah, the exhaustion of his flight. He just ran and ran. Branches cut at his face. He tried to keep in view and aim for the peaks that marked the valley entrance, but otherwise he ran heedlessly, screaming for Sarah as he went.

Then he tripped and fell hard on the uneven ground. Someone leapt onto his back. He struggled, kicking out. A hand grabbed tight over his mouth.

"Silence!"

It was Wadjet. She rolled him over. She bared her fangs, angry. "Silence, fool!"

She withdrew her hand when he stopped struggling.

"The false god—"

"I know. I tried to circle round, to warn you, but I was not fast enough." She stood.

Chance climbed to his feet. "Sarah—"

"Stop!" Wadjet hissed. She pulled him behind a low bush, and crouched beside him. As Chance had climbed, the cover had begun to thin, though looking down the hill they could see nothing coming, and hoped that nothing could see them. "Think! The god does not know where the ship is. It doesn't even know there is a ship. We must go to the airship. Your mate is wise, and will do the same. We can meet there. If we circle around in these woods, looking for each other, we'll only lay a scent trail for wolves."

"I won't lose Sarah," Chance hissed. "I—" And he could not bring himself to say, I already lost Seth. I lost the Guardian—the Guardian! He felt a wave of despair sweep over him. How weak they were, without the immortal to defend them.

But first, he reminded himself, find Sarah.

"She will go to the ship," Wadjet told him. "Where else can she go?"

"Looking for me."

"When she sees you are free, she'll go to the ship. She probably already knows. That opening was easy to see from many places. I watched the whole battle. She likely did also."

"And the Guardian?" Chance asked.

"In that thing," she said. "Swallowed by the blue light."

Chance rubbed a dirty hand over his cut face, smearing soil into his tears. He saw the fierce determination drain out of Wadjet's expression, as her lips covered her fangs. Chance found her look of pity worse to bear than her chastisement.

"Let's go," he said, roughly. "But keep watch out for Sarah."

"Aye, Puriman."

CHAPTER

40

"Sarah!"

The voice was distant. Annoying.

"Sarah!"

A dull ache hammered at the back of Sarah's head. She put her hand to her face, and felt it wet with blood: one of her scars lay torn open. She opened her eyes. Thetis stared down at her.

"Chance!" she shouted, sitting up. They were on a hillside. With one hand she felt the leaves and dirt mixed into her hair. "What...?"

"I saw the god throw you up here," Thetis whispered. She backed fearfully into a low bush blooming with purple flowers. "And I came to you."

Sarah looked around, and found that, amazingly, her swords lay nearby. So, she had not let go of them as she sailed through the air. Good.

She bent her knees and sat forward. None of her bones seemed to be broken. But all of them were sore.

"Chance?" she croaked again.

"I stopped at that peak, over there." Thetis pointed. "When I realized you weren't behind me. I could see the clearing from there. Chance escaped, Sarah, he escaped. Seth and the Guardian fought, they gave him—"

"You said Seth was dead."

"I thought he was, but. . . ."

Sarah finished the thought. "But now he is." She slowly stood and retrieved her sword. She sheathed them carefully. "Which way did Chance and the Guardian go?"

"Just Chance."

She looked down the hill, wondering why there was silence. "The Guardian still fights?"

"No. The Guardian was . . . trapped. They had one of the lost Numin Jars."

"What is that?"

"A thing—ancient—made to trap a god. With it they trapped the Guardian."

Sarah's shoulder's fell. She closed her eyes. "We lost the Guardian?"

"Yes."

"How will we fight it now? How?"

"Sarah, we have to go. There are bears and wolves. They're chasing Chance."

"Where is he?"

"Get down." Thetis motioned for Sarah to crouch like herself. "Get down. Chance ran that way." She pointed higher in the hills. "He'll be running to the airship, surely."

"To the airship," Sarah said. "Let's go."

"But the bears . . . we should. . . ."

"We'll climb up, first. High on the hill." Sarah pointed straight up the steep slope. "Then cut around. We'll avoid the bears, most likely, if they are following Chance's scent. But we'll be able to run down on them in a hurry if they catch up with Chance."

"So be it," Thetis said. She got to her feet, though she still crouched over in caution. Sarah frowned at her.

"Come," Sarah said. "Be strong. We'll die if we are not."

Thetis did not answer, but rather set off immediately, leading the way, her robe catching noisily at low branches.

"No back up," Sar mumbled bitterly. "No alternative. No choice but to die, food for bears, if the plan doesn't work."

A good engineer never puts herself in such a situation, but Sar had not had the time to be a good engineer.

She had watched carefully as the airships began to drop. She peered down through the vent, seeing the white Sæwall, the black tower Ymbringhen, the twin mountain peaks and the plateau beyond. She knew this place, by fame: this was Lethebion, the cursed and abandoned island of the cursed and destroyed guild. Then she saw the boat, anchored in shallow clear sparkling water. The boy was here.

The airship set down on the beach roughly, digging hard into the sand. The bears roared for their lives, terrified. She heard the other two airships crash down on either side, scraping the soft beach with a hard crunching sound so brittle it seemed they had crashed onto stone.

Instantly the bears tumbled out onto the sand. Wolves howled and barked nearby. Silence fell when the god shouted—a voice she recognized well now. Sar waited and heard distinctly a shout from farther down the beach, the guttural growl of a bear.

"The boat is empty!" the bear called.

"Up the hill!" Hexus commanded. "We must find them as soon as we can and bring them here. The boy must not be harmed. Do not hesitate to kill any of the others."

There was talking then, but Sar could not hear it. After a while, the howls and barks retreated up the hill. She listened as they diminished into silence. Then just two bears trudged noisily back onto the airship, their nails clicking on the hard floor.

"Might be food here," one bear growled, just above where Sar lay. "Food to find."

"Two with each ship," the other bear answered. "You leave, only one with this ship."

"I leave and come back with food. Two and food in this ship."

"Shut up," the other bear growled.

"Two on each ship," Sar mumbled. "Six total on the beach. Not bad."

She crawled forward under the hatch to the cabin, pushing a tall cone of paper before her. The steps of the bears were loud now. They were a handspan above her.

"You smell that," one of the bears growled, as she positioned the cone below the door. "Human. Human. Right here now. Smell it!"

She had found in the ship's cargo stores: matches, paper, and short rods of wood. She had arranged these into a cone of fuel, filled with a loose pile of the old stuffing of a life jacket. She had set it on a crate lid for a base. It was enough. She lit a match now, and put it to the top of the cone.

"Here," the bear growled. "I smell it. I smell it. Human meat! Through this!"

She heard the fumbling of claws at the hatch. She was not a moment too soon. The cone exploded into billowing hot smoke, shooting up through the hatch as it opened.

"Step one," Sar mumbled to herself. "Fumigate bears."

The bears roared, stumbling and rolling about the cabin. They ran to the back of the ship, to the front again, tumbling noisily over seats, and then again to the back and out of the cabin. Sar heard their paws thud down on the sand. She had breathed with her face pressed to a small side vent, and now took a deep breath and crawled forward as quickly as she could. She ignored the pain as she planted a hand on hot embers from her smoke bomb and crawled out of the hatch. She slapped it closed. The cabin was filled with smoke, opaque with it. She stumbled toward the door, slammed it shut, and threw the deadbolt. She ran to the controls and threw open the window, and then she could hold her breath no longer.

She fell to the ground, breathing the tiny handspan of clean air that was there. Two breaths. She sat up, eyes blind with tears, and opened the cover on the emergency tether release.

"Step two," she said aloud. "Free the airship." She threw the switch.

She fell back to the floor, gasping. The airship lifted, then jerked against its tethers for only a second before it pulled free. Using the emergency tether release was dangerous, given her plan to ditch the anchor: it meant the ship would have no way to anchor, and they would have to ground the ship at their destination. But Sar could think of no other choice.

The air in the cabin began to clear. Her smoke bomb had been made to be short lived. She leapt up, hurried to the back of the cabin, opened another window, creating a cross breeze, and crawled to the controls again.

"Step three," she said. "Disable the other ships."

The ship drifted toward the trees, a huge green wall rising before her. She turned on the engines and jerked down on the control that set them in full reverse. The ship shuddered and then reluctantly began to slow. The shift was enough to drive the smoke back, billowing into her face. She got a lungful of it, and dizziness swept over her, then passed as the air cleared again.

"I'm too old, too old, too old," she protested, coughing with harsh bursts that scraped her throat raw. The ship listed sideways, not slowing quickly enough. It slammed into the forest canopy. Colorful birds, green and black and yellow and blue, screamed in outrage and took flight, abandoning their nests before the onrush of the airship. A tree branch creaked and broke, then another snapped. Slowly the ship backed away, turning, as it bounced off the trees.

She grabbed the controls and found the ship responded to her now. She turned it. Below, on the beach, six bears clustered between the two remaining ships, waving claws and looking up at her. She drifted over them, waited till she was just above one of the ships, then pushed the engines to full down thrust, and reached for the emergency anchor hook control. She took careful aim—she had only one shot—letting the airship sink slowly down until the other airship took up the entire view of the front windows.

She fired the hook. The dull explosion and the hissing of rope paying out were followed by an audible tear as the spiked anchor hook punctured the other ship.

She cut the engines and dropped ballast. Seawater splashed down on the roaring bears. The ship rose, then jerked and bounced when the tether in the ship below caught and twisted into the balloon fabric. She put the engines into full reverse. It worked: the ship below rocked, turned, came free. It had lost most of its lifting gas from the anchor cutting the balloon, and so it dragged now across the sand as her airship pulled it along, scraping loudly as it shuddered and jumped over small dunes. The bears chased it, uncertain what else to do but roar at her.

Sar dragged the ship into the other parked ship. Her ship jerked, making the anchor cable ping and vibrate. Once, twice, three times she bounced the ship against the tension. Finally the hook cut through the parked ship's fabric and tore into the other ship. She pressed down on the engine control, but they were already in full reverse. Back and forth the ship tossed, straining at the anchor cable. Then the cable broke, and she shot into the air.

Below, she saw the two airships, laying on their sides in mangled heaps, deflating.

"Step four," she said. "Save the boy."

The god and his warriors had run up the trail on this side of the mountain. Best to avoid Hexus. She would circle around the mountain's other side and hope to catch the boy and the Guardian in retreat.

Sar turned the ship toward the west.

CHAPTER

41

Hexus tore the dead coyote from his throat and tossed him aside, drew the great spear from his ribs, and slowly reassembled his body. He was getting fast at this, his power growing, but his skill could not slow the decay of this host, nor did it reduce the agony he felt, the sharp mortal pain, each time he was hurt.

He turned and looked over the clearing. The Potentiate was gone. Apostola, her head smoking, her black eyes inscrutable, pulled on her helmet. The bears lay broken around the clearing. Vark sat in the trees, arms wide and gaze fixed on the Numin Jar as if he had only just been thrown back by it.

And there, on the edge of the clearing, the Numin Jar shook. A blue-green glow spread out thickly through the crystal sides. It hummed, vibrated, and a spark here, then there, sprang from the metal that bound the crystal sides together.

Hexus frowned. Was it meant to do that, to tremble and cast bolts like that? Something seemed wrong. The Jars were made to hold the gods for eons. This one seemed to be shaking apart as he watched.

But it didn't matter, he reminded himself. The Jar need only hold the Guardian a few days while they captured the Potentiate and took him to the Numin Well.

Hexus smiled. There was nothing now that could stop him. Without the Guardian, the Potentiate was helpless. He had no defenders left except for a few mortals with no weapons other than swords.

Three more bears and a wolf ran up out of the woods. The last of his forest group. They skidded to a stop in the clearing, looking and sniffing about in panic, eyes wide at the sight of their dead fellows.

"Fear not," Hexus told them. "The Antigod killed your brothers, but the Antigod is bound now and cannot harm us."

He pointed at the quaking Numin Jar. The soulburdened beasts looked at it uncertainly.

"You," Hexus called to Vark. "Bring that down to the ships. The rest of us will follow the Potentiate. The wolf will show the way."

"My god," Vark said, stepping forward. "I do not think that I can—"

"Do as I say!" Hexus commanded. He was not pleased that the Hieroni had proven unable to sway the Potentiate, though he had claimed a special influence over the boy. "The old books tell that the other jars were carried by Engineers, to be secreted away throughout the Earth. You can carry it."

Vark hesitated, but Hexus watched him, hand in the air, the god's black eye glaring. Finally Vark turned. He stood looking at the shuddering blue jar. And then he whispered, so quietly that he thought none could hear him, although Hexus caught his words, "This is what I have always tried to do. To grab hold of thunder, and wield it. How can I say no now? How can I admit I had been wrong?"

And with panicked determination he strode forward and seized the metal handles along the sides of the jar.

His face was lit a moment in the deep, otherworldly blue glow. Again, the bright sunlight seemed to dim.

And then the leader of the Hieroni screamed, and exploded into flames. He fell to his knees, but his limbs clung rigidly fixed to the Jar, as if his hands were unable to release it. He shook with convulsions. His skin bubbled and turned black. White fire shot from his mouth, his nose, finally his eyes. The bears roared and turned in place, terrified. Somehow Vark continued to scream. Blue flames shot across his skin, and turned to yellow fires in his clothes.

Hexus reached out and broke the man's neck, silencing him.

It seemed a long while before silence settled again into the clearing.

"It is not meant to be like that," Hexus whispered. Had something broken the Jar, over the years? And yet it had been forged by Threkor himself, to withstand the relentless passage of millions of years.

"Leave it," Hexus said. "It can work as well here as elsewhere. The Guardian is bound. Let us go. Follow the boy!"

Fearfully, the wolf lowered its head and started up the hillside, smelling at the earth.

When Chance and Wadjet came into the valley, they found the ancient sleek airship fully inflated, its long blue shape rigid with pressure. The cabin's entrance, where the whole back wall hinged down and lay on the ground, formed a ramp that led into the small cabin. Mimir stood at the bottom of the ramp. She seemed to Chance strangely taller than she had appeared before.

Coughing from the long run, Chance stumbled across the stream and to her side. He put his hand on his knee, bending over, exhausted. Wadjet, beside him, was panting but otherwise unaffected.

"Sa-Sarah?" Chance asked. "Is Sarah here yet?"

"No," Mimir said.

"Thetis?"

"No," Mimir said.

"The Guardian. . . ." he gasped, unable to finish the sentence.

"I feel it," Mimir said. "I can touch the Machinedream." And her voice betrayed something like satisfaction. "What has happened to the Guardian?"

"Trapped. In something. A Numin Jar."

Mimir nodded. "Yes. That explains much."

Chance stood straight, his knees still trembling. He scanned the top of the valley. "We have to be ready to go as soon as they come."

"We shall go now," Mimir said.

Chance turned sharply. He took a step back. "No! Absolutely not. We wait for Sarah."

"If the god comes, we will be lost."

Wadjet nodded. "The Makina speaks harsh counsel, but right counsel."

"No," Chance repeated. But a spike of fear hit him: the Guardian was not here now. He could not depend upon Wadjet. That meant he was alone with this machine. There she stood, in her clean suit of black clothes, like the preposterous formal dress of some citizen of Disthea on the way to a wedding, and eyed him with cool indifference. Her face and form showed no tiredness, no weakness, no susceptibility to any hardship. Her silver eyes looked on him with a cruel indifference to his pains and cares. He had not feared Mimir when the Guardian had been there. But now, gazing at her, he saw the hint of great and ancient powers, bound to cold purposes.

"I judge it expedient that we leave immediately," Mimir said calmly. And in a flash she reached forward and grabbed Chance's shoulder.

Wadjet hesitated, and then ran onto the ship. Chance understood the decision: she would not stay out here and let Mimir decide perhaps to leave her behind.

"No, wait but a moment or two. Sarah must be near," Chance protested. But Mimir did not answer. With an iron grip she dragged Chance toward the ship.

Chance twisted, and kicked out. His foot struck Mimir's leg. Mimir's grip on him slipped, and in a second she was holding only his sleeve. Chance jerked free. The sleeve tore off.

Mimir dropped it. "Consider," she said. "What would be the likely outcome if you and I fought here until the god found us?"

Chance hesitated. And then in a shot Mimir was on him again. She seized his good wrist this time, and dragged him into the ship. With one arm, she pulled the door closed. Then Mimir merely stared at the controls, and the tethers released, the engines screamed into life, and the ship rose.

She can control it without touching it, Chance thought with horror.

"Let me go!" he demanded. But Mimir held him tightly until they were high above the plateau. Wadjet sat in the back of the cabin, looking back and forth from the windows to Mimir, her dark green eyes wide, betraying fear.

What does Wadjet know, or see, that I don't? he wondered. Why is she so afraid of Mimir?

Finally the Makina released him, after they were over the churning whitecaps of the sea.

Chance sank to his knees. "Sarah," he gasped. "Sarah."

CHAPTER

42

"What is it?" Hexus demanded.

The wolf had stopped on a steep part of the hillside, where gravel broke out of the thin soil.

"Four scents," it said. "One, two women go up the hill here." The wolf pointed its snout. "One man, one woman go this way." He pointed his snout along the side of the hill.

"Follow the boy," Hexus told him. "The boy."

The wolf lowered her head in submission. She started forward on the slope, when a dull hum sounded out before them. The bears froze. The wolf lifted its head.

A black airship floated out of the valley before them. Its design was strange, the cabin small and narrow, with two engines as large as the cabin roaring on each side of it. The balloon of the airship was long and dark. It rose quickly, faster than any airship the bears or wolf had seen, and then the ship leaned forward and shot out over the forest, the wind behind it.

Hexus hesitated. He could try running on the air—but as he considered the possibility of attempting the feat, the ship moved out of sight over the tree tops. It would be bad if he pursued it some distance and then fell into the sea.

"Ah!" he howled in rage. This crippled, rotting body made him so weak, so doubting. And surely the Potentiate was on that airship. Chance had escaped again.

The bears cringed at the shattered howl of Hexus.

"Be calm," he told them, not wanting to lose their faith. "I am impatient, but the Potentiate goes where we want him to go. Nothing is lost. You four, search the woods. Make sure the Potentiate is gone. Bring me any other humans you find. I will go back to the beach and take one of the other airships and follow this one. You may come later in the others."

The wolf set off, huge feet padding silently over the hard ground. The bears followed.

Hexus turned and disappeared in a blur.

The ship strained as Sar drove it up against the mountain winds. Perhaps taking it around the mountain had not been a wise plan, for she was not sure it hid her for long—some bear would report to the god soon—and the slow climb against the shifting katabatic winds made the airship drift toward the rocks and cliffs, then back, in unpredictable ways. Below, the forest gave out to shrub and then bare stone.

Finally she maneuvered the ship in among the jagged black peaks of stone. It seemed that the ship stalled there, and might just drift into one of the spires of sharp rock. The engines were on full but only held the ship in the icy headwind—but then the wind shifted and the ship shot ahead, over the lip of a narrow crest, and the black teeth of the peak scraped just below the cabin.

Then the ship flew through clear sky. She had made it over the crest.

The ship descended quickly now into a valley filled with shards of shale, spotted here and there with a tuft of grass.

This was the weakest part of her plan. She hoped that the boy and his group, driven up into the hills, would be between her and the god. She would have to bring the ship down and call out with the ship's loudspeakers, hoping to get the attention of the sensitive ears of the Guardian or the coyote or even the makina.

The valley sloped gently down, turning as it went. She pointed the engines slightly down also, pushing the ship toward the earth, to keep it low. She had dropped all her ballast to make the quick retreat, so it took the force of the engines to descend.

As she turned around a tall spire, a large green bowl opened before her, and beyond it the valley stretched down to forest and to the grassy plateau beyond. In the center of the bowl, two figures stood back to back, surrounded by a cautiously circling group of bears and a wolf. The humans were women, she could see: one in the black robes of the Gotterdammerung, and the other in pants. The Mother, and the Puriman warrior, Sar concluded.

The Ranger had her swords drawn. The Junior Mother held awkwardly in both hands a heavy stick. The soulburdened beasts seemed unusually wary. All now looked up at the ship. The god did not appear to be nearby.

Sar took a chance. The bears were unlikely to know the guild language of the Gotterdammerung. But Sar could speak it. She fumbled with controls, found the loudspeaker.

"*I am Sar,*" she called out in the Mother's guild language. "*I stole this airship and am alone on it. I have no anchor. I'll drive it down near you, and then you must rush the door.*"

She watched as the Mother leaned back, head turned sideways. She was whispering to the girl, translating. Good.

Sar let the ship drift toward them, then abruptly shifted the engines to full downward. The airship protested, the fabric snapping and fluttering loudly in the turbulence. But after a moment of turning hesitation, the ship dove for the ground. The soul-burdened beasts backed up, opening their circle, expecting that there were reinforcements on the airship that they recognized as their own.

The ship hit the ground, hard, scraping on stone. Sar leapt up and ran for the door. She fell when the ship bounced and then slammed into the ground again. Then, on her knees, she threw the door open, revealing the open field, the confused bears, and Thetis and Sarah. Thetis dropped the stick she held for defense and ran for the open portal. Sarah came behind, moving quickly but mostly backwards, swords out.

The bear on that side of the ship howled in anger when it saw the Mother run into the ship, past Sar. He ran for Sarah. But the confusion of the other bears slowed them too much. Sarah was in the doorway by the time the one bear was on her. She leapt back, out of the way of a swipe, and stabbed her points out. The bear fell back, dodging. Sar was in the control seat then and turned the engines over. The ship shot up. The bear leapt and grabbed the frame of the door, but Sarah kicked his paws off the edge, and then pulled the door shut.

"Where are the others?" Sar called.

"Seth is dead," Thetis said, gripping the edge of Sar's seat. "The Guardian is trapped, we think. The others are trapped or on another airship, ahead of us." She pointed north.

"The boy?" Sar asked.

"On the airship," Thetis said.

"And you say the Guardian is trapped?"

"They had a Numin Jar."

Sar hissed in anger.

"Wadjet!" Sarah protested. "Mimir! We're not sure Wadjet or Mimir are on that ship."

Sar glanced at her. They rose quickly now, racing north.

"But you're sure the boy is on the ship?"

Sarah held up a strip of cloth. A sleeve. Sar recognized it: a sleeve of Chance's Puriman-made shirt. "This was on the ground, where the airship had been parked. We saw it leave. He has escaped the false god."

"Mimir was with the ship. And someone is flying it," Thetis said. "She must be on it. And we cannot look for the Steward, when she is likely on that airship. Go! Follow! To Yggdrasil!"

Sar nodded. She agreed with Thetis. The boy was what mattered most now.

She saw then the Ranger's cheeks were streaked with tears. Blood flowed freely down her cheek from her broken scab.

"I can't believe Chance left without me," Sarah whispered. "Why would he do that? I'm his protector."

"He may have had no choice," Thetis said. "The makina may have made him go."

"The makina," Sar mumbled, ominously, as the sea came into view, and beyond it the northern reach of the Sæwall. "The makina may be alone with him. That is ill news."

Chance sat on the floor of the narrow airship, stunned, staring at nothing.

After a long while, Wadjet came and put her hand on Chance's head.

"I lost Seth," he said. "He died saving me. He died horribly. In terrible pain. I lost him. I lost him. Another death on my conscience. Why did he die for me?"

"He loved you," Wadjet explained.

And that was it, of course. But this only made Chance's burden heavier.

"And Sarah's alone with that false god!"

"The god will come after us," Wadjet said. "Sarah can hide, escape, and you can return and save her, when this is over. When you've killed this rotten thing. I will come with you, to get my ship."

Chance grabbed her hand and squeezed it.

Seth is dead, he thought. Sarah is lost. Thetis is lost. The Guardian is bound, perhaps dead. My arm is broken. My village is soon to be burned, its people eaten. My brother will soon be beyond saving, if he is not already so.

"Oh great God," Chance whispered. "Have pity on me. Have pity on us all. Our way cannot get worse. It cannot get worse."

"Yes it can," Wadjet said.

Her hand suddenly gripped tightly back on Chance's palm. He looked up at her through his tears. She stared with wide eyes toward the front of the ship, the points of her fangs just showing behind her open lips.

Chance climbed to his feet and looked at Mimir.

The makina stood with one hand out. She gazed at her palm in reverie. On it rested two dice of bone.

PART III
YGGDRASIL

CHAPTER

43

"**W**hy are you doing that?" Chance demanded.

Two days had passed. Chance paced and turned in the narrow back of the cabin like a trapped animal in a tight cage. All the people he loved had died or were threatened with death, and he could do nothing but fret the limits of this tiny cabin as they glided slowly over a tossing sea, deafened by the roar of the ship's loud engines. Sometimes he stopped and wept when he remembered Seth or worried over Sarah. Other times with Wadjet he picked at their meager scraps of food. And through it all, Mimir maintained a terrifying concentration as she rolled her dice, hour after hour, over the controls of the airship.

A division of the space arose. Mimir crouched in the front of the cabin, silent, ignoring them, studying the results of her dice as if they were surprisingly complex. Chance and Wadjet stayed in the back half of the cabin, by the door. They sat on crates or—one at a time because the space was so narrow—lay on the floor. Most often, Wadjet sat while Chance paced.

The end of the second day, the sky turned gray, and sheets of light rain fell on the airship, making a susurration sometimes audible over the monotonous howl of the engines.

Finally, Chance could bear the makina's silence no longer.

"Why do you do that?" he demanded again. He rose and walked toward her when Mimir did not answer. She only rolled the dice again. Chance slammed his hand down over the bone cubes. The makina looked at him, as if just recognizing him.

"Stop," he said. "That solves nothing. You yourself explained to us how empty it is."

Mimir put her hand on his chest, and smoothly but with unstoppable force pushed him back. Chance stumbled, his broken arm hindering his balance, and fell beside Wadjet.

Wadjet, who had been mostly silent for the two days, spoke to him as she helped him to his feet. "She will kill me soon." She did not bother to whisper.

"Surely not!" Chance said.

"Soon. But she won't kill you. You're useful."

Chance's bitterness overwhelmed him. "May God damn every person who finds me useful." It hurt his heart to utter such profanity, but his anger had won over his restraint.

Wadjet raised a lip in a defiant smile: she approved of the sentiment.

"Why does she take us to the Well, if she means to betray us?"

Wadjet shook her head. "I don't know. But remember this. She will fear the modbarrows."

Mimir looked at Wadjet sharply, her silver eyes turning voluntarily from the dice for the first time that day. She stood. Chance held his breath, expecting an attack. But behind Mimir the clouds had parted, the gray pillars of rain falling on the sea before them were divided, and through the gap Chance saw now a dark shore lined with hills. Behind these rose mountains, densely forested and, beyond, a black cord stretched higher than he could have imagined possible, from the horizon up through clouds and into a remoteness where it became invisible. It seemed to stretch all the way to the stars.

He pointed. "What...?"

"Yggdrasil," Wadjet said. "The World Ash."

Mimir turned her back to them, looking over the sea and the controls at Yggdrasil, clutching her dice in a fist.

"Yggdrasil," Chance said. And at its foot, Chance knew, lay the door to the Numin Well. Would he know how to find it? Would he know how to open it? And how was he to face this thing Ma'at? Would he be able to pass through the door that Ma'at guarded?

He had assumed that Thetis and the Guardian would be with him when he reached the end of his journey. He could curse the Guardian's distrust, to have told him so little. Now he had to hope the makina would take him there, and then allow him to complete his mission. Given Mimir's sullen transformation, this seemed to him unlikely. A terrible battle with the machine was coming, and he would have to fight this battle alone. And if by some miracle he won, he would not know what to do next: how to find the door, how to face the gatekeeper Ma'at, how to get beyond Ma'at....

The ship began to drop, moving closer to the approaching shore.

"Why are you in exile?" Chance asked Wadjet.

Hours had passed, as Mimir stood unmoving with her back to them. The ship crossed low over the sharp black peaks of the steep mountains. Before them, Yggdrasil split the darkening sky, but seemed to grow no closer.

Wadjet and Chance sat on the floor, a dried fish between them. They broke off flaking white pieces with their fingers and then chewed slowly on the salty parched flesh. They passed a cup of water. Chance hesitated over the intimacy: after her first sip, he could taste the smell of Wadjet in the water.

Wadjet looked at him, seemingly deciding what to answer. Finally, she said, "I killed a chimpanzee."

"Was he soulburdened?" Chance asked.

Wadjet nodded.

Chance marveled at this a moment. He had never known of a Truman—or any man in any community of which he'd heard—being punished because he had killed one of the soulburdened. But then he thought: yes. Yes. Seth's death had been murder.

"Why did you kill him?"

"He was a...." She searched for the word in Common. "He beat a friend, another chimpanzee."

"And there was a fight?"

"No fight. Chimpanzees are very strong. I had to defeat him before there was a fight."

Chance found himself morbidly longing to know the details. Wadjet's teeth were fierce, but she was thin, with lean arms and legs, and she never carried a weapon—at least not one that he had seen. How did she kill some strong soulburdened beast? He remembered the immovable solidity of the bear that had attacked him by the riverside, after he had fled the Guardian. He flexed his bicep, naked after Mimir had torn away his sleeve, feeling the stiff skin there from the scar the bear's claw had scraped into his arm.

But instead he asked, "If you cure this disease, will you be forgiven?"

Wadjet showed her fangs. "I don't ask anyone to forgive me. I am not sorry. I do not want to be a Steward. They've done no harm to me, with this punishment of exile."

"But...."

"I want to show the Stewards what I can do, without their help and their rules and their endless counsels. And I want to cure friends, so that they might live their lives a while and have children as they want, and those children can live their lives a while. After life, there is nothing, Puriman. Or so I believe. You have to live your life now, as wild and well as you can. The Stewards are like your 'wise' Elders, like that fretting guild woman, and these old beings—" she waved the back of her hand at Mimir contemptuously. "They have their puffed worries and their struggles and their rules and their schemes and their histories—always they have their histories, their rotting books and old tales, as if nothing was ever dead and done. They think all of this history turns on their choices. They never live a day wild. They live in a cage." She looked around their cramped cabin and she sneered at it as if Mimir had constructed the little space for the very purpose of confining them.

"You can't be sure that there's nothing after death," Chance said.

"You can't be sure that there is anything after death."

Chance opened his mouth to answer, then hesitated.

"You can't," Wadjet repeated. "Now ask yourself, which is more likely? You've seen how the world goes, Puriman. It's not made for men; it's not a nursery for human beings. It's not made for anyone."

"God's world is our home," Chance said, paraphrasing one of the New Psalms of the Purimen.

"No. We're all without a home. Once you have the idea of a home, once you understand the world that much, that is the moment you become homeless."

That sounded absurd to Chance. But also, somehow, disturbing. He pictured his home on the shores of Walking Man Lake, the tall walls with graying shingles. Now, of course, his house and village both would seem tiny to him, after having seen Disthea. He thought of the cool plaster of this own room, with its familiar cracks. The dark warmth of the kitchen. The smell of the lake. The cacophony of the frogs in spring, singing in the swamp just down the hill from the road. The sound of the church bell echoing in the Valley on a Sunday.

Would that still be home to him? Without his parents? Perhaps with the rejection of the Purimen? Would it still be home after all he had seen, after he knew of the suffering and anger that seethed outside the valleys—and also the great beauty and accomplishments outside their realm?

If not, he had no home.

Wadjet tore off the head of the fish, stuck it in her mouth, and crunched away at it, grinding the skull as she glared angrily at Mimir.

Night fell. The airship roared through the dark. Mimir seemed to see as well at night as in the day, for she continued to stand with her back to them, as still as a statue, and to stare out the black windows as if guiding their ship. Every few minutes she threw her dice, and snatched them out of the air on the second bounce to read their faces.

Chance slept fitfully, after exchanging glances with Wadjet that conveyed somehow the agreement that the two of them would trade time sleeping. He slept first, and Wadjet awoke him in the dark by pressing gently on his shoulder.

He sat up and looked about sleepily. Mimir still had not moved. Without warning, Wadjet stripped off her pants and shirt and rolled them into a pillow, and, wearing only thin briefs and a top, lay down to sleep, stretching out like some wild animal.

After it seemed that Wadjet was asleep, Chance knelt in the very back of the cabin and prayed.

"Dear God, please protect Sarah. Please give grace unto Seth, first known as Psuche.

"I know that Purimen say no soulburdened will dwell in Heaven, but that's one of the things they said in the Valley I'm going to have to just give up on, God. I hope that doesn't mean I'm picking and choosing scripture. I just can't believe you'd let Seth suffer for me and battle the wicked and earn no grace. I just can't believe Seth had no proper soul. No, Lord, I've got to give up on that one.

"And by the by I'm giving up on the one about all unmen being wicked. And the one about the Barren being the work of the False Gods. And a few others. No need to go into those now."

He sighed and looked at Mimir's silhouette before the window, visible against the stars. "So. This is the worst of it, God. I thought my father dying was the worst, but it wasn't. This is the worst. Can't get any worse now. And I'm trying hard not to be angry at your silence. Your absence. With a powerful effort, I can almost see how I should feel joy: I did my best, and maybe you notice that worth thinking on. Soon I'll succeed and then most certainly die, or die trying to succeed—I'm not going to let this machine stop me from trying. And then Sarah and Seth and I will be together with our parents in some place closer to you. I can hope on that.

"So I'll keep on. Just a little way now. But it's hard, God. Hard. Suffering prepares the heart for future grace; it says so in the Book. Well, suffering has prepared me for a while now, but it seems the grace just stays in the future. Always over the edge of this huge, tired Earth.

"I'll stop here. I know it's petulant of me to ask again for an answer to my prayers. So I'll think it but not say it.

"Amen."

He stood and paced in the narrow width of the back of the cabin for an hour, before he finally sat on a box and propped himself against the side of the cabin, and then very deliberately stared out the windows at the stars, trying to keep his eyes open without resting them on Wadjet, who lay stretched out like a cat at his feet. In a short while the first fingers of dawn reached pink and purple out of the west. He watched the colors grow as they lit the white fog that lay over the dark green forest below them. It was a beautiful sight.

What if, he wondered, as Wadjet claims, all this wonder were just there, without a beginning, without a beginner? Would that be so evil, so hopeless, so bad?

Looking at the purple sky, the swirling, glowing mists in the trees, he could no longer believe that it would be. Seth dying horribly, before he lived a full life—that was horrible. Sarah alone in a dangerous place, Sarah maybe dead—that was horrible. Paul denied his body, his life, his chance to be a man—that was horrible. But if all this beauty were alone, all of it without design—that was not horrible.

Still. All this, all this beauty... it could be the truest sign of the love of The One True God.

He sighed. How strange these days. How beyond the understanding of any mortal man. He looked down at Wadjet. She lay on her back, arms stretched over her head. He let his eyes follow her lines, along her legs, the fine shape of her hips, her breasts. Then he saw that her eyes were open, that she stared up at him. Neither of them smiled; they gazed fiercely, almost hungrily, at each other.

I should turn away, Chance thought. I should turn my back. But he did not.

Wadjet lifted her chin slightly.

"So, Puriman?" she said.

Chance stared at her a long time. He swallowed. "Sarah," he said. "My wife."

He stood. He turned his back.

CHAPTER

44

There should be no time, the Guardian thought.

But for long hours he howled, holding to Threkor's Hammer as it shuddered and turned white-hot in his hand, searing his stony flesh, driving blinding bolts of burning lightning into his body, his face, his eyes.

He saw in a flash, in a memory, great Threkor, bent over his monstrous anvil, affixing the lid to the last Numin Jar. Sweat beaded on Threkor's dark, bald head. His black eyes squinted in concentration. A crack of blue light poured from the jar and diminished to a bright band, like a crack in the world, as Threkor pressed on the lid. He forced the lid down and the glare shrank to a single beam, then a glimmer—then darkness. The massive demigod's profound voice echoed through the great hall of Uroboros as he stood over his finished creation. "Inside," Threkor had told him. "They will be trapped beyond time, in no time. No pain, no suffering, no true existence. Just waiting, for the end of our sun and world." There had been pity in his voice. Threkor had had doubts. The Guardian, taking the Jar from his hand, had had none.

But there was pain. There was suffering. There was time: a long, slow existence in agony.

How could that be? Threkor had not made mistakes of this kind, mistakes of engineering.

Lightning shot again from the hammer into his eyes. The Guardian howled.

It is the hammer, the Guardian realized. Threkor's Hammer harmed him, and hindered the binding of the Numin Jar. The Guardian could not let go of it—lightning fused it to his hand. But he would not have let go if he were able.

What had Sar told him? The hammer is both here and elsewhere. The hammer must not touch the shield of the binding. The Hammer hindered the shield, it burned through it. And it was the shield of binding that formed the other place inside the Numin Jar.

The Guardian swung Threkor's Hammer.

It struck at nothing, at something, and thundering bolts of power blasted through the tiny no-place where he floated. The bolts cracked his hard flesh.

He swung again. Smoke rose from his eyes, his mouth, from the splits in his scorched and blackening skin.

He swung again. Through the blue light, a yellow glow shone for a second, before being swallowed in blue again. The Guardian fixed on that place and struck again. And again. And again.

He lost his hearing, as his ears were blasted away.

He lost his breath, his mouth, as his face was blasted away.

He lost finally his eyes, cooked away in white heat.

But still he struck, and struck, and struck at a wall that stood invisible, seemingly impenetrable, between two worlds.

And then came the explosion. It rent the Guardian into a hundred parts, and cast these, with the fragments of the bursting Numin Jar, through the dark grass of the jungle clearing. The mind-destroying pain died, as the Guardian died.

✚

Wind rustled dry blades of grass. A bird cried in the distance. Hearing returned to the Guardian.

Next came his sight. He looked at the sky. Round white clouds passed. They seemed to him beautiful. Timeless. Clouds like this had passed over Lethebion when he had walked there as a man, as Treow. Clouds like this had passed over the island before the Age of Guilds. Clouds like this had passed over the island when its stones were young, and humans did not exist, and not a single flower had ever opened its petals.

After a while an airship passed over too. A wide, red airship. One of those airships he had seen on the beach. He should throw a stone at it, fell it from the sky. The god was on that airship. He could ken the foul thing, hurting space.

But he had no arms to lift a stone.

He had no legs to stand and carry him to find a stone.

And his own reasoning, his own voice telling him what to do, seemed so far away. He could hardly hear it. His reason was like his pain of being broken into parts: it goaded him, but it also felt so far away that it harmed him little.

The airship passed. The sound of its engine receded, like the passing clouds.

The Guardian closed his eyes.

The Guardian put his fingers against his face.

And leapt up. He was awake. And whole. His body had slowly managed to reassemble itself, and reforge what had been blazed away in the Numin Jar and the violence of Threkor's Hammer. He stood, naked and gray, in the blasted clearing.

In a great circle, four paces in radius, the ground was black and scorched. Shards of crystal, fragments of the Numin Jar, lay scattered all around—some were driven into the face of the stone wall nearby, as if they were spikes of steel hammered into the rock. A scorched black cinder of a human body lay beside him. No one he knew, by the shape of it and by the clothes. It must be the man who had wielded the Jar. Just deserts for a Hieroni.

Then he saw Seth. The coyote lay crushed, half torn away, eyes open. The Guardian froze, almost stumbled. He remembered now this death, and felt it as a harsh new hurt. No carrion eater had taken the corpse away—larger animals had kept away from the Numin Jar in fear, no doubt. But ants covered the body.

The Guardian knelt and brushed the insects from Seth's face, and then closed the coyote's eyes as gently as his hard gray fingers of stone could manage.

"Psuche, known as Seth, Apprentice of the Hekademon, you undertook great deeds from love and from faithful oaths. Child of Wealtheow, and so in part a child of mine own, I am sorry I failed and let you die. But I shall make it so that your name is sung. Not forgotten will be the greatness of your soul."

He thrust his hands into the dirt and turned dark handfuls of sandy earth over on the coyote. In moments he made a funeral mound.

Then he stood. Nearby lay Threkor's Hammer, whole but scorched all over as black and gray as ashes. He lifted it. Then he ran in a blur up the hill, into the valley.

His airship was gone. The chipped shards of gray slate that covered the ground were not blemished with blood, but many footprints and bear prints had been set with tracked mud on the pale flakes. It might well be as he hoped: Chance could have escaped, with the god in pursuit.

How could the Guardian follow the airships? He could not cross the sea bottom on foot. Wending the thick water would be far too slow. And there was no other airship that he knew of secreted on Lethebion.

It would have to be Wadjet's ship. He lifted the abandoned machinery that they had scavenged from Wadjet's engine onto his shoulders, and shot back as he had come, and beyond, toward the beach.

But when Aegweard first came into view, he saw, through small gaps in the tree cover, the red of an airship. He stopped and set the parts of Wadjet's engine on the trail. Then he moved more slowly, more quietly, down the slope.

There was a single ship tethered to the sand. Bears milled about it. They had a machine making lifting gas and were feeding it sea water in buckets dragged up from the surf. A large blue patch covered the side of the airship: the ship's hull had been torn and mended.

The bears roared as the Guardian strode out from the trees. There were four of them. And a wolf.

"Where is the Potentiate?" he asked. "Where is the boy that the god seeks?"

The bears, as he expected, attacked. He killed them in a flash and tossed their broken bodies into the shallow surf, for crabs to pick their bones.

The wolf, too wise to fight or to run, waited, front legs askew, back legs bent, tail between her legs, ears flat.

"I would rather not harm you, woodwarden. I am the Guardian, once Treow, once husband to the mother of many of your kind. You do ill to fight me, and wrong in serving the god."

The ears of the wolf twitched, but she said nothing.

"Tell me where the boy is, and then I shall take this airship, and you shall have your life, and you shall have leave of this island."

After a moment's hesitation, the wolf rolled onto her back, a show of submission.

"Rise," the Guardian said.

She got up and told the Guardian what she knew.

CHAPTER
45

The ship skimmed but a hundred paces above the tree line. Chance saw now how fast they were moving, with the trees as reference. During the night they had finished crossing the mountains and most of the forest beyond. Shortly after dawn, they passed the edge of the forest and sailed out over a great plateau of small hills, one after another, covered with tall grasses. Something moved among them. Herds of deer, it seemed, but Chance also thought he saw several times the steely glint of a machine twisting through the grasses.

"These are the modbarrows," Wadjet told him. "In each little hill, a soul is bound. By choice, they say. It was endless life that they sought. But now they are mad and envious of the living."

The barrows stretched off all the way to Yggdrasil. After their night of travel, Yggdrasil did seem slightly wider to Chance's eye, a single black trunk rising forever.

Wadjet touched Chance's arm, and then pointed out at the horizon. Chance followed her aim. A black cloud was forming far before them on the plane.

"What is it?" he asked.

"Like birds," she said.

And Chance knew then what it was, as they approached.

"They are Makine," he said. "A black flock of flying Makine." Like the makina he'd seen the Guardian destroy above the river—it seemed a year ago, though it had been only weeks.

The flock sped toward them quickly, a growing black cloud— and then suddenly the glinting black beings flew all about the ship. In a huge speeding band they circled the cabin twice. If they made a sound, it was inaudible above the engines. But the sharp black wings darkened the sky, and the dense flock seemed to spin them into some other world for a moment, as it whirled with blinding speed, filling Chance's view.

And then they were gone, flying off toward the west.

"Where are they going?" Chance asked, suddenly concerned. He turned to the back of the cabin, where a row of windows covered the raised door, and looked at the black flock as it hurried away in the direction from which they had come.

Mimir did not answer. She looked down at the rolling hills beneath them, then out at Yggdrasil. Chance followed her gaze: he could see now where the great trunk of it met the ground, and where what appeared to be buildings were clustered. Then Mimir turned toward Chance and Wadjet.

Mimir drew her dice from her pocket and tossed them, still standing. They rolled all the way to Wadjet's feet. Both Wadjet and the makina looked at them. The symbols on their faces were mean-ingless to Chance.

"What is this?" Chance demanded. "It's time you talked, and treated us as your allies—"

Mimir moved in a flash. In a moment she was between Chance and Wadjet, one hand flat on Chance's chest, the other gripping Wadjet's arm.

The steward twisted in a way Chance would not have thought possible, running her feet up the side of the cabin, leveraging her arm out of the gap between Mimir's thumb and fingers, while also flipping over to land behind the makina.

She kicked the makina in the head, hard.

Mimir bent forward but did not fall. Quickly, Mimir turned and stood erect, facing Wadjet. Wadjet held up her hands like claws. But then Mimir vomited a silver liquid out of her mouth in a narrow stream, straight into Wadjet's face.

Chance shouted, horrified. The silver substance clung to Wadjet's face. Chance had seen quicksilver and this was something like that—and yet it seemed granular, like sand, as if made of small moving things. Wadjet growled but choked immediately as the silver stuff rushed into her mouth and nose.

Chance hit Mimir under her arm with his free hand. His punch was weaker with his left, but he could still hit hard. It was like striking a bag of wet sand. He knocked Mimir forward slightly, but she seemed unharmed. She reached out with one hand and seized Chance's free wrist before he could strike her again.

The silver slime was gone from Wadjet's face. All of it crept into her mouth and nose. Wadjet fell against the side of the cabin, bent over, retching, trying to cough the stuff up.

Chance twisted and pushed, but could not get his arm free to hit Mimir again. He leaned back and kicked Mimir under her arm, awkwardly but with a solid hit. He kicked her again.

But in a single swift motion Mimir swept her foot under his feet, and Chance, with his balance impaired by his sling, fell back. Mimir released his wrist and he toppled onto the hard floor.

"Why did you wait so long?" Wadjet gasped.

"I am not sure how long the emotive bonding agent will operate effectively," Mimir answered. "And so I delayed until we were nearly ready to tether this vehicle beside Yggdrasil. I am sorry if the delay was stressful for you." Her voice had a calm, matter-of-fact tone.

"What have you done?" Chance shouted at Mimir. He got to his feet, and stumbled to Wadjet's side. He put his hand on her bent back.

"Can I help?" he whispered. "What...?"

Wadjet coughed, retched painfully. She looked up at Mimir. "Why not just kill me?" she managed to croak.

"I have no desire to execute any sentient being."

"Liar. There's some other reason."

Mimir watched Wadjet writhe in pain. "You may be useful."

"May God damn every person who finds me useful," Wadjet said. And Chance understood, somehow, that this quoting of his own curse was Wadjet's way of saying goodbye.

She moved in a flash. She pushed Chance into Mimir, and the makina and Chance stumbled back as Wadjet leapt forward. She yanked at a red cord in the wall, and two loud snaps—small explosions—sounded out. It was the emergency release for the door. The door fell open, laying itself down like a ramp. Wind roared in, swirling bits of stray cloth and detritus about the cabin before these were sucked out into the sky behind the ship. Wadjet grabbed a rope that hung coiled on the wall, and leapt out into the air.

"Wadjet!" Chance called. He hurried to the edge of the door and looked down. The line paid out as Wadjet fell. She wrapped the cord around her arm. He saw then how clever the daughter of Stewards had been. The rope had hung there, seemingly untouched, for days. But when they had been moving boxes of stores, Wadjet had tied one end of the line down, and run the other end under a bench so that the rope would drag through a bend of two pipes, paying out slowly.

Mimir reached for the rope. To cut it, Chance thought in a flash. He bent back and twisted, getting all the bound force he could muster, and then struck her again, in the head, as hard as his twisting, leaping body would allow. Mimir fell. Wadjet's line ran out to the end. Chance put one foot out on the door so he could look over its edge. He saw Wadjet twisting on the end of the line as it reached its full length. She dangled perhaps four paces from the ground. And then she let go.

She hit the ground with cruel force and bounced into the air, her limbs flailing.

"Wadjet!" he cried out. There is no way she survived that, he thought. Or she is surely hurt, many bones broken, and will be crippled there.

He would have to go back for her. He was not leaving anyone else.

Mimir seized the back of his shirt, pulled him away from the door, and threw him on the ground. Chance landed hard. He put his hand down and found something pointed under it. The dice. He clutched them and held his fist up, showing their square faces to Mimir.

"You cannot escape your decisions, Mimir. This is your fault, your wrong that happens here."

He threw the dice through the open door.

Mimir watched them fall. Chance had for a moment the thought that she would jump out after the dice, to see how they landed in the grasses below. But then, after standing frozen a moment, Mimir pulled the door up and tied it with a rope.

Then she turned toward him. She opened her mouth.

"This is not going to be easy, Mimir," he said. He got to his feet, snatched a grappling pole from the wall of the cabin, and held it back, a long club. "I'm going to make this hard. Very hard. You might puke that filth on me, but there is no way you can knock me down so as I won't get right back up and fight you again."

"Chance Kyrien, it is not my intention to knock you down or harm you in any other way. I only want to ensure that you perceive certain opportunities in a favorable way, as I believe that you should."

Chance backed toward the front of the cabin.

"You cannot do significant harm to me with that rod, Chance Kyrien. It therefore does not have a deterrent effect."

"Oh, we'll see," he said. And, with all the speed he could manage, he turned and smashed the controls of the airship. Mimir leaped on him, but he struck the small control box twice more with the rod before she pulled his head back, and spat her choking quicksilver machines into his mouth.

The whine of the engines had changed. The ship listed, dropping.

Chance tasted metal. Lead. Tin. He coughed. The quicksilver stuff crawled over his eyes. A horrible sensation of choking, as though he were drowning, overcame him. But he struck out again, and again, both times hitting something hard, solidly. And then his air was choked off, and he fell onto the deck, unconscious.

CHAPTER

46

"It's beyond anything I imagined," Sarah said. She stood, with her mouth open, looking out the front windows of the airship at the sky-cutting height of Yggdrasil. From this distance it was little more than a thin black slit in the horizon, rising from Earth to beyond her vision, but she could see both that it must be huge in circumference, and that it stretched beyond the clouds.

"Yes," Thetis agreed. "It was once the most important thing that human beings had ever built. It was going to give them the stars."

"It stretches to the stars?" Sarah asked.

"No," Sar answered. "But it stretches beyond the air, and beyond the reach of the heaviness of Earth. That's the hardest part of getting to the stars: getting up that little way."

Sarah shook her head in wonder.

They had traveled for three days; most of that time Sarah had stood impatiently with her hands on the back of the seat where Sar sat and steered the airship. A hundred times, Sarah asked, "Are you sure this is the right way?"

"Yes, girl," Sar had answered.

"But then, where is the black airship?"

"It must be faster. We'll catch them. I'm more worried about what's behind us."

But no ship came into view either behind or before them. They finally broke through clouds over a shore where great waves crashed white on black rocks and black sand. Beyond this narrow and broken shoreline, a green forest stretched to low but steep black mountains, its canopy so thick it seemed they could land and walk on it. They rode on, the engine howling, vibrating the whole cabin with monotonous, maddening dullness, until they passed over the mountains and the forest beyond.

A long grassland of small, regular low hills or mounds lay before them, rolling all the way to Yggdrasil.

Thetis pointed now at the hills.

"Those are the modbarrows, as the Guardian called them," she explained to Sarah. "In each of them dwells the mind of a modghast."

"What are they?"

Thetis hesitated. "Sar can tell you more. But they were once human beings," she shouted over the roar of the engines, so that both Sarah and Sar could hear her. "And to escape death they had their...their souls saved—preserved there, in those mounds. They feed off of power that Yggdrasil provides for them."

"What...?" Sarah hesitated. "What do they do?"

"During the age of the guilds, they created worlds in which they lived. But that all ended during the Theomachia. Now, it is said, they are trapped in their barrows, and are completely mad, and all are desperate to escape somehow. For this reason, crossing the modbarrows is dangerous. Some of the souls trapped there have managed to make crude bodies for themselves, and to possess those bodies. Those might see you, and try to seize you, to make use of you. They will try anything, it is said, to escape the darkness of their bodiless immortality."

"That's horrible," Sarah said.

"Bad engineering," Sar agreed. "But this had nothing to do with my guild," she added, defensively, holding up one hand. "Nothing. Other guilds made the barrows." She pointed at the base of Yggdrasil. "Nor was Ma'at ours. The Orderlies Guild did not want to trust the Dark Engineers, so they demanded that they alone build and control the gate keeper to Bifrost. I don't trust their engineering. I don't know what we'll find there."

As Sarah looked out over the endless mounds, horrified now to see that there were so many—stretching off, it seemed, forever—she noticed on the distant green horizon a cloud of black.

"What's that?" she asked.

Sar and Thetis both followed her gaze, searching for a long while before they saw it.

"Keen eyes, girl," Sar said.

"It looks like a flock of birds," Thetis said.

Sarah nodded. "But it's so...straight. And fast. Too fast. Coming this way."

The cloud did not change shape, but grew as it approached directly, too orderly and round, it would seem, for birds.

"We've not far to go!" Thetis shouted. "Whatever it is, if we can just cross the barrows!"

Sarah could not judge the distance to Yggdrasil, not knowing the thickness of the monstrous structure. It looked like it was still a day's walk away, over the up and down slopes of the small knolls.

She realized that they ought to be able to see the black airship, if it were still aloft. Chance must already be down. If the makina could be trusted, Chance might already be entering that other space where he could kill the god. If she could not be trusted, then.... Sarah could not imagine what use the makina might have for Chance. She did not know what the makina might be doing to him right now. She gripped her sword handles tightly.

"This does not look likely to work well for us," Sar shouted. For the black cloud was now close, filling a good quarter of their view, and it suddenly opened and spread. It was more like a flock of birds now than it had seemed before.

And then the flock was on them. Black things shot by, flapping their wings. They were birds—crows, Sarah thought, from their big black bodies and wings. But there was something wrong also about the erratic, sharp paths they flew, and something too harsh about the cold glints of reflected sunlight that cut across them.

"Makine!" Sar shouted.

And then they heard the first tear, a rough ripping above. The airship lurched.

Another tearing sounded out, barely audible over the engines. They were starting to drop.

"Take us down! Down!" Thetis cried.

But they were already falling. Sar put the engines on straight downward thrust, to slow their fall, and drove them to full power, so that they roared in protest. But still the airship dropped. The Makine and the wind both now tore at the hull. The black cacophony of wings and glinting metal bodies spun around them, so that Sarah could not see clearly out of the windows, could not tell how high they were, how far they'd fallen, how far Yggdrasil remained. And it seemed that they were starting to spin, as the dizzying flock swallowed their view.

"Lie down!" Sarah called, flopping backwards.

Thetis followed her example.

And then they hit the Earth.

The cabin bit into the ground and dragged forward. Sarah and Thetis both lay with their feet toward the front of the cabin, and this saved them, as they shot forward and hit hard with knees bent, their feet flat against the front panels as the cabin crunched and folded.

The ship then leaned far back, bouncing and skidding across the ground. The engines screeched and crunched, and then fell silent.

The ship shuddered and settled. The silence, after days of the engines roaring, was palpable.

"Thetis?" Sarah asked. Her ears rang.

The Mother lay with her eyes closed and mouth open, and did not answer. Sarah was stunned but she clung to the tilted side of the cabin and managed to lift herself to her feet. The ship tottered, then settled again.

The front of the cabin was crushed. Through the broken windows, Sarah could see that the black makina birds circled them still, but they remained perhaps a hundred paces above them in the air.

Thetis opened her eyes as Sarah bent over her.

"What happened?" she asked.

"We crashed." Sarah looked to the Engineer, still strapped in her seat. "Sar?"

No answer.

"The Makine?" Thetis asked.

"Still circling above. Waiting to see if we're dead, perhaps."

"No," Thetis took Sarah's hand and let herself be helped up. "They're afraid to come down here. They're afraid of the modghasts. It is said that the Makine are easy to... possess."

They stumbled to the side of the Engineer. The crushed control panel was torn in the center. Two long metal rods that had been somewhere inside it had thrust through the folded and torn steel and into Sar's stomach. Only then did Sarah notice that they went through the seat, and came out its back. Sar held one in each hand, slick with red blood. She looked up at Sarah, then Thetis.

"This is fatal damage," she whispered. "I'm broken beyond repair, for this workshop." She nodded at the stark cabin around them, the empty grasses before them.

"Can't we...." Sarah faltered. But what could they do, here in the middle of a barren waste of grass?

They heard a sound now, like a humming mixed with the sound of the wind in the grass. Their ears rang with the silence, after two days with the roaring engines, but this strange sound was clear. Thetis and Sarah both leaned forward, looking out of the smashed windows, expecting the Makine to make a second attack. Sarah gripped her sword handles.

But the black Makine were flying away, back toward Yggdrasil. Yggdrasil itself looked very near to Sarah, but again she could not tell. A cloud passed over, darkening the green slope of grass before them.

And then the sound grew, and Sarah saw a shimmer of bright, sparkling lights above the grass atop a mound about two dozen paces before the ship. Slowly, the lights coalesced into a human silhouette.

"Is that," she whispered, pointing, "a modghast?"

"No." Thetis whispered also. "That's one of the Sidhe. I believe that's one of the Sidhe."

"The Sidhe?"

"Lucenfolk," Thetis explained. "You call them Lucenfolk."

Other lights appeared over the crest of the mound, a whole crowd of human forms solidifying out of a vague mist of sparkling light. They floated down the hill.

"Lucenfolk," Sarah whispered, awed. "Lucenfolk."

"Leave me," Sar croaked. She coughed, winced in horrible pain from the jerking of her chest that the hacking caused. She spat blood. "I know these ones. I know them. I'm not afraid of them." Blood ran now in a broad stream from her feet down under the console. Her face turned ashen. "I say goodbye to you. Save the boy. I'll have a talk with these ones. Go. May your days be peaceful and creative."

Thetis looked at Sarah. The Mother's hands shook, and the hint of tears started in her eyes, but she said, clearly, "Chance," as if to echo Sar's reminder that they had still to race forward and fight to save the boy. "We know now that the makina has turned on us, because she sent these birds after us. We must hurry."

Sarah nodded. She put her hand on Sar's shoulder, feeling tears come herself.

"Thank you," she whispered. "And goodbye. May God have mercy on you."

Sarah scrambled to the back of the cabin, which sloped slightly up. Glancing often back at the slowly approaching Lucenfolk, she gathered into a sack what food they had left, then slung it over her shoulder. Thetis pushed open the door, which fell open with a clang. Then she stopped with one hand on the door frame. They both looked at Sar.

"Go," Sar said. She could not turn to look at them but somehow she knew from the silence that they hesitated because of her. She still gripped the metal rods in blood-slick hands. "I've built a lot. I built a lot."

Thetis nodded. Sarah leapt out the door, and Thetis followed.

In a moment, they were surrounded by the shining, blinding shards of light that comprised Lucenfolk bodies.

Sarah jerked back in surprise when one appeared before her, just an arm's length away.

"Blood pledge," it said.

"Blade pledge blade," another sang behind her. And then all around they seemed to be singing, and none of the words was clearly before or after another.

"Blood pledge blade pledge blade pledge blood pledge blade...."

"What do you mean?" she whispered.

Thetis pulled at her hand.

"We must hurry," Thetis said. And she added, "They never explain themselves."

Sarah let herself be pulled along, not looking where she was going but looking rather around at the crowd of lights, the Lucenfolk.

Their chant continued, following them. "Blood pledge blade pledge blood pledge blade pledge blood...."

Sarah had long doubted they existed. And she had long wanted to see them. She felt a roiling of emotions, convinced now that her mother had told the truth, surprised to admit to herself that she had ever considered that her mother had lied when, years ago, she had told tales about the Lucenfolk.

She turned her head, letting Thetis tow her along, and called out, "What does it mean, 'blade mother'?"

They gave no answer but "Blood pledge blade pledge blood pledge blade pledge...."

And then, after a few more steps, Thetis and Sarah passed beyond the crowd of Lucenfolk and ran free, into tall grass waving in a mild wind. The sun shone down over the edge of a single voluminous white cloud directly above.

Yggdrasil cut the sky in twain before them. The wreck of their airship lay behind them, and all around it the Lucenfolk seemed to dance and run and flicker in and out of being.

"What does 'blade mother' mean?" Sarah called out again.

But they gave her no answer and only continued to chant, "Blood pledge pledge blade pledge blood pledge...."

That last October when Sarah's mother lay in bed, a few months from death, Sarah had sat at her side and held loosely her burning hand. Her mother's fingers and palm were worn smooth and had always been cool before, like a breeze; her mother had often brushed Sarah's cheek as she passed by on some busy chore or other. Fever made the hand hot now.

Sarah had just started her apprenticeship. Her father and brother were in the fields, the grandparents were walking the grounds, and her mother relaxed to be alone with her only daughter.

They shared a secret honesty together, as sometimes a child and a parent may share when they are very close. With the men of the house, Sarah's mother spoke with the optimism and the caution one reserved for a child or a sensitive aunt. But she treated Sarah, when they were alone, as an equal.

"You and I understand that the world doesn't fall apart if it turns out that some of our ideas aren't quite right," her mother had once told her. "Men don't understand that. Men need you to protect every little hope and every little notion they've got. Their souls are like pottery, like fired clay—try to change its shape and it breaks."

Sarah laughed. "What are our souls made of?"

"Earth and water. Our souls are like wet clay. We can bend and change."

It made Sarah feel special, and strong, and mature, to share this confidence. It also made her feel lonely. Her mother had been raised a Truman but not a Puriman until she was fifteen, when her own father, Sarah's grandfather, had converted. Sarah's mother had never complained or spoke an ill word about an Elder or a custom, but a sigh here, and a frown there, had made it clear to Sarah that her mother found some Puriman rules a burden. By sharing this with Sarah in her tone and weariness, Sarah's mother had lightened her burden by shifting it a bit onto her quickly maturing daughter.

That day, Sarah had piled pillows behind her mother, propping her up in bed, and had thrown open the window so that her mother could look out at the hills turning gold with autumn. The cool air that blew in carried just a hint of the fine smell of piling red and brown leaves. The sun struck down with brief clarity against the house.

"I always loved autumn," her mother said.

"I know."

They sat in silence for a long while as her mother stared at the hills. Sarah looked out there also. Part of her itched to get up and go out. The air smelled sweet with cut hay, the sky glowed bright, and some of the other girls had told her they were riding horses by the lake today. Sarah was fifteen. It was hard to sit still on such a day.

Then she looked over at her mother and saw that a hint of tears reddened the woman's eyes. Shame shot through Sarah as she realized again that her mother was dying, and that they both knew it. In a short while she would be gone. Sarah would lose this woman whom she loved deeply, and she would be alone in the house with a quiet grandmother and three men whose souls were brittle as fired clay.

"What is it, mother?" she whispered.

"I know that people have said spiteful things, about how I talked so many times, for so many years, about the day I saw Lucenfolk in those hills."

"Tell me again," Sarah said. For her mother had not told her the story in more than five years, and she knew her mother longed to tell it once more.

"You had been born not long before. A beautiful baby, but tiny. Not big like you are now—couldn't hardly imagine you'd grow to be a tall girl.

"I went up into those hills, just past where old hermit Sirach now lives. Had you in a sling, looking for mushrooms. Mostly I just hankered to walk. It was like today. Fifteen years ago. The fine end to a fine year, a year to remember. A very good harvest in our fields and everyone's fields. Great vintages at the crofts. Four babies born that summer, other than you. And that was the year a witch brought the Kyriens a boy, too.

"I had walked a while there where the trees grow on the terraced earth, where there had been vineyard rows a long time ago. I wasn't much looking, but I'd found a few mushrooms. And then it happened. First the silence. It'd been kind of noisy. It'd not rained in weeks, and a wind was blowing, so the dry leaves were shushing this way and that. But suddenly they all stopped. The wind was still. Birds quieted. There was a feeling around us like the air was being squeezed. You'd been sleeping but your eyes popped open wide.

"A sound came up out of the silence that I can't describe. Like a little stream going over rocks. Like thousands of tiny soft bells. But not really like those things at all.

"I looked around and it all grew darker, though there was still not a cloud in the sky. Then I saw the first of the Lucenfolk. It stepped right out of a tree. Or so it seemed. I thought later that it had somehow stepped out from behind the tree maybe, but that really makes no more sense than it stepping out of the tree. The tree wasn't big enough to hide it—it was a little scrappy maple like that."

She held her fist up feebly: a trunk as round as a woman's clenched fingers.

"The Lucen was silver and white and shining. It looked just like the water sparkling on the lake, but just imagine the shape of a woman or a man like that. And more came out of trees, out of nothing, then, all around us. Tens of them. And that beautiful sound was all about us."

Sarah's mother looked at her.

"They were beautiful. Like nothing you could imagine." She blinked out two tears. "And they spoke to me. They spoke to me."

"You never told me that."

"I never told anyone. Never anyone, all these years. But now I'm telling you. Before I...." Her voice faltered. After a few seconds she continued, "They spoke. It was hard to understand, and it frightened me, but they all spoke, all of them, all at different times, talking over each other but also kind of like the chorus at church talking with each other, and they said...."

"What?"

"'Blade mother.'"

Sarah just stared.

"Or 'mother blade.' But strange and like music. Blade mother blade mother mother blade mother. All mixed up. Can't tell which word came first. I expected you to cry out. I think I squeezed you hard in fear and surprise and all. But you didn't. And neither did I.

I don't know how long I watched them. They just walked all about us. This way and that. Until they walked back into the trees. Or behind them. And were gone."

"What does it mean? 'Blade mother'?" Sarah asked, in a whisper.

"I don't know. I never understood. It scared me. So I never told a soul about that. Though I made the mistake of telling everyone I'd seen the Lucenfolk. But this year, when you took the Ranger apprenticeship, I thought, maybe—maybe it means you'll get your swords."

Her mother looked back out the window at the hills.

"Lying here now, dying, those Lucenfolk are what I think of. Isn't that strange? I long to think of God, but I'm tired, and thinking pious thoughts is hard work, sure. And I don't really know how to think about God. I try picturing things like they talk about at church, but that isn't much to picture, really. It's a struggle.

"So, when my mind wanders, it wanders into that dark fall forest and the Lucenfolk singing, singing, and their shining skin, and their shining eyes."

She squeezed Sarah's hand. "Oh, Sarah, why didn't God make the world more like they are—the whole world? Why'd God make our world so hard and painful? Instead of beautiful and shining like the Lucenfolk?"

Sarah had looked out at the hills and had not answered, because she did not know.

CHAPTER

47

Inside the airship, Sar grew lightheaded. She well knew this was a mortal loss of blood, and that the last of her life was spilling out onto the floor.

"Threkor's heir," a distant, hollow voice called out. She lifted her drooping eyelids. A Sidhe floated there, glowing.

"I know you," Sar said. "No poetry for this old Engineer, Sidhe. I know you. I've read Threkor's Apocrypha. And in my family, some things are passed down, mouth to ear. 'Ants in the walls,' Threkor called you. 'Ants in the walls of the world.'"

She coughed blood. A crowd of Sidhe glittered in the cabin now. They whispered all around her. A faint smell of ozone cut through the odor of oil and blood.

"Would you join us, Threkor's heir?"

The old woman smiled. She had never expected that. Never.

"Join us join, join, us join us," the other Sidhe whispered all around her.

Sar fixed one of the shimmering figures in her fading gaze. "Tell me this," she said. "Tell me this first."

The shimmering form bent forward, attentive to her question.

"Do you make anything there," Sar asked. "In the little cracks between, the cracks between the walls of the world? Do you make things there?"

The Guardian stood in the front of the airship, gray hands on the controls. He stared out over the sea. Nothing lay before him but the distant black line of land and the tossing caps of sea waves stretching to every other horizon. No airships!

He felt the god slipping farther and farther ahead. Hexus sped closer to Chance, somehow speeding the airship faster, driving it forward. Each minute the Guardian fell farther behind.

He had one opportunity he could foresee. He watched the land approach. The black edge of the coast grew, resolving first into an uneven line, then into gray surf with black mountains rising beyond, seeming pale and flat in the humid air.

He would be faster on foot.

The Guardian waited impatiently for the line of breaking surf to approach. When the airship was nearly over the shore, the Guardian gripped Threkor's Hammer and let his power grow. His eyes began to blaze. Light leaked from his mouth. He swung the hammer at the door, smashing it off its hinges. Wind roared through the gaping entrance. The blue-green sea beneath crashed on white reefs before tumbling onto black sands, too far below to be audible. He heard only the wind ripping through the door, and the hum of the engines.

The airship flew over the beach.

The Guardian leapt.

When he hit the ground the beach exploded, and everything went black, as his raging momentum broke his body and crushed it down into the sand.

In a few moments his senses returned. He bit down, grinding a mouthful of shells and sand, gnashing through the agony of his body reassembling and twisting together again through the hard sand, his limbs scraping against the razor teeth of the buried black rocks.

When he felt whole enough, he reached up, for the sky. His hand broke through heavy sand into the inconsequential air. He gripped at the surface, then pulled down against the earth. He dug out of the black beach, dragged himself up into the broad crater he had formed, and lay a moment in the hot sun. His reformed body throbbed in pain.

Threkor's Hammer stood nearby, the handle stabbed down through a black volcanic stone. The Guardian stood and wrenched it free, cracking the rock.

Then the air exploded as he ran, faster than he had ever run, toward Yggdrasil.

Sarah stopped and waited for Thetis, who looked back toward the wreckage of their airship, no longer visible behind the dozens of barrows covered with tall green grass that they had crossed.

"I liked her," Thetis said. "She was one of the greatest of her kind. Did you know that she was descended from Threkor himself? She was of the line of the demigod." Thetis turned toward Sarah. "But I guess that means nothing to you."

Sarah squinted angrily. After they had passed the last of the Lucenfolk, they had run a long while, the loose bag banging hard under her arm. They ran until pains bit their sides and they had to spit thick saliva. It was easy to keep on course, with Yggdrasil cutting the whole horizon in half before them, but after a long run it appeared no closer. Finally they stopped on the peak of a mound, hands on knees, catching their breath.

"Here's what means something to me," Sarah said. "She gave her life for us. She was kind and good. She saw, after only a few hours, that Chance was good and deserved her allegiance, and she gave it freely. That is what matters. That is what needs to be said."

And, to Sarah's surprise, Thetis nodded sadly. "You are right, Puriman Ranger. What matters is what she did. And she did well."

Sarah looked around. In each direction, there was only softly waving grass rising and falling from one mound to the next, seeming to stretch on forever.

"Mimir sent them? Those bird things?" Sarah asked.

"Who else?"

"Chance is in danger."

Thetis nodded. "And yet," she said. "I think Mimir wants him for some reason. Otherwise she could just kill him and let us hurry on, our quest hopeless. To try to kill us, she must fear us, and that means we can interfere, and that means that she has some plan for Chance."

"Let's interfere, then," Sarah said. She stood erect, squaring her shoulders.

Thetis looked around. "Yes. We'd best hurry on. If a modghast sees us, we'll be in great danger."

They began to walk.

"What do the Lucenfolk have to do with all this?" Sarah asked.

Thetis shook her head. "They just appear sometimes. No one really knows why, or what they want."

Sarah frowned. "I swore to my brother I'd head out to get him the minute I saw Lucenfolk, and take him to see. That's an oath I must break."

"Yes," Thetis said. "Maybe some other day you'll. . . ."

"Maybe."

They walked in silence a while. The wind in the grass smelled fresh and green. It reminded Sarah of the smell of a hay field at home, ready for mowing. A good smell. Ironic given the horror that lay beneath the grass. Sarah pictured corpses, wrapped in some strange guild cloth, buried just below the reach of the knotted roots of the grasses. She shivered.

Thetis sighed. "Things are in one way better. When the Guardian lived, there was no hope. No hope for Chance."

"How can you say that?" Sarah spat. "The Guardian would have protected Chance."

"Yes, and sent him into the Well and waited while he returned, to ensure he returned a mortal."

Sarah stopped in place, and planted her hands on her sword pommels. "I warned you! Chance wants to be a mortal. He wants to go home, and tend his vineyard, and make his wine, and father my children. Do you hear me? If you try to convince Chance he must change in this hell beyond Earth, I'll kill you, witch."

There was a long pause, while the two women stared at each other. And then Thetis stepped forward, wading through the tall grasses, stopped close to Sarah, reached far back, and slapped Sarah hard across her unscarred cheek. Sarah's head snapped aside, and she stumbled back.

"I am a Mother of the Gotterdammerung." Thetis's hands shook, but her jaw clenched hard when she paused in her speaking. She seemed a mix of the frantic fearfulness Sarah had seen before now and a grim determination. "I am one of the last Mothers. My guild is ancient. You will address me as Mother, or Junior Mother."

Sarah unsheathed her swords. "And I am a Ranger of the Purimen and I am tired of your disrespect, witch! And—"

Thetis stepped forward again. Sarah, holding her swords but unwilling to cut Thetis, was helpless as Thetis slapped her a second time.

"You are a child. I never treated you with disrespect. I only treated you as my junior. I don't accuse you of ignorance or incivility— I accuse you of being a girl—"

"I'm no younger than you!"

"I am sixty-seven years old, Sarah Michael."

Sarah stumbled back, stunned, the points of her swords drifting far apart.

"Your face," Sarah whispered. "But your face." She thought of her own grandmother, who was more than one hundred years old. Even the stoutest, long-lived Purimen grew wrinkled and gray. But Thetis had the smooth face and raven hair of a young girl. She appeared younger than Sarah.

"You may be a Ranger of the Purimen," Thetis continued, "but you are to me a child. A little girl. Now listen to your elder. Chance cannot live another ten years—probably not another five years—as a mortal."

"You lie!" Sarah held her swords up and crossed them, as if to ward off a falsehood.

Thetis spoke slowly and clearly. "The changes that make a Potentiate are small, and they serve only one purpose: they allow the sarcophagus in the Numin Well to capture and freeze a moment of the Potentiate's life—the moment when he enters the sarcophagus. Without this change, the body rebels and resists and dies before the soul, the form of it, is captured. But this thing that makes someone a Potentiate—it also alters how that person ages. It allows him to grow but not to stay as he was. As soon as Chance stops growing, stops maturing, he will begin to die. And when will that be? Twenty-three? Twenty-four? He must become a god or perish."

"You lie," Sarah gasped.

"That is why the Guardian feared Chance so," Thetis said. "He feared that Chance would discover the truth, and then—"

"No," Sarah's swords slowly drooped in her hands, until their points lay in the grass. "You lie! You lie because you want Chance for your own plans. You're one of the Hieroni! Or you love him and you want him for yourself!"

Sarah fell to her knees.

For a long moment, there was only the sound of the wind in the grass, whispering as Sarah wept. Finally Thetis spoke.

"Yes," she said, very softly, "I am one of the Hieroni.

"And yes, I love Chance and I want him for myself.

"For I am Chance's mother. He is my son."

CHAPTER

48

This is going to take all my strength, Wadjet thought.

She lay in the tall grass, just where she had landed after her tumble from the airship, face down, unable to see anything but the green blades waving before her. She cut the pain—there was no use to feeling that, she knew she was hurt: her left shoulder was dislocated, two ribs were broken, both wrists were sprained.

She gripped her left arm as well as she could with her right hand and, driving her shoulder into the ground while pulling at it, yanked the arm back into its socket. She felt the pain only distantly, but knew it would be overwhelming, enormous, if she were not suppressing it.

She rolled over. The ribs next. She closed her eyes and concentrated. They were in place, not separated, and not fully cracked through. She made the two ribs begin forming bone at an accelerated rate, working to bind them as quickly as possible.

Now the makina's invasion.

Thinking of the makina made her feel a rush of pleasure. They were such good creatures, with such good goals. Creatures of light, wanting only knowledge and the freedom of the stars!

"Then they won't care if I clean their machines out of my skull," she whispered. It took a long time, but she taught some cells within her to attack the tiny machines that were knitting themselves into the weave of her brain. She let those cells spread through her body, where they could breed before attacking.

Slowly, slowly, the makina seemed less good, less interesting, less deserving of her love.

Wadjet stood weakly, wobbling on her feet. Yggdrasil rose, monstrously huge, before her. She was close. She could not see the airship, but it could not be far. Ahead, less than half an hour's run, stood some low buildings that appeared to surround the foot of Yggdrasil.

She let the pain return, slowly. Her shoulder stabbed at her with a sharp ache. Her head throbbed. It would be hard to run, and harder to fight, with such aches.

She could leave the boy. Leave him to his fate. The makina was not going to kill him, but rather send him into the Well and make a useful tool of him. What concern of hers was that?

She hesitated a long time, standing in the tall grass, her bruised body throbbing.

If the makina were going to kill Chance, Wadjet might turn her back and start walking to the shore. She might start looking for a way to find passage to Lethebion, and back to her ship, leaving all this behind.

But it was the idea that the makina was building a cage for the boy that Wadjet could not bear. She hated cages. Especially the cages made by these ancient, lost beings. They would bind everything, everyone, into their plans, if they had their way. They would strangle the world into their own shape, killing it in the act.

No, she could not bear it.

She set off running, toward Yggdrasil and the fallen towers at its root.

✚

Wadjet was almost to the scarred and pitted buildings that stretched across flat grounds that surrounded Yggdrasil, where hardy grasses cracked through bleached and ancient stone, when the modghast saw her.

Something dark flitted between two mounds to her left. She saw it in the corner of her eye, as she ran at her full stride. She was exhausted, spent from the effort of fixing her bones and of cleaning herself of the makina's machines, and now from the added effort of running between the mounds in a long zigzagging dash across the whispering grass.

She did not slow or stop, but ran straight up, instead of around, the next barrow, to get the view from the top.

And there it was, running along not far behind. She took the sight in a flash, before she was over the top of the mound.

The modghast looked like a spider, nearly twice as tall as her, hacked together from odd bits of iron and old machines and, unmistakably, some parts of animals. She could not smell it yet— the wind was in her face—but as she pressed on harder, she began to hear it, a dull but rapid clanking as it chased behind.

It was big for a modghast, or so she gathered from the stories she had been told and the things she had read in the Traveler's Library of the Stewards. That was very bad. It meant the modghast was one of the hungry ones that had grown skilled at possessing other forms. It would be hard to fight, hard to flee, hard to fool.

The clanking grew louder, closer.

She came around another barrow, and there before her she could see the top of a low stone building. She had come to the center of the grassland and of the modbarrows, where Yggdrasil rose up. A long slope reached to the flat concrete ground that stretched around Yggdrasil.

Her breathing came in dizzying gasps now. She needed food and more air. She cut the pain and raced as quickly up the slope as she could, her long strides pounding at the grass.

She risked a look back. The modghast ran at her from just a hundred paces away, but was still to her left, starting up the beginning of the slope. She saw that three deer heads had been affixed on top, facing in different directions. The eyes in one of the heads blinked. Another flicked its ear. The eight rusted legs of the modghast gouged at the ground, tearing up clods of earth and grass.

Wadjet's legs were rubbery, distant, starting to feel useless. She might pass out, she realized, from the low sugar and insufficient air. That was the danger of cutting off pain—you could not tell when you were finished, when your body could take no more.

Her last step off the grassy slope sent her leaping over the hard white ground. She skidded but continued on, faster on the stone.

Would the modghast stop at the end of the grass? She knew they could not venture far from their barrows.

A sharp metallic hammering behind answered her question. The modghast was speeding up also now that they were on the concrete, its legs cracking loudly against the hard ground.

Before Wadjet, a two-story building stood. There was no door on this side, but a low narrow window gaped in the pitted and stained wall. She raced for it, using the last of her strength, and leapt.

She just cleared the bottom of the window: her upper body sailed through, but her legs scraped the frame as she passed over. She touched ground on the other side with her hands first, sending jabs of distant pain through her sprained wrists, and then she rolled, twice, before coming to her feet, gasping for air.

The building was a large, empty room, with an empty doorway in the far wall letting in the bright daylight.

The modghast collided with the window. Three of its twisted, skeletal metal legs shot through the gap, but the body struck the frame of the window and crashed to a halt. Metal screamed and twisted. One deer head thrust through the window. The others were bent back.

The modghast was stuck. It flailed its legs, smashing at the floor. Chips of stone sparked off where its spiked feet scraped. Dust fell from the ceiling as the building shook.

Wadjet could see the modghast would get free soon. But she needed to slow. She let the pain return and nearly fell to the ground when it overwhelmed her. In a moment she adjusted to it, and then stood straight, and walked quickly away, not running, saving her energy. She dug out of her pocket a bit of dried fish that she had saved, struggling with thumb and forefinger because she could not bear the pain of pushing her whole hand with its sprained wrist into the tight-fitting pants. She chewed the fragments of fish as she hurried from the room.

Once outside, Wadjet looked back. The modghast was still stuck, flailing its limbs.

A dark shadow passed over. The air all around grew dim. Wadjet looked up, expecting some thick storm cloud. But instead, the sun seemed to be shrouded somewhere beyond even the blue sky.

The shadow of Yggdrasil, she realized, or some part of Yggdrasil, fell now over this place.

But there was no time to wonder at it. She raised her head, and sniffed.

Yes: there. She could smell Chance. A weak, sweet scent of the boy hung in the wind. He'd been through here. Or he stood some distance not far upwind.

She followed the scent, ears twitching as she listened for the sound of the modghast, when it should break free.

CHAPTER

49

"What have you done to me?" Chance asked.

He had awoken sitting in a flat, white expanse of stone ground. Scarred and empty shells of buildings surrounded them. Mimir stood beside him. Chance got to his feet and looked about. The ground was cracked and here and there tufts of green grass had broken through the pale stone. Clouds of tiny gnats swirled over the ground, but no other life was visible. The air was warm, but a soft wind blew. And before them, seeming to bend the sky over them, stood Yggdrasil. It was terrifying to see the World Ash this close. The deep, featureless black of it now stretched wider than any building here, and it rose, piercing the sky, up to infinity. Chance bent his head back, stared up, and then turned away, head reeling. How awesome, what the guilds had wrought!

"What have you done to me?" he repeated.

"I have altered you to make your emotional perspective more favorable to my goals and my interpretation of our situation."

Chance thought about that. The words were strange but he could grasp their meaning well enough. It was a bad thing to do, he didn't approve, but he understood why Mimir had done it. She only wanted to be understood. Who could blame her for that?

"We should be expeditious," Mimir said. She looked at the sky. "I receive information from other Makine. There are modghasts in pursuit of us. I have carried you this far but we can move more quickly if you walk also. Should the modghasts capture us, they will cut you to pieces, after they do the same to me."

He felt glad that she was so concerned about him. And he knew, following this thought, that whatever she had done to him caused this feeling of good will. But this made it no less strong. He understood how Mimir thought and planned reasonably, how she cared properly. She strove for a noble goal: to rise among the stars. Even if he had been forced to see these things, he now saw them. Making him see them was a reasonable thing for her to do.

"Why would they do that?" he asked.

"They would seek to make use of us, by harvesting and integrating our components." She began to walk.

Chance followed.

They crossed long stretches of barren stonework, winding a path between many great empty shells of buildings where black birds nested and squawked in surprise when they passed. It struck Chance that this abandoned place was like the modbarrows: an empty expanse, with buildings instead of barrows, and the dead more present than the living. Yggdrasil now seemed to rise vertically above them, dominating the sky, hiding the horizon. It was oddly terrible, a black spire without human ornament and beyond human scale, rising beyond everything.

They walked quickly, but without running. After some minutes Chance asked, "Are we still being followed? I can go faster."

"The modghasts that stalked us have turned back. It appears that easier prey has their attention."

"What? What prey?"

Mimir did not answer.

They came around the shattered corner of a leaning building, to see before them a broad stair, hundreds of paces wide. They climbed up. Atop was a great square, marked with a grid of holes, each about twice Chance's height in diameter. Beyond these, another stair rose again, thirty or so steps, and Chance could just see the top of a building there, at the very foot of Yggdrasil.

Chance looked back. Behind lay the long wasteland of shattered buildings, and beyond, the green barrows stretching off to distant mountains. The waxing crescent moon glared over the mountains, squinting at them in cold analysis.

Then a shadow fell over them. Chance saw the edge of it race across the ground away from them. The air grew dark.

"What?" he cried out.

"It is only the shadow of Yggdrasil. Yggdrasil has great light gatherers high above the Earth. At noon, they cast a shadow here."

Chance looked up at the dark ring of the eclipsed sun. "It has leaves. Like a true tree, it has leaves. And we are in their shade now."

"Yes," Mimir said. "This is an appropriate analogy. These artificial leaves gather the power of the sun, as do the leaves of living trees. Though now only the modbarrows, and their modghast bodies, utilize this bounty of power."

Chance looked back toward the barrows.

"It's like we are at the center of the world," he whispered. Yggdrasil, the world ash, shot down into Earth like an axis, and around it this broken city, a land of the forgotten and lost accomplishments, was ringed by the land of those who cannot forget, the trapped dead. And encircling that: the suffering, confused, aimless globe of men and the many living things that thrived after men. He stood nearly in the center of it all. "I wanted only to return to my farm. But all the world is our vineyard, isn't it? We're always at the center of it, and must tend or neglect the vines."

"There is insightful meaning in this simile," Mimir said.

Chance smiled at Mimir, pleased that she approved. And he knew, again, that she had put something in him that made him pleased by her. But that was just her way of trying to be understood. And she deserved to be understood.

They started across the square.

"What will happen when we reach the Well?" he asked.

"You will eliminate the god, and then you will take his place. Airships of the Makine are hurrying here now. Makine of my syndicate will take us away. Then we can save your village, and you can help us escape the confinement the Old Gods have set upon our globe."

They were walking between two rows of the holes in the ground. Some had steel lids closed over them, with long bars of steel set through eye-holes in arms that held the lids in place. On most others, the lids had been pushed aside, swiveling away on a single pivot hinge. Chance walked over to one of these open holes and looked down. Even with the sun occluded, the air was still bright, and he could see dimly the bottom, a flat expanse of dry stone a hundred paces below, where some dry grass struggled to survive against one side of the curved wall.

"Were these wells?" he asked.

"No," Mimir said. "Come."

When they reached the other stairs, Mimir stopped and looked at the sky awhile. Then she looked at her empty hands. Chance thought suddenly that she was longing for her dice. What decision, he wondered, did she not want to make now on her own?

She turned to Chance. "Please remain here a moment while I ensure that the entrance to Ma'at's hall is safe."

Mimir ran up the stairs, her legs stretching into impossible strides.

Chance turned and walked back to the nearest of the open pits, where the bar to seal it shut lay cast aside nearby on the ground. He picked that up, and went to the next well, and used the bar to lever open the sliding door: he set one point of the bar on the ground, wedged against the protrusion where the eye-hole on the door stuck out. He got his shoulder under the rod and pushed. The door resisted, then began to grind forward more easily. He pushed it open about half the way. Then he laid the rod against the top of the next well, which was closed, and he sat beside it. Only two strides lay between the wells.

Mimir came to the top of the steps.

This is the first test, Chance thought.

"Come," she called.

He did not move.

So, Chance thought. I can disobey her.

Mimir came down the steps.

"Chance Kyrien?"

He did not answer. She crossed the smooth, cracked stones of the square, and stopped between him and the well he had opened.

As fast as he could manage using his left arm, Chance seized the bar and leapt up, swinging at Mimir. It struck Mimir solidly, and she staggered back, toward the open well behind her. He struck her again, and she fell over the lip of the well, down into its depths. He hurried to the side, wedged the metal rod under the edge of the eye, and began to lever the cover closed. As the last handspan of open space was closing, out of the depths of the well echoed the sound of metal cracking into stone. Mimir had gotten up, and prepared now to climb out. The sound of steel fingers hammering into stone rose quickly toward the opening, a scrabbling, raging ascension toward the little crack of light he had left open there. But then, shouting with the effort, he managed to drive the door closed all the way. He threw the bar into the aligned eye holes, locking it.

A loud bang sounded against the lid.

"Chance Kyrien!" Mimir called. Chance did not answer, but leaned on the well cover, exhausted. It felt cold against his naked arm.

"Chance Kyrien, let me out. Consider my position! Have sympathy for my perspective!"

"Yes," Chance said, speaking quietly, knowing that Mimir, clinging with metal claws to the wall, ear pressed to the door, would hear his every word. "Yes, Mimir, I have sympathy for you. I even feel love for you. Your... attack worked."

"Then understand that this is not what I want. I want to be liberated of this place so that we may proceed now together!"

"I understand," Chance said. "But the first thing a Puriman learns, and learns well, is that sometimes—often—you must deny even the people you love the things that they want. It is a loving service, to help them see beyond their own desires, to help them begin to see God in the world. Suffering prepares the heart for future grace."

"Please open the door, Chance Kyrien."

"I don't believe that would be best for you, Mimir. You don't need a god that is your slave. You would lose sight of the beauty of what is, of what the One True God has given you. It would make things worse for you. And I don't want things to be worse for you. I'm very sorry that is painful for you." He turned to go.

"Stop!" Mimir shouted.

Chance crumpled to the ground.

He tried to move his arm. He could not. He tried his legs. They were useless. His limbs were not his own. He could not control them.

Ah, he though bitterly. She cannot command me, but she can stop me.

He found he could move his head, and speak. He turned and looked at the black metal lid over the well. "Mimir, this does no good. Let me go. The false god will come, or these modghasts you speak of, and I will be lying here, helpless. Let me go."

"I will let you go when you agree to open the door. I will be able to stop you again if you do not."

"I won't do that Mimir. Because you are better off if I escape the god and kill him."

"I believe that you will submit to my demands before the god can get here."

"No, Mimir. No. I won't."

Mimir was silent a moment. Then she struck at the steel lid.

"Mimir," Chance called. "I know why you picked up the dice again."

She struck the lid again. "There were complex incomputable contingencies that required the contribution of random input in order for any potential undertaking to be determined in a suitable time."

"No," Chance said. "I don't really know what you just said, I don't know anything about that, but I know that ain't why. You don't want to be responsible for what you do. That's the problem with this world of yours, this Machinedream also. No one is responsible for what they do. It's all the dice, the dice. You hide behind the dice, Mimir."

She hit the lid, hard.

"Remember," Chance said, "that Hexus murdered your father. You may let him be victorious, keeping me here. You may undo your father's work, keeping me here."

Mimir hit the lid again. The edge of it bent very slightly.

"I think I would have liked your father. You failed him when you picked up the dice this second time. When you asked the dice if you should betray me. At that moment you betrayed him. But you can make amends. Let me go."

"You will free me," Mimir answered. "Because it is in your best interest and my best interest that you do so."

"I told you I don't think it's best for you. And as for me: I'm not going to be shoved this way and that any more. If I kill the god, my people will die. My wife may already be...." He choked on the words, and couldn't say them. "My dearest friend died a horrible death at my feet, and before I could make amends for his years of unappreciated kindness. My parents were murdered on my birthday, standing before me, defending me. The Guardian was bound, imprisoned forever, before me. My brother is ruined, rotted. If I kill the god, none of that will change. If I don't kill the god, none of that will change. I've got no good choices left. Except the choice to make my own choices. No guide for me, Mimir. No elders. No dice. No Makine crafting inside my brain. I'm making my own choices."

Mimir hammered at the door. It moved slightly again, the metal bending. Chance realized that, given enough time, she would be able to bend up an edge of it and reach through to unlock the door.

And then Chance heard footsteps on the stone.

"Mimir," he said. "Something is coming. Do you still want to test my will?"

Mimir said nothing, but hammered again at the lid.

"Too late," Chance said. The steps ran up behind him.

Wadjet stepped into his view.

"Wadjet," he said with relief. "I am glad you live."

"Stop, Wadjet!" Mimir called. Chance held his breath—but Wadjet did not fall.

Mimir resumed hammering at the cover.

Wadjet knelt before Chance. She took his face in her hands, and she bent over and kissed him on the lips, hungrily, her mouth open.

If Chance could have done so, he would have wrapped his arms tight around her, though it would have been an infidelity to Sarah. In this moment when he expected soon to die, in this moment when he felt he'd lost everything—his friends, his love, his family, his place among the Purimen—this wild, beautiful woman embodied something he now painfully wondered what it would be like to have: the desperate, joyous hope of freedom, of passion, of wilderness. A life unoppressed by history.

Then she bit his lip, hard.

"Ah," he cried out in pain. She pulled back, and bit into her own bottom lip, the fang piercing the pouting pink flesh. Blood beaded there immediately, to fall down her chin. She kissed him again, mouth open, mixing their blood, pressing hers into his mouth and then into the wound behind his lip.

She grabbed his free wrist and bit it too, and rubbed her bleeding lip over the wound.

Chance twitched a finger. Then closed his fist. He began to feel his feet, then his hands, then his legs and arms. He moved his limbs, first a twitch, then deliberately.

"I taught my blood to destroy her tiny machines," Wadjet explained, as she stood.

"You taught your blood to destroy her tiny machines," Chance repeated in wonder. He took her hand and she pulled him up. "You taught your blood to destroy her tiny machines."

Chance shook his head and looked up at the terrible wonder of Yggdrasil, dwarfing anything and everything he had ever imagined men could make.

"Thetis spoke the truth," he whispered, thinking of days ago when she had taken his head in her hands and pressed her forehead to his. "Though I was angry at her when she said it, I understand nearly nothing of what is happening here. Nearly nothing."

Mimir hammered at the door, slowly beating the edge of it up.

"We must run," Chance said. "The Well should be just above. She'll be free soon."

"You go," Wadjet said.

"But Mimir...."

"A modghast hunts me. I'll draw it here. It will find Mimir far more interesting than it finds me. Else, the makina will be on you in minutes. Go!"

Chance hesitated.

"Puriman boy," Wadjet growled. "I don't want to face Ma'at and the Anubin warriors any more than I want to face this makina and a modghast. You don't offer me any fine choice!"

Chance nodded. "Thank you," he said. And then, surprising both Wadjet and himself, he leaned forward and kissed her, quickly, again. He turned to the stairs. At their foot lay one of the metal bars like the one he had used to lever and lock the cap of the well. He picked it up and hefted it.

Then he ran.

At the foot of Yggdrasil a ring of buildings stood. All but one of them was a broken, empty shell. The door to the Numin Well was a square, stout block of heavy black stones, covered over with gilt writing. On the south side of the squat building, double doors of gold were open a hand's width. Through the open crack Chance could see a bit of a smooth stone floor that descended at a gentle angle into the ground.

Down there, in the dark, Chance knew, Ma'at waited.

Something was written over the massive square entrance in the guild letters of the Gotterdammerung. He could not read it. He levered the door open with the metal bar. It scraped noisily over the stone threshold, but otherwise moved miraculously smoothly for an ancient and disused portal. He pried both doors all the way open to let some of the shadowy light down into the darkness.

But as he stepped into the descending path, dim lights in the ceiling began to glow, revealing a long, narrow hall that sloped down and ended at another double door of gold. The walls on each side were covered with inlaid writing of gold, all of it in the indecipherable Gotterdammerung guild letters. It seemed that glass walls had once shielded these ancient writings, because thick triangles of crystal shards lay covered in dust the entire length of the way. Chance started down the hall quickly. His steps crunched on the glass and echoed ominously.

When he was half way down the hall, he stopped and looked back at the open door behind him, a bright rectangle of light. He did not know whom he expected to see there. Wadjet? Mimir? Some monster? But he was alone. Completely, totally alone.

He looked at the metal bar in his hand and frowned.

He cast it down, the clatter of metal on stone echoing in the long hall.

Chance continued, almost running now. He clenched his one free hand, fingers flat on the palm, in an attempt to form something like a single hand pressed into prayer, and whispered, "Oh One True God, I beg of you to give me the strength to pass into this terrible other realm of blasphemy, and do there your will. Give me strength, Oh God. Give me strength to serve your ends on Earth, to kill the god and return here as I leave here."

He reached the two smooth gold doors. He pressed them open, hand trembling. The space beyond breathed out dank, musty air. Lights flickered on in a round room with red stone walls lined with narrow black pillars. A huge single mirror hung on the far wall, a shimmering oval. In the center of the room stood a mirrored pillar—or, it seemed, a pillar made of quicksilver. Four statues of dogs sat around the pillar, facing in the cardinal directions. They were made of black metal, ravenously thin, with exposed deep lines in their frame, so that they seemed more the skeletons of dogs than dogs.

Chance stepped inside and approached the pillar. Whispering, the doors behind him closed.

One of the dogs turned its head, emitting a loud, grinding sound of rusted iron on iron.

Chance jumped back in surprise. These, then, were the Anubin warriors. But the dog seemed frozen again, unable to move farther.

Creaks and moans sounded out of the other three dogs now, loud protests of seized metal limbs—they were trying to move, he realized, but time had corroded them into place.

The silver faded from the pillar, revealing a crystal cylinder filled with pink liquid, in which floated knotted gray forms. Chance took another step forward. The things in the pillar looked like ocean creatures from a rosy sea caught in a black and gray net of wires.

Chance stared a moment, not comprehending what he beheld. Then he realized that the complex visceral mess inside was a collection of brains. He had seen, as any farmer's son would, all the parts of animals. He knew brains, even the brain stem and the long spinal cord that descended from it and rooted in the body. But these were large brains, with long spinal cords floating down like fronds of waterweed in the lake shallows.

Human brains, he realized with horror.

"I am Ma'at," dozens of voices, some speaking at different times and speeds, said from every corner of the room.

Chance swallowed. He trembled all over. He was exhausted. Hungry. Thirsty. And the energy of his fear evaporated now, leaving just terrified fatigue. It was cool in the room, so that his sweat felt icy on his skin. He wiped the back of his one free hand across his forehead. The skin on skin felt gritty, filthy.

"I am Chance Kyrien."

"Are you a Potentiate?"

Chance hesitated. He would loathe saying the words, but perhaps he must speak them. "I am a Potentiate. I must pass into the Numin Well."

"Step into the circle."

There was a ring of gold on the floor before the cylinder. Chance stepped into it. A thick yellow light fell on him.

"He is a Potentiate," a single mechanical voice said.

He waited while the light pulsed.

Then the light died.

"You cannot pass," the collection of many voices pronounced.

"I must pass!"

"Your arm is broken. You have eighty-seven bruises. Three of your ribs are fractured. You are undernourished. There are metallic impurities in your central nervous system. You need to drink water."

"I must pass! So much depends upon my passing!" If Sarah still lived, alone on that island—or if she were held now, prisoner of the false god! Only by killing Hexus could he hope to then save her.

"Heal your wounds," the voices said. "And eat properly. Drink water. Then you may pass. Only a Potentiate in perfect health may pass, lest the Aussersein form be flawed."

Chance ran. He ran around the brains and between two of the frozen dogs of Ma'at. A shrieking grinding of metal sounded from all four of the iron dogs as they struggled to step forward, to chase him, but could not. One managed to turn its head and snap black metal teeth at his passing leg, but nothing more.

Chance ran at the mirror on the far wall. He had recognized the strange otherworldly sheen of it, like the shimmering surface of the Dark Engineers' trap for Hexus. That, he realized, must be the door to the stars.

He flung himself against the mirrored door—

And hit an immutable surface. He fell to the ground. His broken arm throbbed in pain. "Ah!" he howled in frustration.

"You may not pass," the many voices said again. "Potentiate, you may not pass."

CHAPTER

50

S arah could just see the tops of buildings ahead, when she heard the shriek of metal on metal before them and realized that there were other modghasts now besides the one that, almost timidly, had been following them, just out of view behind them, for a long while.

She and Thetis had run as much as they could, walking only when Thetis needed to slow and catch her breath. The hot dry air of the plain did not help. They sweated profusely and had finished their water. A dark shadow fell on them—"it is only the shadow of Yggdrasil," Thetis explained when Sarah looked up with fear, expecting another attack from the sky—just seconds before the clattering metallic sounds reached them. Sarah led the way with an extra burst of energy and they mounted one of the barrows.

Just a few hundred paces before them was the long slope that rose to a plateau of shattered buildings and fractured concrete where Yggdrasil was rooted. But between them and that flat place, five ominous heaps of rusted metal, each of different size and shape, scraped through the grass, leaving a broad, torn trail of shredded vegetation and plowed dark earth. Sarah looked to one side and saw the deer-like modghast that had been following to their left. It now sprinted ahead to join the others. They all seemed to grow—no, to stand and rise. Sarah realized that they were looking at her and Thetis.

"We'll have to run down, and circle to one side," Sarah commanded. She dropped the pack of food she had been carrying. Then she drew one sword and took Thetis's hand in her free hand. "Run!"

They bounded down the barrow, as if fleeing back the way they came, but then cut to the side, to what had been before their right.

Sarah sprinted on her long legs, sword swinging, in the narrow path between barrows.

"Sarah!" Thetis called.

Sarah ran on, not looking back, pulling Thetis along.

"Sarah!" Thetis sounded sharply urgent now. She pulled her hand free. Sarah stopped and looked back.

"We can't outrun them. Not both of us," Thetis gasped.

"But...."

Thetis drew from within her robes a gray metallic egg and held it out, balanced on her palm. "This is something I'd been saving for...." She didn't finish the sentence. Sarah didn't ask. Some weapon, of course. Thetis could have prepared it for the Guardian, for Hexus, for Mimir.

"You must go," Thetis said. "Save Chance. And tell him... tell him his mother was fearless, in the end."

"I cannot—"

"Listen, Sarah. I betrayed Seth."

"What?"

"I could have saved him, and didn't. No—it's worse. I... I pushed him off the rocks. I meant to betray him. He knew I was Chance's mother. I told myself I did it to save Chance, so that I could be on the airship, so that I could prevent the Guardian from learning from Seth that I was Chance's mother. But really I did it because I was afraid of the Guardian."

Sarah stood, silent. She did not know what to say. She did not know what to think. Seth!

"But you've made me want to redeem myself," Thetis continued. "You must go. You must. It's the only way."

Metal clattered somewhere behind them.

"They're coming," Thetis hissed.

Sarah drew her other sword. She turned, took two steps, and then stopped. A preposterous vision came into her head in a flash: she pictured Thetis at the kitchen table of her home in the lands of the Purimen, with her mother and herself, eating pie, sipping wine, talking quietly of Chance and the year's crop and maybe of a grandchild. And—she believed, just as suddenly—her mother would have liked Thetis. Her mother would have accepted the Junior Mother out of the solidarity of women, and because Thetis was like herself: quiet, a good listener, someone who spoke of her own accord only in intimacy.

Sarah went back to Thetis and fell to her knees in the tall grass before the Junior Mother of the Gotterdammerung. She turned her swords and planted their points, then bowed her head.

"Mother," she said. "Give me your blessing."

Tears fell from the eyes of both the women. Thetis put a hand on Sarah's head.

"Go with my blessing, Sarah Michael—Sarah Kyrien, Ranger of the Purimen, wife of my son . . . daughter now of mine."

Sarah sobbed once. And before she lost her will to leave, before she felt unable to quit Thetis to her fate, she snatched up her blades and turned and ran, ran to save Chance.

She heard Thetis calling out behind her, "I'm here, Modghasts! Useful, full of life!"

Sarah turned around one barrow, then another, and was starting up the long slope to the abandoned buildings when a light flashed. She looked back. A shockwave shot across the grass, a white wave of turning blades. It hit her and threw her on her face. Then dirt, and shards of metal, rained down all about her.

When the shower of smoking earth and shattered iron stopped, she rolled over. In the sky above, through a ripple of twisted air, she saw a red airship float over, descending as it sped toward Yggdrasil.

"Damn you, false god!" she shouted. "So many did not die to let you get there first!"

She gripped her swords more tightly, stood, and ran.

Sarah had almost caught up with the red airship, which was turning slowly in the air now as it descended, when she came into a huge square spotted with open wells. She stopped, gasping. At the far end, a huge modghast stood, a spidery heap of sharp and twisted metal. It did not move. Beside it, a disk of metal was bent high into the air, bright cracks of steel showing through the black and gray weathered surface of the metal, indicating that it had been bent and broken recently.

She stole to the side. She would go around. As she came to the edge of the square, crouched over, chest heaving to regain some strength after her frantic run, she got a different perspective on the spidery modghast, and froze. Now she could see that Mimir stood before the modghast, one hand held up, arm outstretched. The modghast also had one of its eight legs held out, the brutal rusted tip of it thrust right through the flesh of Mimir's upturned palm. They were frozen there, linked where iron pierced makina flesh, both transfixed: Mimir, erect, seeming calm, in her formal black and white suit; the modghast, a still heap of rot and corrosion and refuse.

"Sarah!" a voice called.

She started and turned. The shell of a broken building stood just a few steps away. Wadjet waved to her from one of its gaping windows.

Sarah ran to Wadjet, sheathed her swords, and climbed through the window. Inside she found a stripped, empty space, like all the other buildings she had passed here. Half of the roof had rotted away. Shadowed clouds shot past overhead. She held out her hand, and Wadjet took it.

"Where's Chance?" Sarah asked.

"In the Well, I hope. Mimir betrayed us. But I helped Chance escape. How did you get here?"

Sarah told her briefly.

"Then where is Thetis?" Wadjet asked.

"She is dead."

Wadjet pressed her lips together in frustration.

Sarah pointed toward Mimir and the modghast. "What's happening? They seem paralyzed."

"They fight."

"They're fighting?"

"A terrible, terrible battle, I suspect. Modghast against makina."

"Who will win?"

Wadjet shrugged. "If we are fortunate," Wadjet said, "the god is too late. Chance may already be beyond Earth and deep inside the Well."

Sarah began to walk toward a hole in the opposite wall. "We've had no good fortune. I cannot wait. I must help Chance."

"But the god...."

"I've faced him before and spitted him on my swords. He said I shan't do so a second time, but I aim to show him wrong."

"I...." Wadjet had not moved.

"You've done much," Sarah said, understanding Wadjet's reluctance. "Thank you for helping Chance get this far, escaping Mimir."

This was enough for Wadjet. A reminder of what she hated about the god: he was another builder of cages, another one to bind the boy.

"I'm coming," she said.

Sarah reached behind and pulled out her knife. She flipped it, held the blade, and offered the handle to Wadjet. The exile of the Stewards took the handle, then tossed the knife, feelings its weight, and said, "It's a good knife."

CHAPTER

51

C hance pulled the gold doors open. The dim hall rose before him to a bright square of sky. Even in the shadow of Yggdrasil, the sky shone brilliant now that his eyes were adjusted to this dim place.

He started up the slope, walking slowly, favoring his suffering broken arm that he had yet again bashed.

It was impossible. His arm would need a month to heal, or more. Nothing to eat or drink could be found in this empty plain. The modghasts roved all this land: the stark, scoured emptiness of the buildings around them revealed how thoroughly the modghasts hunted for anything that they could tear apart and make use of. The danger to Sarah grew each day—each hour—that passed. All this—and the god could not be far behind. Chance could not wait here, to heal. But what else could he do?

Halfway up the long hall, he stooped and picked up the metal rod he had dropped there. He hefted it, slipping his hand down its length, until he had it balanced in his grip.

A shadow fell across the door. Chance looked up. He could see only the figure of a human being, silhouetted against the sky.

"Wadjet?" His voice echoed.

"No, Potentiate," his brother's voice responded. "No. It is I, Hexus."

Another, low figure stepped next to Hexus. The gorilla, in her armor.

Chance took a step backward. And then, instantly, Paul stood before him—Paul's body stood before him—holding up one arm blistered with running red sores, and in the rotting palm of it the eye of Hexus glared at him.

"So we come together at the end," Hexus said. "On the threshold of the new world, the reforging of the Ultimate Age."

Chance backed away. The gorilla walked down the hall behind Hexus, slow with solemn dignity, her armor clinking.

"And even now, shrinking away from me, you move toward the Numin Well, where I would send you."

"Where is Sarah?"

"Ah, the Ranger? I do not know. Still on Lethebion, perhaps. Waiting for you to return a god."

Chance sighed with relief. Sarah was safe. He could die then, here, and she might find still a way back, working with Thetis. He could die and he would not be abandoning her to the will of Hexus.

"Now, come," Hexus said.

"I will not yield," Chance whispered.

"Oh, you have no choice, Potentiate. I admire you, I honor your accomplishment. Look at you. The Guardian is bound, your friends are dead or far away; you stand here alone, broken, dirty, starving and thirsty, and yet you made it all this way from your tiny little quiet nursery corner of the world. You have done something heroic. Truly you reveal your heritage."

The gorilla, now at the side of Hexus, held her spear close in both hands and eyed Chance with her head tilted back. She tightened her grip on her spear, twisting it in her strong black hands as though she longed to thrust it through him. Chance noted that it was made of ash. Then she sniffed and turned her face away. Her meaning was clear: *I see nothing heroic.*

Chance swung the bar, but before the long sweep of it had crossed half the distance to Hexus, it froze in the air, as if Chance had struck at a mound of sand. The gorilla shouted in outrage.

"Stop," Hexus whispered. Chance felt the air tighten around him. He could not move.

Hexus stepped forward. Chance saw that his brother's body now had the appearance of someone mortally ill. The familiar lines of Paul's face were etched, haggard. He had lost much weight. His eyes were yellow and bloodshot. His hair had thinned to an unhealthy nest of brittle red strands. The breath that fell on Chance's face reeked of foul, rancid meat.

One, then two bears roared behind them. Their voices echoed down the hall.

Hexus did not take his eye off of Chance, but he turned Paul's head and told the gorilla, "See what is happening there."

The gorilla ran back up the ramp.

"I will defeat you," Chance said. "Even if the final battle is in my soul, where my soul must fight your soul, I will defeat you. I swear to you, as the One True God is my witness, I will not yield. I will not yield."

"Be careful what you threaten, Potentiate," Hexus said. "Or I may leave nothing, nothing of you."

He pressed his hand to Chance's head. Chance shivered with revulsion as he felt the horrible wetness of the running sores and of the eye pressed against his filthy forehead. A terrible, screaming pain raged through Chance's skull, a feeling that his brain might explode. Then the visions, and the memories, began to eat their way into his soul.

Hexus released the tight grip on Chance's body, seeming to put all his effort into cutting through Chance's mind. Chance fell to the hard ground, the palm of his hand reflexively thrusting out and scraping hard over the shards of glass across the ground as he fell onto his right shoulder. Hexus crouched down over him so he could press the hand again to Chance's head. Paul's eyes were closed.

Writhing, Chance gripped a long narrow blade of crystal. He saw again the tower of the Hand that Reaches, whole and shining in the bright sun, high over a Theopolis teeming with white towers beyond which the Crystal Wall, polished and gleaming, held out a crashing sea. Chance clutched the broken glass so tightly his fingers bled, and the pain in his hand anchored him to this older world, to this empty dirty hall below the ruins of that age.

Then Chance raised the shard and thrust it into his throat.

"No!" Hexus screamed. "No!"

But this voice faded into silence, and Chance's splashing blood blackened the vision of the white city of Theopolis.

CHAPTER

52

Wadjet saw in a flash, before she even smelled them, the soulburdened. Three bears and a wolf. She and Sarah had leapt over the top steps and onto the small square where the entrance to the Hall of Ma'at opened, and where the red airship was anchored with its tail swinging in the light wind, and there the beasts stood, as if waiting for them.

Sarah ran ahead without stopping, her swords swinging, the hard soles of her boots slapping the flat stones of the square. Wadjet would have hesitated, tried to circle around, but that was not possible now that Sarah plowed ahead. Events flung themselves toward a chaotic collision, and Wadjet had no way to shape them. She could only follow, easily matching Sarah's pace with her long legs.

One bear saw them. It roared and charged. The others froze a moment, taking the scene in, before roaring themselves. The first bear came on alone, and then, foolishly, it stopped before them and stood to its full height, waving its claws, twisting its nose, howling. Sarah did not slow, but drove both swords into its chest, precisely aimed up under its ribs and into its heart. It clawed at her, scoring her arms, but fell back. The swords came free. Blood gushed just once from the wounds, and the soulburdened beast was dead.

Sarah pointed to the left. "You go that way. I'll go this way. We'll split them. Try to get to the door, to help Chance."

Wadjet looked to the door. A gorilla in brightly gleaming armor emerged from the dark beyond it and peered over the scene.

Sarah ran off, circling right. The remaining two bears chased her. Wadjet ran in the other direction. The wolf, seeming relaxed, loped toward Wadjet, mouth open so that its tongue lolled out. Wadjet held the knife out toward it, flashing the blade, trying to make the wolf fear her.

The gorilla lifted her spear and started toward Wadjet.

The wolf slowed, looked back, and, seeing the gorilla coming to its aid, slipped to the side.

They will try to get in front and behind me, Wadjet realized.

Wadjet saw, over and far beyond the wolf, Sarah crossing the square. One bear ran toward her and Sarah feinted, turned, and leapt onto it, driving her twin swords down through its back, just behind the neck. The swords came free as she ran over the beast and tumbled onto the hard ground. She rolled and came up, bloody swords swinging.

Lucky, Wadjet thought. She's very good but she's also very lucky. The stupid bears attack her one at a time—that's lucky. And her every sword strike is hitting its true target—that's very lucky.

Wadjet slipped to the side, trying to keep the wolf and gorilla on one flank. But this drove her away from the door, toward the steps. The wolf stalked her, head down and pointed slightly off to her side, as if out of politeness the beast did not want to look straight at her.

She backed up until she had to stop at the top of the steps. To be driven back down the stair would be to leave Sarah to fight all of them. She couldn't allow that. She crouched, held the knife out, and watched her opponents cautiously. Her heart pounded, seeming to shake her whole body. The shadowed but still powerful sun, and the sun-baked rocks, conspired to make sweat fall into her eyes.

I've never been lucky, Wadjet thought. Her master had said just that. When Mjuba had beaten Afukali that last time, Wadjet had found the girl chimpanzee who had been her crib mate crying under green fern fronds. Afukali's nose had been bleeding, and blood matted the hair on her chest and shoulders. Flies feasted on it. Afukali's eyes were swollen shut. Wadjet had been unlucky that Mjuba had been right there, nearby, to catch her rage when it burned white hot. Wadjet had been unlucky that Mjuba faked that he felt no regret, and when she showed him her fangs he beat his chest, enraging her even more. She had set on him hard, clawing at his eyes, surprising him long enough that she could sink her teeth into his throat— thinking, he will beat me till I cannot walk if I let go. I must hold him till he is unconscious. She bit hard, tasting blood, while his long hairy black arms beat and beat at her back.

And she had been unlucky that when Mjuba finally fell still, he had been not unconscious but dead. And she had been unlucky that Mjuba's aunt was on the Council of Stewards. "A Steward must know her powers! She cannot make mistakes!" the old ape had cried.

Now the gorilla and wolf glanced at each other, and then separated further, flanking her. That was bad. They knew what they were doing—again, ill fate. Wadjet pointed the blade at the wolf, but kept her eyes on the gorilla and the gorilla's spear.

The wolf growled. Wadjet noted, with a kind of distant curiosity, how the wolf was all gray, with gray eyes, just as the gorilla was all black, with black eyes. It was so strange to see here a gorilla, at the base of the Numin Well, as if a creature from Wadjet's home were transplanted, like her, to this barren and catastrophic place.

"Now I eat you," the wolf said.

An explosive rattling and clanking roared behind Wadjet. She dared a glance down the steps. The spider-like modghast ran up the steps at her. A clutch of smaller twitching arms bound Mimir tightly to the front of the modghast, as if the makina were some morsel being drawn into the mouth of a giant crab. Mimir's eyes were closed. Thin rods of iron had penetrated her clean, trim black and white suit, the first blemish Wadjet had ever seen on it. Whether this meant Mimir had won or lost their battle, or even whether the battle raged on or was over, she did not know.

Wadjet ran, feet skimming the edge of the top step, moving sideways to avoid the ape and wolf. She had not gone ten steps before the wolf jumped at her. But at that same moment, the modghast loomed up above them, and as the wolf leapt at her, one rusted iron leg slammed down out of the air and through the canine's back, pinning it to the ground with a force that cracked the hard stones. The wolf whined horribly, its back legs scratching away at the hard ground.

The gorilla threw her spear. Wadjet saw the flash of golden wood and dove. The point nicked her back, but passed on, to be lost as it sailed through the air and then clattered down the stone stairs.

Wadjet rolled over—and saw, just in time to roll aside, another of the modghast's pointed spider legs strike for her. It hit the stone by her hip with a spray of sparks. A third leg struck down at the gorilla, knocking the ape onto her back. The pointed foot of it settled on the gorilla's armor, pinning her. The rusted iron point twisted and slid against the metal, trying to penetrate the gold plate that protected her chest.

The leg that had just missed Wadjet snapped quickly sideways, striking her, sending her rolling across the stones. She lost her grip on Sarah's knife and heard it skitter away. Her head hit the ground once, twice, as she spun.

When she came to rest, the world reeled for a moment and she saw the leg strike down at her with swift violence—

And stop.

"Ah!" Wadjet cried. For a long moment, she was sure that the foot had stabbed through her, and that the pain had simply not climbed to her skull yet.

But no. The leg was poised, the tip of it pressed against her but not pushing down. She grabbed the iron limb. Pain shot through her sprained wrists as she tried, without result, to shove it aside, or to shove herself out from under it. Coarse dirt coated the metal, and this close she could see the roots that clung to it and the green streaks of grass stains that had been pressed into the endless tiny scrapes on the metal. A smell of rotten flesh and wet rust and burnt hair filled the air around her.

"I teem with labyrinths, modghast," a voice called out. Wadjet looked up. Mimir's eyes were closed, but her lips moved and from both Mimir's own mouth and the modghast the makina's calm voice reverberated, so that Wadjet could feel the vibration of the makina's words in the modghast's foot that she held.

"Your bitter years cannot plumb my depths. You cannot circle my thoughts."

The modghast's foot trembled against Wadjet's stomach, struggling to overcome some resistance that Mimir manifested, so that it might stab Wadjet. The claw began to sink slowly, slowly, into her stomach.

"I am a god, you fool!" Hexus screamed, a harsh sound that cut through the soothing black silence that surrounded Chance.

Pain returned to Chance. A dull throbbing ache in his skull. Then a sharp pang at his throat. He opened his eyes, and light stabbed at his brain.

"Fool." Hexus stood before him. Paul's face was furious. The black eye glowed angrily in the rotting palm held up by his shoulder. "I can fix a simple wound. You only make your suffering last longer."

Chance looked down. Hexus held him erect, his legs and arm bound. His filthy shirt was drenched with blood. He was dizzy, light-headed. His vision clouded a second, and only slowly did the dark lines of the hall begin to form again in the gray blur of his sight.

And through this blur he saw Sarah, running toward him. It's my own dream, he thought. My own dream competing with Hexus's dream. Hexus is just getting started, and in a few minutes I won't be myself any more—but I'll cling to this dream of my wife....

But then Sarah sprinted the last of the distance, pointing her swords straight out before her. She leaned forward, hands close together, so that the parallel blades shone together like one weapon.

And she ran them into Hexus's back and through his chest.

The grip on Chance's body shattered.

Hexus screamed.

"Yes," Sarah said clearly, slowly. "Yes, twice."

Chance saw that Sarah truly stood there. Her short hair was caked brown with dust, her cut cheek inflamed red with infection, her eyes swollen. But she stood with her mouth set in grim determination, both sword hilts tightly gripped.

Chance seized the bar at his feet. He swung it wide and brought it down hard on Hexus, unable to keep from cringing as the heavy iron struck against his own brother's shoulder.

Chance froze again.

Paul's eyes looked at Chance and then squinted angrily.

"Bitch!" he said, in Paul's voice, with Paul's disappointed invective.

A loud *snap* sounded out. Sarah stumbled back, drawing her swords from Hexus. Snap, snap, snap, snap, snap.... The sound went on. As Hexus turned, Chance saw that Sarah's swords were breaking, a finger's width of steel at a time splintering off. A shining pile of bright shards collected on the ground before her feet, ringing as they fell.

In a moment she held only the handles of swords, studded with small torn nubs of steel.

Then Chance heard another *snap*. And Sarah cried out and fell to the ground. Crack, crack, crack. She screamed, writhing.

"Stop!" Chance howled. "Stop, you goddamned foul, filthy devil! Stop!"

Hexus was breaking every bone in Sarah's body. Her legs, her arms, her fingers. Her jaw twisted aside. Her chest heaved as her ribs crumbled. Her hips turned impossibly as her pelvis shattered.

"Oh God, save us, save us," Chance whispered. "Oh God, please have mercy and save her." Tears streamed from his eyes. But Hexus held him tightly.

Hexus turned and faced Chance. He shouted over the sound of Sarah screaming in pain. "Your god does nothing, Puriman! It is silent, impotent. It does not exist. But I—I could save her, Puriman. I could save her as I just saved you. But I will not. There is no god, no god that will save her—*unless*—unless you become that god. Unless you go into the Well and return to redeem. Unless you yield now to me."

CHAPTER

53

This is how I always expected to die, Wadjet thought, as she shoved with all her might at the modghast's steel leg that held her down. I expected to die pinned in some battle between ancient causes for which I care nothing. Murdered by histories I did not choose and long ago renounced.

The foot could not be pushed aside. It slowly sank down against her. Soon it would sluggishly crush her organs. The death of the wolf had been far kinder.

She looked up at the modghast, at the twisted festering nest of wire and iron and old concrete and animal flesh that made its confused and fetid underbelly and face. And there, above it, floated the Guardian.

Ah, Wadjet thought, if only I were that lucky. But I'm never lucky. I am Wadjet the free, Wadjet the wild, Wadjet who smashes cages and spurns the judgment of elders, Wadjet who spits on dead histories—but never am I Wadjet the fortunate. And this hopeful hallucination is a misfortune; it does nothing but distract me.

But the Guardian was not floating. He was paused at the highest point in the arc of a great leap, left arm stretched straight out before himself, fingers open and held out like a blade, and with his right arm high above his head he held Threkor's Hammer from the very bottom of its shaft. And now he was falling, but falling toward her, so that it seemed he was almost still. He came more quickly, accelerating, swinging the hammer down.

Still caught in the modghast's mouth, Mimir in that instant opened her silver flashing eyes and smiled.

The metal claw lifted away from Wadjet as the modghast began to rear up. Wadjet crawled out of the way, scrambling backwards frantically, and fell onto her back again.

And as she did so, an explosion of tearing metal boomed, and the modghast was torn open. Huge shards of steel and iron burst from it. Wadjet watched, unable to escape, as one round thick panel spun down onto her.

Her world went black.

"Oh God, please have mercy and save Sarah," Chance cried. Tears streamed from his eyes. Sarah cried out in pain, writhing on the floor behind Hexus.

"Yield, Puriman," Hexus said. "You cannot win, and the sooner you submit, the sooner she could be saved."

"You—" Chance hesitated. "You give your word? If I yield, you'll save her?"

"Yes. My word."

Chance bowed his head. "I yield."

But then the air rushed out of the hall. Dust stirred over the desiccated ground. An explosion of tearing metal sounded in the distance, and then instantly upon the sound of it a hulking naked shape occluded the light falling through the doorway, and a voice called out, shaking the ground, the walls, the column of space that formed the hall.

"I am very angry now, Hexus. Very angry. I'm going to hurt you."

"Atheos!" Hexus spat.

A minute before, Chance would have cried out with joy, but now he could care for nothing but Sarah, twisting in agony on the ground, broken and dying.

Hexus stepped over her. Chance was released. He fell to the Earth and crawled toward Sarah. Just steps away, the immortals smashed into each other with such force that powdered stone fell from the ceiling and rained down, laying a corpse-like color over Sarah's hair and face.

"Sarah, Sarah!" Chance called, shouting above the explosive thundering of the battle.

She hissed.

"What?" Chance asked. "What, my love?"

"Go," she managed to get out through her broken mouth. Chance saw then that Hexus had cracked even her teeth. The fractured bloody stumps of them broke unevenly from her gums, and the splinters of her front teeth were spread on her lip. Blood covered her tongue.

"Oh my love," he whispered, touching her hair. "It cannot end like this. It cannot end like this."

"Go," she whispered. "Forget... Guardian. Do it. Save yourself. Save us."

Chance touched his forehead to hers.

"I'll be back in a moment," he said.

He stood. Before him Hexus and the Guardian twisted about each other, hammering and tearing at their bodies and at space and time. They were visible only as a gray and black blur.

Chance picked up the steel bar and ran for the hall of Ma'at.

"Are you a Potentiate?" Ma'at asked Chance, as the lights flickered on and he ran toward the pink cylinder with its school of brains. And then the voices began, "You have returned—" but said no more, as Chance slammed the steel bar into the pillar of glass.

It cracked. Pink fluid beaded on the gnarled fracture.

Thetis had told him, "It is said that one voice gives passage, and the other voices deny passage."

"Stop!" the voices called.

Chance struck it again. The frozen dogs of Ma'at struggled at their bonds of ages, screeching, biting at the air, twisting their heads. But they remained fixed in place still by eons of corrosion.

"Stop!" the voices demanded. "We are the many voices of the Numin Well, Gatekeeper of Bifrost, immortal of the Penultimate Age! Who are you to harm us? Young Potentiate, you know not what you do!"

Chance held the metal rod far behind his back, his torso fully twisted. "I hear that often these days." Then he swung with all his strength.

The cylinder shattered, sharp fragments of crystal scattering across the room. The fluid gushed over the floor. Some of the gray brains fell to the stones in shapeless heaps, each with a wet slap. A sweet smell that reminded Chance of fermenting wine rose from the smoking pink liquid. Other brains, still suspended from wires that now cut into their flesh, bent and began to tear. Chance smashed through the few standing glass shards of the cylinder, cutting all the wires, severing every connection.

He tossed aside the heavy bar. It clattered loudly on the stones of the floor. He stepped back into the circle.

The yellow light shone on him.

"You are a Potentiate," the lone, mechanical voice said.

"Open the Well," he told it.

The mirrored door before him shimmered, turned transparent. Through it, Chance saw a tunnel of stars, spinning. And perhaps a hundred paces ahead, another door. The door he had seen in his dreams.

He ran past the snapping teeth of the iron dogs, and leapt.

And fell.

"Ah!" he cried. He reached out for something to grip to, and touched a smooth wall of clear glass that separated him from the black and the stars beyond. He could get no purchase, he fell still—

And yet, he did not fall away from the wall.

He was floating, he realized. Not falling.

After a moment Chance adjusted. It was hard to move, like floating in the center of the lake—like floating in water, he realized, but being unable to swim because air is too thin to kick against.

He tentatively stretched, turning in place. The stars spun by. A salt taste rose in the back of his mouth. If there had been anything in his stomach he would have vomited. But after a minute the nausea passed. He found that he could touch both walls with his feet and his one free hand, and by pressing against them get enough hold to move himself. It was cold in the hall. He began to shiver.

He looked over his shoulder. There was the hall of Ma'at, the Anubin warriors, and the broken cylinder, but dim now, as if the door were half closed. Then the passage between places turned opaque, and then became a mirror. Chance gazed only upon himself reflected in the closed doorway.

Slowly, he managed to pull himself forward to the other door. It was featureless, white and oval shaped. A round red disk was set in the wall beside it. He touched this. The door slid aside. As it passed he saw that it had no width: the edge was invisible. He remembered Thetis's warning. *The door is like the sharpest blade imaginable.* Blood-warm air poured out from the room beyond.

Chance looked back—and caught his breath in shocked amazement. The door was there, at the end of the short tunnel, but beyond it, visible through the tunnel walls, a blue globe floated in the stars, with blue seas over which swirled delicate wisps of white cloud. It filled his view.

Was this the world? The whole world? Where all men and all their trials and pains and hopes dwelled? It seemed so small, almost insignificant, set here floating in the vast black of God's creation.

But down there Sarah suffered. He could not pause now to marvel at it.

He pulled through the doorway. On the other side he floated in another hall, this one not of glass like the hall behind, but of white metal. There were seven bright shimmering surfaces, like oval pools of water, along one side of the corridor. These were the Aussersein membranes, as Thetis had called them. From these the gods emerged. Past these, no god could go.

He pulled himself down the hall.

One door. Another. Another. He drifted, as quickly as he could push himself, down to the penultimate door. The symbol that Thetis had told him meant *six* was cut into the metal above the shimmering surface.

Chance looked back at the other shimmering surfaces. He remembered the Guardian's plea: *you could kill them all, after you kill this one*. Or, he realized, *before*.

"Sorry," Chance said. "But I don't have the time to kill them now. And after...."

He pushed through the surface. The hair on his head and skin stood stiffly up, and he felt a slightly painful prickling all over, but then he was through. Dim lights flickered on. He floated in an oval room, little bigger than a closet, with a single black door opposite the Aussersein membrane. It was even warmer than in the hall outside.

A small, simple handle was on the black door. He turned it, and pulled it open.

A white sarcophagus stood behind it, with a lid of thick crystal. Within lay a naked, hairless boy, only a few years younger than Chance, perhaps, but pale and without any scar or even a callus. Wires and tubes covered him. As Chance watched, one of the tubes twitched.

Chance touched the top. After fumbling for a moment, he found many small handles along the edge. He seized one in his fist, and it turned easily. He turned each, one after another, working from bottom to top. Then the massive lid slid aside.

He reached in, and grabbed the sleeping child by the arm, and pulled on him. Slowly, reluctantly, the body came out. He pulled harder. Some of the white cords, like retreating worms, began to pull away and slip back into tiny orifices in the casket.

He dragged the boy into the room, and the last of the lines separated, retreating.

Chance let go of him.

The boy opened his eyes. He reached out, clawing at Chance, a look of panic on his face. Like a drowning man, he scratched at Chance's face and arm, trying to grip on to him, to grip into him.

"Stop!" Chance howled.

The boy clawed at him, in panic screaming words that Chance could not understand.

And Chance thought: this was Hexus. Murderer of Seth. Murderer of my parents. Torturer of Sarah.

He grabbed the boy by the throat and smashed him against the wall. The motion started slow but gained momentum, his strength leveraged because his feet were planted firmly between two corners of the panels in the floor. The boy's head connected hard. The boy stopped clawing. He shouted in anger, a guttural growl.

"God damn you," Chance cried. Tears pooled in his eyes, but having nowhere to fall they gathered on his lashes, to be pressed out when he blinked. He smashed the boy against the wall each time he cursed him. "Damn you, damn you, damn you, damn you, damn you."

The boy was still. Crimson blood leaked from the back of his head. It stained the gray wall, stained Chance's hands, and floated in thick globs in the air. Shaking with weeping, still holding the boy's throat, Chance pushed him away and through the Aussersein membrane.

"Oh, God, I've lost my way," Chance whispered. "Please help me."

Chance pulled off his shoes. His socks. His pants and under-clothes. He pushed these through the membrane also, not wanting them floating about in the little space, clotting the close air. He tore his shirt open, not bothering with the buttons, and pulled it over his good arm. Then he carefully worked the splints off his broken arm and pulled the shirt after them.

He stood naked, filthy, bruised blue all over, thin from hunger, head pounding from the makina's metal poisons and the assault of the god and from lack of water and loss of blood. And he was about to spend eternity like this.

"Dear God, One True God," he whispered, pressing his hands together. "Take me and make of me an Erthengle, an instrument of your divine will on Earth. I do not mean to tempt thee God but rather beg thy mercy when I plead: speak to me, now, please. Give me some sign. That I might not become a thing of evil. Give me the power to become a thing of your will."

There was no answer. But he was not surprised. He had not expected one.

He climbed into the coffin.

CHAPTER

54

The door closed over Chance. White snakes sought their way into his flesh. He would have screamed, but in seconds he was asleep.

And then awake.

He opened his eyes. He was looking at the bloody, broken body of Hexus—of the true boy that had become Hexus—floating before him, in the gray hall. Chance's own clothes, looking like trash falling from some terrible height, floated around the naked, hairless corpse of the ancient boy.

Chance had done it. He felt different, but only a small bit different. He did not feel powerful. He was clean, naked, but his arm felt still broken, his head still ached, though it ached less.

Chance turned. The Aussersein membrane was behind him. In its silver he saw himself: a shape he recognized but also did not. His face, his form. But his skin was nearly silver. It pulsed, changing to a human shade as he watched.

"Is this me?" he whispered. "Am I Chance?" *Or something else? Something that only dreams it is Chance, and may awake some day as something else, and forget Chance as one forgets a dream?*

He reached out to touch his reflection and touched the membrane. It was hard, unyielding.

Sarah waited. Sarah was dying. He had no time.

The door between worlds was still open, at the end of the hall. Still open.

"Please God. Forgive me. Make me your instrument."

Now the hard part. Now the real struggle. Now he must split the vine, must plant each of twin cuttings in separate soil. One cutting would grow strong in shelter, and feed its strength to the other. The other cutting would face hardship.

Thetis had said it was impossible. That no one, not even a god, could bear the pain. But the ancient Puriman prophets, the great martyrs, had borne pains like no others had known, and had done so because they had the strength given them by their faith in the One True God.

Chance could not save Sarah if he could not survive the Guardian, who would attack instantly. He must be able to face the Guardian. *You would have to be a god for five hundred years before you had the power to face me, even to flee me*, the Guardian had said. So Chance would take a thousand years.

He would not hesitate. He had taken too long already. He pulled himself down the hall and then lay in the open doorway between Bifrost and the Numin Well. He reached back and touched the red button that controlled the door. The infinitely thin edge between spaces slid forward, and cut him evenly, precisely, in two.

In the Numin Well, long decades passed in which a formless half of a man screamed in pain, howling and writhing, learning, with impossible slowness, how to think first a single thought, then another, in a grinding agony.

Then years passed as he learned how to create the image of his whole body, hollowing out his own form to make the other half of himself. More years passed as he learned to see, to hear, to move again. Then more years as he learned to think clear thoughts through the blaze of pain.

Trembling between form and formlessness, barely able to withstand the thought of the nine hundred years still before him, he opened the door to Bifrost, stepped into the tunnel of stars, and gazed out at the Earth and the universe....

And he set about now to begin to discover his powers, in that narrow column of air, floating above the world. He would spend nearly a whole millennium here, exploring possibilities, finding what the universe could reveal to his new potency, and communing with his past and his present and his future. Alone wresting from ignorance the vast powers of a god.

Chance screamed. And screamed. And screamed. The pain was impossible. It consumed everything. He reached for the door—it was not possible to survive without the rest of himself—he would open the door and reunite. But he could not form himself enough even to touch the switch. His body—trying to find its shape while at the same time curling into a shapeless rebellion against its division—seethed and twisted, more formless than formed.

But then Chance heard, or felt, the voice—his voice, his own voice—reach out to him. From this very column of air, this Bifrost. From a future impossibly far away. He cried out even more fiercely then, unable to hear it, horrified at the impossibility of waiting so long before he could reunite his halves.

But he did hear it. It spoke of power. It spoke of how to be as if whole, and how to move through space and time.

Chance began to learn.

Chance stepped out of the shimmering door into the Hall of Ma'at and accelerated to a hummingbird's pace. He shot past the shattered brains clumped wetly on the floor and into the hall beyond.

Sarah lay there, frozen in slower time. He could see the warmth of her body and the motion of her heart: she still lived. Relief flooded him.

The Guardian stood, clutching Paul's broken body in one hand. The power of Hexus's god flesh was fading, Chance could feel. The Aussersein fragment of Hexus was losing its shape, losing a little bit of itself with each blow from the Guardian, and there was no soul in the Well linked to it, informing it so that it could reshape itself. In seconds it would be formless matter. Paul's legs were twisted impossibly, his chest pulpy and torn and red. His blood stained the dark walls of the hall. The Guardian held the hammer over Paul's face, ready to smash the skull. The hand with the god's eye was rising, but at a human speed, too slow to intervene.

But Hexus looked at him. And somehow, Chance realized, Paul looked upon him also. Time stopped. Hexus and Paul reached for him, and Chance reached for them too. Between them they folded a moment of space, clasped a bubble of shared time together, hidden for an instant from the Guardian.

Chance saw the many hidden folds of space and time. He reached out and cleaved two folds, and then Hexus floated before him, turned mostly out of Paul, a diaphanous cloud in human form wrought of thin shimmering veins of Aussersein, a single eye in the palm of one ghostly supplicant hand held high.

And Hexus said, shaking the very air, in a call of joy, "All praise to my victory! Behold! Hexus is triumphant, and a new god is born! Now humankind can be redeemed! I have won!"

Chance stared, horrified, but then he felt the thunderous approach of the Guardian and he pushed Hexus aside, folded that space away, and Paul stood before him, one arm thrust in darkness trailing after Hexus—but the rest of his brother still there.

And Paul said softly, his voice pleading and intimate, full of regret and sorrow, "Chance, Chance, let me be free. Let me...."

Chance reached his hand out. "Paul—perhaps I can—I can...."

Paul did not take his hand. "Let me be free," he moaned.

Chance's mouth twisted in despair. But after a moment he nodded.

"I love you, Paul," he whispered.

"Tell Sarah," Paul said, "tell the folks back home, tell them I died like a Puriman." He drew his broken body erect. Unable to tug on the cuff of his one torn sleeve with only one hand, he shook it out, then pulled at it with a bend of the wrist, his fingers catching the cloth against his palm. He straightened as best he could the ripped collar of his white shirt. He smoothed back his dust-thickened hair.

And then the Hammer of Threkor smashed through Chance's folded glade of space and time, and Hexus collapsed into Paul, snapping together again, as the otherworldly metal tore into their intertwined flesh.

Paul's heart stopped.

Suddenly Chance was back in the hallway, Sarah at his feet, Paul dead in the Guardian's grasp. Chance still moved at a hummingbird's speed. But the Guardian, holding Paul's body as the world crawled around them, raised his head to look at Chance. His expression of unbridled rage collapsed. He gazed at Chance with weariness and, it seemed to Chance, something like misery.

"Oh, Chance," he said, his quick voice a buzz in their fast motion. "Why?"

Chance did not let his own despair, nor the Guardian's despair, take hold of his heart. He stepped forward, bent space, and raced out of that world and time. The instant fell away. He chased the past.

✜

Before Chance, the snaking path of the Guardian's life stretched backwards through time and space like a long cord knit of the toils that shaped history. At a furious pace, racing toward eons before, Chance followed the Guardian's life.

The experience reminded Chance distinctly of something: the one summer that Chance's father had taken him canoeing for the first time. His father was a master with the canoe, but he sat in the front, facing backwards, his dripping paddle held out of the water, and told Chance what to do. The boy took the advice, and it was good advice, but he acted slowly, unevenly, uncertainly. Chance learned then that you couldn't know what advice like that really meant until you tried it out for yourself. Knowing what to do and knowing how to do it, and do it well, were different. And so, just as his father had advised him in the canoe, his own future self told him what to do, but could not teach him how to do it. That he had to learn by trial and accident.

He shot backward wildly, clumsily, hurtling nearly out of control, as time lay before him like a vast land, and the Guardian stretched across it to the horizon. No—not like a vast land, but like a river. All of time was a river, he realized. And you could climb out of it, and run along the bank, before stepping back into it. And there were rapids, and still places. And there were moments, like some of the acts of the other gods, which were like boulders in rapids—you couldn't get near them because the flow of time broke over them and turned you away. His father, who had taught him to canoe a river, and to fish from a canoe, had prepared him well.

Chance kept his distance from the shining, massive life path of the Guardian, lest the immortal see him in this place behind space, but he still marveled at the ages the Guardian had known.

And nowhere in this sweep of vast time could Chance see the One True God.

Chance flew along beside the Guardian, unable to take in the sight of everything—

And then he saw his home, and his father, where the Guardian's path and that of the Puriman crossed, and in an instant, because his attention shifted to his father and away from the Guardian, Chance was thrown off his course, and he shot along his father's path—and then, drawing himself up, realizing his mistake, he fell into time and space at the feet of John Kyrien.

He stood near the vines, by the great boulder on the hill. His father stood with a pruning knife in hand, his pants and shirt soiled with soft dirt, his face still caught in an expression of uncertain surprise.

Chance almost cried out, "Father!" But then he realized the danger of that. It was years before his own birth. His own path could be ruined by such an act.

Dusk was spread out across the sky above his house and its fields. Dark storm clouds crowded together overhead and shot quick and low over the hills, threatening dark rain. Wind shook the vines. Chance drew himself back—but not all the way back. He stood, half out, half in, time and space.

"Puriman," he whispered.

His father stumbled and dropped his pruning knife. He fell to his knees and put one hand on an aged, gnarled Ries vine to steady himself.

"It's the devil," he groaned.

Confused, painful emotions roiled through Chance. He felt shame, to be this thing his father found now infernal. But he also felt a surge of near joy, to see his father again. Here was his father, alive and young! Why should this good man be lost?

"I could give you a second life," Chance said, thinking aloud with wonder or maybe hope about his new powers.

"Only the One True God can give a true second life."

"That's right." Chance hesitated. "It would not be like this life. I could not make it like this. Not yet. But something."

"Go away, devil," his father pleaded.

Devil? Chance felt dizzy. Who was he? He feared again that he had lost himself. That he was watching another life through a dream. Or that Hexus had won and he was actually Hexus and had only tricked himself—some part of himself, some fragment?—into thinking that he was Chance.

Who can help me? Chance wondered despairingly.

"Why...." Chance started. "Why does the One True God not speak to me?"

John Kyrien frowned, uncertain at this question. Finally he said, "Why should he speak to you?"

"To one of my power, perhaps, he should...?"

"You are as small to Him as I am. Why should he speak to you, and not to me, or anyone else?"

Chance nodded. That was right, wasn't it? At least, it was possible. It was something. A hope. A chance for faith. "You are wise," he said. In part trying to convince himself.

His father cringed.

Chance closed his eyes. He should cause his father no more fear. His visitation pained the man, and shamed him. Though it was terrible to leave his father a second time, and again without saying goodbye, Chance stepped out of space and time and ran backward. His course was clear to him now. He knew what to do.

CHAPTER

55

The bent intrusions into time of other gods were like stones in a stream. Chance could see that it would take the greatest effort even to press close to where the Younger Gods had passed in the world. He found again the Guardian's history, followed it back, saw also the paths of gods, and avoided them, passing unnoticed, until he came to a black tower—Hroth—in a wet forest, in a world full of machines and people.

Two fearsome, frightening intrusions cut through this time and place, and between them lay only a tight gap where Chance could fit, in a small children's room. The knot in time's past he could clearly see stretched back just a short while toward the far south. Primus, the false god. The knot in the future was as black and inscrutable as night: the Old Gods. Chance could not see their path, except that the dim image of it stretched into the future with his own path—they twisted around each other until they both disappeared into darkness.

Another dizzying thought struck Chance: what if I am the Old Gods? In the farthest future?

I do not know how to make a thing like the Guardian, he told himself.

But what if I learned? His own fear answered back.

A nauseating vertigo seized Chance. The forest and tower that lay before him, the dim past and the dim future, all in that instant became brute, intrusive, alien things, absurd in their meaningless solidity, their equally meaningless malleability. Not only could anything be done here in the world, but anything might be done with him. He was free to become, and to do, anything. But did that mean he was nothing?

What could it mean, all this sweep of time, these bright flashes in a vast darkness? There was no up, no down, no anchor. He could walk through walls with a thought—so were they really walls? He could leap through time—so did the past set anything, did the future promise anything? He could build a new world, take away the machines, remove the unmen from Earth—or make them pure, perhaps, if he studied them long enough—but would it mean anything to be a Puriman then?

And where, in all this darkness and possibility, was God? Why didn't the True God shine like a beacon at the end and beginning of time, showing him the way?

As this despair seized Chance, he fell back into space and time, into the narrow place between the Younger God and the Old Ones.

And there stood Primus, first of the Younger Gods. He held a woman by the throat. She was thin, strong, with severe but beautiful blue eyes. Two children, a boy and girl, trembled in a corner, clinging to each other and to a black and white animal that had wide, frightened eyes.

Chance was in the children's bedroom. Bright cloth hung down in nets over two low beds. Colorful feathers and flowers were hung here and there on the walls, decorating the dark stone. It would have been a clean, soothing place at any time other than this murderous moment, when Primus held a woman suspended by her throat, her neck stretched to nearly breaking.

The woman gripped and twisted the pale, unreal flesh of Primus's forearm. A rush of smells hit Chance: baking bread, the wet humus of the rain forest, a clean scent of rain after a thunderstorm.

In an instant Chance comprehended the entire scene. And in that instant he overcame his despair. He could chose to stand here, with gravity pulling him down, with the floor holding him up, with the walls solid and obscure, with his heart aching for these children. And though it was terrible to know that he would remain free to choose otherwise—and though it was terrible to see further and so see that the One True God was that much more remote, more remote than he could ever have imagined—even so, he would *choose* to act like a Puriman. He could and he would choose, and accept his choice, and keep to his choice.

In that instant Wealtheow spit into the face of Primus.

Primus snapped her neck.

"Ah!" Chance howled. There was nothing he could do. The space around Primus was gnarled, hard, resistant. Chance could not penetrate its past. He could not save the woman.

Primus looked at him. "Who are you?" he demanded.

"I am the wrath of the One True God," Chance hissed, furious at the casual murder that he had just witnessed. "And I shall make sure that you shall come to nothing."

"I have dreamed of you," Primus said, the boundless arrogance of his voice never wavering. "We shall fight at the end of time." Primus still held the dead woman, dangling her without concern, indifferent to the bitter finality of her mortality.

"Should God will it, I will crush you out of all creation," Chance said. He glanced at the children.

Primus saw then how to harm Chance: he snatched at the children, trying to bend space around them. Chance was faster. He leaped for the children, bound them in his own arms, and rushed out of space, and far, far into the future.

Chance exploded into the air behind the Guardian, one second after he had disappeared from the hall of Ma'at. Paul's body lay in three broken fragments on the floor. His blood was sprayed over the walls. Sarah twitched on the floor nearby.

The Guardian did not hesitate for a thousandth of a second. He turned, swinging Threkor's Hammer in a savage sweeping blow at Chance.

Chance flung himself against the Guardian, getting too close for the Hammer to hurt him, and, seizing the immortal, ran up the hall and out of the door, nearly out of time again, but spinning, as they both absorbed the force of the hammer's swing and the great momentum of Threkor's Hammer set them in motion.

The Guardian reached back one hand and struck Chance's cheek, hard, smashing the godflesh, the Aussersein. The pain was impossible, but Chance now lived with pain that was infinitely worse, infinitely more impossible. He clung still to the Guardian and sped forward, accepting the blows.

Chance had discovered that Hroth Tower was not far from Yggdrasil, just over the horizon to the north. In moments they were there. He bent space to pass them up into the air and then through massive stone walls—and they fell back into a dark room with a single window covered over with leafy vines. Dust exploded from the ground where they landed on their feet. Chance let go of the Guardian and fell back, flung away. The Guardian raised Threkor's Hammer far above himself, preparing to strike at Chance.

"Ah!" a child cried out.

Threkor's Hammer froze. It seemed for a moment that Chance and the Guardian had fallen again into that timeless place behind time and space, while the Guardian stood with the hammer high above his head, frozen, and Chance lay on the floor below. Then the Guardian turned his head. In a dark corner of the desolate ruin of the room, a small girl, a small boy, and a lemur crouched. The Guardian stared at them.

"Some foul, some evil wile," he whispered.

"No, Guardian," Chance said. "I saved them from Primus. I would have saved Wealtheow, but that the god was impenetrable to me, his deeds done beyond my power to fix."

"I...."

Chance floated away, back, out of the range of the hammer. Slowly, very slowly, the Guardian planted the hammer at his side.

"Beo," he whispered. "Una."

The children look at him in terror but also in hope.

"It is I. Treow. It is your father. I know I've changed. But it is I. Still me."

The lemur leapt. The boy reached for it, but too late, it scampered out of his reach and bounded to the Guardian. The lemur climbed the Guardian's bare leg, ran up on his shoulder, and looked at his eyes.

"Changed," it piped in a small voice.

"Changed," the Guardian said. "But still your friend, and still their father."

The lemur whooped.

The children ran to him then, and clung to his gray legs. The Guardian put his hand on the boy's head, then the girl's, looking down at them.

Chance backed away.

"I go," Chance said. "I must save a young coyote, years ago. And then I must save Sarah, minutes ago."

"Puriman," the Guardian said. "Chance...."

They looked at each other a long time.

"Come for me if you must," Chance said. "You know where to find me. But first raise these, your daughter and son, heroes of the heroic age. Let them rebuild some part of this world with peace, not with war as the false god had dreamed."

The Guardian's brow trembled. Chance knew that if he could weep, the Guardian would have done so.

"One thing," the Guardian said, after a long moment of silence. He held Threkor's Hammer out. "I made oath to the Creator that I would give back this when the god was killed."

"No," Chance put his hands up. "I should not. You return it, when these are grown."

The Guardian smiled.

Chance disappeared.

CHAPTER
56

Wadjet woke. Green leaves, far above, waved in the wind. Blue sky stretched beyond them, cheerfully full of light. A single voluminous cloud passed. The air smelled of salt water, and dry leaves, and life.

Wadjet pushed herself up. She sat in a forest, on a slope, surrounded by great trees, huge ferns, low bushes. High above, hidden in the tree tops, insects thrummed, thrummed, thrummed, a song of great and vibrant industry. Surf shushed across sand nearby. Wadjet stood and discovered that she trod on a dark and narrow trail, pressed smooth by the regular passage of some small animals. She walked down it, taking big, quick strides. The smell of the salt sea, of the sea wrack decaying on the beach, of the forest behind her, all filled her now with a swelling sense of life. She burst through a wall of dense shrubs onto a beach of black sand.

The high sun was blinding, so hot and alive that for a moment, after the dark forest, she could sense nothing but white light and the sound of surf. Slowly her eyes adjusted, revealing a bright and beautiful world.

Not a hundred paces out in the sea, her ship sat, anchored, restored, bobbing on gentle waves.

On the beach before it, a large, black shape huddled just beyond the reach of the surf. Beside it, a heap of golden metal plates shone blindingly in the bright sun.

Wadjet walked down the beach and stopped a few paces away. The creature there was a gorilla. The gorilla. Champion and herald of the god. The gorilla's salt-encrusted armor lay piled beside her. The gorilla did not look up. Her black fur was matted and caked white with brine.

Wadjet realized, suddenly, that the gorilla must have tried to drown herself, and then given up on the attempt.

"I am Wadjet."

The ape did not answer. For a long time, they listened to the surf.

"That is my ship," Wadjet said finally. "I'm going to sail far away, to a place where no one has feared or hoped of gods in a thousand years, and where there is no war between soulburdened and humans, and where most of your kind are sterile. If you would come with me, you could be mother to a whole future race."

The gorilla looked up at Wadjet.

"Don't," she grunted. "Don't make promises."

Wadjet listened to the surf a long time before she bowed her head and consented, "That is wise counsel."

She sat down beside the gorilla. She brushed at the hot sand with both palms, while the gorilla stared out over the waves. Finally, Wadjet said, "This, then: would you come with me, if only to see the ocean and see a new land?"

The gorilla nodded. "I've lost all hope," she whispered in a coarse, grinding voice. "But I still live. I still want life. I will see what comes of living."

EPILOGUE

Chance Kyrien stood at the end of a row of Ries vines, on the hill above the Kyrien Vincroft house. He looked down the length of Walking Man Lake. The sun had almost completely set, but light still diffused through the sky and lit the valley dimly. A thin layer of gray clouds hung low over the lake. A mild wind set the first tiny buds of leaves on the vines and trees trembling. It was proving a mild spring after a mild winter.

Sarah walked up the path between vinrows, hand on her growing belly. When she came to his side, she put her other hand on Chance, breathing heavily.

"I don't have much wind today."

"How is my daughter?" he asked.

"What makes you think it's a girl?"

Chance only smiled at her.

"Kicking," Sarah finally answered. She tapped his right arm. "You're still favoring that arm."

"I always will."

Sarah turned and leaned against him, and looked also down the length of the lake. "My father came by just now. Said he's sorry to miss you. He wants some help with his vines."

"I shall go down there tomorrow."

"That'd be nice. He also said most people in town are used to having us back now. I'm glad the talk is dying down."

Chance nodded.

"And guess who else stopped by? Jeremiah Green."

"No." Chance laughed.

"Yes. Wanted to say hello, he told me. I could have fainted. I think he wants to buy any Ries grapes we have left next season. He asked if we expected a surplus."

"He shall have some, then."

Sarah pressed her head against his shoulder. "It's good to be home."

"Yes," Chance said, reaching his arm around her. "It's very good. Let's not leave."

She laughed. "I was not planning on another trip to Disthea."

Their return had been a small matter, much smaller than Chance or Sarah had imagined it would be. While Chance and Sarah had been at the foot of Yggdrasil, the soulburdened of the Forest Lakes had begun raids on the edge of Purimen lands. The Purimen, Trumen, and some refugees had joined with the Rangers to beat the soulburdened back. The Trumen of the lakes were all convinced that no greater battle had been fought in centuries. The return of Chance and Sarah seemed insignificant after that. When Chance had first gone to church, holding Sarah's hand, a few had grumbled and stared. Now, months later, folks treated Sarah and him like any others when they arrived for the service.

Chance's house was cleaned up. It had not taken much work. The vines were in fair shape. The wine that his father had already started had not gone sour. There would be a batch of wine this year after all.

They were home. They were mostly accepted. It was clear that eventually everyone would accept them. They had been raised here, after all, in this tiny place, this valley. They were its people.

And here Chance chose to fix his feet, here where he would relent and respect the flow of time and the pull of the Earth on matter. Here he would stay planted, as long as he could. At least for a human while.

Sarah pointed at the glowing cloud. "Full moon. We'd be under the Eye, if it weren't for that cloud." She said it lightly, a joke, but Chance's reply was serious.

"I'm not ready to walk in the gaze of the moon. Not yet."

Sarah frowned. With an effort Chance smiled at her, to dispel the grim tone he had taken. He pulled Sarah closer. An owl cried in the forest behind them. A distant coyote howled, as if in answer. Two bats flitted past overhead.

"It's as beautiful a place as any we've seen, isn't it?" she asked.

A few bright stars began to appear in the darkening sky and their twinkling light reflected in the lake. A warm, gentle wind whispered through the forests behind them and stirred about them. It smelled of damp soil, and the first green tendrils of plants, and of the wetland below the farm, and of the lake beyond that. It smelled of spring. All the fecund land begat now the creatures of spring that started life with the conviction that life was new.

"It's fair, that it should be ours a while," Chance said. "This small and human share of heaven on Earth."

-THE END-

ACKNOWLEDGMENTS

I have many debts. Foremost to Nancy Kress, my teacher and mentor and friend. Next to both Jonathan Sherwood and the members of the D309 East Side Novel Group: Lyndsay Calusine, Ben Chapman, Kim Gillette, Therese Pieczynski, Aaron Micheau, and Gary Mitchell. Thanks to Sarah Higley for help with Old English, and to Michael Boylan for help with Ancient Greek. Special thanks to Janice Carello. Writers & Books was an essential locus for much of my writing and learning. The artist Jeffrey Carr inspired my first dim idea of the Numin Jars and then of the gods of Earth; he also offered valuable advice on early drafts of this novel; I thank him for both. A shout-out to Dr. Stanley Schmidt for being the first editor to believe and invest in me; and to David Pomerico at 47North for believing in this book. Thanks to Aletheia DeLancey for inspiration and to Lorena Ferrero DeLancey and Nancy DeLancey for their support.

ABOUT THE AUTHOR

Craig DeLancey is a writer and philosopher. He has published dozens of short stories in magazines like *Analog, Cosmos, Shimmer, The Mississippi Review Online,* and *Nature Physics.*

He also writes plays, many of which have received staged readings and performances in New York, Los Angeles, Sydney, and Melbourne, to name just a few.

His stories have also appeared in translation in Russia and China, and his writing has garnered numerous awards. His short story "Julie Is Three" won the Anlab Readers' Choice award in 2012. "The Man Who Betrayed Turing" was named by *Cosmos* magazine one of their Top 12 Science Fiction Short Stories of 2012, and his short play "My Tunguska Event" was a finalist in 2011 for the Heideman Award, given by the Actors Theatre of Louisville.

DeLancey enjoys oceans and forests, hiking and gardening, reading and talking, and imagining other worlds.

Born in Pittsburgh, PA, he now makes his home in upstate New York and, in addition to writing, teaches philosophy at Oswego State, part of the State University of New York (SUNY).

Made in the USA
San Bernardino, CA
15 September 2013